TITLES BY KERRY REA

The Wedding Ringer
Lucy on the Wild Side

Lucy
on the
Wild Side

KERRY REA

BERKLEY ROMANCE
NEW YORK

BERKLEY ROMANCE
Published by Berkley
An imprint of Penguin Random House LLC
penguinrandomhouse.com

Copyright © 2022 by Kerry Rea
Readers Guide copyright © 2022 by Kerry Rea
Penguin Random House supports copyright. Copyright fuels creativity,
encourages diverse voices, promotes free speech, and creates a vibrant culture.
Thank you for buying an authorized edition of this book and for complying with
copyright laws by not reproducing, scanning, or distributing any part of it
in any form without permission. You are supporting writers and allowing
Penguin Random House to continue to publish books for every reader.

BERKLEY is a registered trademark and Berkley Romance with B colophon is a
trademark of Penguin Random House LLC.

Library of Congress Cataloging-in-Publication Data

Names: Rea, Kerry, author.
Title: Lucy on the wild side / Kerry Rea.
Description: First Edition. | New York : Berkley Romance, 2022.
Identifiers: LCCN 2022008081 (print) | LCCN 2022008082 (ebook) |
ISBN 9780593201862 (trade paperback) | ISBN 9780593201879 (ebook)
Classification: LCC PS3618.E213 L83 2022 (print) | LCC PS3618.E213 (ebook) |
DDC 813/.6—dc23
LC record available at https://lccn.loc.gov/2022008081
LC ebook record available at https://lccn.loc.gov/2022008082

First Edition: September 2022

Printed in the United States of America
1st Printing

Book design by Kristin del Rosario
Title page art: Leopard print © Dakin / Shutterstock.com

To Chris,
for holding my hand through all of it.

And to Finn,
our wildest dream come true.

Lucy on the Wild Side

Chapter One

I wish I were a Humboldt squid.

Everyone thinks chameleons are the best camouflagers, but a Humboldt squid can change its colors as fast as four times a second. If I could do that, I'd transform myself into the rain cloud gray shade of my office walls. That way, Elle wouldn't be able to find me and remind me of my four p.m. assignment.

But I'm not a squid, and I jump when my office door bangs open.

"Lucy." My best friend Elle pops her head inside the doorway, a mass of black curls framing her face. "You cannot hide from the children."

I sigh and shut my laptop, where I've been updating the daily feeding log. The gorillas ate their regular afternoon snack of popcorn, cereal, and sunflower seeds, with peanuts added in as an extra treat. As a keeper, part of my job is maintaining detailed records of the gorillas' dietary intake, social interactions, sleep habits, and vital signs. I've got at least an hour of data entry left today, but that will have to wait.

I don't want Elle to kill me.

"I know you hate doing the Critter Chats, but they're important. I've got twenty-six second-graders out there who can't wait to learn about primates," she says, sticking her neck farther into my shoebox-sized office. It's so tiny that between my cluttered desk and stuffed mini fridge, I can't lean more than three inches back in my chair without smacking my head against the door. Elle has no chance of getting in.

"Did you say twenty-six?" I ask in disbelief. "That's a fuck-ton of kids."

When she raises an eyebrow at me, I grab a fresh can of Diet Coke from the mini fridge and pop the tab open. I'm going to need a serious caffeine fix to make it through the next half hour.

"And it's not that I hate the Critter Chats," I continue, letting the cold deliciousness of my drink soothe me. "It's that I hate the *four o'clock* Critter Chats."

Three times a day—nine a.m., one p.m., and the dreaded four p.m.—a zookeeper from the primates department hosts an educational Q and A in front of the outdoor gorilla exhibit. I enjoy the Chats most of the time, since they're a great way to share my passion for gorillas with the public. During the morning and early-afternoon sessions, the kids who attend are in cheery, inquisitive moods. It's early enough in the day that the zoo is still fun for them, and they've got a day full of camel rides and ice cream Flamingo Pops to look forward to.

But by late afternoon, the excitement and sugar highs have faded, and the exhausted children have sunk into cranky moods. If they're little, they've gone all day without their usual naps, and if they're teenagers, it's late enough in the day that their phone batteries are dead and they have to suffer through the oppressive June heat without access to TikTok.

It's not a great situation.

"I know they can be challenging, but you're the only primate keeper available today. Jack's assisting over in Asia Quest, and Lottie has to go to her grandmother's funeral. Plus, it'll get you extra brownie points from Phil."

I clear my throat. "It's Lottie's grandmother's *cat's* funeral," I clarify, narrowing my eyes at Elle. "And I bet she could make it back in time."

Elle's dark brown eyes flicker with exasperation. "You know I don't assign keepers, Luce. I just make sure that somebody's out there to educate the children."

She's laying it on a little thick with that whole educate-the-children line, but she's not wrong. As an associate activities director, Elle's responsible for coordinating events for the public, including Zoo Camp, the painting-with-penguins fundraiser sessions, and Critter Chats. If I refuse to be a good sport, I'll be making her job harder. And because we've been best friends since the first day of ZooTeen volunteer orientation fourteen years ago, that's not an option for me. Plus, she has a point about my boss, Phil. He's looking to promote a junior primate keeper to senior sometime this year, and I want that job more than anything.

"Okay, okay," I relent, standing up from my chair to stretch my legs. At five-nine, I tower over Elle's five-one frame, and I bounce on my heels to increase blood flow to my long limbs. "Just tell me, this second-grade class—are there any girls with flower names? You know, Tulip, Rose, Iris? Because girls with flower names always give me the hardest time. Along with boys with bougie names, like Brantley or Oakley or Banks."

I'm not pulling those names out of thin air. Last week, a five-year-old named Tulip tried to stick gum in my hair, and a six-year-old Banks screamed at me when I explained to him that gorillas aren't monkeys. I've learned to maintain a ten-foot distance between myself and children at the afternoon Critter Chats, lest any of them have a tantrum and decide to fling a Capri Sun at my head.

Elle scrunches her nose. "Who names a kid Tulip? Anyway, it's almost four, so let's go, please. And if the kids get too rowdy, just tell them that filming starts next week, so if they come to the zoo again over the summer, there's a chance they'll get to be on TV. Kids love TV."

Kids love launching full juice boxes at innocent zookeepers' heads more than they like TV, in my experience, but I don't argue. Elle's mention of filming inspires a flutter of excitement in my stomach. Next week, the Columbus Zoo and Aquarium will be the site of a months-long documentary project produced by wildlife expert Kai Bridges, host of *On the Wild Side with Kai Bridges*. *Wild Side* has taken viewers like me—I've seen every episode, including the famous one about the last grizzly bear in a small Montana county—from the ice shelves of Antarctica to the volcanoes of Hawaii, showcasing animals in every biome. Now, his production company wants to show audiences the magic of wildlife right in their own backyards, starting with our zoo.

I'm so excited about the docuseries that not even the memory of Tulip and her aggressive bubblegum antics can lessen my enthusiasm. I'd rather die than be on camera—my fellow keepers Lottie and Jack can have that glory to themselves—but I'm looking forward to meeting Kai. He's the son of famed primatologist Dr. Charlotte Kimber, who's half the reason I'm a gorilla keeper, and meeting her offspring is probably the closest I'll ever get to meeting my idol herself. Plus, at least on TV, Kai looks like Tom Hardy's twin, if said twin wore a Crocodile Dundee hat and said "Wowza!" in a South African accent every time an apex predator appeared.

The docuseries will put our zoo on the map, and my heart skips a beat when I imagine people all over the world getting to know the gorillas I've dedicated my career to.

But first, I have to survive the Critter Chat.

"All right, let's go," I say, taking another swig of Diet Coke and surrendering to the inevitable. "But I swear to God, if any second-graders launch spit wads at me, I can't promise not to retaliate."

Elle shakes her head but smiles as I follow her out of my office and through the administrative section of Ape House. She loves kids, which is a good thing, since she and her husband Nadeem are expecting their first baby in six months.

"C'mon." She lifts her employee ID to grant us access to the hallway leading toward the gorillas. "And while I have you, don't forget about that benefit picnic this weekend. You don't have to wear a dress, but you *cannot* wear your work uniform."

I sigh. Like the Critter Chats, attending zoo fundraising events is part of my job, but I don't enjoy it. It's the actual *work* part of my career that comes easily to me: building relationships with the animals, researching advances in gorilla care, keeping impeccable records of every aspect of their lives so that conservationists can use the data to bolster outcomes for gorillas in the wild. But making agonizing small talk and eating tiny appetizers at a rich donor's house doesn't appeal to me. I'd much rather be knee-deep in hay getting real work done.

"What's the picnic for?" I ask, trying not to let my annoyance show. It's not Elle's fault that zoos, like other nonprofits, rely on the support of the community to thrive. "And I wouldn't wear my work uniform. I'm not a moron."

As we approach the behind-the-scenes animal area, the unmistakable odor of hay and gorilla fills my nostrils. It smells like a barnyard exploded, and it's my favorite scent in the world.

Elle rolls her eyes. "It's to raise money for a lemur rescue in Madagascar. And I'm not saying you're a moron. I'm saying that sometimes you're so focused on work that things like general self-care fall to the wayside. Remember that gala at the art museum? The one for the giraffe blood bank? You showed up in khakis and a polo shirt. With gorilla shit on your boots."

I glance down at the black polo, khaki shorts, and hunter green rain boots I'm currently wearing. There's not a cloud in sight today, but the boots are essential footwear for a long day scrubbing exhibit floors.

"Piper was born the night of the gala," I explain, remembering the night the zoo's youngest gorilla entered the world. "So excuse me for not missing the birth of a *critically endangered creature* so I'd have time to shower."

"Nadeem and I had to sit next to you at that gala, so you are not excused." Elle reaches an arm out to give me a friendly swat, and I hop sideways to miss it.

"Point taken."

I push open the heavy metal door that leads us out of Ape House and into the warm June sunshine. We emerge on the keepers-only side of Gorilla Villa, the twenty-six-thousand-square-foot outdoor viewing area. Currently, the members of silverback Ozzie's troop roam the space, enjoying what's left of an afternoon scatter feed. Ozzie, the four-hundred-pound leader of the group, rests on a wooden platform above us while he munches on a head of lettuce.

"Hi, handsome," I say. Ozzie's eyes dart toward me, but he continues enjoying his snack. With the distinctive smattering of red hair on his forehead, the proud, observant look in his eyes, and trademark silver hair on his massive back, Ozzie never fails to stop me in my tracks.

"He looks so majestic," Elle says, craning her neck to look up at him.

"That's because he *is* majestic." The silverback, the dominant male of a gorilla family, is the cornerstone of a troop's survival in the wild. He mediates conflicts, leads his group to feeding sites, and will even sacrifice his own life for the safety of his kin. Ozzie, in all his lettuce-munching glory, is no different.

The rest of Ozzie's troop is scattered throughout the Villa. Thirty-one-year-old Zuri, my favorite member of the troop, basks in the sun on an overhead ledge. Her fellow females Tria and Inkesha doze on a beam tower in the center of the exhibit while Tria's daughter, one-year-old Piper, sleeps on her mom's chest. On the public side of the Villa, youngsters Tomo and Risa engage in a wrestling session, and young male Mac sticks his head into the opening of a tunnel on a grassy hill, probably foraging for more greens.

The outdoor exhibit, a massive structure of interconnected beams and wire mesh, serves to give the gorillas as much choice in their whereabouts as possible. Overhead transfer chutes connect the outdoor space to Ape House, allowing the troop members to move freely between their indoor and outdoor habitats, and a labyrinth of ropes, ladders, and tunnels provides opportunities for playing and napping out of the public eye.

"Ready?" Elle asks, passing me a headset mic and sliding hers on.

"No," I mutter as we approach the shaded viewing area, where a crowd has gathered to watch Risa and Tomo's playful antics. My stomach drops when I see that the twenty-six kids Elle mentioned are wearing matching purple T-shirts with *St. Thomas Day Camp Superstar* printed on the front.

"Dammit, Elle. You didn't tell me they were day camp kids!"

She bites her lip in guilt. She knows as well as I do that a four o'clock Critter Chat with day camp kids is the worst scenario of all.

Not that I have anything against camps—I'm not a monster, and I was a child myself once—but the sheer ratio of exhausted teachers to unruly, even more exhausted kids is a recipe for disaster.

"It'll be great," Elle whispers as we approach the group. "I promise."

I shoot her a dark look but take my place at the glass window in front of the exhibit. The thick humidity in the air does no favors for my wavy, white-blond hair, and between the frizz and the loose pieces of hay stuck in my ponytail, I probably look like a deranged Targaryen.

"Welcome," Elle says, waving her arms at the assembled group of children and flashing them her most patient smile. Between the kids' chatter and the birdsongs floating through the air from the nearby aviary, her voice is lost in the commotion.

"Welcome!" she repeats, louder this time. For a petite person, Elle can really project.

"For this afternoon's Critter Chat, we've got junior keeper Lucy to teach us about the gorillas who call our zoo home. And if you use your very best listening ears, I bet she'll even answer some questions for you."

I try not to hold my breath as Elle winks at the crowd. Something tells me their listening ears got switched off somewhere around lunchtime.

"And remember," Elle continues, "no tapping the glass, please." She smiles and motions toward me with a dramatic sweep of her arm, as if we're on a game show and I'm the prize behind door number three. "Let's listen up while Lucy tells us all about gorillas!"

"Hello," I say, taking my cue. I swallow hard, and my gaze darts from Elle to the group of purple-shirted children. I know I'm not about to deliver the Gettysburg Address, but my palms have already grown slick with sweat. Public speaking, even when it's about my life's passion, has never been my strong suit. I'm great at chatting with small groups of zoo guests, but any more than that triggers serious stage fright. I'd rather shovel gorilla dung.

"*Your mic*," Elle mouths to me, motioning to her headset.

It takes me a second to realize my mic isn't turned on, and my cheeks heat up as I correct the error. I spot my boss Phil making his way toward Ape House from the bonobo exhibit, and he stops to observe the Chat.

"Hello," I repeat, trying to calm my nerves. "I'm Lucy, and I've been a keeper here for four years. Right now, you're looking at Ozzie's troop. Ozzie is the big, beautiful guy chowing down on lettuce over there."

I point to him and introduce the other members of his troop. The crowd listens as I go through my educational spiel, telling them about troop social structure, what makes a healthy gorilla diet, and how western lowland gorillas are faring in their native lands. (Hint: not well.)

Just before I can launch into the most important part of my speech and explain how people can support gorilla conservation in the wild, a gap-toothed boy from St. Thomas Day Camp raises his hand.

"Do gorillas fart?" he asks, prompting a roar of laughter from his classmates. His teacher rolls her eyes and gives me a sympathetic glance. I'm guessing gorillas aren't the only thing he asks that question about.

"They do, actually." I answer his question smoothly, as if it's no big deal. And it isn't. Kids are naturally curious, and I've found it's best to give them simple, honest answers. "Most animals experience flatulence. Except for octopuses. And birds. And according to researchers, sloths."

Elle side-eyes me as if to ask how I know that as another St. Thomas kid raises her hand.

"Why did you become a keeper?" she asks, shifting her weight from one skinny leg to the other.

I smile at her. It's a question I could spend hours answering.

"Well, when I was little, my grandmother bought me a very special book called *Majesty on the Mountain*, by Dr. Charlotte Kimber. She wrote it about her experience studying mountain gorillas in Rwanda. I loved that book so much that I took it with me everywhere. In fact, I'd spend hours in the woods pretending I was her research aide."

I remember stuffing my Lisa Frank backpack full of Goldfish crackers and twist-cap Sunny Delights and traipsing into the woods outside my grandmother's house. I'd gather leaves and sticks and even dead bugs and glue them into my "research notebook," where I'd write detailed logs of my outings. I couldn't exactly track gorilla dung or observe their behavioral patterns like Dr. Kimber. So instead, I counted elderberries and made meticulous notes about the urinary patterns of the neighbor's poodle Clancy.

On Friday nights, when my grandmother Nona microwaved popcorn and let me pick a movie, I always chose the film version of Dr. Kimber's book. At the end, when the actress playing Dr. Kimber sobbed over the death of her favorite gorilla, Nona and I would cry our eyes out until she swore never to let me watch it again. But she always relented, and if she thought I was weird for stalking around in the woods with a Dr. Kimber–like braid in my hair, she never let it show.

"That book introduced me to the magic of gorillas," I continue. "I'd go through *National Geographic* magazines and cut out pictures of gorillas and monkeys and chimpanzees and put them up on my bedroom wall." I'd also displayed seven posters of a *Titanic*-era Leonardo DiCaprio, but that's neither here nor there.

"When I was old enough, I joined the ZooTeen program right here at our zoo." I explain how I studied biology in college and did several internships before landing my dream job. "For me, it all really started with Dr. Kimber's book. I wouldn't be here today without it."

Unmoved, the gap-toothed kid from St. Thomas raises his hand again. "Do gorillas puke?"

After I assure him that gorillas share ninety-eight percent of our DNA and thus have the same basic bodily functions, Elle twirls her finger subtly to get me to wrap things up. I breathe a sigh of relief. Nobody's tossed so much as a gum wrapper at me, and Phil was here to witness every second of my successful Critter Chat.

But before I head back inside to my sweet, sweet celebratory Diet Coke, I want to drop a line or two about conservation. "Dr. Kimber, who the mountain locals called *Nyiramacibiri*—'the woman who lives alone in the forest'—wrote that the building block of conservation is love. Love for gorillas and the earth that sustains us all. We don't have to be 'people who live alone in the forest' to make an impact. We can do that right here in Ohio, whether we're keepers or second-graders."

I describe the zoo's partnerships with international conservation programs, and how global demand for palm oil has accelerated the deforestation of great ape habitats. I encourage them to download the zoo's palm oil shopping guide so they can ensure the products they buy, from cooking spray to ice cream, contain sustainable palm oil.

The boy who asked about gorilla bathroom habits pretends to snore loudly, but I'm satisfied with the session. If I've done my job right, and I think I have, the kids will go home with a little more knowledge about gorillas and compassion for their plight in the wild.

And I'll go home without gum in my ponytail.

Elle turns off her mic as the crowd disperses. "Great job, Luce." She glances at her smartwatch and frowns. "Shoot, we went five minutes over. I've gotta run to the Tasmanian Devil Chat next. Text me when you're leaving, okay? Sam mentioned getting dinner at El Vaquero tonight."

The prospect of enchiladas with my best friends is almost enough to make my stomach growl, and I wave good-bye as she trots off. I still have a lot of data to work on today, along with drafting plans for Ozzie's upcoming birthday.

Remembering that I've got a question for Phil about Ozzie's cake, I scan the crowd for him. I spot him next to the surly-faced, six-foot-tall bronze statue of Rock, one of the zoo's original gorillas. Phil's deep in conversation with an auburn-haired man who's an inch or two taller than the Rock statue and looks about as pleased.

"Lucy!" Phil calls when he notices me observing them. "Come here. I've got somebody for you to meet."

Following my boss's orders, I approach the pair. Phil, with his salt-and-pepper hair and all-khaki outfit, looks like he could pass for Steve Irwin's dad. Unlike my neatly groomed boss, the auburn-haired man looks like he hasn't seen a razor in months. His full beard bears streaks of blond, and a scar over his right eyebrow leaves a centimeter of it bare.

"Hello," I say, trying not to stare at the scar. "I hope you enjoyed the Critter Chat."

I'm used to making niceties with the occasional donor who stops by for a behind-the-scenes tour with Phil. But instead of the awe-struck expression most people wear when they're up close and personal with gorillas, his lips are curled into the deep frown of someone who just stepped in dog shit.

His gaze shifts from Phil to me, and I force myself to look into his hazel eyes instead of at his eyebrow.

"I'd hardly call a gorilla a critter," he says in a deep voice.

His words bear the trace of an accent, but I can't quite place what it is, and his gruff tone catches me off guard. I glance sideways at Phil, but he doesn't seem to pick up on any tension.

I shrug. *Critter* is probably a better term for a pygmy slow loris than a great ape, but I don't name the programs.

"Well," I say, "I hope you found the talk informative. Education is a big part of what we do here at the zoo."

Phil beams, and I award myself a mental brownie point. Take that, Jack and Lottie.

The bearded man says nothing in response. Phil glances from me to the sour-faced guy and clasps his hands together, and I start to wonder if he called me over to help him escape from this dreadful conversation.

I should get double brownie points for that.

"So, Phil," I say, giving him a meaningful look. "When you're done here, I wanted to talk about Ozzie's birthday cake. He didn't like the pumpkin puree frosting last year, so I was thinking we could try strawberry this time."

Before Phil can respond, the grumpy man turns toward me again. "You were wrong, you know."

He watches me with a steady gaze, and I blink at him in confusion. What the hell's he talking about? Wrong about what? I wasn't wrong about any of the facts I laid out during the Critter Chat. I know more about these gorillas than anyone, except for maybe Phil. I spend upward of sixty hours a week tending to them and researching every possible method for improving their care. I miss family dinners and nights out with friends because my work with the gorillas always comes first. I love it. I love them.

And I know my shit.

"Wrong about what?" I ask. I manage to keep my tone calm, even though I want nothing more than to reach out and yank his stupid beard. I've dealt with enough mansplainers who think watching a single documentary on Animal Planet makes them a zoologist.

He nods toward the spot where I stood to lead the Critter Chat. "You said the locals called Dr. Kimber *Nyiramacibiri*. 'The woman who lives alone in the forest.' They didn't."

It takes real effort to keep disdain from crossing my features. My cheeks have a tendency to go fire-engine red when I'm annoyed, and I don't want to give this guy an inch. I force myself to take a deep inhale and think about enchiladas.

"I'm not wrong." I've read *Majesty on the Mountain* at least twenty times and watched the movie way more than that. I know everything there is to know about Dr. Kimber, down to her favorite color (green) and what she liked to cook for dinner in her tiny mountain hut (jasmine rice). While other kids my age collected Beanie Babies and played Nintendo 64, I sent my Barbies on gorilla-tracking expeditions and had fake conversations with Dr. Kimber in my head.

So Mr. Eyebrow Scar can take his know-it-all attitude and his stupid beard and shove it. Hard.

"You are wrong," he insists, running a hand through his thick waves of hair. If I didn't loathe this dude so much, I'd ask him what conditioner he uses.

Instead, I run my fingers over the zoo badge on my waistband, as if to remind myself that I'm the one in charge here. Technically, Phil's the one in charge, but I refuse to be condescended to in front of my boss by a mid-thirties manbaby who never learned to double check his facts. Especially when I'm gunning for a promotion.

"I'm not, actually," I reply. "And I'm one hundred and ten percent confident in that." I lift my chin slightly, trying to look as proud and noble as Rock the gorilla statue.

He raises his eyebrows and opens his mouth to respond, but a chiming noise stops him. While he grabs his smartphone from his pocket and presses it to his ear, I glance sideways at Phil to see if he's picking up on the serious douchecanoe vibes. But Phil just smiles at the dude like he's the second coming of Jane Goodall.

Whoever this asshole donor is, he must be worth a lot of money.

"I've gotta give someone a lift from the airport," he says to Phil after the call ends. "We'll talk more next week."

"Looking forward to it." Phil sounds almost breathless with excitement, as if this guy just handed him fifty-yard-line tickets to the Super Bowl.

I glance from a radiant Phil to the surly bearded man and back to my boss. What in the world am I missing here?

The man turns to leave, but before he reaches the walkway toward the main zoo path, he pauses. He turns back to give me a curt nod, as if he's remembered to at least *act* like someone who has manners.

I don't nod back. Instead, I fix him with a steely glare.

Because I'm not wrong.

After a moment, perhaps when he realizes I'm not going to back down, he turns away. I breathe a sigh of relief and utter a silent prayer that he trips on his way out.

"What a jerk, huh?" I ask when he's out of earshot.

Phil, still staring after the man like he's about to walk on water, doesn't seem to hear me.

"Can you believe it?" he asks. "Kai freaking Bridges! It's going to be quite a summer, Lucy."

My heart drops into my stomach. "What did you say?"

Phil grins at me. "That was Kai Bridges. He stopped by to get a feel for the zoo before production starts next week. Sorry I didn't give you a proper introduction."

I'm so surprised that I take a step sideways, as if to regain my balance. *"What?"*

That was Kai Bridges, son of my all-time, number one, I'd-die-to-meet-her idol? That's the guy whose wildlife programs have won three Emmys? That's the guy whose docuseries about our zoo is supposed to make the world fall in love with Ozzie and his troop?

What. The. Hell. The on-screen Kai Bridges is a chipper, clean-shaven adventurer who's always saying "Wowza!" and flashing a trademark toothy grin. The on-screen Kai has a strong South African accent and isn't a major asshole.

"Where's his accent?" I ask Phil. "Why's he look like he hasn't shaved in a month?" *Why is the incredible Dr. Kimber's son a total, colossal jerk?*

Phil shrugs. "I'm sure he presents himself differently for the show. I met Lady Gaga in an elevator once, and she looked really different than she does in her music videos."

I'm surprised that my boss is familiar with Lady Gaga's videos, but not as surprised as I am by the man I just met. Minutes ago, I was beyond excited for *Wild Side* to start filming. Over the past month, I've put together spreadsheet upon spreadsheet of data and created a seventy-slide PowerPoint to help the production crew get acquainted with each of our gorillas.

But the man I just met doesn't seem like a PowerPoint kind of guy. He seems like a cocky, ignorant mansplainer who tried to embarrass me in front of my boss and doesn't know basic facts about his own mother. And there's no way I can trust him to capture the magnificence of the gorillas I love so dearly.

Forget wanting to be a Humboldt squid. I wish I were a great white shark.

Chapter Two

Screw the enchiladas. I have a point to prove. After Phil finishes a lengthy monologue about the merits and drawbacks of strawberry topping for Ozzie's cake, I rush back to my desk with cheetah-like speed and whip open my laptop.

Dr. Kimber Nyiramacibiri, I type into the search bar, my fingers flying and my heart pounding. Despite that awful Kai Bridges's insistence, I know I'm not wrong. I can't be. I've read *Majesty on the Mountain* so many times that I almost know it by heart, and I distinctly remember Dr. Kimber's description of her tenuous friendship with the Virunga Mountain locals.

"But through it all," she wrote, recounting a spat with local tribesmen over their attempt to hunt deer near gorilla territory, "they never called me by my given name. They called me *Nyiramacibiri,* 'the woman who lives alone in the forest.' It amused me, for they know better than anyone that a person in the forest is never alone."

I'm *definitely* not wrong. Right?

I skim the search results until I land on Dr. Kimber's official website. The homepage features the same breathtaking photo that graces the cover of *Majesty on the Mountain*: a mid-thirties Charlotte Kimber sits cross-legged in front of lush vegetation, wearing a long-sleeved, pickle green button-up and jeans. Her raven hair, braided into her signature plait, hangs over one shoulder, and a notebook rests in her lap. Beside her, a young gorilla with thick black fur and wide eyes reaches for her pen with an outstretched hand while Dr. Kimber's lips curl in amusement. She looks like the jungle version of Snow White, minus the woman-on-woman hate and Prince Charming bullshit.

I tried to re-create the image often as a kid, using my American Girl doll Molly as a stand-in for the gorilla. I'd beg Nona to snap Polaroids while I scribbled in my journal and giggled, pretending that the lifeless, glasses-wearing Molly was about to rip my mechanical pencil away. Looking back, it's a wonder Nona didn't get me professional help.

I speed-read the site, looking for evidence that I'm right and Kai Stupid-Face Bridges is wrong. Before I can find it, my phone buzzes, and I see a text from my grandmother: Squirrel emergency!!! Hurry home.

I roll my eyes. Nona hosts my half sister Mia's Girl Scout troop meetings on Thursday afternoons, and she's always coming up with bullshit reasons for me to attend. Once, she pretended she'd fallen and hurt her hip. Another time, she claimed I should rush home because her hot fireman neighbor was washing his car shirtless; he was not. And last month, she committed the unforgivable sin of threatening to feed my family-size box of birthday cake Oreos to the Scouts if I didn't show up.

Nobody fucks with my Oreos.

Not falling for it, I text back, proud of myself for finally seeing through Nona's dramatics. It's not that I have anything against Girl

Scouts or my ten-year-old half sister Mia. I love Thin Mints as much as the next girl, and Mia's an okay kid, even if she does ask tons of questions and once accidentally let her Saint Bernard eat my favorite flip-flops. But even though Nona's offered me free Starbucks for a month if I come to a Scout meeting and teach the girls about my job, I refuse to do it. Because wherever the Scouts go, Mia goes, and wherever Mia goes, my mother Karina goes.

And I'd rather get stung by a jellyfish than spend my free time with her.

I'm serious this time, Nona writes back. I need help.

I send her an eye roll emoji, along with a picture of a wolf. Seconds later, my phone rings, and I contemplate sending Nona to voice mail before thinking better of it. After all, she knows where I live.

"Nona," I say, not bothering with niceties. "I'm working. I can't come to the Brownie meeting. And no fake squirrel emergency will change my mind. Did you not understand the wolf pic I sent? Because, you know, you're the lady who cried wolf—"

"I understand the reference, Lucille," Nona says in a clipped tone. She has the raspy voice of a longtime smoker, even though I've never seen her touch a cigarette in my life. "I can assure you that I'm not, nor have I ever, cried wolf. And the girls are Juniors, not Brownies."

I let out an indignant huff. "Really? What about the time you pretended to break your hip? Or the time you said Joey Macoroy was hosing down his Mustang without a shirt? Or when you threatened to give the *Juniors* my entire stash of Oreos?"

There's a long pause before my grandmother speaks again. "I never claimed to have broken my hip. I simply said I injured it, which I did. I had a bruise the size of a softball! And it's not my fault you didn't get home in time to see Joey wash his car. We both know you drive at the pace of a convalescent turtle."

I don't point out that if Nona drove more like a turtle and less like a total psycho, she'd have a lot fewer speeding tickets.

"And the Oreos?" I ask.

She sighs. "I'll give you that one. Threatening to give your cookies away was a dick move."

I hear a gasp in the background. Clearly some of the Juniors—or their parents—aren't accustomed to my seventy-three-year-old grandmother's colorful use of language.

"My apologies, ladies," I hear Nona whisper, followed by the sound of a door opening and closing shut.

"You'd think I was leading a Puritan girls' club," she grumbles. "I had to walk outside so I can curse without Avery Thompson's moms looking at me like I'm an ax murderer."

I don't blame Avery's moms for their reaction. Nona's pretty much my favorite person in the whole world, but she's a lot to handle.

"Anyway," she continues, "I need your help. I'm serious about the squirrel emergency. Dynamite caught one in the backyard. Mia got him to drop it, but I think he broke the squirrel's leg or something. There's a lot of missing fur and a *lot* of crying ten-year-olds."

I picture Mia's 170-pound Saint Bernard trotting up to a bunch of preteens with a half-dead squirrel wriggling around in his mouth. Then I glance at my mini fridge, wishing I had a nice cold bottle of something stronger than Diet Coke.

"I'm not a vet, Nona. Sorry, but I don't know how to fix squirrel legs."

"You're a zookeeper, Lucille! I bet you know more about squirrel legs than I do."

I drum my fingertips on my desk, praying for patience. "I'm a *primate* keeper. You need a vet who sees rodents."

A wailing sound pierces my eardrum from the other end of the line, and I hold the phone away from my ear, wincing.

"Do you hear what I'm dealing with?" Nona asks, her tone turning frantic. "Half the girls are in hysterics, and poor Ava Walker got so upset, she had to use her inhaler. And don't get me started on Penelope Rocht. She tried to do CPR on the squirrel, Lucy. He wasn't even unconscious!"

"Nona," I protest, "I really don't—"

"Can you call Nick?" Nona interrupts. "I know it might be a little awkward, but I bet he could help."

I sigh and lean back in my chair, bumping my head against the door. "Ow. No, I cannot call Nick. I refuse."

Working at the same zoo as my veterinarian ex-boyfriend already presents plenty of awkward moments. It's been five months since our breakup, but I still found myself diving behind a Dippin' Dots stand last week to avoid crossing paths with him. I'm certainly not about to contact him for nonprofessional reasons.

"You sure?" Nona asks. "I bet he'd be happy to help. He still carries a torch for you, and—"

"Whatever torches Nick carries are none of my business. Besides, he's dating Margo from Guest Relations now."

A surge of annoyance washes over me. I'm supposed to be proving that I'm right and Kai Bridges is wrong, not thinking about my ex and his budding relationship with the perpetually smiley Margo.

"Anyway, Nona—"

"Penelope! Get your mouth away from that squirrel, I swear to God!"

I wince, regretting my decision to answer the phone.

"Sorry," Nona says after muttering an impressive stream of curses. She sighs, and I can hear the weariness in her voice. "I don't mean to bother you. I know how busy you are. It's just that Mia's worried sick over the squirrel, and Karina's not answering her phone. Anyway, I'll figure something out. Maybe Joey Macoroy can help. Firefighters rescue kittens sometimes, right? Squirrels can't be that different."

Her resigned tone pokes at my resolve, and I fish a piece of hay out of my ponytail. Nothing upsets Nona more than seeing either of her granddaughters cry, and few things upset me more than Nona being upset. It's also no surprise that Karina isn't answering her phone—my grandmother and I have a long history of showing up for each other when my mother fails to do so.

I glance at my smartwatch. I've been at the zoo for eleven hours, and it's Jack's turn to hose down the exhibits. I guess it won't be the end of the world if I leave before dinnertime just this once.

"I'll come home," I relent. "But if I get there and there's no squirrel, I'll change your Netflix password to something you wouldn't guess in a million billion years. I mean it."

"There's a squirrel," Nona promises. "Scout's honor."

She hangs up, perhaps to stop Penelope from trying to resuscitate the already-conscious squirrel again, and I put my phone down and press my forehead against my desk.

If I get the senior keeper position, maybe Nona will finally respect my schedule and stop strong-arming me into attending Mia's events. *When* I get the senior keeper position, I mean. Nobody wants it more than me, and I'm gonna keep working my ass off until it's mine.

You can bet all the birthday cake Oreos in the world on that.

I didn't always live with my grandma. Once upon a time, I was a responsible adult with my own Netflix account and a charming town house I shared with Nick. But when he broke up with me, leaving me and my vast khaki pants collection with nowhere to go, I accepted

Nona's offer to move back into my childhood bedroom. After all, my pittance of a salary made living on my own a less viable option, and if I had to have a roommate, one who baked mouthwatering cherry pie and loved me enough to put up with my after-work gorilla odor sounded tolerable enough.

That's why, for the past five months, I've stayed in the same pink-wallpapered bedroom where I lived from ages ten to eighteen. So yes, I'm a thirty-year-old professional who sleeps in a canopied bed with a forty-inch poster of *Titanic*'s Jack and Rose on the ceiling. For now. Once I land the promotion and the accompanying salary bump, that will change.

I turn out of the parking lot, joining the army of SUVs heading from the zoo toward Riverside Drive. Unlike the sleek Range Rovers and BMWs inhabiting the driveways of Nona's neighborhood, my decade-old Chevy is not living its best life. The overhead mirror fell into my lap last week, and a yellow maintenance light on the dashboard's been begging for attention for months. But unlike Nona's neighbors, most of whom are surgeons or executives or lawyers who make bank suing the surgeons, I'm not rolling in cash. Nobody goes into zookeeping for the money.

Luckily, I don't have to stare at the maintenance light for long. Nona lives a half mile from the zoo, close enough that if I listen hard, I can hear the gibbons' calls from my bedroom window. Her house, an egg white Spanish revival, sticks out from her neighbors' Cape Cods and Dutch Colonials like a sore thumb. With its stucco exterior, red tile roof, and arched corridors, it looks like a movie star's home in sunny California. I throw the car into park and jog through the front courtyard, passing rows of lavender bushes and apricot-toned Marilyn Monroe roses. As if on cue, the lawn sprinklers switch on, and I pick up the pace to avoid getting soaked.

"Finally!" Nona says when I step inside, shaking water droplets out of my hair.

I see my grandmother every day, but somehow I'm still struck by her air of effortless glamour. A semi-retired cardiologist, she once posed for the cover of *Columbus Monthly* magazine wearing a red sheath dress that, according to Elle, "probably inspired a thousand new Viagra prescriptions." This afternoon, she's wearing a peach chiffon blouse with a deep V-neck tucked into palazzo pants. The silk scarf knotted around her neck and gold bangle on her wrist only add to her elegance.

If I wore those pants, I'd look less like a Hollywood star and more like a hired party clown. It's weird having a grandma who's hotter than you.

"How do you always look like you're on the set of a Nancy Meyers movie?" I ask, marveling at her. "And why didn't I inherit that gene?"

Instead of answering, she grabs my arm and pulls me across the foyer. She doesn't give me a chance to slip off my work boots, so I leave a trail of dirt on the Saltillo tile floor. When I was a kid, we spent a lot of time sliding across that floor in our socks, imitating Tom Cruise's famous scene from *Risky Business*. We still do it on occasion, after we've had a few too many cocktails.

"Damn," I say, impressed by Nona's strength. "Somebody's been keeping up with her Pilates."

She shoots me a look as we practically sprint toward the living room, and it doesn't take me long to figure out why. Before we're even halfway down the hallway, I hear the wracked sobs of a dozen ten-year-olds.

"It's Herbert," Nona whispers. "Things aren't looking good."

She thrusts me into the living room, where a small army of girls clad in green vests gather around the fireplace, crouching over a shoebox.

"Lucy!" my half sister Mia cries, leaping up to grab my hand.

Unfortunately for Mia, the effortless-beauty gene that blessed our grandmother and mother Karina seems to have skipped both of us. Instead of their silky blond tresses, she's got a headful of unruly dark curls that she refuses to let Karina straighten. Where Nona and Karina are long and lithe with perfect, gleaming teeth, Mia's got the small potbelly and before-braces tooth gap of prepubescent girlhood.

In other words, she looks like a perfectly normal kid. Karina must hate it.

"Dynamite hurt him." She points toward the shoebox on the floor, where a brown squirrel rests on the tie-dyed Zoo Camp shirt I wore as a teenager.

"Sorry," she whispers. "I borrowed your shirt."

Beside her, a redheaded girl with French braids holds a smartphone on a selfie stick, recording a video. "We didn't know Herbert long," the girl says in a somber, choked-up voice, "but he was a special squirrel. He taught us so much about life and death, and—"

"He's definitely still alive," I interrupt, watching as the squirrel wriggles around in the box.

The redheaded girl lowers her phone and narrows her eyes at me. "I'll get more likes on TikTok if I pretend he's dead," she says, all the mourning gone from her tone. "It's more dramatic."

"Olivia has six thousand followers," Mia whispers. "She's an influencer."

"She's ten!" I protest, fishing a pair of gloves from my backpack.

The pint-sized influencer juts her chin out in my direction. "I'm ten and a *half*. And how many followers do you have?"

Mia glares at Olivia like she just might cut a bitch. "My sister is too busy to care about followers. She has an important job, and she's gonna be on a TV show."

The mention of a possible brush with fame piques Olivia's interest, but Mia's comment reminds me of how rudely Kai Bridges treated me. Enraged all over again, I take a deep breath and focus.

"Looks like his leg got fractured," I say, peering at the squirrel. I don't find any blood, but his hind right leg is bent at an awkward angle.

Mia and her fellow Juniors watch with wide eyes as I fish around in my backpack for a container of seeds and berries that I borrowed from the Ape House kitchen. I set the container in the shoebox with Herbert, and he perks his head up for an instant before lowering it again.

"What are we gonna do with him?" Mia asks, her arm touching mine as she peers at Herbert.

I glance at my watch, frowning. It's after six, which means the local wildlife center is closed for the evening. "We'll just have to keep him comfortable until morning. Then we can take him to the wildlife rescue in Powell."

Red-haired Olivia hoists her phone into the air and beams for her followers. "Time to place your vote, guys: Will Herbert cross the Rainbow Bridge tonight? Share your guesses in the comments below!"

"You've gotta be kidding me," Mia whispers. I start to laugh at her mortified expression, but a familiar voice sucks all the humor from the room.

"Mia?" Karina asks. "What's going on?"

I turn to see my mother standing in the arched doorway to the living room, her forehead furrowed in confusion. With her pink button-down, linen pants, and suede loafers, she looks like every pretty, suburban forty-something on her way to Whole Foods. The formfitting dresses and waist-length hair she wore when I was a kid have been traded in for Talbots blouses and a smooth blond bob, and if you stood behind her in line at Starbucks, you'd never guess that she once dated Tim Allen and had a starring role on a popular TV show.

These days, she looks like a *mom*, and it still catches me off guard.

"Hi, Luce." Her silver Pandora bracelet jingles when she waves at me.

I nod and give her a brief smile before turning back to the squirrel. *This* is why I don't come to Mia's meetings.

I place a towel over Herbert to keep him warm, trying to stay busy as Karina listens with rapt attention to Mia's narration of events. It's been more than a year since Karina, her husband Alfie, and their daughter Mia moved from California to a slate gray Craftsman home five blocks from Nona's. You'd think I'd be used to this version of Karina by now—the sober, Peloton-riding woman who buys organic produce and reads every title in Reese Witherspoon's book club— but I'm not.

I might never be.

"Come on, buddy," I whisper to the squirrel, lifting the shoebox off the ground. "Let's get you someplace quiet."

While the Scouts dry their tears, I carry the box to my bedroom. My desk is cluttered with half-empty Diet Coke cans and old editions of the *Journal of Zoo and Aquarium Research*, and I push them aside to make room for Herbert. Before I can text Elle and Sam to ask about their plans for the evening, someone raps lightly on my bedroom door. "Luce?"

I turn to see Karina standing in the hallway, one hand perched on the doorknob.

"I wanted to say thanks for helping Mia with the squirrel. I know you've got your hands full with work."

I nod but don't say what I'm really thinking: that there's no need to thank me, because I'm not doing anything for her. I'm not even doing it for Mia, really. I'm doing it for Nona.

"I also wanted to mention," she continues, her voice wavering a little, "that we're going to dinner for Alfie's birthday tomorrow. Nona and Mia are coming, too, of course, and I made the reservation for five in case you're able to join. We'd love it if you came."

She's too polite to mention that she's already texted me twice about attending, and I'm not bitchy enough to point out that I ignored both messages. It's not that I have anything against her husband Alfie, even if he is named *Alfie* and pronounces *gyro* with a hard *g*. He seems like a good dad to Mia and once helped me fix my laptop when it crashed. It's just that I can't force myself to wear a fake smile while Karina sings "Happy Birthday" and cajoles Alfie and Mia into taking another sweet family photo for Facebook. I can't watch her run a loving hand over Mia's hair or plant a kiss on Alfie's cheek without thinking of all the birthdays she missed. All the times I sat in Nona's kitchen, a chocolate fondant cake with pink flowers and candles in front of me, wishing for my mom to show up.

It's not that I don't want to try. It's that I can't.

I smooth the corner of a decades-old *NSYNC poster plastered next to my vanity mirror, making intense eye contact with Joey Fatone instead of Karina.

"I have a fundraiser on Saturday," I tell her. "And tons of work to do before filming starts next week." I'm sure Mia, who's never missed an episode of *On the Wild Side with Kai Bridges*, told Karina all about the upcoming docuseries.

"I understand," she replies. "But if you get done early, there'll be a lettuce wrap appetizer with your name on it."

I half expect the poster version of Justin Timberlake to roll his eyes. If a *lettuce wrap* appetizer is the carrot she's dangling, it's no wonder my mom and I haven't made peace. She could at least offer spicy buffalo wings or a goddamn Bavarian pretzel.

"Anyway," I say, peering into Herbert's shoebox, "I better see what I can do here."

Karina nods. "I'll leave you to it," she says, her shoes clacking against the hardwood as she heads downstairs.

Relieved that she's gone, I head for my bookshelf. On the top row, tucked between my middle school yearbook and a Kamala Harris biography, is my dog-eared copy of *Majesty on the Mountain*. I grab it and flop onto my bed, my pulse quickening as I flip through pages and pages of Dr. Kimber's witty observations, detailed data logs, and family tree diagrams of the gorilla troops.

Finally, on page 182, I find the evidence I'm looking for.

"They called me *Nyiramacibiri*," Dr. Kimber wrote. "'The woman who lives alone in the forest.'"

Aha! I snap the book shut so hard that Herbert pops his head up from the shoebox. I *knew* I was right. I knew I was right and Kai Bridges was wrong, and I'm annoyed that I ever doubted myself. There are lots of things I don't know: Why my grandmother can pull off hotpants but they turn me into a walking billboard for camel toe. Why Nick changed his mind about everything I thought we wanted in life. Why Karina, who abandoned me at Nona's when I was ten so she could play a sexpot PI on the soapy *Guilty Pleasures* without having to drag me along with her, transformed into Super Mom the second Mia was born.

But work stuff, gorilla stuff, Dr. Charlotte Kimber stuff—*that* I know like the back of my hand.

And I'll make sure Kai Bridges knows it, too.

Chapter Three

On Saturday afternoon, after depositing Herbert at the wildlife rescue, I arrive at Picnic for Paws wearing a blue gingham sundress that's too heavy for the ninety-degree weather. It's a fact I don't realize until sweat has pooled in my armpits, leaving me with two highly visible stains, and I tug at the layered cotton as I scan the sprawling backyard belonging to zoo donors Frank and Alice Forrester. The Forresters, owners of central Ohio's largest luxury-home-goods empire, have hosted Picnic for Paws for a decade, and they have the event down to a science. To my left, a throng of people exit the catering line, their plates loaded with burgers and savory baked beans. Across the lawn, families with young children spread picnic blankets on the grass in front of a portable stage, sipping rosé and lemonade from plastic cups as a cover band belts out a folk rendition of "Baby Shark."

I take a deep breath and adjust my name tag, on which I scribbled HI, I'M LUCY. ASK ME ABOUT GORILLAS! But since my handwriting sucks and I ran out of room toward the end, it looks more like HI, I'M LACY. ASK ME ABOUT GIRLS! Even though the whole point of keepers attending fundraisers is to chat up donors and charm them into writing the zoo fat checks, I'd rather listen to six straight hours of "Baby Shark" than field any questions. Because, unlike my fellow keepers, adorably button-nosed Lottie and smooth-talking Jack—who once got a Columbus Blue Jackets player to donate five grand to an exhibit redesign project after three minutes of small talk in a Starbucks line—I'm a horrible schmoozer. At my last fundraiser, a 5K for cheetah conservation, I went into excessive detail about bonobo mating habits when a runner asked a simple question about the primate reproductive cycle.

"Bonobos engage in sexual activity like you wouldn't believe," I'd rattled off to her while poor Phil died slowly in the background. "Group conflict? They have sex. Excitement about a new feeding area? Sex. Sex, sex, sex. And in virtually every partner combination you can imagine!"

The runner, her face beet red when I'd finished explaining how long bonobo sexual relations typically last (about twenty seconds, which is pretty much on par with my college boyfriend Roger's performance), did not ask further questions. Nor did she donate a single dollar to Ape House.

The memory makes me want to chuck my name tag into the nearest bush, but before I give in to the temptation, I spot Phil waving at me from the face-painting station. He's sporting a Hawaiian shirt with pineapples so neon yellow they make my eyes hurt, and his young daughter bounces on her toes beside him, a Popsicle in one hand and a stuffed tiger in the other.

Shit. I want him to see me mingling with donors, not standing around like an antisocial party pooper.

"*Ultrasound machine*," Phil mouths, giving me an encouraging nod. He motions to the rows of blankets and picnic tables, then rubs his fingers together in a show-me-the-money gesture.

I wave back and return his nod. If we meet this year's funding goal, we'll be able to purchase a new cardiac ultrasound machine for Ape House. And if I solicit enough donations to help, Phil might reward me with my desired promotion. I wipe my palms on the folds of my dress and search for an unsuspecting donor I can corner. I might lack Jack's charisma or Lottie's disarming sweetness, but I can do this. I can fundraise without scarring anybody with bonobo sex descriptions.

I have to.

Wishing I was at Ape House with the gorillas instead of surrounded by middle-aged rich guys in Ray-Bans and Sperrys, I spot one of those very guys approaching.

"Hi!" I greet the man brightly, trying to channel Jack's easygoing manner. "Do you have a moment to hear how your donation to the zoo can support gorilla heart health?"

My words come out in a rushed, awkward tangle, but the guy thrusts his hands into his pockets and smiles at me anyway. Maybe he'll be charmed by my nervousness. Maybe he's a Forrester heir, a prince to the throne of Columbus home goods, and he'll be so impressed by my dedication to my work that he'll whip out his checkbook and make a generous donation.

"Um, actually," he says, adjusting his sunglasses as he gives me a bashful smile, "can you tell me where the bathroom is?"

"I think that way," I say, pointing. "But if you can spare a moment, the information I want to share with you will only take a—"

"I, like, really need the bathroom," Sperry Sunglassface interrupts, his easy smile fading fast. "Too many IPAs, you know?"

Dammit. I hope this guy and his stupid boat shoes fall straight into a Porta-Potty. Sighing, I motion farther down the lawn. "Just past the popcorn bar."

He flashes me a relieved grin before he trots off. "Thanks, Lacy."

Screaming internally, I put on my most determined smile and stroll past the ice cream stand, trying to engage picnic goers in conversation. I'm unsuccessful except with a petite woman in aquamarine yoga pants, who listens for ten seconds before turning the tables and trying to recruit me for her multilevel marketing scheme.

"You seem to have a real girl-boss attitude," she says, slipping her glossy business card into my hand. "I'd love for you to join my team."

When Phil gives me a thumbs-up from across the lawn, I wave the card at him in celebration. Poor guy probably thinks I netted a hefty fundraising promise, and I'm not about to rain on his parade. Finally, after a dozen more people reject my awkward attempts to talk about gorillas, I spot Elle and her husband Nadeem strolling past the children's bounce house. Elle, wearing a violet dress with polka dots and gladiator sandals, looks like she stepped right off a Pinterest board. Nadeem, in a white button-down and lavender chinos, is no slouch, either.

I resist the urge to break into a sprint as I hurry toward them, relief flooding me.

"Hi, Lacy," Nadeem greets me. "Why should I ask you about girls?"

I groan and cover my name tag with my palm. "Don't start."

"Holy crap, Luce," Elle says, doing a double take of my outfit. "You didn't even try to wear your work clothes!" Her tone holds the same amazement a proud parent would use when describing their child's first steps, and a warm blush creeps over my cheeks.

"Did you really doubt me that much?"

"No," she replies, her tone too firm to be sincere. "Of course not."

"Yes," Nadeem confesses. "She packed an extra outfit in case you showed up in khaki."

I can't blame her. The gala for the giraffe blood bank wasn't the only event I showed up to with dirt on my boots and hay in my hair.

Before I can respond, I'm engulfed by a pair of arms from behind, and I turn around to find my other best friend Sam wrapping me in a hug.

"Lucy in a dress," she marvels, releasing me from the embrace. "Never thought I'd see the day."

Sam, wearing a bow knot hat and a coral romper that complements her caramel skin, looks like she just stopped by on her way to the Kentucky Derby. With her enviable cheekbones, expert smoky eye, and silky dark hair that ends at her waist, she's the kind of flawless pretty that I can only dream of achieving.

I glance from Sam to Elle to Nadeem, suddenly feeling like a wilted dandelion in a garden of roses. "How do you guys always look like you're straight out of a Ralph Lauren ad?"

Nadeem grins and tilts his head toward Elle. "It's all her. Before we started dating, I owned exactly three pairs of pants. Two of them were stained jeans. Besides, I don't think there are a ton of Indian guys in Ralph Lauren ads."

He lifts Elle's hand to his mouth and presses a kiss to it. When they first started dating, I never guessed that it would lead to marriage. Civil engineer Nadeem, with his lean frame and quiet steadiness, was so different from the guys Elle usually dated—fast-talking, peacoat-wearing consultant types who used a lot of hair mousse and were never clear about what they consulted—that I thought it might be just a fling. But when Elle got bit by an ornery goat during a shift at the petting zoo, Nadeem rushed to meet us at the ER like she was getting open-heart surgery instead of a few minor stitches.

That's how I knew he was the real deal. And now, six years later, their little family of two is about to become three.

"How are you feeling?" I ask Elle.

She places a hand on her belly. "Okay, I guess. But if we get any closer to the catering tent, I might lose my breakfast. Nobody warns you that morning sickness lasts all day."

Ugh. I add food aversion to my list of reasons for staying childfree.

"Speaking of the catering tent," Sam says, adjusting the brim of her hat to block out the sun, "I saw you making the rounds with donors over there, Luce. How was it? Did you sweet-talk anybody into pledging a million dollars?"

I roll my eyes. Sam, the zoo's assistant director of communications, could probably sweet-talk the teeth off a great white shark.

"Please. I gave more directions to the bathroom than information about gorillas." I relay my failed attempts at inspiring donations, including my painful interaction with the woman who tried to rope me into her MLM.

Sam laughs. "Just promise to name a baby gorilla after anybody who donates enough money. That always works. Why do you think the zoo has a koala named Dilbert Dort?"

"*Dilbert Dort?*" Nadeem repeats, his mouth dropping open. "You gotta be kidding me."

"I'd name a gorilla after Voldemort if it got me the senior keeper job," I say with a shrug. "Hell, I'd rename *myself* Dilbert Death-Eater Dort if it meant I got that promotion."

Sam nudges me with her elbow. "You're a badass keeper, Luce. I don't think you need to change your name to impress Phil."

Sam's one of the most impressive people I know, so her compliment means a lot. At thirty, she's one of the youngest leaders in the communications department, and during her off hours, she runs a blog that features workplace tips and career advice for professionally minded women. We've been friends since I asked her for a tampon two years ago in one of the employee restrooms, and not a day goes by that I'm not grateful to my mistimed period for bringing us together.

"It's not your fault that public speaking makes you nervous," Elle adds. "Besides, you've gotten way better. Remember your first Critter Chat? You fainted before you even introduced the gorillas."

"I hit my head on the Rock statue," I recall, cringing. "I was lucky I didn't need stitches."

"Well, forget the public speaking and the fundraising and everything that stresses you out," Sam says. "Because next week, when *On the Wild Side* starts production, you'll have a brand-new opportunity to shine."

Sam and the rest of the communications department played a huge role in getting our zoo selected for the show, and I can hear the excitement in her voice.

But once she meets the scowly Kai Bridges, she'll lose that enthusiasm real quick. The thought of him makes my blood boil all over again, and I pat my purse to ensure my copy of *Majesty on the Mountain* is tucked inside. Once Phil finishes guiding his daughter through the picnic festivities, I'm going to show him the hard evidence proving that I'm right and Kai was wrong.

"The *Wild Side* crew stopped by the zoo on Thursday," Sam continues, waving away a bee. "I met some of the camera guys and Kai Bridges's co-producer. I heard that Kai stopped in, too, but I was stuck on a call with the mayor's office. Selena from Marketing took him on a golf cart tour of the grounds, and she said she was so nervous that she almost crashed into the sea lion pool."

"I wish he'd crashed into the tiger habitat," I grumble.

Sam's eyes widen, and I realize I haven't told my friends about my tense conversation with Kai. I relay the entire interaction: his gruff, unpleasant attitude; how he insulted the name of the Critter Chat; and his disrespectful, offensive, and *totally incorrect* insistence that I was wrong about Dr. Kimber's nickname.

"The worst part is, he made me look like an idiot in front of Phil," I continue. "But look, I have proof that I'm right."

I whip my copy of Dr. Kimber's book out of my purse so aggressively that Nadeem steps back to avoid getting smacked in the face.

"I'm sure it was just a miscommunication," Elle says. "According to Kai's Instagram, he was in Nova Scotia last week supporting a research project on pilot whales. He was probably just jet-lagged and exhausted when he met you, Luce. That doesn't excuse rudeness, but can a guy who's that devoted to whales really be so terrible?"

Nadeem glances sideways at her. "You follow him on Instagram? You don't even follow me."

"You have three posts, honey," Elle says with a shrug. "Besides, I care very deeply about pilot whales."

"Don't let her fool you," Sam tells Nadeem. "Kai has his shirt off in half his posts, not that I'm complaining. Did you guys see his reel about rescuing that stray puppy in Texas?"

"How could I miss it?" Elle asks. "The puppy was so tiny, and Kai had her all curled up against his chest—"

"Okay, I'm with Lucy here," Nadeem says, frowning at the dreamy look on Elle's face. "He sounds like a major douche."

At least someone's on my side. I'm not surprised by Elle's inclination to give Kai the benefit of the doubt, because she's the sweetest person I know. The harshest criticism I've ever heard her give was to the universally panned *Emoji Movie*, which she scathingly described as "not the best thing I've ever seen."

But I'm not her, and I don't owe anyone a second chance.

"I don't know," I say. "Maybe Kai's not really the friendly, cheery,

'Wowza!'-shouting guy he plays on TV. I think we should consider that he might be a run-of-the-mill asshole who built his career off riding on his mother's coattails."

"Lucy," Elle chides, but I'm not finished.

"Maybe instead of the chummy stone-cold fox he pretends to be, he's just a C-list celebrity with a bad attitude and lazy grooming habits. Honestly, when I met him yesterday, his beard looked a little bit like Tom Hanks's in *Cast Away*. *After* Tom's cargo plane crashes into the Pacific."

"Luce, seriously," Elle interjects, but I wave her off. We can't all be adorable, polka-dotted-dress-wearing versions of Mother Teresa.

"All I'm saying," I continue, drumming my fingers against the book's spine, "is that we shouldn't be surprised if he turns out to be nothing but an overhyped, overpaid—"

"Luce," Nadeem says with an edge to his voice.

I narrow my eyes at him. I thought we were on the same team here. Traitor.

"—egotistical moron," I finish, my insult so cutting that Elle's cheeks turn a furious shade of red.

"Lucy," Sam hisses, looking at me like she's about to smack me upside the head with her Sprite can. "*Stop talking.*"

I stop talking. Sam doesn't sugarcoat anything. If she thinks my words are too cruel, then I've gone too far.

"Sorry," I offer, the hardness evaporating from my tone. "He just really pissed me off."

"It's not . . . you don't . . ." Sam gives me a mournful look, and I wonder if she's just realized that the gingham pattern of my dress makes me look like a walking picnic table.

Elle clears her throat, and Sam stares at her Sprite like the label holds the solution to world peace.

"What is it?" I start to ask, but I stop after *what*, because Elle's cheeks are practically scarlet, and Nadeem grimaces like he's waiting for a bomb to go off.

"Shit," I whisper, squeezing *Majesty on the Mountain* to my chest. I no longer need an answer to my question, because the sheer mortification on my friends' faces tells me everything I need to know.

Kai Bridges, the overhyped, overpaid, egotistical moron, is standing right behind me.

Chapter Four

I don't have to turn around. There's no rule that says I must. I could stand here all day with my back to Kai, pretending like I didn't just unleash a torrent of insults on his character. In fact, if I stand here long enough, something might happen to get me out of this nightmare. Maybe a tornado will appear out of the clear blue sky and we'll all have to run for our lives. Maybe Nick will propose to Margo from Guest Relations and everyone will pity me. Maybe the aquamarine yoga pants lady will swoop in and poison me with a hibiscus-flavored skinny tea.

"So, *Cast Away*," Nadeem says loudly, gripping Elle's hand like he's holding on for dear life. "Great movie, huh?"

I pray for the Forresters' yard to open and swallow me whole.

"Remember the scene where the volleyball falls off the raft and floats away forever?" Nadeem continues in a heroic effort to fill the silence. "Soul crushing."

No one responds except for the bee buzzing around Sam, oblivious to the disaster unfolding in its midst.

"Wil-*son!*" Nadeem mimics in his best Tom Hanks impression, glancing from Elle to Sam to me in desperation. "Wilson, I'm sor—"

"I haven't seen *Cast Away*," a baritone voice behind me interrupts. "But I do like Tom Hanks."

Cringing, I glance toward the sky in hopes that my longed-for tornado might appear, but only a bluebird flies overhead.

"Don't forget about *You've Got Mail*," Nadeem adds, and I take a deep breath before he can compare life to a box of chocolates in a terrible Southern drawl.

I'm an adult. I'm a professional. And there's no tornado coming to save me.

My cheeks blazing with embarrassment, I force myself to turn around slowly, like a spinning ballerina on a winding-down music box. Maybe if I move at a glacial pace, Kai will be gone by the time I finish.

He's not. Instead, he stands before me with his arms folded across his chest, wearing a scowl so deep that Severus Snape would look downright gleeful in comparison. And instead of Thursday's untamed beard, Kai's now clean-shaven, with just the hint of a five o'clock shadow darkening his jawline.

"Hello," I say, the word coming out half-choked. "I . . . um . . ."

He stays quiet, studying me as I scramble for a way to extract my foot from my mouth. Finally, once I've uttered three more "ums" and a last-ditch "so . . . ," his gaze flickers to my name tag.

"Lacy, is it?" he asks with disgust, his nose scrunched up as if my name were *Vomit* or *Aboveground Swimming Pool*.

Damn that tiny tag. "It's Lucy, actually."

He gives me a brief nod, his stern expression unchanged. "Lucy . . ."

Ricardo, I imagine myself lying. *Lawless. Lucy In-the-Sky-with-*

Diamonds. If he doesn't know my last name, he can't run straight to HR to file a complaint.

Sam nudges me with her elbow.

"Rourke," I say finally. "Lucy Rourke." It's not like he won't find out anyway.

"Well, Lucy Rourke," Kai says, his voice thick with abhorrence, "I bet you're wondering just how long I've been standing here."

He crosses his arms tighter over his chest, and I concentrate hard on not looking at the biceps muscles peeking out from underneath his gray T-shirt. The possibility that he heard every awful comment I made makes me want to barricade myself in a Porta-Potty. Just how long *has* he been standing there? Did he hear me reenact our conversation from Thursday, when I impersonated him in a cartoonishly thick South African accent? Did he watch me hoist *Majesty on the Mountain* over my head like it was the Stanley Cup and I was a championship hockey player?

Dear God, did he hear me wishing that he'd landed in the *Amur tiger exhibit*?

"Rosha the tiger is actually a very even-tempered girl," I say quickly, just in case. "For, you know, a tiger."

Kai raises his eyebrows. "I bet she is."

"I'd like to say," I announce, hugging Dr. Kimber's book to my chest so tightly that my boobs would cry out in protest if they could, "that I'm . . ."

Sorry, barks the voice of reason in my head. *Tell him you're sorry! Apologize before he tells Phil that you're not allowed within a hundred yards of him! Plead for forgiveness lest he sic his three million TikTok followers on you!*

While Kai was rude to me on Thursday—and worse, he was *wrong*—

I did go fully balls-to-the-wall on my tirade of criticism. Calling him an asshole based on a single interaction was probably overkill, and it was a low blow to make fun of his beard. Besides, if Kai rats me out to Phil, I can kiss my chances of a promotion farewell. And from the way he's glaring at me like he's a raging elephant and I'm the evil hyena that slaughtered his whole family, I'll be lucky if I still have a job by the end of the picnic.

But try as I might, I can't finish my apology. As Kai's dismissive treatment of me after the Critter Chat replays itself on a loop in my head, the words vanish from my tongue.

"I'm . . . surprised to see you here," I finish lamely.

His scowl deepens. "Clearly."

Before I melt into a puddle under the scorching hatred of his gaze, Sam extends her hand toward Kai.

"Hi, Mr. Bridges. I'm Samira Rahimi, assistant director of communications." She gives him her best please-forgive-my-insane-friend, she-knows-not-what-she-does smile. "Lucy's right about one thing: your presence today is a wonderful surprise! We're honored to have you."

Kai somehow restrains himself from pointing out what's glaringly obvious: that I've given zero impression of his presence being anything resembling *wonderful*.

"Pleased to meet you, Ms. Rahimi," Kai says, shaking her hand. "You helped write the zoo's proposal, correct? I remember your name from the submission."

Sam, who's usually so unflappable that I once watched her yawn on Cedar Point's Top Thrill Dragster while Elle and I screamed our lungs out, nods in surprise. "I did. I'm shocked that you remember."

"I reviewed every proposal myself. Your team's was exceptional."

An infinitesimal fraction of my hostility dissolves at Kai's kind words to Sam. She spent months designing a proposal that would convince Kai's production company to pick Columbus for its first zoo-centric season, and I remember a grueling three-week stretch when her meals consisted solely of triple-shot coffee and microwaved Lean Cuisines in the break room.

"We're thrilled about the show," Elle says, getting in on the help-Kai-forget-that-Lucy's-a-monster action. "I'm Elle, an activities director at the zoo. And when I say *thrilled*, I mean that we're, like, over the moon." She blushes as Kai shakes her hand. "By the way, how's the puppy you rescued from that sinkhole? What was her name— Peaches? Paisley?"

"Penny," Kai answers. "Because she was a good luck charm." For the first time, the hint of a smile crosses his face, and it's like watching Mia's massive Saint Bernard transform into a kitten.

Nadeem, observing the fawning expression on his wife's face with a look of mild horror, points across the lawn. "Mr. Bridges, have you checked out the dessert tent? You don't want to miss out on Jeni's ice cream. It's a Columbus specialty."

I remind myself to hug Nadeem later. Unlike Elle and Sam, who are studying Kai like he's a man-sized scoop of Jeni's Buttercream Birthday Cake ice cream, he understands that we need to get Kai as far away as possible—before I say anything else to implode my career, and before Elle tosses aside her marital vows and rides off into the sunset with Kai and a gaggle of puppies.

Kai shrugs. "Line's a little long."

From the corner of my eye, I spot Mrs. Forrester, a silver-haired woman in a scalloped pink pantsuit, strolling past the catering tent with Shira Woodrow, the zoo's CEO. Full-fledged panic rushes through me as they walk toward us, and I'm desperate to distract Kai from noticing Shira and telling her about my furious rant.

Flustered, I point toward the dessert tent with the sweeping arm arc of an overcaffeinated air traffic controller. "I'm sure you could cut the line. Because you're, well, you know." I gesture toward Kai in the same royal wave motion that Julie Andrews teaches a young Anne Hathaway in *The Princess Diaries*, and Sam whimpers beside me.

The shadow of a grin that crossed his features disappears, replaced by the hateful glower of someone who just learned that his favorite hair gel brand went bankrupt.

"Why could I cut?" Kai asks, sneering. "Because I'm a C-list celebrity? A stone-cold fox? I suppose I *could* ride on my mother's coattails to the front of the line, but that's not really my style."

Shame crawls up my skin when I realize that Kai heard every one of the vicious insults I rattled off to my friends, and I contemplate sprinting into the path of an approaching man on stilts, who's wearing a sleeveless giraffe costume and just might be able to squash me. Surely it's only a matter of seconds before Kai runs to Phil or Shira to tattle on me. I picture the giraffe on stilts dragging me out of the picnic while Margo from Guest Relations records the scene for Snapchat. I'm sure the clip will make its way to the six o'clock news: Deranged zookeeper harasses beloved TV personality, the ticker will read, underneath a video of me furiously trying to escape the giraffe's clutches.

I'm in deep shit.

"About calling you a C-list celebrity and all that other stuff," I say, my pitch reaching a Minnie Mouse level of squeakiness, "I'm really sorry."

Kai's glare doesn't waver. If anything, the angry smolder he's giving me only intensifies, and it's so disarming that I wonder if he practices it in the mirror before bed every night.

"If you really think about it," I continue, the deepening lines of his scowl sending me to the verge of a panic attack, "celebrity is just a matter of perspective. Like, there are only a few people who are A-list without question. Oprah, for example. Beyoncé. Taylor Swift. But after that, it gets a little murky."

I realize I'm rambling like I do whenever I'm nervous. Elle lets out a less than subtle cough to warn me to slow my roll, but she has no chance of stopping me now; I'm a cheetah chasing a lure at sixty miles per hour. I'm a horned lizard spraying blood at my predator. I'm Linda Blair from *The Exorcist* spewing nonsense instead of vomit.

"Take Chris Pratt," I continue as Elle coughs again, this time so loudly that Nadeem checks to see if she's choking. "Is he A-list? You might say yes, considering the success of the *Guardians of the Galaxy* franchise and his marriage to Katherine Schwarzenegger, but the little old lady down the street might confuse him with Pine or Hemsworth or one of the hotter Chrises. So she'd say he's B-list. And that little old lady probably isn't familiar with someone like Big Ed from *90 Day Fiancé*, and neither is your average neighborhood mom, so that puts Big Ed somewhere between D and F. But if you're, like, an avid reality TV fan, then you might consider him more of a D+ star, which is way lower than the Kardashians but higher than, say, the crazy alkaline diet family on *Seeking Sister Wife* . . ." I trail off, realizing I have literally no clue what just came out of my mouth.

"I'm going to be honest," Kai says, blinking at me like I just shined a laser beam into his eyes. "I have no idea what you just said."

Maybe getting dragged out of here by the giraffe stilt guy wouldn't be the worst thing.

"What I was trying to say is," I continue, "I'm really sorry for what I said. I shouldn't have called you names or compared you to Tom Hanks."

Even if you humiliated me in front of Phil, I add silently. *And even though everything I said was true.*

Kai raises his notched eyebrow. "A homeless Tom Hanks, you mean."

"To be precise, Tom Hanks wasn't technically homeless in *Cast Away*. He took shelter inside a cave." I try to give him a conciliatory, please-don't-get-me-fired smile, but it's like grinning into the face of an unnervingly handsome piranha.

"I stand corrected," he says, his tone holding the same quiet anger that Nona's does when it's her cheat food day and I've eaten all the Bagel Bites. "You said I looked like a *cave-dwelling* Tom Hanks."

The growing urge to dive headfirst into the children's bounce house and let a storm of toddlers trample me to death threatens to overwhelm me. "In all fairness, you have shaved your beard since Thursday. So that observation no longer applies."

Kai clenches his jaw so tight that he's probably about to strain at least six different ligaments. "What about your observation that I'm nothing more than an overhyped, overpaid, egotistical moron? Does that still apply, *Lucy*?"

His words hit me like bullets, assassinating any chance I have of not getting a formal written report—or God forbid, a pink slip—added to my employee file. Beads of sweat trickle down my hairline, and my stomach now lives somewhere around my ankles.

"I . . . um . . ."

"You report to Phil Sanders, correct?" Kai asks.

I flinch. Once he tells Phil what I said, it's game over. It won't matter that I've dedicated my life to my job, because it's Kai, not me, who has the potential to earn the zoo a boatload of dollars. After all, he has his very own TV series and a yearly Earth Day special on Animal Planet, and I've got a knack for giving directions to the shitter.

"Yes," I admit, my voice just above a whisper. "But please—"

"Great," Kai says in a tone that is not great at all. "Take care, Lucy."

He nods to my friends before turning away, and I'm tempted to fling Dr. Kimber's book at the back of his head to make him stop.

"By the way," Kai says after a beat, turning back to glance at Elle. "Penny's doing great. She was adopted by a family in Corpus Christi, and she's learning to be a reading therapy dog for kids. She might be missing a leg, but she's got plenty of spirit."

He grins, and it's like watching a Crayola-bright sunrise after spending decades in darkness. The tight lines of his jaw relax, transforming his face from that of Snape's enraged younger brother into the open, easy look of a man who holds doors open for old ladies and doesn't blare his horn when someone cuts him off in traffic. For a fraction of a second, I'm jealous of Penny and her three-legged ability to soften his heart.

But as Elle practically convulses with delight, Kai's gaze shifts back toward me, his sunrise smile replaced by that old familiar scowl. Forget my brief, imaginary glimpse into a lighter side of Kai; he probably mows through school zones in a Maserati and only helps old ladies when there's a camera crew to witness it.

He should be *honored* to be compared to Tom Hanks. But before I can tell him that—or more accurately, before I can beg for his forgiveness so that he doesn't rat me out—the singer of the cover band pauses his rendition of "Sweet Home Alabama" mid lyric.

"Sorry for the interruption, everybody," the tattooed singer announces, raising his hands for pardon. "But I've just learned that we have a celebrity guest!"

My throat tightens as a murmur of excitement spreads through the crowd. Cornhole players and dads chasing toddlers glance around the lawn, searching for a retired OSU football coach or the cherished local meteorologist who lets his Pomeranian chill under the green screen during broadcasts.

But while everyone else peers around for the mystery celebrity, Kai's gaze stays on mine. We're like gun-slinging, Wild West cowboys staring each other down before a duel, except one of us has appeared on *Anderson Cooper 360°* and the other might be unemployed come Monday morning.

"It's Kai Bridges, host of *On the Wild Side!*" the singer declares with such jubilance that you'd think Kai just gifted everyone a baby bottlenose dolphin.

The hate-fueled fire in Kai's eyes dwindles, and for an instant his shoulders slump in what looks like exhaustion. But then, quick as the switch of a light, the scowl plastered onto his face morphs into a megawatt smile so warm and effervescent that it would make even his toughest critic go weak in the knees.

I make a mental note to strengthen my knees.

We don't get many celebrities in Columbus—our biggest home-grown star is the rapper Lil' Bow Wow, who skipped town long before he dropped the *Lil'* from his name—so I'm not surprised when people react as though Dwayne the Rock Johnson showed up. The crowd whoops and hollers, and I spot Phil's daughter Maya jumping up and down with excitement, going so absolutely apeshit that she drops her candy apple on the ground.

"*Move*, Edgar!" an elderly woman near the photo booth cries, jostling her cane-bearing husband out of the way to get a better glance at Kai. "I want a selfie!"

"What do you say to coming up here and welcoming everybody to Picnic for Paws?" the singer asks, motioning for Kai to come on-stage.

Grinning, Kai shakes his head in fake hesitation, as if he's not loving the attention. As if he's not soaking up the roaring applause of the crowd like a sandgrouse soaks up water in the desert.

"Kai! Kai! Kai!" the crowd chants.

Stop applauding that self-satisfied jerkface! I want to scream. But the chant only heightens in volume, and I half expect a flock of Sperry-wearing dads to hoist Kai in the air and carry him to the stage.

Before I can alert the crowd to Kai's poor manners, he turns away from his doting disciples and strides toward me. His movements are lightning quick, like a lion springing into action to chase down his prey, and before I can think to sneeze on him and pass it off as an accident, I'm inhaling the heady scent of campfire and Old Spice.

Huh. I'd pegged him for an Axe-body-spray kinda guy.

He's close enough that I could smack him upside the head with Dr. Kimber's book, and I might seriously consider that option if there weren't several hundred people here to witness the crime. But my murderous instincts must flash across my face, because Kai reaches forward and takes my copy of *Majesty on the Mountain* right out of my clenched hand.

"Hey!" I protest, but before I can threaten to tell *People* magazine about his thieving ways, he's holding the book just out of reach.

"Mind if I borrow this?" he asks, ignoring my attempts to grab it back. "By the way," he says, tilting his head toward me so I'm close enough to spot the tones of cognac and flecks of forest green in his eyes. "I know I'm no Beyoncé, or—what did you call him? Large Ed—but my fans sure seem to like me."

He smirks as the chant of "Kai! Kai! Kai!" rings in my ears, and the lazy smugness of his face makes me long for the moments when he glared at me like I was a discount bottle of drugstore shampoo.

"Cheers, Lucy," he adds as he heads toward the stage. "Maybe I'll see you around."

"It's *Big* Ed!" I yell after him, not sure if he hears me over the cries of his worshiping stans. "And get Beyoncé's name out of your mouth!"

But instead of listening, Kai struts toward the stage.

"He stole my book!" I lament to my friends, gritting my teeth as I spot Phil punching the air with the excitement of a rave goer who's high on life and Molly. "And did you hear the last thing he said— *maybe I'll see you around*? As in, maybe he *won't*? As in, he's going to tell Phil what I said and get me fired?"

But my friends don't hear me, because the crowd's volume swells as Kai takes the stage. A heavy dread settles in my stomach as the singer hands him the microphone, sending Phil and every Lululemon-sporting mom around into an even bigger frenzy. The admission makes me want to throw up, but Kai was right: he hasn't uttered a single word yet, and the crowd already loves him.

My heart falls into my stomach, where it joins my nerves in a churning, simmering mess. Because it doesn't really matter why Kai's accent mysteriously comes and goes, or whether he's actually an over-paid moron. It doesn't even matter that we both know I'm right about Dr. Kimber's nickname, or that he stole the book that proves it.

All that matters is that it's him, not me, who's running this show. Literally. And that makes one thing clear: I am totally, royally, *wildly* screwed.

Chapter Five

I'm so nervous the rest of the weekend that I can barely breathe. Every time my phone buzzes, I'm convinced it's Phil calling to fire me, or Mario Lopez, cohost of *Access Hollywood*, angling for an interview with the unhinged gorilla lady who went full Karen on the world's most beloved puppy rescuer. On Sunday afternoon, I burrow into the soft cushions of the living room couch and sip a glass of wine as I obsessively refresh Kai's social media pages. If he decides to publicly drag me, I want to see the post right away, so that I have time to pack a go-bag before any of his rabid fans show up to seek revenge.

"Whatcha watching?" a voice behind me asks, startling me so badly that I almost spill wine all over the cream-colored couch.

I turn around to see my grandmother's best friend Trudy studying my iPad over my shoulder, and I tilt the screen away from her quickly. "Oh, nothing. Just browsing."

The last thing I want to do is get stuck in a conversation with Trudy, whose two favorite hobbies are collecting embroidered blouses and bringing up the sore subject of my ex-boyfriend. She and Nona grew close after meeting at a widows' support group twenty years ago, and while I admire their long-lasting friendship, I try to avoid Trudy's gossipy inquiries whenever I can.

"How was the fundraiser?" Nona asks, following Trudy into the living room.

"Is that what you wore?" Trudy asks, eyeing my ratty Ohio State T-shirt with obvious surprise. "It's not khaki."

I sigh and take a generous sip of wine. "The picnic was fine," I lie. "And of course I didn't wear a T-shirt with holes in it to the fundraiser. I didn't wear khaki, either. I'm not totally inept."

Trudy, who's currently sporting a collared sweatshirt with a beaming basset hound on it and has zero right to judge my fashion choices, shrugs. "If you say so. Was Nick there?"

I take another swig of wine. If I keep drinking at this rate, I'll be seeing two-headed basset hounds before the conversation is over. "I'm not sure. And if he had been, I would have avoided him anyway."

Trudy helps herself to a handful of Cheez-Its from the box beside me. "That's too bad. I always liked Nick. Such a nice young man. Do you know he changed a flat tire for me once?"

I wish the iPad was a book so I could slam it shut, because pulling my index finger away from the screen doesn't have the same effect. I'm fully aware that Nona, Trudy, and their entire social circle liked Nick. Loved Nick. Their friend Shirley was so disappointed by our breakup that *I* had to hand *her* a wad of Kleenex at Nona's Galentine's Day party. If I have to listen one more time while Trudy rhapsodizes about the time Nick said her perm looked nice, I might lose my shit.

"Yes, Trudy," I say, making a concerted effort not to grit my teeth. "I helped him change the tire, remember?"

"And he had such nice buttocks," she adds, grabbing another

cracker and ignoring my response completely. "It's really a pity he doesn't come around anymore."

"He's not dead, Gertrude," I snap, running out of patience and Cheez-Its. "If you like his ass so much, why not ask him out yourself? He was a big fan of your perm."

She lets out a high-pitched whistle, as if to say, *My, my, somebody's testy,* but Nona places a soothing hand on the top of my head.

"Speaking of nice buttocks," my grandmother says, nodding toward my iPad. "He's quite the looker, eh?"

I know she's only trying to change the subject so that Trudy and I don't rip each other's heads off, but I scramble to pause the video playing on the screen.

"Oooh, *On the Wild Side!*" Trudy chirps, batting my hand away from the iPad. "Love that show. That Kai Bridges sure is a tall glass of water."

My petrified refreshing of Kai's social media led me down a YouTube clip rabbit hole of his greatest hits, and I seriously regret not doing my Insta-stalking in the privacy of my bedroom.

"He's not *that* tall," I protest. "And I wouldn't call him a looker, exactly."

Nona blinks at me and then at the iPad, where an on-screen Kai traverses through a grassy plain in a military green Jeep. Wearing a gray Patagonia jacket, a safari-style hat, and a mischievous grin, he keeps one hand on the wheel and rests the other on the back of the passenger seat. It's very *Crocodile Dundee* meets *GQ,* and by the time he stops the Jeep next to a watering hole and removes his jacket, both Trudy and Nona are practically salivating.

"You were saying?" Nona prods as the camera swoons over Kai, zooming out so that the waning rays of the sunset shine on his auburn hair.

"Wowza!" on-screen Kai says in a lilting accent as an elephant approaches the hole and lowers its trunk into the water.

"Wowza," Trudy repeats, pressing one hand to her chest. "Magnificent."

I'm not sure if she's talking about the elephant or the annoying human who's probably going to wreck my career, and I pause the clip as Kai removes his safari hat and runs a hand through his hair like he's a star-crossed lover in a Taylor Swift video.

Before Trudy can protest, I hear the patter of footsteps in the foyer, and I down the remaining contents of my wineglass as Mia and Karina enter the living room, Mia's perpetually slobbery Saint Bernard Dynamite trailing behind them.

"Lucy!" Mia greets me. She's wearing her hair in twin braids high up on either side of her head, and between those and the mound of curly bangs piled on her forehead, she looks like the love child of Pippi Longstocking and Curly Sue.

I wince as Dynamite places his enormous front paws in my lap, but I'm grateful for a distraction from listening to Nona and Trudy wax poetic about Kai's rear end. "Hey, Mia."

"Want to come to lunch with us, Luce?" Nona asks, grabbing Dynamite's collar before he can curl into a gigantic ball on my lap. "We're going to the Pearl, and I know you love their fried oysters."

I do love fried oysters, but the hopeful look on Karina's face when Nona invites me makes my stomach clench. I'd rather get a root canal than join in on an unnecessary outing with my mother, and besides, I have big plans to spend the rest of the day hyperventilating about my job security.

"Thanks, but I have a ton of research to do."

Karina's face falls, but she quickly recovers with a half smile.

"We're stopping for ice cream afterward. I'll bring you something from Handel's. The butter pecan cone is your favorite, right?"

"Bring one for me, too," Mia tells her. "I don't want to go to lunch, either. I'd rather stay here and help Lucy with her research." Before I can protest, she unzips her backpack and retrieves a handful of pencils and a notebook bearing JoJo Siwa's beaming face. "See? I've got supplies and everything."

Her expression is that of a shelter puppy hoping to be loved by a new family, and I can't bring myself to point out that I don't need pencils or notebooks. I'm not writing a Kai Bridges–themed burn book, after all—not that it's the worst idea in the world.

"Um, well," I stammer, trying to think of a gentle way to break her heart, "I actually don't—"

"That's lovely, Mia," Nona interrupts, shooting me a look that says, *How do you like your free rent and 24/7 access to my wine cellar?* "I'm sure Lucy can use your help."

I curse my grandmother silently, but I know she's right. Lots of people would kill for the generosity she's shown me, and the least I can do to repay her is not be an asshole to innocent Mia.

"Really?" Mia asks, her face lighting up.

The fact that spending time with me is worth skipping dinner threatens to fill me with guilt, but I push the pang away. It's not my fault that Mia and I aren't close, and I can hardly be expected to rearrange my busy schedule to accommodate her.

But I guess I can let her sit next to me while I panic.

"Sure," I reply, not sounding sure at all.

Mia doesn't seem to notice my reluctance. "Every good research team needs snacks," she declares, skipping toward the kitchen. "I'll be right back!"

57

As Dynamite lumbers after Mia, Nona runs a hand over my hair. "Thank you. Spending time with you means the world to your sister."

Half sister, I'm tempted to correct her. *Sister* implies that Mia and I grew up fighting over clothes and toys and the remote control and entrusting each other with our deepest, darkest secrets, but that's a bond we'll never have. After all, I'm nineteen years older, and before Karina showed up in Columbus with a dad-joke-machine husband and a gangly preteen in tow, Mia was barely a blip on my radar. And while it's not her fault that the same mother who lovingly stitches Girl Scout patches onto her vest dropped ten-year-old me like a hot potato, it doesn't change the fact that spending time with her makes my chest ache.

"I'll bring you back two scoops of fudge ripple," my grandmother promises, lowering her voice and pressing a kiss to my cheek. The silver locks of her hair tickle my ear, and the scent of vanilla and Chanel No. 5 lingers when she pulls away.

I nod toward the iPad. "Thanks. Better get back to it."

I don't need to tell Nona, who knows I haven't touched butter pecan in years, that I'll have another excuse ready the next time Karina invites me out, just like I blamed my busy schedule for skipping Alfie's birthday meal. Because as much as I try to pretend it doesn't bother me, Nona understands that seeing Karina and Mia together for an entire dinner reminds me of the inescapable fact that will forever set my *sister* and me apart: we might have the same mother, but we had very different moms.

And there's not an ice cream cone in the world that can fix that.

Within minutes, Mia's assembled a pile of lopsided sandwiches on the coffee table.

"It's fairy bread," she says, pointing to the slices of bread loaded with peanut butter, sprinkles, and marshmallows. She plops onto the couch and slides an iPad out of her backpack. "So, what are we researching?"

I watch as Dynamite sniffs the bread, coming dangerously close to dripping slobber onto the stack of sandwiches. "It's not what, it's who," I explain. "And when did you get an iPad?"

"Last week. Mommy said she'd get me one if I promised to stop practicing my harmonica before sunrise. I'm trying to learn the Mario Brothers theme song." She snuggles closer to her dog, and it occurs to me that if it weren't for my strained relationship with Karina, I might like Mia a hell of a lot.

"Do you play any instruments?" she asks, wiggling her toes against my hip. The casual familiarity of the gesture unnerves me, and I slide farther away and place my iPad between us.

"No. I took voice lessons when I was little, but I wasn't very good."

Just as Karina's TV show *Guilty Pleasures* took off, back when my mom fantasized that she could fashion me into a young Melanie Griffith to her Tippi Hedren and we'd be the next mother-daughter duo to take Hollywood by storm, she signed me up for singing lessons with a lady who'd trained half a dozen Nickelodeon stars. But by the third session, when I still couldn't squeeze out a round of the *Mommy made me wash my M&M's* vocal warmup without making my own ears bleed, Karina gave up on my musical abilities. I'll never forget the mortified bewilderment she studied me with as I followed her to the car after class, like she couldn't possibly fathom how she, who performed with the tenderness of Judy Garland and the hip flexibility of Jennifer Lopez, birthed a creature who sounded like Alanis Morissette being tortured underwater.

"Sounds fun," Mia says, not even flinching when Dynamite licks a glob of peanut butter off her chin.

"It wasn't," I say flatly.

Her eyes widen like I've scolded her, and I instantly regret my harsh tone. It wasn't Mia who treated me like I was a disappointment. But her excitement returns full force when she points at my iPad, where on-screen Kai's face is frozen into a grin that could, despite my reluctance to admit it, melt the hardest of hearts.

"Wait, you're researching Kai Bridges? I love him!" Mia coos. "The episode where he gets licked by a sun bear is hilarious. And look, have you watched his dance with Ellen? My friend Abby almost fainted when she saw it."

Before I can say "sun bear," Mia hoists her iPad in front of my nose, and I'm watching Kai strut onto the stage of *The Ellen DeGeneres Show*, his hips snug in a pair of dark-wash jeans that show off the bulk of his thighs. He sways from side to side, moving with more rhythm than I'd expect from a man who has a large stick up his ass. When he turns his booty toward the audience, gyrating in a hypnotizing fashion that helps me understand why Abby got light-headed, I have to take a bite of fairy bread to stop myself from panting.

But that easygoing, ass-shaking Kai is nothing like the guy who stole my book.

When the dance is over, Mia types Kai's name into Google and scrolls through a dizzying number of hits. She reads aloud from an *Interview* magazine article detailing his remarkable childhood: he had twelve stamps in his passport by the age of two, and his parents, American primatologist Dr. Charlotte Kimber and South African wildlife photographer Alexander Bridges, had divorced, remarried, and divorced again before Kai was old enough to read.

"Did you know Kai's mom saved a bunch of gorillas in Rwanda?" Mia asks. She points at an image of a tiny, gangly-limbed Kai poking his head out of a canvas tent, a notebook-toting Dr. Kimber looping an arm around his shoulders. "Virunga National Park, 1997," Mia reads. "Wow."

Mia asking if I'm familiar with Dr. Kimber is like asking Harry Potter if Voldemort was bad, and I nod. Kai's mother isn't just my professional idol; she was my childhood vision of the perfect mother. After Karina shipped me off to live at Nona's so she could enjoy *Guilty Pleasures'* success without me dragging her down, I fantasized about what it would be like to have a mom who loved me. My first pretend mom was Nona's neighbor Mrs. Elgine, who styled her daughters' hair into matching French braids and always carried Skittles in her purse. Then it was the *Lizzie McGuire* mom, followed by the ever-patient and awesome-haired Marge Simpson. Finally, after Nona took me to visit Zuri at the zoo and kickstarted my gorilla obsession, she bought me a copy of Dr. Kimber's *Majesty on the Mountain*. After that, I retired my fantasies of being the fourth Simpson kid and reimagined myself as Dr. Kimber's only daughter. In my daydreams, Mommy Kimber and I wore matching braids and traipsed through the jungle hand in hand, eating beef jerky and berries and tracking mountain gorillas until our feet ached. Sometimes Kai, whose childhood adventures at Dr. Kimber's research camp are documented in her book, came, too.

Carrying a satchel full of Goldfish crackers and Hug juice barrels through the woods behind Nona's subdivision, I'd spot a white-tailed deer and pretend it was a gorilla. In my fantasy, Dr. Kimber and I would return to camp after a hard day's work, and we'd cook stew and play Uno, and she'd never force me to suffer through humiliating singing lessons or call me a disappointment.

She'd sic a mountain goat on anyone who tried.

"Whoa, there's even a movie about her," Mia continues, unbothered by my silence. "Have you seen it?"

"Uh, yes. Probably a hundred times."

The movie, titled *Majesty on the Mountain* like the book, starred a glammed-down Diane Lane and followed Dr. Kimber's attempts to study a gorilla troop led by the proud silverback Taji. In the film's most famous and heartbreaking scene, a band of poachers murders Taji, and eleven-year-old me was so scarred by it that I almost vomited up my popcorn.

"Well, if you like it, then I know I'll like it, too. Let's watch," Mia says, grabbing the Fire TV Stick remote. "For research."

"You might have nightmares," I warn.

"Don't worry, I'm brave." Ignoring my protests, Mia hits the play button, and the opening credits roll on Nona's TV.

I know the dialogue by heart, and I find myself mouthing the characters' lines as we watch the actor versions of Dr. Kimber, Kai, and her research team trudge through the thick Rwandan forest. At first, Taji's troop runs for safety anytime Dr. Kimber approaches, but by the second half of the movie, she's earned their trust, and Taji looks on as a young gorilla drops tree bark onto Dr. Kimber's head and playfully cuddles into her lap.

Mia gasps at every plot twist that threatens the team's quest to save the gorillas from extinction—tense skirmishes with poachers, run-ins with corrupt governments, Dr. Kimber's bouts of malaria and depression—and coos at every shot of the majestic animals. My heart races as we get closer to the pivotal scene, and when the gap-toothed actor playing a young Kai and a sweating Diane Lane zip up their raincoats and head out to find Taji's troop, I grip Dynamite's paw for comfort.

"Oh no," Mia whispers as the score reaches a haunting crescendo and young Kai steps on a poacher's snare, dropping to the ground and screaming in pain. Diane Lane turns back to help him just as a band of gun-wielding poachers cuts between her and the gorillas, and the camera lingers on her terror-stricken face as she recognizes the gut-wrenching decision before her: leave her son in agony and risk the poachers finding him, or abandon Taji's troop to the same fate.

"Mom! Help!" little actor-Kai screams as Taji roars a warning to his troop, and poor, tortured Diane Lane takes three steps toward the gorillas before turning back toward her son.

By the end of the scene, Mia and I are both in tears, and Dynamite uses his long tongue to lick Mia's away. But our heartache is nothing compared to the tragedy played out on-screen, where Dr. Kimber saves Kai but Taji, her beloved friend, dies trying to protect his troop from the poachers. Nona and Karina get home just as the movie flashes forward several years to the opening of the Charlotte Kimber Research Center near Mount Karisimbi, a conservation station dedicated to noble Taji's memory.

"Crap. I don't think we brought enough ice cream for this," Nona says when she finds us crying into our shirtsleeves.

"I'm too sad to eat," Mia announces, and when she scoots Dynamite off the couch so she can slide closer to me, I don't protest.

Because what I just witnessed on-screen—the decision of a mother who loved her child so dearly that she sacrificed everything for him—hits me as hard now as it did when I was little. The thought of having a mom like that, a mom who wouldn't abandon her kid, whether to a snare or to achieve her dreams of stardom, fills me with a heavy longing.

"You know, I met Diane Lane at a casting call once," Karina says, as if I needed the reminder that she's no Dr. Kimber. "Super nice lady, and she had the shiniest hair I've ever seen."

Mia, who doesn't seem to give two shits about the sheen of Diane's hair, blows her nose into the collar of her T-shirt.

My phone pings, and I realize I got so sucked into the movie that I forgot about my job-related panic. But it rushes back to me when I glance at the screen to see a text from Phil: Please meet me in my office at 8am tomorrow.

My heart plummets to my knees, and my fingers tremble as I unlock my phone to type out a response.

"You okay, Lucy?" Karina asks, studying me with a look of concern. "You're shaking."

"I'm just upset about what happened to poor Taji," I lie, doing my best to steady my hands. "It makes the Shadow-gets-stuck-in-a-hole scene from *Homeward Bound* look lighthearted."

I try to sound calm, as if my world's not on the verge of imploding, but I can't hide the flood of panic that makes my voice waver. Because unlike my mother and Diane Lane, I'm not an actress.

And after tomorrow, I might not be a zookeeper, either.

Chapter Six

That night, I toss and turn and dream of things that make me break out in a cold sweat: Kai's impermeable scowl. Phil snatching the Dr. Kimber bobblehead off my desk and flinging it into the trash. Trudy chasing me around Nona's backyard, peppering me with questions about Nick and my impending spinsterhood as the basset hound from her sweatshirt leaps off the polyester blend and lunges at me. I know they're ridiculous dreams—who ever heard of an aggressive basset hound?—but they rattle me enough to have me out of bed by five a.m. and inside Ape House by six, my hair still wet from a hasty shower.

I'm not on breakfast prep duty today, but I head to the kitchen anyway, where I fill paper cups with biscuits and raisins for the gorillas' morning snack. For safety, I need to wait for another keeper's arrival before moving the troop to their daytime exhibit, so I carry the cups to their sleeping quarters. I sit cross-legged in front of the mesh barrier that separates me from the gorillas and tug a surgical mask over my face to protect them from germs. The troop is still asleep, so I set their snack aside and fish a sketchpad from my backpack.

When I dated Nick, I rarely arrived at the zoo before sunrise. Instead, we'd sip coffee in bed while he reviewed his daily lineup of procedures and I brainstormed activities for gorilla enrichment. We'd drive to work together, and he'd drop me off at Ape House with a kiss before heading to the animal health center. I thought we'd spend the rest of our lives like that, climbing the career ladder as a team. I thought we were happy.

I was wrong. Just after our second anniversary, Nick's younger sister had a baby. On the drive home from meeting the little tyke, a red-faced bundle of joy whose screams made my teeth clench, Nick reached across the passenger seat and took my hand.

"I think I want kids," he said, his tone perfectly casual. Like he'd said, *I think I want tacos* or *I think we're out of detergent.*

I'd been thinking the opposite—that I was elated to return to his quiet townhome, where we could have sex and send emails without a tiny human disrupting us. I'd been honest from our first date that I didn't want kids, and maybe not even marriage. That I'd witnessed how children could hinder a woman's career, and I wasn't about to have a kid and then resent her so much that I ship her off to her grandmother's. And Nick was on the same page, until he wasn't. Until that one-sentence grenade he flung in the car exploded, and suddenly he was talking about engagement rings and ovulation strips and ring sling baby carriers. Until he realized that I wasn't going to suddenly transform from a workaholic caterpillar into a beautiful butterfly of motherhood, wasn't going to ooh and aah over tiny baby onesies like Elle.

So when he dumped me and started dating Margo from Guest Relations three weeks later, I needed something to fill my early-morning hours, and something to do with my hands besides scroll through Margo's Instagram for evidence of their abundantly hashtagged bliss. At Nona's suggestion, I bought a sketchpad and a charcoal pencil set and have spent the predawn hours of the past four months trying to draw the gorillas. Unfortunately, my artistic ability is about on par with my people skills, and my recent sketch of Mac, the troop's eight-year-old blackback, looks like a portrait of a chubby dog with oversized pecs.

I flip my sketchbook to a fresh page to start over, and when I look up from my work, I spot Zuri knuckle-walking past her sleeping troopmates toward me.

"Morning, Z," I greet her as she settles across from me on the other side of the mesh. "Want a snack?"

She scratches her chin in response, and even though I look at her every day, I can't help but marvel at the pronounced ridge of bone that juts out over her remarkably human-looking eyes. A thin blaze of copper fur stretches from her brow ridge to the top of her head, as if someone ran a paintbrush over her with an elaborate flourish, and the slight upward curve of her lips makes her look perpetually amused.

"Touch." I ball my hand into a fist and place it on the mesh. When Zuri places her dinner-plate-sized hand against mine, I pass a biscuit square through the netting.

"Smart girl!" I cheer. "Now, arm." I press my other fist to the mesh, and she leans one thick arm into my touch in exchange for another treat.

Using biscuits and handfuls of raisins as enticement, I ask Zuri to show me everything from her chest to the inside of her mouth so that I can note any physical changes, from a patch of dry skin to an infected tooth. Western lowland gorillas in captivity can live into their fifties, and at thirty-one years old, Zuri is in excellent health. As I conduct her daily health check, the familiar routine loosens the knot of anxiety in my belly. When I'm working, whether I'm interacting with the gorillas or traipsing around Ape House with a bucket and a mop, I don't have the mental bandwidth to worry about my scuffle with Kai Bridges or contemplate the fact that Nick replaced me in no time at all. I can concentrate solely on the task in front of me, and practicing Zuri's operant conditioning training gives my mind a break from the inconvenient stressors of my personal life.

After Zuri clambers off to fluff up the hay in her night nest, I return to my sketchbook. Mac's still asleep, which makes it tough to work on his portrait, so I focus on perfecting the unruly bit of fur that sticks up from the back of his head. But I've barely touched my charcoal pencil to the paper when my phone vibrates, and I grab it out of my satchel to find a text from Elle.

Drinks at Liberty Tavern later no matter what happens at your meeting. You got this, Lucy! And by drinks, I mean you guys can get margs while I cry into my sparkling water.

I fire back a thumbs-up, but the calm that came over me during Zuri's training session dissipates instantly. I'm grateful for Elle's support, but I don't think she and Sam realize how devastated I'll be if Phil fires me. They love their jobs, too, but if Elle got laid off or Sam moved to a corporate gig, they'd adapt just fine. Unlike me, they have thriving social lives and actual hobbies that don't involve dreadful attempts to doodle primates at six a.m. So when Elle says I've got this, no matter what, I know she's wrong: my keeper job is everything to me, and without it, I'll be lost.

After all, while Sam was buying her luxury townhome and Elle and Nadeem were deciding to start a family, I was knee-deep in hay in Ape House, poring over journal articles and research data and

Excel spreadsheets until my eyes ached. Sam has her five-thousand-hits-per-day blog and impressive investment portfolio, and Elle has her doting husband and growing belly, and Nona has a flush retirement account and a seemingly endless ability to forgive Karina for her sins.

I have Zuri. I've got bonobos and Suma the orangutan and a perfect work attendance record, and that's all I ever wanted.

But if I lose that, I'll have nothing.

Chapter Seven

At exactly seven fifty-eight a.m., I tap my Dr. Kimber bobblehead for good luck and make the short but agonizing trek from my office to Phil's. When I find the door closed, the pit in my stomach opens wider. He only closes the door when he's packed hard-boiled eggs for lunch or when he's doing uncomfortable Boss Things, like explaining to Scotty the intern that yes, Parkour is cool, but no, it's not acceptable to leap backward off the coffee kiosk and land on an unsuspecting Lottie. I imagine him rehearsing my firing on the phone to his wife while he listens to "Eye of the Tiger" and throws little punches in the air to psych himself up.

Bracing for the worst, I take a deep breath and knock. I hear muffled voices, and my pulse races as I consider who might be in there with Phil. Maybe it's the suspenders-wearing HR rep who stops by every year to drone on about ethics compliance, except today he's here to oversee my termination. Or perhaps it's my buddy Norm the security guard, ready to escort me out of Ape House like a ref dragging a streaker off a football field.

I really hope it's not Norm, because I'll fight him if I must.

Before I can practice a karate chop, Phil opens the door. "Morning, Lucy," he says, his ruddy cheeks showing the effects of a weekend sunburn. "Come in."

I don't need to ask who's waiting for us in his office. Because as soon as Phil waves me inside, I glimpse a flash of hair so auburn and maddeningly lustrous that I'd recognize it anywhere.

It's Kai Bridges, loyal friend of sun bears and Ellen DeGeneres and enemy of me. And he's here to seek revenge.

Regret burns in my belly as I step into Phil's office, my organs melting into a puddle of goo. Why in the name of all that is holy did I run my mouth about Kai in public? Why couldn't I take Elle's sunshine-and-rainbows approach and recognize that one negative encounter with someone doesn't necessarily mean they're a complete and total asshole?

And most important, why is the real-life Kai Bridges—unlike the smooth-talking, swashbuckling, clean-shaven adventurer he portrays on TV—such a complete and total asshole?

I slide into the chair next to Kai's while he ignores my arrival in favor of typing on his phone, his fingers flying. He's left his keyboard sounds turned on like a psychopath, and the flurry of annoying clicks grates my fried nerves even further. I can only imagine the plight of the poor souls forced to sit next to him on transatlantic flights.

"Freya's on board," Kai tells Phil. "She says we're good to go."

"Who's Freya?" I ask, convinced she's the hotshot attorney Kai hired to annihilate me in court when he sues me for slander.

An angry beeping sound from the printer drowns out my question, and if Kai hears me, he doesn't bother to answer.

I tuck my trembling hands under my legs and decide that before this goes any further, I should make a last-ditch effort to salvage my career. I'm sure Kai told Phil a convincing sob story about my tactlessness at the picnic, but I bet he left out the fact that he was wrong about *Majesty on the Mountain*—and that he stole my book.

"Before we start," I say, trying to swallow the mousiness out of my voice, "I'd like to share my version of the events that transpired. And to be fair to everyone involved, I want to apologize for my role in what happened."

Kai glances up from his phone, and the hint of a smirk tugs at his lips. He must be chomping at the bit to watch my life go up in flames. How is this evil maniac the same guy who swayed his hips so seductively on *Ellen*? The memory of his booty wiggling back and forth is enough to warm my cheeks, and I find myself glancing at the generous thighs currently taking up Phil's finest swivel chair.

He doesn't deserve to look that good in slacks.

Kai's gaze follows mine to his lap, and the hint of a smirk turns into an all-out snicker. "Are you all right, Lucy? You seem to be sweating a lot."

I tear my gaze away and make intense eye contact with Phil's Swingline stapler. "I'm fine, thank you. Again, Phil, about what happened—"

My boss leans across his desk and lowers his voice conspiratorially. "If you're apologizing about that clogged toilet last week, don't worry. Maintenance sent a couple guys down with an auger, and they fixed it in no time."

From the corner of my eye, I note Kai's broad shoulders shaking in barely contained laughter. Fabulous. Now in addition to getting fired, everyone will think I suffer from GI distress.

"No," I say, wishing an asteroid would drop from the sky and finish me off. "That, um, wasn't me."

"It's my fault, really," Phil continues. "I should have known better than to let Scotty participate in the staff chili cookoff. He's a great kid and he's learning a lot, but I don't think he has a full understanding of meat refrigeration protocols."

"Right," I say, scratching at the itch crawling up my arms. "Again, wasn't me. I was actually talking about what happened at Picnic for Paws."

Phil blinks as if he has no idea what I'm talking about.

Puzzled, I glance at Kai, who leans back in his chair and shrugs like he's just as bewildered as my boss. "I had a blast at Picnic for Paws," he says easily. "Great crowd. Good vibe. Did you not have a blast, Lucy?"

He cocks his scarred eyebrow at me, and that's when I realize: he hasn't said a word about my tirade to Phil.

"I, um . . . no, I did have a blast," I stammer, trying to hide my confusion from Phil. I was so convinced Kai ratted me out that my brain can hardly process what's happening. "The vibe was, as you said, quite excellent."

"Great." Kai beams at me and then at Phil, and I wonder what happened to the man who scowled so deeply on Saturday that I thought his face might get stuck. Maybe he found the Lord over the weekend. Maybe he got laid. Or maybe he knows that if he keeps my outburst between us, he's got the upper hand.

Whatever dastardly plan he's crafting, he gives Phil a Boy Scout–wholesome smile and taps the desk with his palm. "Let's get down to business, shall we?"

Phil grins at Kai like he's Jesus Christ and Barack Obama rolled up into one person, and jealousy surges through me. *I* want to be the one on the receiving end of Phil's approving smiles.

"Yes, let's get down to business," I agree, tucking a hand under my chin in what I hope is a confident pose. "What's the business?"

And why the heck is Kai here for it?

"Yesterday I got a phone call from Alexandra St. John, lead curator at the Miami Zoo," Phil explains. "They've been trying to match Keeva with a surrogate."

I nod. I know exactly who Alexandra and Keeva are. Keeva, a four-month-old infant gorilla born at the Austin Zoo, was the only survivor of a disastrous *E. coli* outbreak that killed three adult gorillas in her troop, including her parents. Little Keeva was transferred to Miami in hopes of connecting her with a surrogate mother, and I've followed her story closely.

"So far, Alexandra's team hasn't had any luck getting one of their females to act as a surrogate," Phil says. "They're worried for Keeva, and they want to move her here."

If my heart had legs, it would leap out of my chest with excitement at this incredible news. "Here? To Columbus?"

Phil nods. "Exactly. And I want you to help lead the charge on her transition."

The nervous butterflies that conga-lined in my stomach earlier take flight again, but this time out of elation instead of terror. Not only am I not getting fired today, but Phil wants me—me!—to help integrate an orphaned baby gorilla into our troop. I feared today might be the worst day of my life, but instead it's Christmas and Halloween and the time I spotted Ali Wong at the O'Hare Airport all at once.

"It'll be a team effort, obviously, but I want you to see this as a chance to step into a leadership role," Phil adds.

My brain translates his words into *I want you to see this as an audition for the senior keeper job*, and I'm tempted to cartwheel around his office.

"Obviously, the plight of an orphaned baby gorilla will be catnip to viewers, and I want to capture every second of Keeva's journey for the show," Kai says. "So get ready for your close-up."

A prickly sensation creeps up my spine. The breezy way he describes "Keeva's journey" makes him sound like the host of *The Bachelor* describing the fantasy suite escapades of an airheaded twenty-something. I imagine him sporting a designer tux in the Ape House nursery, offering the terrified baby gorilla a rose if she'll do him the honor of reeling in a million viewers.

But Keeva's not entertainment for the fans who shell out for Kai's exclusive T-shirt line; she's a living, breathing creature who lost her entire troop—the very foundation of her existence.

"What do you mean, close-up?" I ask, imagining a team of frustrated stylists trying to blow-dry the frizz out of my hair. "You're the host of *On the Wild Side*. I'm just a keeper."

I planned on spending the summer safely behind the scenes, far away from the cameras.

Kai shakes his head, and his hair's so magnificent that he looks like a majestical Andalusian horse shaking out his mane. If I weren't half convinced this was all an elaborate plot to tank my career, I might ask if I could touch it.

"I'm the host, yes, but I don't want this season to be about me," he says.

What a regular Mother Teresa.

"I understand that most people don't have the opportunities I do," he continues. "They'll never get to swim with tiger sharks in the Gulf of Mexico or bottle-feed baby bonobos at a rescue in the Congo. But most people *can* experience the magic of wildlife at a zoo, and keepers are an essential part of that magic. So I don't want this to be another regular season of *On the Wild Side with Kai Bridges*. I want it to be *On the Wild Side with Keeva. On the Wild Side with Lucy. On the Wild Side with Phil.*"

He fixes my boss with a smile that could blind the sun, and Phil beams back at him.

"Yeah, so, the thing is, I don't do cameras," I declare, causing Kai's dazzling smile to deflate like a balloon.

"Like, they're in opposition to your beliefs?" he asks, crossing his arms over his chest.

"No, nothing like that. I did read the *Say Cheese and Die!* Goosebumps book a few too many times as a kid, but I'm not, like, ethically opposed or anything."

Kai doesn't laugh. Instead, he glances at his watch like my rambling is keeping him from something important. "So, what's the problem?"

"I . . . well . . ." I trail off, glancing to Phil for help. He saw me pass out at my first Critter Chat, coming dangerously close to smashing my head on the outstretched iron hand of the Rock the gorilla statue. He witnessed the 10TV anchor's annoyance as I tried, take after failed take, not to choke on my words while filming a news clip about the zoo's new red ruffed lemur. He watched Jack take my place and deliver his lines like a natural-born star while I dry-heaved in the bathroom.

He knows that when it comes to anything performance related, I'm an unmitigated disaster.

"I'm not comfortable on camera," I explain, leaving out the more excruciating details of my history. "The thought of being on TV makes me nauseous."

Kai, probably puzzled by the existence of a human being who doesn't want to be the center of attention, shrugs. "You'll just be doing your day-to-day work. Nobody's asking you to be the next Meryl Streep."

Phil knits his hands together and gives me an encouraging nod. "I'm going to be frank with you, Lucy. You're the most dedicated junior keeper I've got. You're sharp, you're focused, and I think you could run this place with your eyes closed."

He pauses, and I hear the *but* coming a mile away.

"But," he continues, adjusting his glasses, "you don't take risks. You don't put yourself out there. Like at the picnic this weekend: how many donations did you get?"

I blanch, not wanting to admit the only success I had was getting myself recruited for an exciting career as a skinny tea sales rep. "None," I say finally. "But—"

"I know how passionate you are about our animals, but passion doesn't pay the bills," Phil says gently. "If you want to be a senior team member someday, I need you to show me that you've got what it takes. And that means being able to get donations and serve in a public-facing role. And this summer, it means working with Kai and Keeva and, yes, being on camera."

He raps on his desk and nods at me. *"Capisce?"*

It's not *capisce.* It's not the least bit *capisce.* It's *capisce* if *capisce* set itself on fire and jumped off a cliff.

My fingers tingle, and a pulsing sensation throbs at the back of my head. I'd rather Phil assign me to perpetual poop-scoop duty with Scotty the intern than ask me to be on camera.

It's never going to happen.

"Don't worry, we'll do some practice camera work to get everybody comfortable," Kai says.

Phil nods. "We'll start this afternoon. Can you let the team know to be ready to roll at the bonobo exhibit at three?"

I'm ready to roll right into an anxiety attack, and my head suddenly weighs too much on my tired shoulders, but I force myself to nod. "Ready to roll. Right."

Ready to rock, ready to roll. Ready to humiliate myself and the zoo I love and lose any shot of getting my dream promotion.

"And I need the nursery set up for Keeva by the end of the week," Phil adds. "Can you organize a team to help you with prep?"

"Of course," I say, trying to muster up a facade of confidence.

"Thanks, Lucy." My boss, perhaps registering a fraction of the terror I'm trying to hide, gives me a reassuring nod. "This is a big opportunity. Seize it, okay? I know you've got what it takes."

"Right. Thank you." Of course I'm going to seize this big opportunity. Of course I'm not going to be such an epic disaster that Jack and Lottie and even Scotty the intern will have a better chance of getting the senior keeper job than me. Of course I'm not going to panic so badly that I break out into hives the size of golf balls.

Of course my dream isn't dead.

"See you this afternoon, then," Phil says, politely cueing my dismissal.

Kai, who doesn't seem to notice that I almost fall sideways as I stumble out of my chair, doesn't glance my way as I head for the door. Instead, he crosses one leg over the other and leans forward to ask Phil about exhibit lighting.

When I leave the office, I barely make it to the coffee kiosk before I fling myself into the chair of an intern cubicle. Cold sweat trickles down my hairline, and I press a hand to my chest to slow the thudding of my heart.

Phil might think he's simply asking me to step outside my comfort zone, but he's asking much more than that. Managing to stay conscious during a Critter Chat is outside my comfort zone. Asking me to appear on an *international television show* is like asking Stubby the manatee to cartwheel into the sky.

It's impossible.

My phone vibrates, and I wrench it from my pocket with shaking fingers. Maybe Phil, sensing that I'm three seconds away from having a heart attack, has come to his senses. Maybe he'll let Jack and Lottie steal the show and spend their summer tolerating Kai's incessant smirks while I do the real, behind-the-scenes grunt work of welcoming Keeva to the zoo.

But it's Sam, not Phil. Hell yes to Liberty Tavern, she writes in the group text. How'd your meeting go, Lucy? Everything OK?

I clutch my phone to my chest and close my eyes, trying to steady the frantic pace of my breathing. Elle and Sam will be thrilled to learn that Kai, for whatever reason, had enough mercy not to rat me out to Phil. But try as they might to see things from my point of view, they won't understand why spending my summer on camera feels like a career death sentence anyway.

Well, Kai didn't snitch and Phil didn't fire me, I write back.

But considering the bomb they just dropped on me, they might as well have.

Chapter Eight

I wish I were an Arctic tern. Terns, black-crowned birds with elegant white wings, have the longest regular migration of any bird species and fly over twelve thousand miles, from the Mendenhall Glacier to the southern oceans, every winter. If I could do that, I'd be somewhere over the Atlantic right now, hauling ass to escape Kai and my impending close-up.

Instead, I'm huddled over my computer, conducting a frantic Google search for "how to fake appendicitis." I'm midway through a helpful checklist probably written by a high school kid trying to get out of algebra when my fellow junior keeper Lottie pops her head into my office.

"Please tell me you have a hair straightener," she says, her tone desperate. "If you let me borrow it, I'll take your deep-cleaning shifts for two weeks."

It's a tempting offer, but the only beauty products I keep at work are a hairbrush for overnight stays and a half-melted tube of Chap-Stick. The best heat tools in the world couldn't stop my hair from poofing up at the first hint of humidity, so I've learned to wear a ponytail all summer.

"This is all I've got." I offer the brush to Lottie, who steps into my office and starts combing out her shoulder-length locks.

"Thank you, Lucy. I just can't believe that shooting got moved up to today." She runs her fingers through her bangs. "How am I supposed to look half decent on TV when I didn't even use dry shampoo this morning? If Phil had warned us there might be cameras around this early in the week, I'd have done a skincare routine yesterday instead of spending three hours on a photoshoot for Ernest."

Ernest, Lottie's pet hedgehog and her pride and joy, has twelve thousand Instagram followers and a paid partnership with Pete's Pet Supplies Inc. Every week, she shares elaborate themed photoshoots of the little guy, and last week's welcome-to-summer post, where Ernest lounged by a Barbie pool in a tiny sun hat, went viral on TikTok.

"What's this week's theme?" I ask, watching Lottie wage a tense battle with her bangs. At barely five feet tall, with soft waves of sandy blond hair and brown eyes as big as craters, she's like one of Trudy's Precious Moments figurines blown up to adult proportions.

"Ernest Goes to Summer Camp." She winces as she brushes out a knot. "It sounded fun in theory, but do you have any idea how long it takes to make a lanyard for a hedgehog? And don't get me started on the mini campfire. Ernest does *not* like open flame."

Not sure how to respond, I go back to reading checklist item number five: Complain about pain near your belly button, then in the lower abdomen. But my concentration is broken again when Jack, the third member of our trio, follows Lottie into my office.

"No luck with the straightener?" he asks, granting himself the liberty of grabbing a Diet Coke from my mini fridge. With his burly frame, muscular neck, and horn-rimmed glasses, he looks like an Olympic powerlifter who moonlights as a college professor. "I've got baby powder in my locker. You can try that as a substitute for dry shampoo."

"Maybe." Frowning, Lottie grabs a fine-tip Sharpie from my desk and holds it up to the light. "Think this could work as eyeliner?"

Jack and I reach for the Sharpie, and he manages to wrench it out of her grasp first. "No, Lottie! Get a hold of yourself."

"Sorry," she says. "I just can't believe I'm going to meet *Kai Bridges* looking like a mess."

Jack reaches up to scratch the top of his bald head, and my office is so small that he bumps the back of my chair in the process. I let out an exasperated sigh, wishing I could focus on rehearsing a fake medical emergency in peace.

"Kai's not *that* big of a deal," I grumble, not sure if I'm trying to comfort Lottie or myself. "I know his show is popular, but it's not like Jesus Christ himself is coming to Ape House. I think we all need to relax."

I'm the opposite of relaxed—the pit sweat marks under my arms are probably visible from a mile away—and Lottie looks at me skeptically.

"You must not have seen the *BuzzFeed* article '25 Pics of Kai Bridges Guaranteed to Make You Weak in the Knees,'" she says. "It's a must read."

"Is it wrong that I'm more excited to meet Kai than I would be to meet Jesus?" Jack asks, popping open the soda tab. "I might go to hell for saying this, but Kai seems like more fun. And he's got a killer accent."

Based on my experience, Kai's about as fun as a Pap smear, and it's obvious that he exaggerates his accent for his show.

"And what would your fiancé say about that?" I ask, wincing as Lottie accidentally elbows me in the back of the head.

Jack laughs. "Patrick would say the same thing I'd tell him if he ever ran into Jason Momoa: Go for it, babe. You only live once."

"I actually think we live several times," Lottie says. She grabs a red marker from my desk and examines it, probably wondering if she can use it as lipstick. "You know, like reincarnation. I think I was a peasant washerwoman in my former life."

I'd like to be reincarnated as a European hornet so I can sting Kai and anyone who fawns over his ridiculous *BuzzFeed* pics. I grab the marker from Lottie and tap my desk in frustration. "Would you guys mind giving me some privacy, please? I'm on the verge of losing my shit here."

"Oh, Lucy, I'm sorry," Lottie says, setting the brush down and patting my back in sympathy. "I didn't even think about your stage fright."

She was at the presentation I did for Ohio State students on gorilla enrichment, when I tried to describe the paintings a group of elementary school kids made for a pregnant gorilla's baby shower. I mixed up *shower* and *art* and instead said *shart*, and Lottie felt so bad that she baked me two batches of rocky road cookies.

Jack gives me a gentle pat on the shoulder. "Phil's email said today is just practice getting comfortable with the cameras," he assures me. "Try not to stress."

"You'll be great," Lottie promises. "You're an expert on our zoo, and everybody knows it. Soon Kai will, too."

"Thanks, guys." I snap my laptop shut, not wanting them to catch a glimpse of my checklist of fakery. I get along with Jack and Lottie, but they're my colleagues, not my friends. They're nice enough to invite me over for game nights and out for Thirsty Thursday karaoke, but I rarely go. For one thing, I can't shake the feeling that they're pity invites—they'd feel bad leaving out poor, work-obsessed Lucy, who got dumped by her boyfriend and has nine Instagram followers, one of whom is her preteen half sister—and they don't really want me to come anyway. After all, I'm one of those freaks who like to talk about work outside of work, and I once seriously killed the vibe at Jack's backyard BBQ when I cried about a dying vervet monkey.

But the major reason I don't confide in Jack and Lottie is that no matter how many bar trivia nights they invite me to or leftover cookies they bring me after lunch outings to Subway, they're still my competitors. We're all candidates for the senior keeper job, and I can't stop myself from thinking that behind their comforting shoulder pats and soothing words, they're grateful that when it comes to public speaking, I'm a total train wreck.

We all know why they've each appeared in a half-dozen news clips and I've appeared in zero, and it's no secret why Phil assigns me to oversee the interns' scut work while the rest of the team mingles with donors at ZooClue Mystery Dinner fundraisers. Jack and Lottie must know as well as I do that as soon as Kai points a camera at me, it's game over for my promotion dreams.

"We'll leave you to your work," Jack says, glancing at my laptop in a way that tells me he saw my appendicitis plan. "But if you feel like stress-eating gummy bears, you know where to find us."

He shuffles out of my office, and Lottie waves and trails after him. I wish I were like her, more worried about gaining followers for my hedgehog than humiliating myself on camera. I wish I had the easy friendliness that lets Jack be buddies with everyone from CEO Shira Woodrow to Poppet the lemur.

I wish I weren't quite so very me.

Chapter Nine

The problem with faking appendicitis to get out of a public performance is that the very act of faking it requires a public performance. I'm about as talented at acting as I am at sweet-talking zoo donors, so by the time the primates team gathers at the outdoor bonobo exhibit, I've abandoned my pretend medical crisis plan. Instead, I position myself as far from the *Wild Side* crew as possible, hoping that Kai and Phil and God Herself will forget I exist.

Fanny the bonobo, a twenty-year-old female with a propensity to start a ruckus in the group by running around and smacking other bonobos on their heads, spots me hiding in the corner and knuckle-walks toward me.

"Hi, Fan," I whisper. "Behaving yourself?"

She probably can't hear me over the booming voice of one Kai Bridges, who's sporting a ridiculous safari hat and delighting Jack, Lottie, and the gang with the harrowing story of how he once broke his leg in a remote Rwandan forest.

"My team carried me on their backs through six miles of steep terrain, and when we got to the hospital, the doctors weren't sure if they could save the leg," Kai says, as if he was a courageous James Franco in *127 Hours*. "Moral of the story: Watch your step, and always pack a flask."

I squint at Kai's assistant, a pint-sized twenty-something whose name tag reads *LARS* and who looks like he couldn't carry a sack of flour for six hours, let alone his six-foot-two, probably two-hundred-something-pound boss. I hope Kai gave him a nice Christmas bonus.

"Wow," Lottie says, breathless at the dramatic tale. "You must have been so brave."

I snort so loudly that it startles Fanny, who lets out an annoyed *waah* sound and runs off to smack her little brother over the head.

"Lucy, there you are," Phil says, waving me toward the group. "Come on over."

"Dammit, Fanny," I mutter, but I force myself to join the cluster of people gathered around Kai.

"Let's get started," Kai says, grinning at the group. "For those of you I haven't met yet, I'm Kai Bridges, producer and host of *On the Wild Side*."

Jack raises his hands toward the roof like we're at a high school pep rally, and Lottie lets out a soul-piercing shriek of excitement. She's sporting a pink Columbus Zoo and Aquarium hat, and she leans closer when she notices me looking at it.

"Baby powder is *not* the same as dry shampoo," she whispers, tugging the hat tighter over her hair. "Take it from me."

"Our show has won Emmys, a Peabody, and even Nickelodeon Kids' Choice Awards," Kai continues. "Prince William called it 'a masterpiece,' and Michelle Obama made a guest appearance last season. But the best prize we've earned is the trust of viewers around the globe. When people want to laugh and cry and learn a bit about the world around them, they tune in to *Wild Side*. And I'm thrilled for you all to be part of our team."

Kai's braggy name-dropping habit prickles my ears, but I can't tear my eyes away from him because he's magnetic when he speaks. It's not just that the afternoon sun shines on him like a spotlight, lending him the ethereal dazzle of one of those dumb vampires from *Twilight*. And it's not that his stupid hat, which has strings that he's tied underneath his chin like an overgrown toddler on beach day, somehow doesn't look half bad. It's the way he shifts his gaze to make eye contact with everyone around him: not just Phil or Shira Woodrow or the stunning woman next to him, a lithe thirty-something in cornrows and a lilac summer smock.

Kai makes sure he speaks to all of us, even security guard Norm and the summer interns. Even me.

He'd make an excellent skinny tea salesman.

"I know some of you might be thinking, what's this bloke doing at our zoo?" Kai says, rolling up the sleeves of his button-down to reveal a muscled set of forearms. "What's he know about our animals and our lives? He's just an overhyped, overpaid, egotistical moron who was born on third base and thinks he hit a triple."

His gaze settles on me, and I wonder if anyone else picks up on the tension.

"We would never," Lottie whispers, clutching her chest as if Kai said, *Some of you might be thinking, let's go kick some baby ducklings.*

"But if you're not sold yet, hang tight," Kai says, grinning at Lottie. "I'm not everybody's cup of tea, but I'm focused, I work hard, and I know how to make great TV."

"You're my cup of tea!" Katie the summer intern hollers, and I'm surprised when she doesn't take off her bra and launch it at Kai's head.

"This season is going to be different," he says, zooming right past Katie's flattery. "You guys are the experts here, not me. And I want to step away from the camera so you can take my place."

Lottie raises her hand like we're in third grade. "Wait, do you mean you're not going to be on camera at all? You're the face of the whole show!"

She makes a great point, and I don't think that just because I'd rather eat my own fingernails than watch myself on Animal Planet. When people tune in, they'll expect an hour of entertainment from Kai, his tight-fitting T-shirts, and the plight of whatever adorable animal he's featuring that week. I imagine people like Trudy settling in for a new episode and realizing they're in for a season of close-ups of Scotty the intern, who has a penchant for wearing *Rick and Morty* tees and the sleepy-eyed look of someone who just smoked an extremely potent blunt.

I don't think the wine-sipping moms at Picnic for Paws will go for that.

"Don't worry, I won't be disappearing from the show," Kai says, sending a wave of relief through the group. "But I do plan to be behind the camera more than in front of it."

He grins at the woman in the lilac smock, who looks like a longer-haired Lupita Nyong'o, and introduces her as his co-producer Freya Framingham. "This season, while I focus on big-picture stuff like which plotlines to follow, Freya will assist with the day-to-day parts of shooting."

Kai's use of *plotlines* sends a shockwave of annoyance down my spine. Ozzie and Zuri aren't characters he can manipulate to garner high ratings or win another Peabody Award; they're complex creatures whose numbers in the wild are shrinking every day. And my task of connecting Keeva to a surrogate mother isn't a *plotline*, either. It's a crucial step in restoring a young gorilla's chances for an enriching life.

"If you have questions about anything, big or small, ask me first," Freya says in a butter-smooth voice, politely warning us not to bother King Kai. "I'm here to help, whether by arranging call times or teaching you guys how to wear a microphone without dropping it in the toilet—which happens more often than you'd think."

She glances at Kai, and they share a knowing look.

"Long story involving a latrine in Thailand," he says, his quarterback-sculpted shoulders shaking with laughter. "Don't ask."

"And this is our crew," Freya says, motioning toward the group of people clad in matching blue *Wild Side* T-shirts. She introduces Kai's personal assistant, a boom operator, and a production assistant. When she points to four camera operators, including a grown man with blue hair who legitimately introduces himself as Skippy, the sweat that's been dripping off me since my meeting with Phil turns into a downpour. As Skippy hoists his camera up and waves at us, an airy lightness swirls through my limbs. I try not to pass out as I envision Kai barking orders at me in the Ape House nursery while Phil cries into a handkerchief, cursing the day he hired me.

"Lucy, he's calling on you," Lottie whispers, nudging me with her elbow.

I blink myself back into reality to see Kai motioning for me to step away from the bonobo exhibit, where I've practically plastered myself to the Plexiglass. "Earth to Lucy," he says. "C'mon, practice time. You're up first to bat."

Fear fills up the hollow spaces of my body, and anger quickly follows. After I explicitly told him about my discomfort with cameras during the meeting, his decision to make me go first is downright cruel. Like he can read my thoughts, Kai cocks an eyebrow at me as if to say, *I'm in charge, and there's nothing you can do about it.*

"It might, um, be better for someone else to start," I say, my voice cracking on every other word. "I don't feel very well."

He only glances at his smartwatch. "I didn't ask someone else. I asked you. C'mon, let's get on with it."

I can't help but glare at him, because he didn't do any *asking* at all. He's ordering me around like I'm Lars the assistant and I messed up his ridiculously overcomplicated Starbucks order. But before I can remind Kai that I'm a zookeeper, not his personal bitch, I spot Phil in the background and force myself to take a calming breath. If showing my boss that I have the chops to be in charge means doing what Kai says, then I have no choice but to do it.

I'll make a voodoo doll of him later.

I peel myself off the glass and walk toward Kai with Jell-O legs and a racing heart. But halfway there, I trip over Scotty the intern's skateboard, and I barely catch my footing in time to stop my face from smacking the cement.

Freya gasps, and I mentally roll my eyes at her as I regain my balance. She ain't seen nothing yet.

"Let's get your mic set up," Kai says, not bothering to ask if I'm all right.

He grabs a slim black wire from a bag at his feet and steps toward me, so close that I'm hit with a gentle, infuriatingly pleasing wave of campfire-and-aftershave scent.

"Did you roll around on the floor of a Bath and Body Works to-day?" I ask, not able to hold back my frustration.

Ignoring me, Kai attaches the wire to the collar of my polo. I hold my breath so as not to inhale another drop of his scent, and he fiddles with my collar like we're awkward prom dates and he's having a hell of a time adjusting my corsage.

"There," he says after a moment. "That's a LAV, also known as a body mic."

And he's a raging asshole, also known as a narcissist.

"My goal today is to get everyone comfortable with the mic and the camera," he says. "None of the footage we shoot here will make it past the cutting room floor, so there's no reason to be nervous. Okay?"

"Okay!" the group echoes back at him.

Kai leans toward me. "Okay, Lucy?" he asks, quietly enough that only I can hear.

I wish I could impress Phil and reply with bubbly enthusiasm, but I can barely breathe. The mic on my collar is small and light, but I imagine the wire coiling itself around my neck like a reticulated python, squeezing and constricting until I can't get any oxygen.

"I, um, actually," I whisper, desperate for Kai to have mercy on me and let me slink back to my spot in the corner, "I'm, um, no. I'm not."

"Hey," he says, all the scowl and smirk gone from his face. "You're good. You've got this." His expression is firm, certain, like he really believes I'm going to nail this. Like he's not purposely setting me up for failure.

But I don't believe it for a second. He stole my copy of *Majesty on the Mountain*, and now he's going to steal my chance at winning a promotion—the slow, tortuous, enjoyable way. He could have done it in an instant by telling Phil about my tirade, but then his fun would have been over too quickly.

After Kai rattles on about the mechanics of the equipment, he motions for me to step in front of Skippy's camera. "For practice, I'll ask you a few simple questions. Remember, this is about establishing your comfort with the camera."

He might as well say, *This is about establishing your comfort with this highly poisonous box jellyfish*, and I shudder and wrap my arms around myself. It's the protective pose I adopted during dodgeball games in middle school gym, and Skippy gives me the same wary glance as my PE teacher Mrs. Edmunds.

"Relax, Lucy," Kai instructs. "Like this." He demonstrates how I should roll my shoulders and shake the stiffness away, and I try to imitate him. But he looks like he's warming up for another sexy dance on *The Ellen DeGeneres Show*, and I feel like a floppy inflatable advertising noodle stationed outside a car dealership.

"Now look at the camera and state your name and job title," he instructs.

Blinking, I try to look at the camera, but it's like staring into the open jaws of a great white shark.

"I . . . I . . ." I stammer, letting out an alarming wheeze.

"Take a deep breath," Kai says. "What's your name?"

"It's, um, Lucy," I mumble. "Lucy Rourke." The words come out high-pitched and breathless.

"Good. Now say that again, along with your job title, but try to make it sound natural," Kai instructs. "Conversational. Like it's just you and me having a chat."

The only thing that would feel natural right now would be curling up in the fetal position and dying, but I won't go down without a fight. I have to try to impress Phil.

"Lucy Rourke," I say, eking out the words like a movie character trying to impart a critical message from her deathbed. "Junior keeper."

"Huh," Kai says after an uncomfortable pause. He casts a brief sideways glance toward Skippy, who's watching me go down in flames in open-mouthed awe. It's amazing, really, that swimming with stingrays and chatting with Oprah can't rattle Kai, but two minutes of trying to coach me on camera is enough to throw him off his game.

I really am that hopeless.

"Remember, it's a camera, not a crocodile. I promise it won't bite," Kai says.

Scotty the intern and some of my colleagues snicker, but Kai doesn't look away from me. His tone is sincere, placating, and I realize that at least in this moment, he's not making fun of me. He's trying to help—or at least make sure that I don't single-handedly tank six seasons' worth of killer Nielsen ratings.

"Tell me a fun animal fact," he instructs, adjusting the position of Skippy's camera a few inches. "Remember, it's just you and me. The camera's not even here."

I snort. Sure it isn't—and Kai wasn't blessed with butt cheeks that I could bounce a quarter off. Please. The fuzzy sensation in my head grows stronger, like an army of cobwebs creeping over my brain, and I can't remember what year it is, let alone pull a fun animal fact out of my ass.

"Hyenas," I say finally, the word mush in my mouth. "A fun fact is that, um . . ." Mia watched a marathon of *The Lion King* movies at Nona's last week, and she knocked on my bedroom door afterward to pester me with questions about the species.

"Female hyenas have a pseudopenis," I say, trying so hard to speak above a whisper that I practically shout. As soon as the words leave my mouth, I wish I could reach into the air and snatch them back. But it's too late; I yelled "pseudo" and I yelled "penis," and the damage is done. I should have shared a cute, G-rated fact like, *Guess what, kids? Honeybees communicate through dance*, but it's too late.

"It's nearly indistinguishable from the male penis," I continue, blinking into the camera. "They, um, urinate through it. And give birth through it. And, um, when female hyenas fight, the loser gets an erection to show that she's, like, submitting."

I wipe sweat off my cheek, and my skin is so warm to the touch that I won't be surprised if it melts off. Then nothing will be left of me but a skeleton, and Lottie and Jack can bury my remains in the zoo topiary garden with a headstone that reads, HERE LIES LUCY, WHO RAMBLED ABOUT HYENA ERECTIONS TO THE MAN DIANE SAWYER CALLED "A NATIONAL TREASURE."

Kai watches me for a long moment, like he doesn't know what to say, and I wonder if that inscription is too much for the Ape House budget. HERE LIES LUCY, WHO COULDN'T SHUT THE FUCK UP would be cheaper.

"Okay," he says finally. "Good start. Who's next?"

It was an abominable start, and Jack gives me a sad, sympathetic smile as I stagger back toward the group.

"I'll go," Lottie says. After Freya fixes her with a mic, she beams and puts her hands on her hips with a cheerleader's bouncy confidence.

"I'm Lottie Devins, junior keeper," she says proudly, and even her baby powder–coated hair can't dim her exuberance. "My favorite fun animal fact is that a single elephant tooth can weigh as much as nine pounds."

She nods at the camera, and I almost expect her to launch into a backflip and thrust her arms into the air. She's good at this—she's great, actually—and her ease makes my pathetic ineptitude more glaring.

"Great work, Lottie. You're a natural," Kai says as the sinkhole in my stomach opens wider.

Jack goes next, and his wide smile and deep, narrator-perfect voice give Lottie a run for her money. After two senior keepers take their turns, Scotty the intern follows, and even he—a twenty-two-year-old who eats Cool Ranch Doritos for breakfast and has thrice locked himself inside the Ape House refrigeration unit—does a better job than me.

I thought staring into the camera was unbearable, but watching my colleagues do it with minimal discomfort, and many of them with obvious enjoyment, is even worse. I can't do this. I can't spend an entire summer hyperventilating while a squad of baby-faced interns outpaces me in the race for the senior keeper job. I can't blink into a camera while I'm caring for baby Keeva, trying to claw back at the panic blazing through my heart.

I just can't.

"That's a wrap for today," Kai says as Freya disassembles a trifold lighting system. "Great work, everybody!"

What he means is, *Great work, everybody but Lucy,* and the simmering nausea that's bubbled in my stomach since this morning boils over.

"Excuse me," I whisper, jostling past Lottie. Once I'm away from the group, I sprint the rest of the way to Ape House and scurry into the employee bathroom, slamming the door shut behind me.

The vomit comes hard and fast, and so do the tears. Because even if I were a Humboldt squid or an Arctic tern or the fastest cheetah on earth, I couldn't escape the harsh truth in front of me, the one I learned from Karina as a kid and Phil's going to realize this summer:

No matter how hard I try, I'll never be enough.

Chapter Ten

"Lucy? Are you in there?" A knock sounds on the door, and I scramble to flush the toilet.

"One second!" I bark as someone knocks again. "I'll be out in a sec."

I turn on the tap and splash cold water on my face, and when I glance up to look in the mirror, my reflection looks like Mischa Barton's sweaty ghost in *The Sixth Sense*.

"Lucy?"

Grumbling, I wash my hands and fling the door open to find Kai waiting in the corridor, one fist raised to knock again.

"Can I help you?" I ask. What I need right now is alone time with my feelings and a bottle of mouthwash, not a condescending earful from America's Jeep-driving golden boy.

"Are you all right?" He's removed his Crocodile Dundee–esque hat, and he runs a hand through his mussed hair in a way that would have Trudy salivating.

I wipe my mouth with the back of my hand. "I'm fine. Now if you'll excuse me, I need to feed the gibbons and start preparing the nursery."

I move to strut past him, but he shifts sideways to block my path. "Lucy, I n—"

"What?" I hiss, worried that I'm gearing up for another round of vomit. Whatever he wants to say—*I've never seen someone crash and burn so hard; I'm going to blast an Auto-Tuned clip of you saying "pseudopenis" all over social media; what happened out there is just the first course of revenge for what you said at the picnic, and I'm gonna serve up hot dishes all summer*—I don't have the energy to listen. I need to feed Titan and Snowdrop, then retreat to my office to lick my wounds and game-plan a way to salvage my standing with Phil.

"If you followed me in here to gloat," I tell Kai, "don't waste your time. You can't possibly make me feel worse."

A scowl crosses his face, and he furrows his brow. "Gloat?"

I forgot he wasn't a big reader. "Yes. To gloat. You know, to rub my failure in my face and tell me I deserve it for what I said at the picnic." I twist my features into an imitation of Kai's deep smirk and try to mimic his lilting accent: "Ahoy there, little lass, but did you really think you could insult me without penalty? I'm Kai Bridges, friend of bottlenose dolphins and the royal family, and you're a right little nobody. Wowza!" I run a hand through my ponytail with a flourish like I'm auburn, silky-haired Kai, but I didn't brush the knots out after my shower this morning, and my fingers get tangled up.

"Wowza," I repeat lamely, wrestling my fingers from my hair.

"You sound like the Lucky Charms leprechaun," Kai says, looking more bewildered than offended. "With a dash of pirate thrown in."

"Sick burn. Mind if I go do my job now?"

He doesn't even try to hide his smirk. "I'd rather hear you try to imitate me a bit more. And just so you know, I'm not friendly with the entire royal family. Just the princes."

"Right. Well, you and the princes can have a big laugh at my expense. You win, okay? You humiliated me. Frankly, you could have just ratted me out to Phil and saved us both some trouble."

The flicker of amusement in Kai's eyes vanishes. "I humiliated *you*? I'm sorry, but did you or did you not refer to me as a homeless-looking D-list celebrity?"

"As I already explained," I say through gritted teeth, "the concept of celebrity is complicated. And I apologized. Besides, if what I said bothered you so much, why didn't you just tell Phil? He'd have fired me without a second thought."

"Because I'm not a snitch," Kai says evenly. "And because I don't let personal feelings interfere with my work."

"So why did you make me go first today?" I ask, my voice growing louder. "I told you I wasn't comfortable on camera, so you knew I'd be a disaster. You set me up!"

"Yes, Lucy," Kai says dryly. "It's all my fault. I forced you to trip over a skateboard and relay facts about hyena penises. How very callous of me."

"*Pseudo*penises," I retort. "And you made me go first because you knew I'd suck."

"Did it ever occur to you that I was trying to help?" he asks, crossing his arms over his chest. "That I heard what you said about not liking cameras and figured that standing around watching your co-workers go first would only give you time to panic? That maybe I'm not just a regular, run-of-the-mill asshole after all?"

His questions slow my roll of rage, and I can only stare at him in response. The truth is, I was so certain Kai was set on revenge that I didn't consider other possibilities.

"Right," he says after a beat. "That's what I thought."

What Elle said to me at the picnic—*He was probably just jet-lagged and exhausted when he met you, Luce*—rings in my ears. What if

Kai's telling the truth, and he actually was trying to make today easier for me? What if *I'm* the asshole here?

"Whatever," I say, rubbing my eyes in frustration. "It doesn't matter now. We both know I was a disaster."

"Yes, you were," Kai agrees, sounding more matter-of-fact than malicious. "But I can help you get better."

"Trust me, you can't." And after the names I called him, I'm not sure why he'd want to.

He raises his scarred eyebrow at me. "I've hiked Mount Kilimanjaro with a fractured ankle and spent a week on an ice ridge of the East Antarctic Plateau. I think I can teach you to relax in front of a camera."

He's so cocky that it makes me want to scream, just like it did when he so confidently—and incorrectly—accused me of being wrong about Dr. Kimber's nickname. A man who can't be trusted to know basic facts about his own mother has no chance of shaping me into a docuseries superstar.

"Are you always so sure that you're right about everything?" I ask, jutting my chin out toward him.

He smirks. "Are you always so afraid of a challenge?"

I gasp as if he's cursed at me. I've been called a lot of things—a workaholic, a commitment-phobe, even a disappointment—but no one's ever accused me of being a chicken.

"You don't know anything about me," I say, stepping an inch closer to him. I can only hope that I reek of vomit and the bonobo exhibits I power-washed this morning. "I *live* for challenges. I eat them for breakfast."

I'm aiming for a badass, chew-him-up-and-spit-him-out vibe, but I sound like an actress from a corny action movie.

"And lunch," I add, hoping it'll make my previous comment sound cooler. It doesn't.

"I know more than you think." Kai steps a fraction closer to me, too, and I wish he were still wearing his dumb hat so I could reach up and knock it off his head. "I know you haven't missed a day of work in four and a half years. I know you write the most detailed observation logs I've ever read, and that you've been named Employee of the Month nine times. I know you're the only primate keeper who stores an air mattress in her office in case she needs to stay overnight."

"Excuse me, who gave you my observation logs?" I demand, hating the self-satisfied look on his face. "When were you in my office?"

I haven't always been obsessive enough to keep an air mattress in there. It started two years ago when Zuri came down with an intestinal blockage that almost killed her. After her emergency surgery, when things were touch-and-go, I couldn't bear to leave her side.

"I know you're the only keeper who doesn't appear on the zoo's YouTube channel," he continues, ignoring my questions. "I know that while your colleagues travel to Rwanda and Uganda to study gorillas in the wild, you've never done so much as a two-week stint at the Cincinnati Zoo. I know a senior keeper's retiring at the end of the year and Phil wants to give you that job, but he worries that your colleagues have something you don't: nerve."

The accusation strikes me like a lightning bolt. It's not my fault that I don't belong on center stage like Jack and Lottie and Raquel from Small Mammals, who make regular smiley appearances on *Good Day Columbus!* with vervet monkeys and porcupines in tow. It's not my fault that the thought of leaving Zuri for a month to fly off to the jungle makes my heart pound in fear that something terrible will happen to her while I'm gone.

But I don't tell him any of that. Instead, I pull my ponytail tighter and fix him with a steely glare. "Oh, I've got plenty of nerve."

"Then prove it. Meet me at the nursery tomorrow at one. I can spare thirty minutes to work with you."

How very generous of His Royal Kainess to spare a whole half hour on a lowly peasant like me. I suppose I should bow at his feet and kiss the ground he walks on. But I don't care how many times he's hiked a mountain with his eyes closed or whatever braggy bullshit he's on about; I'm beyond anyone's arrogant tutelage.

"You can't help me," I insist. "You're better off trotting back to Hollywood instead of wasting your time."

"Hey, I'm the one with the Emmys here," Kai says, and I wonder just how many times a day he polishes his shiny trophies and tells himself he's pretty. "Not you. So you don't have to like me, Lucy, but don't tell me how to do my job. Either show some nerve or stay in your lane."

I'd love to show some middle finger, but I think back to what Phil said at the meeting this morning: *You don't take risks. You don't put yourself out there.* Kai might come across as a cocky, self-obsessed jerk, but he's basically telling me the same thing Phil did, and the realization that he just might be right hurts worse than the nausea bubbling in my stomach.

"Why are you offering to help?" I ask. "After everything you overheard me say about you, why do you care if I improve?"

He shrugs. "What you said at the picnic doesn't matter to me. It's no skin off my back if some zookeeper in Ohio thinks I'm overrated. But your glaring on-camera incompetence makes you a challenge, Lucy Rourke, and *I'm* not afraid of those."

His dismissive description of me as *some zookeeper in Ohio* makes me wish he'd get stomped on by an elephant, but I can't protest. Because in comparison to Kai's star power, that's all I am, and while he might be an absolute tool, he's not wrong. I *am* incompetent when it comes to the camera. And that pisses me off even more than Trudy haranguing me about Nick.

"You don't know who you're dealing with," I say. It's not a threat; it's reality. He has no clue that I'm incapable of improving my media skills.

Kai fiddles with the sleeve of his oxford, and it strikes me as deeply unfair that he has such thick forearms. He deserves puny pencil arms and a pancake butt.

"Neither do you, Lucy. But you're about to find out."

"Whatever you say, Crocodile Dundee." I strut past him, ready to do some actual work and then find a pillow to scream into.

"Hey, I need your mic," Kai calls after me. "That's the whole reason I followed you inside."

I was under the impression that he'd followed me inside to check on me, and the clarification only annoys me further.

"Here." I try to slide the mic off, but it gets stuck on my top button.

"Stop before you break it, please." Before I can protest, Kai moves closer and reaches for the wire. I drop my hands, lest my fingers cross paths with his, just as the earthy scent of campfire and sandalwood hits me again. It's a light, calming aroma, and if Yankee Candle bottled it up and sold it in stores, I'd buy a hundred wax melts and deny it as long as I lived.

Kai's assistance makes me feel like a three-year-old who needs Mommy to help button her coat, and I refuse to look at him as he untangles the wire. He wrangles the mic off me but accidentally brushes my collarbone with his fingertips in the process.

I jerk away from his touch, but Kai only tucks the mic into his pocket and gives me a breezy "Thanks, Lucy," as he heads for the exit.

If looks could kill, the one I give his back would strike him dead.

"I eat challenges for dinner, too!" I yell at his disappearing form, not caring that a docent entering the building stares at me like I'm unhinged. "And I want my book back!"

My heart pounds as I head toward the gibbon exhibit, and even when I reach Titan and Snowdrop, whose high-pitched songs are loud enough to be heard throughout the zoo, all I can hear is Kai taunting me, accusing me of fearing a challenge. The allegation ignites a fire in my belly and sets my teeth on edge as I grab a bucket of figs from the gibbon building kitchen and carry it toward the animals.

Because I may not have an Emmy or an edge-of-your-seat tale about almost losing a leg in the forest, but I know one thing: regardless of what Kai says, my lane is wherever the hell I want it to be. And we're bound for a head-on collision.

Chapter Eleven

"I've never missed anything as much as I miss margaritas." Elle tucks a hand under her chin and gazes at Sam's spicy jalapeño drink. "I can sniff one, though, right? Margarita fumes can't hurt the baby?"

Laughing, Sam slides her margarita under Elle's nose. "I think it's safe to take a whiff."

We're clustered around a table at Liberty Tavern in Powell, a stone's throw from the zoo. Gleaming wood surfaces and a red-brick wall lend the bar a rustic vibe, and a painting of a disco-dancing Statue of Liberty adds a dash of eclectic patriotism.

I sip my strawberry-basil vodka lemonade and slide a plate of buffalo chicken tots toward Elle. "Here. These will lessen the pain."

Sighing, she pops one into her mouth. "Want to hear something awful? Today I was leading a bunch of day campers to Polar Frontier, and when I sneezed, a little bit of pee came out. I thought that only happened *after* you push a baby out, but I was wrong. So that's where I am now: I can't drink margs or control my bladder. I'm basically a toddler in a grown woman's body."

"I'm sorry," I say, reaching over to pat her hand. "Want me to order some pretzel bread?"

She shakes her head. "Maybe later. But I shouldn't complain. I don't want to bore you guys with my lame preggo problems."

"One, your problems are our problems," Sam assures her. "And two, don't worry about a little urinary incontinence now and then. It'll all be worth it when your kiddo arrives, and then we can pop a high chair right here and introduce Elle Jr. to the wonders of seafood nachos." She pats the open space next to the table like she's patting the head of an invisible toddler.

I chew a tot, trying not to stress about how my friendship with Elle might change once her baby arrives. I'm thrilled for her and Nadeem, but I worry that once there's an adorable baby in the mix, Elle and I will grow apart. After all, even the easiest kids suck up their parents' time and energy, and that doesn't leave much room for hanging out in my office while we eat tacos and gossip about work.

Plus, I worry that my easygoing, fashion-forward friend will transform into an overworked, underappreciated, over-puked-on mombie who refers to kids as "littles" and never gets a break. What if Elle trades her beloved romance novels for spit-covered board books and never picks them up again? What if she gets so beat down by the daily grind of pumping and feeding and diaper changing that she trades her stylish outfits for ratty T-shirts and the khaki pants she's always giving me shit about?

It's fine if she *wants* those things; being childfree doesn't mean I dislike kids or think no one else should have them. But time and time again, I've watched female colleagues and acquaintances trade their cherished hobbies and ambitions for *Mama Bear* T-shirts and *Mommy Fuel* wineglasses. First it was Tracy from Reptiles, who spearheaded a loggerhead sea turtle research project in Mexico until she became a mom and found it too difficult to travel. Then there was Nona's neighbor Akemi, who quit teaching her weekly aerial yoga class and started calling her husband's attempts to care for their kids "helping out." And then, of course, there was Nick, who looked at me like I was missing a femininity chip when I refused to budge on the issue of children.

Babies are great for people who want them. But we live in a world that still expects more of moms than dads, and while I have every confidence in Nadeem's ability to be an equal team player, I don't want Elle to lose her identity to motherhood.

And selfishly, I don't want to lose any of her, either.

"So, Luce, spill: what happened at your meeting?" Elle asks, perhaps noticing the color draining from my face and deciding to change the subject.

I down my lemonade. "I'm going to need a stronger drink."

After ordering a cherry sour, I give them a rundown of the day, from Phil's announcement that I get to work with baby Keeva to how I almost ate shit when I tripped on Scotty's skateboard.

"I don't mean to be insensitive," Sam says when I'm done, "but how in the world did the first animal fact you thought of involve a pseudopenis?"

Groaning, I bury my face in my hands. "I don't know. But now there's video evidence of me talking about how female hyenas get *erections*. I'm not sure I can look Phil in the eyes ever again."

Sam laughs. "Doesn't he have five kids? I'm sure he's pretty familiar with erections."

That's the last thing I want to think about, so I take a bite of my salmon watermelon salad and try to chew the pain away.

"It's cool of Kai to offer his help," Elle says, changing the subject before Sam can unleash her arsenal of dick jokes.

She smiles so widely that arguing with her would be like telling Pollyanna to go fuck herself, so I make my tone gentle. "Did you miss the part where he bragged about his Emmys and called me a coward?"

"To be fair," Sam says, "if I had an Emmy, I'd brag about it, too. I'd carry it around with me and make people kiss it."

"And he didn't call you a coward," Elle adds. "It sounds like he was trying to get you fired up."

"I'm sorry, but aren't you guys supposed to be on my side?" I ask. "It's like the cardinal rule of friendship that if one of us hates someone, the rest of us hate them, too. That's why we all loathe most of Sam's exes and that blond lady at Whole Foods who's always hitting on Nadeem."

"Erika from Prepared Foods," Elle mutters, gritting her teeth like she's saying *Pansy Parkinson from Slytherin*. "May she choke on her unscented organic toothpaste."

It's the meanest thing I've ever heard her say, and she blushes when Sam and I do a double take. "Sorry. Pregnancy hormones."

"I'm happy to hate anyone you do, minus a few exceptions, Luce," Sam says. "Like if you suddenly started hating Malala Yousafzai or Sandra Bullock, I don't think I could agree. Honestly, I'm not sure I can make myself hate Kai just yet."

"Excuse me," I say, stealing the tot Sam was reaching for, "but did you just compare Kai Bridges to America's sweetheart and the girl who stood up to the Taliban?"

"No," she says quickly, sipping her margarita. "I mean, sort of? I'm just saying that some people are really tough to dislike."

"We're on your side, but I think you're being rough on Kai," Elle clarifies. "It's hard to imagine that a guy who rescues dogs like Penny can be all that terrible."

"Ted Bundy volunteered at a suicide prevention hotline," I argue. "John Wayne Gacy threw block parties for his neighbors."

Sam stares at me in disbelief. "Seriously? You're comparing Kai to Ted Bundy?"

My cheeks grow warm as Elle's eyes widen in horror. "No, I'm just pointing out that plenty of people hide shady behavior behind a good public image."

"Come on, look at this week's edition of Kai's newsletter," Sam says, picking up her smartphone. "He's hardly the spawn of Satan." Before I can blink, I'm staring at the image of a beaming Kai posing with an adorably fluffy, wide-eyed baby capybara. Click to learn more about the Reizer Ridge Capybara Rescue!, a caption underneath reads, and the little rodent's so disarmingly cute that I'm almost tempted to click the link.

Instead, I take a sip of cherry sour. "Cool. Maybe after Phil kicks me to the curb, you can frame that picture for me to put in my bedroom."

"It would be a step up from your *NSYNC poster," Elle grumbles, then pats my hand in apology. "Sorry. Like I said, it's the hormones. Anyway, Luce, if you really think Kai's awful, then I think I speak for both Sam and me when I say that we hope he balds prematurely."

"Or gets lice and has to shave all his hair off," Sam adds with a nod. "Including his eyebrows."

"But I think you should consider the possibility that he's not," Elle continues, popping the last tot into her mouth. "Because you do have a tendency to assume the worst of people."

I slide my sweet potato fries farther away from her. "I do not."

Sam fixes me with a skeptical look. "Remember my ex-girlfriend Magdalene? You thought she was cheating on me when you saw her holding hands with another woman at Café Elena, and it turned out the other woman was her grandmother."

"Okay, in my defense, her nana looked really good for seventy," I argue. "And Magdalene *was* a little shifty. Nobody wins that many rounds of Bananagrams without breaking the rules."

"Well, what about that time you found Lottie sneaking into your office after hours?" Elle asks. "You thought she was trying to steal data from your spreadsheets, but she was actually just decorating it for your birthday."

I shift in my seat. "Okay, yes, that was a bad misjudgment. But in my defense, I'd only been working with her for a few months at that point."

"You hate Mr. Rogers, Luce," Sam says. "*Mr. Rogers.*"

"I do not hate Mr. Rogers," I retort. "I just find it unsettling that he's always taking his clothes off and putting new ones on. Like, at some point pick an outfit and call it a day, you know?"

Sam and Elle, who clearly do not know, stare at me with eyes as wide as the baby capybara's.

"But, um, I guess I see your point," I relent, picking at my fries. "I do rush to judgment sometimes."

"And you love a good grudge," Sam agrees.

She's right: I can hold a grudge like nobody's business. It's why I refuse to even meet Karina for coffee despite the hundreds of invitations she's extended, and why I'll never forgive Sarah Jessica Parker for making *Sex and the City 2*.

I'm as stubborn as a wolverine, even if it takes my friends' guidance for me to admit it.

"Don't deprive yourself of an opportunity because you dislike

Kai," Elle says. "If he turns out to be the world's biggest jerk, we'll put Tabasco sauce in his coffee. But jerk or not, he can help you get your promotion."

"Tabasco sauce?" Sam asks. "Hell, I'm going with ghost pepper."

Before I can suggest something a bit stronger, like cyanide, Elle spots Ashley from Aquatics, another zoo employee, entering the tavern.

"Ash!" she calls, waving her over.

When Ashley joins our table, still smelling vaguely of fish from the sea lions' evening feed, the conversation shifts to an upcoming girls' trip to Nashville—one I was invited on but can't swing with my work schedule. As my friends chatter about honky-tonk bars and the Grand Ole Opry, I eat my salad and reflect on their advice.

Maybe they're right. After all, I did password-protect my spreadsheets after I spotted Lottie leaving my office four years ago, and she was only putting balloons and a plate of butterscotch cookies on my desk. Maybe I got so burned by Karina letting me down all those years ago and Nick bailing on me last winter that I've started writing people off before they have a chance to disappoint me.

But so what? There's no rule that I have to like Mr. Rogers or give anyone—even baby-capybara-hugging Kai—the benefit of the doubt. Because I know something my friends don't: that at the end of the day, no matter how good someone looks in a safari hat or how swiftly they change Trudy's flat tire or how sincerely they look into your eyes and promise that they'll be back to pick you up from Nona's in a week, no later, they swear, the only person you can count on is yourself.

Chapter Twelve

At least my favorite gorilla doesn't insist that Kai's an angel. Unlike Elle and Sam, Zuri only grunts and makes a throat-clearing noise when I tell her how much he sucks.

"And then he called me glaringly incompetent," I explain, watching as she uses an enormous hand to swipe a paintbrush across a sheet of butcher paper. "Despite the fact that *he* hasn't even read Dr. Kimber's book."

Zuri blinks at me before plopping her brush in purple paint and dripping some onto the paper.

"And even though I am glaringly incompetent, that's not something you say out loud," I add. "It's just, like, basic manners."

Grunting as if to say, *But didn't you call him an overhyped moron?* or *I want more grapes*, Zuri twirls her brush in the air.

"I know you like the blue paint best," I tell her, passing her a grape. "But you used it all yesterday, remember?"

Painting is one of the gorillas' favorite enrichment activities, and it's a fun way to practice their hand-eye coordination. Unlike Mac, who prefers holding the brush in his mouth, Zuri is a proper artist.

"Waaargh," she vocalizes, abandoning the purple paint for pink.

"I agree. Kai is a rude man, and I'm glad you can see that."

I pass her another grape and try not to think about my upcoming meeting with Kai. I'm not actually an insane person who thinks Zuri understands what I'm saying or cares whether I get promoted. I'm not a deranged Dr. Dolittle. But it feels good to vent to someone without being bombarded with shirtless pictures of Kai in response— even if he does look infuriatingly good without a shirt, and even if the someone is a two-hundred-pound gorilla.

It's one of my favorite things about gorillas: what you see is what you get. When Ozzie the silverback pounds his chest, I know he's angry. And when Zuri turns a grapefruit husk upside down and wears it like a hat, I know she's feeling playful. Gorilla social dynamics are complex, but it's a language I can mostly understand. They don't use words to obscure their true emotions or manipulate each other. A silverback would never say, "I thought my happiness mattered to you," when you declare for the umpteenth time that you don't want to have a baby. A mother gorilla would never look into her youngster's eyes and say, "See you next week," when she has no intention of doing so. They can't use words to hurt or lie to each other, and I have an easier time understanding them than my fellow humans.

Hence why I'm spilling my life problems to Zuri, who probably wishes I would shut up and let her paint in peace. But she's always been a good listener, ever since I was ten and Nona brought me to the zoo for the first time. In the months after Karina deserted me, once I realized she wasn't coming back, I started acting out. First I endangered the life of Nona's pet goldfish Marigold by substituting Pixy Stix dust for fish food. Then I attempted a midnight excursion to the bus station, where I planned to book a ride back to California. When that didn't work, I spent every fourth-grade recess period bragging to the other girls about my made-up voiceover role in an episode of *Kim Possible*. But the final straw for Nona was when I racked up a three-hundred-dollar phone bill making daily calls to Miss Cleo, the honey-voiced TV psychic.

After that, she dragged me to work with her every day after school. She was a cardiologist, so I spent most afternoons hanging out in the waiting room and contemplating ways to ruin her life, but one day she was called to the zoo to help with an echocardiogram on a gorilla. When we walked inside Ape House, I was convinced that Nona was going to feed me to the macaques, but instead, a khaki-clad zookeeper guided us to an exhibit that housed the most beautiful animal I'd ever seen: a gorilla with a strip of copper fur on her head. Zuri. I got to pass her slices of pumpkin while Nona did her ultrasound, and suddenly the girl who lived only to put vinegar in her grandmother's herbal tea had a new obsession: gorillas.

I begged Nona to take me to the zoo every Saturday. I plastered my bedroom walls with pictures of Koko and his famous kitten. The only movie I wanted to watch was *Majesty on the Mountain*, and the only book I wanted to read was Dr. Kimber's. Whenever Nona went to the zoo to assist with a primate cardiac procedure, I'd camp out in front of Zuri and talk her ear off about anything and everything: How much I missed my mom. My undying passion for Chad Michael Murray. An in-depth review of the Disney movie *Treasure Planet*. I was at a phase in my life when I desperately needed someone to listen to me without casting judgment, and Zuri became that someone. And sometimes, even though the Chad Michael Murray thing turned out to be a bust, she still is.

I'm passing Zuri another handful of grapes when my phone vibrates, and I glance at it to see Nona calling me for the third time today.

Zuri lets out a hoot bark, and I know she wants me to pass her the phone. There's nothing she loves more than staring at a screen, and the one time she managed to grab Lottie's iPad through the mesh, she spent three hours watching Netflix on a hammock.

Sighing, I press the phone to my ear. I felt okay ignoring Nona's first couple of calls, figuring that she just wanted to share her thoughts on the newest episode of *Grey's Anatomy*. But a third call might mean something important.

"Hello?"

"Lucy," my grandmother says, relief flooding her throaty voice. "Thank God. I need a favor."

I instantly regret my decision to answer. "No, I will not leave work to watch Joey Macoroy wash his car with you."

She huffs. "Joey washes his Mustang on Saturdays, Lucille. And I know this is a big ask, but can I drop Mia off with you? Please?"

No way, I mouth to Zuri, who resumes painting something that vaguely resembles a three-eyed platypus.

"I wouldn't ask if I weren't desperate," Nona continues, not giving me a chance to shut her down. "I'm supposed to watch her this afternoon, but Dr. Richards is sick, and I have to manage her caseload for the day. Can I drop Mia off with you for a few hours?"

"Have you tried calling Karina and Alfie? You know, Mia's parents?" I ask, not hiding the saltiness in my tone.

"Yes. Alfie's in Chicago for work, and Karina's teaching an acting course in Cleveland. I called Trudy, too, but her boyfriend sprained his ankle at bowling league, and she's taking him to urgent care." Nona sighs. "Look, I'd bring her with me, but we both know that if I turned my back for a second, she'd have a defibrillator cranked up to max voltage on some poor soul who just came in for a checkup."

"And you think dropping her off at a zoo, where there are *wild animals*, is a safer alternative?" I ask.

"I think leaving her under the close supervision of her older sister, for whom I will bake anything she wants, is my best option."

I scan my brain for an excuse as to why I can't help, but Nona's pleading tone weakens my resolve. It's tough to say no to the woman who practically raised me and funds the premium Hulu subscription that lets me watch *The Real Housewives* ad free.

Dammit.

"Tiramisu," I say finally. "With homemade espresso. And no more bugging me to hang out with Karina for at least a month."

"Have I told you that you're the best granddaughter in existence?" Nona asks.

I only grumble in response and mouth *Help me* to Zuri, who presses a hand to the mesh for another grape.

"We'll see you in twenty minutes," Nona says. "And don't worry, Mia promises to be quiet as a mouse."

Chapter Thirteen

Mia is not quiet as a mouse. As soon as she steps inside Ape House, handing me a Starbucks macchiato that Nona bought to assuage her guilt, she lets out a screech that would make a lion's roar sound muted.

"I can't believe I'm behind the scenes at the *zoo*," she says, taking a long whiff of Clorox and hay. "Olivia from Scouts is gonna lose her mind."

I tell myself it's a good thing she's here; the presence of a witness will help deter me from locking Kai in with the vervet monkeys.

"This way," I say, leading her down the back corridor.

The nursery, tucked away on the south side of Ape House, is off-limits to the public. Lottie, Jack, and I spent most of the morning scrubbing its floors and piling them with hay in preparation for Keeva's arrival. We also examined the mesh fencing that separates the nursery from a holding area for the other gorillas, checking for any gaps. The mesh will allow the older females from Ozzie's troop to watch Keeva in the nursery and hopefully spark their interest in rearing her.

I expect to find Kai waiting for me, possibly clutching a pitchfork and a pair of horns, but the nursery's empty.

"Well, well, well," I mutter. "Guess he stood me up." One point for Lucy, zero points for Elle's eternal optimism.

"Who stood you up?" Mia asks, then gasps so loudly that I look over my shoulder to check for an escaped gorilla.

"Lucy, it's *Kai Bridges*," she breathes, her eyes bulging like we've stumbled onto a bow-wearing JoJo Siwa in the flesh. She points down the hallway toward the employee offices, where Kai faces a wall and presses one hand against it as the other holds a phone to his ear. Unlike Mia, who's grinning so widely I think her face might crack, Kai's frowning like Penny the three-legged puppy just peed on his best pair of shoes.

Guess he didn't stand me up after all. No points for Lucy, three points for Sam and Elle and Team Lucy-hates-everybody-even-Mr.-Rogers.

"Wow," Mia whispers, smoothing her Girl Scout vest with the ginger touch of someone determined to look her best. "I didn't expect him to be so . . ."

"Snarly?" I suggest, watching as Kai's mouth puckers in distaste. "Scowly, like Fitzwilliam Darcy if he wore dumb hats and lacked charm?"

"No." Mia doesn't tear her gaze away from him. "Gorgeous."

"Take it down a notch, Trudy," I retort. "Sunsets are gorgeous, okay? Michael B. Jordan is gorgeous. Kai Bridges is not."

I'm not sure if I'm trying to convince Mia or myself, but as if the universe has conspired with Jack to prove me wrong, he cuts through the hallway en route to the lemur exhibit and switches on an oscillating floor fan that sends a sudden gust of air toward Kai. Kai's hair catches the breeze and he tilts his head back in what seems like slow motion, and damn if I don't half expect him to open a bottle of water and pour it over his T-shirt.

Double damn if I don't totally hate the idea, either. Because as much as I want to deny it, Mia has a point. As Kai barks into the phone, probably threatening to fire Lars the assistant for buying the wrong kind of hair pomade, it's impossible not to notice that his gray T-shirt hugs his well-muscled back with just the right amount of snugness. And though I curse the day he was born, the Bad Lucy part of my brain—the side of me that hasn't shared an orgasm with anyone besides my vibrator in months—imagines what it would be like to lean against the wall he's got one hand pressed up on, his tricep flexed mere inches from my body. How it would feel to have his hands pressed on either side of me, his broad shoulders boxing me in until—

No. Fuck no. Bad Lucy is a traitorous little bitch, and I give myself a swift mental kick in the ass.

Kai, who's so lacking in manners that he ends the call without even saying good-bye to the victim on the other end of the line, glances up to see Mia and me lingering outside the nursery. In the blink of an eye, his sulky pout mutates into a smirk, and I can read his thoughts a mile away: here's glaringly incompetent Lucy Rourke, here to provide his daily dose of entertainment and smug superiority.

Oh goody.

"So you came to learn from the best," he says in a silky tone that makes me want to slice my ears off. "Good for you, Lucy."

He winks at me like he knows what I was thinking about his triceps a moment ago, and I can't resist the urge to snap back.

"Actually, no," I say, my voice sugary sweet. "I came to learn from you. But if you know where I can find the best, please point me in that direction."

Kai laughs, and as he crosses his arms over his chest, I shove Bad Lucy back into her cave and force myself to think of decidedly unsexy things, like funerals and Pap smears and the time I went on a date with a guy named Razor who ate pizza with a fork and declared that the gender pay gap was a hoax.

"You look tense," Kai says, running a hand through his hair as I focus, hard, on Razor's misogynistic claims. "Did something bad happen? My God, Lucy, did *90 Day Fiancé* get canceled?"

My cheeks heat up as I remember my meandering rant about celebrities and Big Ed at Picnic for Paws, and I curse Kai to a lifetime of getting stuck behind the slowest walker in a crowded hallway.

"I'm not tense at all," I say in a tone that's undeniably tense. "And for your information, *90 Day Fiancé* would never get canceled. It's a reality TV empire. It spawned eighteen spinoffs."

"And how many of those have you watched?" he asks, reaching up to knit his fingers behind his head like he knows it will make his biceps pop.

"Just two or three," I say smoothly, keeping my gaze locked on his face. I couldn't care less about his bulging biceps.

Kai smirks like he knows I'm lying—which I am, because as a loyal Discovery Plus subscriber, I've seen every spinoff and every spinoff's spinoff. "I bet."

I make a note of all his snarky comments so I can present them to Sam and Elle as proof that he's not a capybara-rescuing Sandy Bullock with a broader frame and too much testosterone.

He's a jerk, plain and simple.

"That didn't seem like a fun phone call," I say, deciding that two can play at this game. "Poor thing, was it Prince William? Did he call to say you aren't his very favorite boy anymore?"

Kai shakes his head. "Good try, but no. It was a producer from *Fresh Air* scheduling an interview for the fall."

"*Fresh Air* with Terry Gross?" I ask, annoyed that I'll have to skip an episode.

He grins. "That's the one. I'm guessing you're a fan? Well, good to know reality TV isn't the only media you consume."

I fix him with a benevolent smile. "I wouldn't be so quick to criticize reality TV, since your show could technically be classified as such."

His smirk disappears, and I mentally high-five myself for managing to hit a nerve. "*On the Wild Side* is an educational docuseries, Lucy," he says tightly. "Let's not compare it to *The Kardashians*."

"I actually think you have a lot in common with the Kardashians," I muse, thrusting the knife in deeper. "Your name starts with a K, for starters. And they've won an Emmy, too."

"They haven't." Kai drops his hands from the back of his head and fixes me with a look that could melt whatever frozen Antarctic ice ridge he bragged about spending a week on.

"Yeah, I'm pretty sure they have." I'm talking entirely out of my ass, but Kai's lips are twisted like he's sucking on a black cherry War-Head, so I wave a carefree hand at him and keep going. "Or maybe it was a Teen Choice Award. Oh well. They're basically the same thing, right? Tomato, to-mah-to."

Kai clenches his jaw like he's on the verge of a stroke, and even though Sam and Elle would seriously disapprove of my behavior, it's too satisfying to stop once I've started.

"Hi," Mia says after a pause in which I patiently wait for Kai's head to pop off his body. "I'm Mia, Lucy's little sister."

I got so distracted by landing a shot on Kai that I forgot she was here, and I watch in horror as she holds her notebook up toward him.

"Can I have your autograph?" she asks, barely meeting Kai's gaze. "I'm, like, your number one fan."

I die a little inside as Kai fixes Mia, then me, with a radiant grin.

He's the human equivalent of Pac-Man, except he survives on praise and attention instead of little white dots.

"Did you hear that, Lucy?" he asks with enough bravado to make my teeth clench. "Your sister adores me."

"I really do," Mia agrees.

Nona owes me a dozen tiramisus for putting up with this.

"My favorite *Wild Side* episode is the one where you visited the macaques in Nepal."

He raises his eyebrows at me as if to say, *Do you hear how special I am? Even this ten-year-old thinks so*, but when he crouches down toward Mia, Kai's smile appears genuine.

"Thank you, Mia. I like that episode, too. Here, how about a hat?" Reaching for a giant duffel bag behind him, he fishes out a blue ball cap bearing the *Wild Side* logo and a Sharpie. "To Mia," he narrates, signing it with a dramatic flourish. "Stay wild! Love, Kai."

I bet signing autographs is his favorite hobby. I bet he practices his signature every night before bed, and his hotel room is littered with T-shirts and hats and black-and-white headshots signed: *To Kai: You're the most handsome, well-traveled man in the world, and everyone who meets you worships you. Stay wild! Love, Kai.*

Mia accepts the hat like it's a diamond ring. "Wow. Thank you."

"You're welcome. And you know what, Mia?" Kai says, resting his hands on his knees as he crouches toward her. "I think your big sister wants a hat, too."

"Half sister," I say automatically, trying not to feel guilty when a fraction of the joy on Mia's face flickers. "And I absolutely do not."

If he tries to stick one of those monstrosities on my head, I'll rip it off and smack him in the face with it.

Grinning, Kai pulls a purple hat from his duffel and scribbles on it while I contemplate how to murder him without getting caught. Then he holds the cap toward me, and before I can smack it out of his hand, he waves at someone behind me.

"Cheerio there, Phil!" Kai greets, and my stomach drops when I turn to see my salt-and-pepper-haired boss striding down the hallway.

"Hello, Kai," Phil says like it's Christmas morning and Kai's a present-laden tree. "I didn't expect you back in Ape House until Keeva arrives."

"We won't shoot until then, but Lucy asked me to help her with some camera training," Kai says, as if this was my idea. "I have a busy schedule, but when she told me how much she wanted to improve, I knew I had to help."

My hatred for Kai grows by the fire of a thousand burning suns, but to my surprise, Phil nods approvingly. "Great idea, Lucy! That's the kind of initiative I'm looking for. And hey, cool hats."

He points at the signed caps, and Kai gives him a sheepish grin. "Anything for my fans. Well, mostly anything. As I was just telling Lucy, no matter how flattered I am by her request, I have a firm policy against autographing body parts. A hat will have to do."

Rage burns inside me, and like he's freaking Mary Poppins with a bottomless suitcase, Kai grabs another hat to hand to Phil. "Can't leave anyone out."

"Wow, thank you," my boss says. He puts the hat on with the reverence of Queen Elizabeth II putting on her most bedazzled crown.

"Kai, can we take a photo?" Mia asks. "Please?"

He nods. "Phil, will you do the honors?"

Grinning, Phil takes Mia's phone from her outstretched hand. Seizing her opportunity, she snakes an arm around Kai's waist and gazes at him like she's planning to snip a lock off his hair and wear it around her neck.

"Hop on in there, Lucy," Phil says.

"Yes, come on, Lucy," Kai says, not even trying to hide the triumph in his eyes. "Get over here and let me make your dream come true."

I stay planted to my spot, wishing Ozzie the silverback could scoop Kai up with his massive arms and fling him back to whatever circle of hell he came from. I glance from Phil to Kai, realizing there's no escape. I can't storm away from the nursery without giving Phil the impression that I'm a bad sport. Swallowing my pride, I force myself to stand beside Kai.

"Atta girl," he says, and when he reaches over to place the autographed hat on my head, it's all I can do not to bite his hand off and slap him with the detached limb.

"Say 'cheese!'" Phil instructs.

"Say 'stay wild!'" Kai adds, oozing with good cheer. Taking pictures of himself is probably his third favorite activity, after signing autographs and manhandling his penis.

I wish I were a hippopotamus and he was sailing the Nile so I could capsize his boat and swallow him whole.

"Stay wild," I mutter between gritted teeth.

I smile for the photo like this is going to be the best summer of my life, and I think that should earn me an Emmy of my own.

Chapter Fourteen

"What is *wrong* with you?" I ask Kai when Phil bids us farewell and heads to his office for a conference call.

"I'm sorry, is that Lucy-speak for 'thank you'?" Kai asks. "Because now Phil thinks that this extra training was your idea, and he seemed impressed. So suck it up and deal." He grabs his duffel bag and strides toward the nursery. "That's Kai-speak for 'you're welcome.'"

Anger simmers in my bones, but he's not wrong. When we reach the nursery, he sets up a tripod and a camera, then pulls a plastic baby doll out of his duffel and tries to hand it to me.

"Um, have you lost your mind?" I ask, ripping my hat off and stepping sideways to avoid the doll. "No."

Kai sighs. "It's a prop. You're going to be shooting with Keeva soon, and I want you to be prepared. So just take the doll and pretend it's her."

"'*Take the doll and pretend it's her*'?" I repeat, narrowing my eyes at him. "Sounds like somebody bought an inflatable girlfriend after his last breakup."

To my delight, the faintest hint of a blush creeps over his cheeks. "Grow up, Lucy. Either you want to get better or you don't."

I eye the doll's wide blue eyes and creepy, open-mouthed expression. "I've seen *Annabelle*, and that thing looks possessed."

Kai stuffs Annabelle into my hands, rolling his eyes. "It would be great if you didn't make it so difficult to help you."

He just made me look like an obsessed fan in front of my boss, and somehow *I'm* the difficult one?

"Helping me?" I ask, hoisting my hat in the air. "Is that what you'd call your behavior back there?"

Kai smirks. "No, that was me having fun." He nods toward the hat. "But those go for $39.99 on my website, so you're welcome."

"Turning quite a profit from that child labor in Sudan, huh?"

Kai's head snaps up from where he's bent over the camera, and he shoots me a look that could freeze his fiery birthplace. "If you knew anything about me, you'd know that all *Wild Side* memorabilia is made through fair trade labels. Sustainability and ethical sourcing are especially important to me."

Mia lets out a breathy sigh of appreciation, and I chalk up another point for Elle and Sam.

"Oh," I say, impressed. "Good to know." Now I feel bad about tossing my hat onto the ground so rudely.

Kai pats the camera. "Think of today as an expedited version of exposure therapy. The sooner you realize the camera is a tool, not a rabid dog, the sooner you can relax in front of it."

If only it were so simple. I don't know how to explain to Kai why I freeze up in front of a camera, intimidated by its power to capture a humiliating moment and make it eternal.

"Look, I'm not asking you to earn an Emmy here," Kai says, noticing the terror written all over my face.

"Our mom has an Emmy," Mia says from the bench outside the nursery, her notebook open on her lap.

There's no subject I'd rather avoid more than Karina, and I shoot Mia a look that says, *Stop talking, or I'll feed your fairy bread to the petting zoo goats.* But she's looking at Kai, not me.

Kai, his interest piqued, glances from me to Mia. "Seriously? Who's your mom?"

"Doesn't matter," I say at the same time that Mia announces, "Karina Katona," with a distinct note of pride in her voice.

"She was on *Guilty Pleasures*," Mia continues, oblivious to my discomfort.

"*Guilty Pleasures*?" Realization dawns across his face. "The show about the private investigators that ended on a cliffhanger?"

"That's the one," I grumble.

Guilty Pleasures was abruptly canceled after its seventh season, leaving a string of unsolved murders and love triangles in its wake. Fueled by a long-standing feud between the writer and the network, the sudden cancellation sparked the start of a decline in Karina's career and an intense fury among fans demanding to know (A) which bed-hopping characters ended up together, and (B) the culprit behind the merciless Malibu Fish Hook Killings.

"Mom played Kitty Conway," Mia adds.

Kai's jaw drops, and I contemplate thrusting Annabelle's plastic hand inside his mouth and using it to rip out his tongue.

"Your mum is Kitty Conway?" he asks, unable to hide his shock.

"No, our mother is Karina Katona, who *played* Kitty Conway," I say testily. "The people in the box are actors, Kai. SpongeBob doesn't actually live in a pineapple under the sea."

He raises an eyebrow at me. "Clever."

Karina's character Kitty, a sweet-faced Georgia peach who moved to California and discovered a passion for stilettos and crime solving, was a fan favorite for her generous bosom and silky blond hair that she never pulled into a ponytail, not even while she chased bad guys down alleyways and through abandoned warehouses. Basically, my mother is super-hot. So when Kai says, *Your mum is Kitty Conway?* in that disbelieving tone, I interpret it as the same question I've asked myself since I was a kid: *Why don't you look like her, you tiny-boobed, frizzy-haired disappointment?*

"You didn't tell me your mum was an actress," Kai says, aiming the tripod at me.

"You're right. I must have skipped that tidbit when we reviewed our family trees. I should also mention that my cousin Bobby's a line cook at Benihana."

Kai rolls his eyes. "I'm just saying, it's interesting that you struggle with the camera, considering your mum was a TV star."

And it's interesting that you struggle with dumbassery when your mom is Charlotte Kimber, I want to snap back, but I don't. Instead, I shrug. "I guess sometimes the apple falls pretty far from the tree."

"Yeah," Kai says, studying me for a long moment. "I guess it does."

"We came here to practice, right?" I ask, refusing to engage in further discussion of Karina. "So let's practice."

Kai nods. "First things first: the mechanics of the camera." He rattles off something about static versus tracking shots, and Mia takes notes while I try not to convulse with anxiety. I'm okay as long as Kai's spouting off terms like *aperture* and *lens* and *boom pole*, but the instant he powers the camera on, it's game over. I'm going to sweat my ass off until I melt into the ground, leaving nothing behind but a pile of khaki and a ponytail elastic.

"Okay, now tell me about Keeva," Kai says. He fiddles with the camera, causing a red light to flash on, and my hands turn so clammy that fake Keeva slips out of my grip and lands on the cement floor with a thud.

I bend down to pick her up, detesting the way the camera steals every ounce of my confidence. But when I straighten back up, I'm shocked to see that Kai's not laughing at my clumsiness. Instead, he gives me a reassuring nod, as if I didn't just drop an endangered baby gorilla on her head.

"You're fine, Lucy."

"Go, Lucy!" Mia cheers, taking a bite of fairy bread and sitting back to enjoy the show.

"So, um, Keeva," I say, a cyclone of nausea swirling in my stomach. "Keeva is a baby. A gorilla. A baby and a gorilla."

"Describe your plan to integrate her into the troop," Kai says, motioning for me to take a deep breath.

I take a long inhale, but it only leaves me light-headed. "Um, okay. Well, we'll, you know, bring her here. To the nursery." I gesture to the space behind me, accidentally smacking Annabelle into the mesh barrier. The blow's impact twists her plastic head to an unsettling angle, and Mia winces.

"Okay, this is stupid," I tell Kai, wanting to die of embarrassment as I wave the nearly decapitated doll toward the camera. "I told you, I can't do this. It's nice that you're trying to help, but let's face it: I'm hopeless."

I can't help but think that Lottie would never knock the head off a baby gorilla. Maybe Kai was right after all; maybe I'm just not up to the challenge. Maybe I'm destined for a lifetime of being stuck in a junior keeper role while Lottie and Jack and Scotty the intern fight their way up the food chain to CEO. I picture myself in ten years, still earning a pittance of a salary and living at Nona's while my new boss Scotty assigns me all the grunt work. Nick will be happily married to Margo from Guest Relations, and their eighteen unruly children will fling bubblegum and juice boxes at me while I try to lead a Critter Chat.

I'm fucked.

"Lucy, stop," Kai says, forming a timeout gesture with his hands. "You're doing fine."

I hold up the gravely injured doll as evidence to the contrary. "Have you seen Annabelle's head?"

Kai frowns, and I wait for him to acknowledge that he was wrong. That my glaring incompetence can't be helped after all, but could I please get Karina's autograph for him?

But he doesn't. Instead, he shuts the camera off and points it toward the opposite wall. "Forget about the camera for now, then. Just show me the nursery. Tell me what Keeva will experience here. Like it's just you and me having a conversation."

"But the camera's the whole point," I argue, praying that Kai will just let me retreat to my office and bury my shame in two sleeves of Chips Ahoy!

"No, Keeva's the whole point," he says. "You're the whole point. It's your connection with the animals that matters. *That's* the story. The camera is just a tool that helps me share it with the world."

Kai's being, dare I say it . . . nice? And it might just be a trick, but the encouraging nod he gives me tells me it isn't, and the pounding of my heart slows a little. I might not know the first thing about being successful on TV, but I know the ins and outs of Ape House. I set the cursed baby doll on the ground and give Kai a tour of the nursery: the scale where I'll weigh Keeva twice a day, the sink where I'll wash and prepare her bottles, and the blankets, balls, and cardboard boxes that will serve as enrichment items and encourage play.

Eventually, I glance away from the nursery to find him bent behind the camera, his face pressed to the lens.

"Hey!" I cry when I see the red power light. "You told me to forget about the camera!"

Kai pops out from behind the tripod, a cocky grin playing at his lips. "And you did. See? You *can* do it, Lucy. I've been recording for the last ten minutes, and you were too absorbed in your excitement to notice."

"You have? Really? But I . . . I didn't even trip on anything," I say in disbelief. "I didn't even lose my train of thought or ramble about hyenas."

Sure, I had no idea Kai was shooting, and I displayed zero percent of Kitty Conway's sultry intrigue, but I stayed upright. I stayed conscious. I didn't sob into my polo or lose my lunch. I did it, even if I didn't realize that I was.

"What I'm trying to teach you is that once Keeva's here, you'll forget the cameras exist," Kai says. "You'll be too caught up in your passion to worry about anything but your work."

I'm not totally convinced, but before I can explain that to Kai, his phone buzzes. Kai's jaw tenses when he glances at the screen.

"I better take this," he says, a hard edge to his tone. "Good work today, Lucy. And it was great to meet you, Mia. Stay wild, okay?"

"Okay!" Mia chirps back, but he's already out of earshot, his phone pressed to his ear as he strides down the hallway for privacy.

"He's awesome," Mia says, watching him walk away. "Don't ya think?"

I glance down the hallway, where Kai's got his hand pressed against the wall again, his head hung low as he engages in what looks like another unpleasant phone call.

"Um, maybe," I say, too confused by the events of the past hour to pull away when Mia wraps her hand around mine.

Because Kai might be an obnoxious braggart who's too handsome for his own good and can't shut up about his Emmys, but he also humored Mia when she asked for his autograph and took time out of his day to help improve my cataclysmic screen appeal. And yes, he might annoy the hell out of me and suffer from a cringeworthy addiction to applause, but he clearly cares about his job.

And for a reason I can't figure out, he seems to care about mine.

I call a mental truce with Kai, but it only lasts about two minutes. Because when Mia and I get back to my office, she sets my new *Wild Side* hat in a place of honor on my desk, right beside my cherished Dr. Kimber bobblehead. Only then do I read the rage-inducing inscription that makes me want to march straight back to the nursery and kick down Kai's camera.

To Lucy, from Kai: Don't get your pseudopenis all bent out of shape.

Chapter Fifteen

I'm the only person in the world who doesn't adore Kai. On Wednesday, he retweets Lottie's Ernest Goes to Summer Camp post, winning her thousands of new followers, and she can't stop gushing about him while we prep dinner for Ozzie's troop. On Thursday, he treats the entire zoo staff to Donatos pizza, and I hate myself for eating four slices of Serious Cheese. On Friday, two Aquatics keepers in front of me in the Starbucks line argue about whether he has twelve or thirteen Emmys, and when I lean toward them and say, "I think it's only three," they glare at me like I sneezed on them.

But I have bigger things to focus on—or one smaller thing, to be precise. Keeva's arrival is set for Saturday, and between nursery prep and managing my usual workload, I'm too busy to worry about Kai's self-satisfied smirk.

Unfortunately, I'm also too busy to remember that I promised Sam and Elle I'd meet them for drinks. Sam learned on Wednesday that a piece she wrote for her women in the workplace blog, Leaders in Lipstick, was picked up by *HuffPost*, and she chose a nearby tiki bar for her celebration.

Lucy! Elle texts me just after seven on Friday, when I'm blinking at yet another journal article on gorilla surrogacy. Where are you? You're late!

I'm about to reply with My office! Where else would I be? when I remember I was supposed to meet my friends fifteen minutes ago.

Got stuck at work, I text back. On my way!

I'm as close to being on my way to the bar as I am to being the next Lisa Ling, but Elle, who undoubtedly knows I forgot, only sends back a thumbs-up. She's too sweet to call me out, and a pang of guilt overwhelms me as I shut my laptop and scramble to change out of my work boots. I know Sam and Elle wish I spent less time in my office and more time hanging out with them, but the fact that I can't join their upcoming girls' trip or make it to Sam's wine and *The Bachelorette* nights doesn't make me a bad friend. It just makes me busy.

Right?

I push away the creeping doubt and grab my car keys. The sooner I get to Huli Huli, the sooner I can buy Sam a drink before heading home to rest up for tomorrow. When I park and hurry toward the bar's entrance, where baby potted palm trees set a tropical vibe, I catch a glimpse of my reflection in a car window and regret not packing a change of clothes. A long morning shoveling hay in the outdoor Gorilla Villa left sweat wrinkles on my polo, and a layer of dirt from the red river hog exhibit cakes my shorts. I look like I got my ass handed to me in a mud-wrestling fight, but I trudge forward anyway.

"I didn't forget," I tell Sam when I find her sipping a cocktail next to the stone replica of an ancient Mayan temple guard. Stacks of bamboo shoots and a papier-mâché parrot lend the lounge a surf shack feel, and Sam tucks a purple tropical flower behind her ear and looks at me skeptically.

"I know you, Luce. You totally forgot. But thank you for showing up." She grins and fingers the festive leis looped around her neck. "I'll accept your apology in the form of a Shipwreck Shirley."

By the time I find my way back to her, clutching her drink and a Blue Hawaii for me, Elle's returned from the bathroom sporting two pink leis, and she peels one off and slides it over my head.

"To Sam!" I say, passing her a drink. "For writing a blog post so kickass that even Arianna Huffington took note."

"To be fair, I'm not sure Arianna's involved in the day-to-day *HuffPo* operations," Sam says. "But I did get tons of new hits on my blog this week, and that's huge."

Pride radiates off her, and as she launches into an analysis of how she'll use her newfound notoriety to woo blog sponsors, I realize I haven't even read her article yet. In fact, I'm a month or two behind on her posts, and I sip my drink and make a mental note to catch up as soon as I have time.

"Oh, shit," Sam says, abandoning her description of cost-per-click ads. "She came."

"Who came?" I turn toward the door, glancing around for one of Sam's exes. If it's Bananagrams cheater Magdalene, I'm going to be a very unhappy camper.

"Quick, how do I look?" Sam takes a swig of her drink and runs a hand over her hair, smoothing her side part.

"Are you serious?" I ask. It always stuns me when obviously hot people doubt their own hotness. "You look like the prettiest member of the *Pretty Little Liars* if she grew up and raided a Banana Republic. You look great."

"Don't look now, but Freya's here," she whispers.

"Kai's co-producer?" I ask, like I know any other Freyas.

Sam nods. "I met with her and Marketing yesterday about branding ideas, and she's, like, a genius. Do you know she grew up really poor in some tiny town in Wyoming? Now she has a bachelor's in environmental science *and* an MBA and runs a whole TV show. Plus, she looks like that."

I glance toward the entrance, where Freya, looking like a dime piece in a sage green jumpsuit and laced sandal booties, is being chatted up by a T-shirt-wearing bro with numerous chins and a blatant disregard for personal space.

"I mentioned I'd be here to celebrate, but I didn't think she'd show up," Sam says. "I'm freaking out."

"Get a grip," I say, giving her the same tough love she gives me when I'm the one panicking. "Why don't you go say hi? Rescue her from that dude before he asks what her sign is."

Nodding, Sam adjusts her leis. "Right. Wish me luck."

"Good luck!" Elle calls after her.

Once we're alone, Elle raises an eyebrow at me. "I want you to know that I see your outfit and am choosing not to comment."

I can't even blame her this time. "Wanna be distracted with lobster rolls? My treat."

Before Elle can answer, her phone buzzes, and she bites her lip when she glances at the screen. "Shoot, Nadeem's stuck at work. I've gotta run home and let Trixie out."

"Oh, let me!" I dog-sit for Elle and Nadeem sometimes, and their nine-year-old Jack Russell mix is a total sweetheart. Plus, letting Trixie out is the perfect excuse to dip out early and head home to get more work done.

Elle shakes her head. "Nice try, missy, but no way. Social outings are good for you. Like vegetables and fresh air."

I hardly think attending happy hour is equivalent to eating my daily dose of greens, but I don't protest.

"Stay," she insists. "Order a drink and chat up a handsome guy and forget about work for twenty minutes. It's been a while since your breakup, and it wouldn't kill you to talk to other men."

"Chat up a handsome guy?" I repeat. "Elle, you've seen my outfit! Plus, there are only two handsome guys at the bar, and one just kissed the other on the neck." I take a sip of my drink. "Also, I've talked to plenty of guys since Nick dumped me. I talk to Phil every day. I talk to Nadeem. And last week I spent half an hour listening to Trudy's boyfriend complain about Rachel Maddow and the mainstream media."

Elle looks like she wants to strangle me with a lei, but she just shakes her head and tries, unsuccessfully, to smooth out my collar. "At least stay awhile in case Sam needs a wing woman, okay? You owe her that."

Waving, she trounces off in her striped romper, and I contemplate sneaking back to my office. But when Sam catches my eye behind Freya's back and gives me a stealthy thumbs-up, I sigh and take a seat at the bar. I might not be a social butterfly, but I can stick around for Sam's sake. I order lobster rolls from the bartender, but as I wait for my food, I peer over my shoulder and see the aforementioned Nick standing at the entrance to the bar. Margo from Guest Relations follows him inside, her hand snaked around his waist.

Dammit. This is what I get for leaving the safe confines of my office, and I can act like an adult and say hello, or I can run for cover.

I run for cover. Sprinting around the left side of the bar, I seek refuge behind a potted plant with blessedly thick leaves. It's not that I hate Nick or Margo, even if they did wait all of twenty-one days after he dumped me to start appearing in each other's Snapchat stories. It's that nobody wants to run into her ex while sporting dirt-streaked khaki shorts, and certainly not while stuffing her face with lobster rolls alone.

As the happy couple heads toward the bar, I wedge farther behind the plant. So much for Elle's advice to go forth and make small talk with eligible bachelors; this little palm tree's getting closer to my naughty bits than any man has in months.

I hear footsteps approach, and I hold my breath in case they're Nick's. But it's a pair of Nikes walking toward me, and Nick, in all his nerdiness, prefers New Balances.

Yes, I'm embarrassed for myself.

"I've told you a hundred times, I don't want to do it anymore. I'm not sure how to make myself clearer." The Nikes are only four feet from the plant now, and I can't peek out to see their owner without exposing my hiding place. But I don't need to, because I'd know that accent anywhere.

It's Kai Bridges, and he's in the middle of an argument.

"So we let the chips fall where they may, then," Kai says. He's either talking to himself or he's on the phone with someone, and I give equal weight to both possibilities.

I glance through the leaves to see Nick speaking to the red-haired bartender. He's probably ordering something exciting to go with his New Balances, like a Coors Light.

"Of course people will talk. Let them. I can handle the fallout," Kai says tersely, and I'm not *trying* to eavesdrop, but it's not like I can just shut my ears off.

Am I listening to him break up with a girlfriend? Or maybe someone discovered a dark secret about him—like the fact that he can't read—and is threatening an exposé. Maybe he paid for his Maserati by selling bonobos on the black market, and he's finally about to get his due.

"I know that, but—" Kai pauses, but even though I'm straining to listen, I can't make out anything from the other end of the line. "I know," he repeats after a moment. "Yes. It's just . . . I want things to be different."

What in God's sweet creation could Kai Bridges, who has the world in the palm of his hand, want to be different?

"No, I understand," he says, and I get the feeling that he's starting to lose the argument. "Yes, I know that, too."

This is some juicy stuff, and it's clear that Kai walked around this side of the bar because he wanted privacy. Guilt creeps over me, and I'm about to cover my ears with my hands when his blue Nikes, pacing back and forth across the floor, take a step too far in my direction.

"Ow!" I cry as he accidentally kicks me. Realizing my mistake, I cower lower under the plant, praying my cry didn't grab Nick's attention.

When I glance up, I find Kai staring at me in shock.

"Cheerio," I whisper, wishing I could sink into the floor. "Fancy meeting you here."

Kai narrows his eyes at me. "I'm gonna have to call you back," he says into the phone before slipping it in his pocket. Then he crouches down until he's eye level with me, his jaw set in a tight line.

"Lucy Rourke, are you spying on me?"

Chapter Sixteen

I say the first thing that pops into my head, which is the very mature answer of "You wish."

"Now go away, please," I whisper, wiggling farther behind the plant. "There's nothing to see here."

"On the contrary. I think there's quite a lot to see." Kai gives me an assessing look, and I can only imagine how I must appear to him, curled up behind a potted plant in my sweaty work clothes.

"I didn't hear anything," I lie. I cringe when Kai raises an eyebrow at me. "Well, I didn't hear a lot. Just something about chips falling and people talking and wanting things to be different. You know, nothing memorable."

Stop rambling, I order myself, but I can't. "My theory is you're either navigating a breakup or trying to extricate yourself from an international crime ring." I bump my head on the ceramic pot and flinch. "I'm leaning toward the crime ring."

I expect Kai to whip out his phone and speed-dial Phil, but he doesn't. Instead, he laughs, and it catches me so off guard that I fall sideways and grab the pot to keep my balance. That only makes him laugh harder, and I duck lower when I peek through the leaves and spot Nick looking toward the sound.

"Be quiet! You're gonna blow my cover," I whisper-hiss at Kai, grabbing his sleeve and tugging him toward the floor.

But I pull too hard, and within an instant his face is mere inches from mine. We're close enough that I can see the hint of dark circles beneath his glinting hazel eyes and the scar crossing his right eyebrow, and when I find myself taking an intentional whiff of his campfire-scented aftershave, I release my grip on his jacket.

Bad Lucy, bad. Back into your cage.

"Why are you still hiding?" he asks in a stage whisper, and I contemplate ripping a leaf off the plant and stuffing it into his mouth. "I already caught you."

His arrogance knows no bounds, and I scoff at him. "It's precious that you think I was crouched here to listen to your phone call. No offense, but you're not that important. I'm hiding from my ex-boyfriend, and you're about to blow it with your big fat mouth."

Suddenly curious, Kai peers through the leaves. "That guy? Wow, I guess you're into beards after all."

Nick can barely grow a smattering of peach fuzz, let alone a beard. Confused, I peek past a leaf to see a white-haired man who looks like a cross between Santa and Father Time's grandfather waving down the bartender.

"Not him," I groan, wishing I could wipe the amusement off Kai's face. "*Him.*" I point to where Nick stands with Margo, smiling as she shows him something on her phone. It's probably a list of adorable names for their hordes of future children.

"Oh, Dr. North," Kai says, scratching the stubble along his chin. "That makes more sense. He was on set yesterday for Brian the rhino's blood draw. Seems like an okay guy."

When he turns to find me scowling at him, Kai seems to realize he's gone too far. Calling me glaringly incompetent is one thing, but speaking tolerably of my ex is another. "I mean, he sucks," he says halfheartedly. "I bet he murders kittens in his basement."

I roll my eyes at him but breathe a sigh of relief when the adoring couple leaves the bar to venture out to the patio. They should be outside long enough for me to wolf down my food and buy Sam another drink before making my escape. Leaving Kai in my dust, I scurry back to the bar and stuff a lobster roll in my mouth.

It's a short-lived moment of bliss that ends when Kai slides into the seat next to mine and watches me eat like I'm a lion shredding an antelope carcass.

"No offense, but can you find someplace else to sit?" I ask. "It's hard to eat when I can feel the judgment radiating off you."

"Where else would you suggest I sit?" he asks, gesturing to the packed lounge.

I take a swig of my drink. "A nice toilet in the men's room, perhaps?"

He signals for the bartender. "If anyone should move, it's you. I gifted you a free hat and helped train you for the cameras. In return, you eavesdropped on my private conversation."

"It's not eavesdropping if I was trapped," I counter. "And you can take your free hat and shove it up your pseudopenis."

The dark cloud that crossed Kai's features during his phone call dissipates, replaced by a satisfied smirk. "I see you didn't appreciate the inside joke. I'm sorry you don't have a sense of humor."

"Oh, I've got plenty of senses of humor," I say, so annoyed that I trip over my words. "And what are you doing here? Shouldn't you be holed up in your luxury hotel room, admiring your own reflection in your Nickelodeon Awards?"

"The Nickelodeon Kids' Choice Awards are tiny orange submarines,

Lucy. They're not reflective." He orders an old-fashioned and a basket of spring rolls and turns to meet my gaze. "But if you must know, I came here with a friend in case she needed a wingman."

Of course. He came with Freya. I glance across the lounge, where I see that Sam has successfully scared off the pasty-looking dude in the Zelda T-shirt and is deep in conversation with Kai's coproducer.

"Fine. If you're going to sit here, can you at least tell me if your phone call was about a drug deal gone bad?" I ask. "I want to be prepared in case a SWAT team shows up at Ape House."

I'm trying to get under his skin, but I'm also curious. Kai's usually full of bravado, but he sounded apprehensive toward the end of the phone call. Who was on the other end of the line? Was it the same person who called him outside the Ape House nursery?

I'm no gossipmonger, but a girl can't help but wonder.

"Frankly," Kai says, "that's none of your business."

He's right, so I shrug and concentrate on my food. But my peace and quiet last all of three seconds before he pipes up again.

"What happened between you and the good doctor?" he asks, sipping his old-fashioned. "I mean, if you went so far as to hide behind a houseplant, it must be a good story."

I give him a sideways look. "Would you want to run into your ex in this outfit? Besides, the breakup is none of *your* business."

"Was it because he wears those white New Balances?" Kai asks. "Or was it something more dramatic?"

I spin my glass in a circle, trying not to remember the heartbroken look in Nick's eyes the day I moved my stuff out of his town house, the look that said, *Why can't you just be a normal woman who wants normal woman things?* with its teary, slack-jawed disappointment.

"Chill out, Gossip Girl. I'm not gonna tell you about the breakup."

I brush my lips with my napkin and push away the memory of the anger I felt the day Nick came home with a zoo-themed baby onesie, somehow thinking that a tiny piece of cotton fabric could convince me to abandon my life plan.

"Do you want to know why my last relationship ended?" Kai asks, examining a spring roll.

"Not particularly," I say, but he's already talking over me.

"She pronounced *wolf* with a silent *l*," he explains. "It was unbearable. Like, what does a dog say? *Woof*. What animal runs in a pack and howls at the moon? A *woof*. One day I just couldn't take it any longer."

"The horror," I say flatly. "And joke's on you, because wolves don't actually howl at the moon."

He peers at me over his drink. "I was being facetious. I dismantled that very myth in Season 2, Episode 6, of *Wild Side*."

"And here I thought your ex dumped you because you stole all her conditioner," I tell him. "Or because she had more Instagram followers and you couldn't handle your jealousy."

Kai laughs, and it's a deep-throated rumble that sends a tingle down my spine. As punishment for finding his laugh attractive, I force myself to watch Father Time's grandfather wolf down chicken wings and wipe sriracha from his beard.

"I have five million followers, Lucy. I'd have to date Justin Bieber to have that problem." He winks at me, and from the corner of my eye, I notice the bartender observing him so raptly that she doesn't notice when the glass she's holding under the tap overflows.

"Congratulations," I say dryly.

He smirks. "Hey, can I ask you a serious question?"

"Will you leave me alone if I answer?"

"I make no promises."

I wait, expecting him to ask me about my terrible stage fright.

"Do you know who the Malibu Fish Hook Killer was?" Kai asks. "On *Guilty Pleasures*?"

I'd rather narrate a play-by-play of the time I said *shart* in front of a bunch of grad students than discuss Karina's show, and I bite into a lobster roll instead of answering.

"I spent most of my summers at my aunt Susan's when I was a kid," he explains. "She lives on a farm in Montana, and there wasn't much to do at night except play Battleship and watch TV. We got very, very into *Guilty Pleasures*, and it kills me to this day that I don't know who murdered all those poor surfers." He raises an eyebrow like I've got insider information. "Just tell me: was it Detective Wiles? Blink once for yes, twice for no."

I'm shocked that Kai spent time hanging out with his aunt and watching soapy dramas. "You spent summers in Montana? I thought you pretty much grew up at your mom's research station."

I remember my childhood fantasies of traipsing through the Rwandan jungle with Kai and Dr. Kimber, a bandanna tied over my forehead and thorns pricking my ankles as we tracked Taji's gorilla troop. I certainly never pictured a tiny Kai bent over a board game while the TV droned on in the background.

"Yeah, well, you thought wrong." He sips his drink and then smiles at me, as if trying to soften his response. "I spent a lot of time on Mount Karisimbi, sure, but that can be a dangerous place for a kid." His expression darkens, and I wonder if he's remembering the fateful day he caught his leg in a snare and they got overrun by poachers. "Plus, we didn't have cable there." If he's having a flashback to the fateful day of Taji's murder, he conceals it by biting into a spring roll. "So come on, Lucy. It was Wiles, wasn't it?"

"I have no idea." The discussion of Karina's show makes me sweat, and I wrap my hands around my cool glass. "I didn't watch *Guilty Pleasures*. Trust me, I know less about the Malibu Fish Hook Killer than you do."

Kai's jaw drops like I've admitted the Fish Hook Killer is me. "How is it that you've watched forty-two seasons of *90 Day Fiancé* but not the show your mum starred in? I mean, everybody's seen *Guilty Pleasures*. It's something you put on in the background while you fold laundry, like *Friends*."

"My mother *co*-starred," I correct him. "And what can I say? I guess I'm not one for overdramatic, underbaked plotlines or nonsensical love triangles."

I'm lying through my teeth; when I was a kid, I'd sneak out of bed just before ten on Sunday nights so I could tiptoe downstairs to the basement and catch the newest episode without waking Nona. I kept a stash of Cosmic Brownies hidden behind a bookshelf, and I'd curl up in the La-Z-Boy and eat them while I followed Kitty Conway into the seedy underbelly of Malibu Beach. It was bizarre, watching the show; there was my mother, right there on the screen, and yet she wasn't my mother at all. Karina looked like my mom and sounded like her—apart from Kitty's folksy southern twang—but she was someone I didn't know anymore.

She was right in front of me, and yet she was two thousand miles away.

"Sorry to disappoint your aunt Susan," I tell Kai, taking a final swig of my drink.

"No worries. I have complete confidence that I'll convince you to give up your secrets by the end of the summer." The knowing look he gives me is playful, almost mischievous, and I can't help but think that a girl would give all her secrets to a guy who looked at her like that.

Hell, she'd give him more than her secrets.

As if she can smell the testosterone in the air, the bartender slides another old-fashioned toward Kai and leans over the counter, her boobs so close to his spring rolls that she's circling health code violation territory.

"On the house," she purrs, tucking a lock of red hair behind her ear. "Hey, you're Kai Bridges, right? From Animal Planet?"

He smiles at her with the smooth congeniality of someone accustomed to getting hit on a lot. "If the answer's no, do I get to keep the drink?"

She giggles when he extends his hand toward her, and she shakes it with all the enthusiasm of Elle at Picnic for Paws. "Hi, I'm Kai."

"Courtney," she says, clutching his fingers for at least three seconds longer than necessary. "I knew it was you. And I just have to say, your episode on that capybara rescue near the Andes changed my life."

It's a good thing I'm done with my food, because the starry-eyed look in Courtney's eyes would have ruined my appetite.

"And don't even get me started on that interview you and your mom did with Oprah way back in the day," she continues, completely ignoring Father Time's grandfather's attempts to flag her down for another order of wings. "When your mom told the story of how she saved you from that snare, and the poachers were able to take down that big gorilla—what was his name? Tiko? Tony?"

"Taji," Kai says, his smile shrinking.

"Taji," Courtney repeats. "That was, like, the saddest thing I've ever seen. Your mom was so brave. And you were just so adorable."

I remember the interview she's talking about: a gap-toothed, baby-faced Kai sitting next to Dr. Kimber on a tan couch as she told the story of Taji's death to a teary-eyed, transfixed Oprah. Dr. Kimber's voice was solemn, steady, and at the end of the episode, Oprah pledged a ten-thousand-dollar donation to the Charlotte Kimber Research Center in Taji's memory.

Kai, shifting in his seat like he'd prefer to go back to talking about capybaras, gives Courtney a somber nod. "He was an incredible gorilla."

"I read that the poachers, like, chopped up his body and sold the parts for thousands of dollars. Apparently his hands were the size of basketballs."

Courtney, who rattles this information off like she's discussing the weather, doesn't seem to notice the hollow, sucked-in look taking over Kai's face.

"What was it like meeting Oprah?" she asks, her enviable boobs now one with the bartop. "Was Gayle King there?"

Kai blinks at her and pushes a spring roll around his plate. "It was, um, a long time ago. I don't remember."

"Well, did you get to meet Diane Lane?" Courtney asks. "When she made that movie about your mom?"

Courtney's questions have grabbed the attention of the people clustered around the bar, and Father Time's grandfather and a couple of guys in basketball jerseys pause their conversations to glance over.

I wait for Kai to wink at Courtney and say something like, *Yes, I did, and Diane Lane said I was the most magnificent boy she'd ever met.* But he doesn't. Instead, he swallows once, twice, three times, and rubs a hand to his throat like his answer is stuck there. One of the guys in basketball jerseys pulls out his phone to snap a picture, and I watch as the color drains from Kai's face.

He's no longer the happy-go-lucky, "Wowza!"-shouting adventurer he plays on TV, or the scowling guy I sparred with at Picnic for Paws, or even the smirk-wearing jerk who signed my hat with a cocky flourish.

He's just a regular person, one who's probably flashing back to the worst day of his life and trying not to picture dismembered basketball hands. I remember the actor version of Kai screaming as the snare tightened around his leg, begging for his mother to help him. I remember the terror in Diane Lane's eyes as she turns back for him, knowing she's leaving her beloved gorillas to a tragic fate.

"Um," Kai says, staring into his old-fashioned. I notice his fingers trembling just like mine did when I looked at Skippy's camera, and I know I have to help. I have to say something to put him out of his misery.

I scramble for something—anything—to say before he passes out, and I utter the first thing that pops into my head. "Scorpions die of constipation after they sting."

Kai turns to look at me with wide eyes.

"What?" Courtney asks, wrinkling her nose.

"Um, scorpions," I repeat, feeling a warm blush creep over me. "When their stinger gets lodged in something, they can, um, tear it off to get away. But the anus is inside the stinger, so when it's gone, they have no way of, you know. Relieving themselves."

Disgust crosses the bartender's features, but like a roller coaster going down a steep hill, I can't stop. I only pick up speed. "And eventually, after, like, eight months, they explode."

The only response to my comment is a silence so heavy, you could hear a pin drop, and considering there's a jukebox only twenty feet away, that's a pretty impressive feat. I die a little inside at the realization that I just informed Kai Bridges and a half-dozen others that scorpions can die of poop explosions.

"So yeah, just a fun little fact about the animal kingdom," I finish, rapping my knuckles on the bar. "Isn't nature grand?"

"Gross," the bartender says.

"Awesome," Father Time's grandfather declares.

Kai blinks at me for a long moment, then pushes his spring roll basket away and stands up. "Excuse me." He nods at Courtney and strides off, and I realize I've finally done it: I've managed to make a situation so uncomfortable that even Kai Bridges, who hiked seven miles through the arid Mojave Desert to track the elusive bighorn sheep, couldn't handle it.

I'm either a walking disaster or a wizard, depending on how you look at it, but I was only trying to help.

I don't know if Kai's coming back, but every second I linger here increases my odds of running into Nick and Margo, and I'd rather be an anus-less scorpion than deal with that. Dropping a couple of bills on the counter, I make my way toward Sam and Freya.

"Lucy, this is Freya. Freya, Lucy," Sam says, and if Freya remembers my disastrous turn in front of the camera outside the bonobo exhibit, she doesn't let on. Instead, she shakes my hand and greets me warmly.

"We're headed to Local Roots for dinner," Sam says. "Want to join?"

I'm not the most socially adept person in the world, but even I can see the sparks flying between Freya and Sam. The last thing I want to do is crash their date, and I have an early day tomorrow.

"Thanks, but I'm going to head out. Unless I can buy another drink for the *HuffPost* star?"

Sam smiles and shakes her head. "One Shipwreck Shirley was enough. Thank you, Luce."

After hugging her good-bye, I wave to Freya and head for the parking lot. I glance toward the bar to see if Kai ever returned, but his seat is still empty. For a moment, I think of his tense phone call and trembling hands and wonder if he's okay, but then I chide myself for caring. Of course he's okay; he's Kai Bridges, son of a real-life Wonder Woman and subject of a thousand fan fictions.

He doesn't need some zookeeper in Ohio worrying about him. I have plenty in my own life to stress about, a fact that becomes especially obvious when I get into my car and slide the key into the ignition. Because no matter how many times I grit my teeth and wrench the key again, the engine refuses to start.

Chapter Seventeen

Crap. I should not have spent the past six months ignoring the yellow maintenance light that flashed to life every time I started the car. I kept meaning to drive to AutoZone for a checkup, but stuff kept popping up on my work schedule, and I never got around to it.

It's a classic Lucy Rourke mistake, and I have only myself to blame. While I try to start the car again, as if the eightieth turn of the key just might do the trick, I run through my options. I can't call Nona for a ride because she's at a salsa dance lesson. I'd feel bad calling Elle, because asking an exhausted pregnant person to bail me out seems like poor form. I'm not about to bother Sam while she's hitting it off with Freya, and I'm sure as hell not going to call Karina.

Damn. I really need to make more friends.

I don't love the idea of paying for an Uber, because I've already blown my weekly budget by eating out twice, but I have no choice. I'm fishing my phone out of my purse when a familiar voice calls from behind the car.

"Lucy?"

No. Please, for the love of all that is holy, no. But sure enough, when I glance into the rearview mirror, I spot Nick waving at me.

"Hey, Luce!"

For a moment, I close my eyes and pretend that I'm a ruby-throated hummingbird. I fly out through the open car window, flapping my wings fifty-three times a second.

"Hi, Nick," I say finally, opening my eyes.

Margo from Guest Relations stands behind him with her hands on her hips, clearly no more pleased by this turn of events than I am.

"Car trouble?" my ex asks, frowning at the high-pitched grinding noise the engine makes when I crank the key. It's the soundtrack to my life, that noise, and if I had a walkout song that played every time I entered a room, this would be it.

"Oh, no, I'm fine," I lie.

Nick, who can't resist the urge to help a soul in need even when that soul is his baby-hating, unmaternal ex-girlfriend, shakes his head and strides toward the Chevy. He rests his elbows on the driver's-side window, and I give him a strained smile and wonder what I did in my previous life to make the universe hate me.

"Lucy," Nick says with the same you-little-rascal-you smile that he wore whenever I tried to make a new word in Scrabble, "tell me you got your engine light checked."

"Of course I did," I lie, annoyed. "It was a problem with the carburetor."

I know as much about cars as I do about ancient hieroglyphics, and I avoid Nick's gaze as I open the Uber app.

"She said she's fine, Nicholas," Margo says, tapping her foot against the pavement.

"At least let us give you a ride home," he insists.

Half of my soul curls up and dies at the thought of sitting in the back seat of Nick's Prius in my muddy shorts while he and Margo hold hands and give each other long, loving glances.

"No," I say so firmly that Nick startles. "I mean, no thanks. I already have a ride."

He tilts his head like he doesn't believe me, just like he did when I tried to convince him that the word *snarkles* should earn me Scrabble points. "Did you call an Uber?"

"No," I say. "I mean, yes. I mean—"

"Lucy," a deeper voice calls, interrupting me. "I thought you were going to wait for me at the bar."

I pop my head out the window to see Kai striding toward the Chevy, his hands in his pockets and a warm smile on his face. Gone is the wide-eyed, frozen stare he gave Courtney moments earlier. He's the picture of calm, cool, and easy-breezy, and he glides past Nick to open my door and offer me his hand like a gallant knight who just won a round of joust.

"Let's take my car this time," he suggests, as if there were other times. As if we leave bars together on the reg and drive off to get up to who knows what.

The stunned look on Nick's face gives me a thrill that starts at the top of my head and travels all the way down between my legs, and I don't stop to think twice. I accept Kai's outstretched hand, and he pulls me out of the car and to my feet in one swift motion.

"Oh," Nick says, glancing from me to Kai and back to me. "Oh. Okay, then."

Kai's hand is warm, steady, and for a split second I forget all about wanting to be a hummingbird. For this brief, shining moment when Margo's head practically spins in a complete circle, I'm happy to be Lucy, mud-covered shorts and all.

"Thanks anyway, Nick," I say.

His gaze lingers on Kai for a beat, and Margo lets out an exasperated sigh and marches toward his Prius.

"See you around, then, Luce," my ex says, glancing back at me as he trails after her. "Don't ignore your engine light anymore, okay?"

"I've been telling her the same thing!" Kai says. "Classic Lucygoosey." As if to really sell the lie, he taps a finger to my nose like my inability to handle proper vehicle maintenance is an oh-so-adorable quality.

"You didn't have to do that," I tell Kai when Nick and Margo drive off, even though I'm glad he did. Except for maybe the "Lucygoosey" part.

Kai nods. "And you didn't have to intervene at the bar. I'm just returning the favor."

He's still smiling that warm, Kai-to-the-rescue smile, one I haven't seen before, and Bad Lucy finds it quite panty dropping. Reminding myself that he's still the guy who stole my book, I drop his hand like a hot potato.

"If you ever boop my nose again," I say, pulling myself back to my senses, "I will feed you to the polar bears."

Kai shrugs. "I thought the boop was a nice touch." He points toward my car. "Want me to take a look under the hood?"

The double meaning of his words sends another tingle southward, and I cross my arms over my chest, refusing to let Bad Lucy out to play.

"No thanks," I say quickly, before he can offer to pump my tires or something that sounds equally dirty. "I'll just call an Uber and get my car towed tomorrow."

"Forget the Uber. I'll give you a lift."

He strides away from the bar, expecting me to follow, and turns back to study me when I don't. "I won't mention my Emmys, if that's what you're worried about."

I don't point out that in promising not to mention his Emmys, he just mentioned them. Because what actually worries me is that being trapped in an enclosed space with Kai's campfire and Yankee Candle scent might give Bad Lucy more evidence for her budding hypothesis that he isn't actually so terrible. My other concern is that Kai's still secretly pissed about my insults at the picnic, and he's going to drive me fifty miles toward the middle of nowhere and abandon me to be eaten by wolves.

Or, according to his ex, *wooves*.

"You can pick the music," Kai adds, as if it's a preference for pop rock, and not the threat of death by apex predator, that's giving me pause.

But I don't have money to waste on an Uber, so I guess I'll take my chances. Plus, I've never been in a Maserati before, and this might be my only shot.

"Okay," I say with a hint of reluctance. "Thanks."

I follow him across the parking lot, realizing that if Kai does murder me, at least two witnesses saw us leaving the bar together. But when he stops next to a blue minivan to fetch his keys from his pocket, I wonder if he's had too many sips of his old-fashioned to operate a vehicle.

"Um, what middle-aged mom are you trying to jack this from?" I ask, peering around the parking lot. "Where's your Maserati or your Lamborghini or your Batmobile?"

Kai squints at me. "A Maserati, Lucy? Seriously?"

I shrug. "I didn't realize we were swinging by the soccer fields to pick up the kids."

He rolls his eyes and climbs into the driver's seat, leaning over to open the passenger door. "If you must know, I rent one of these puppies when I travel for work. They're safe, they get decent mileage, and they can fit plenty of camera equipment."

"True. And if you cover the windows, they're perfect for snatching up children."

Kai ignores my snarky comment. "Did you seriously think I drove a Lamborghini? I produce a wildlife show, not a *Fast and the Furious* franchise."

Well, I certainly didn't expect him to drive the same car as the neighborhood Karen, but I keep my mouth shut as I buckle my seat belt.

After I guide him out of the parking lot, an uncomfortable silence fills the air. I know that Kai's seen me roughly ten seconds after I threw up and watched me humiliate myself on camera, but there's something strangely intimate about riding in the car together. It's bizarre to see someone I've watched chatting with Oprah and helicoptering over a wild elephant herd on Animal Planet do something as mundane as flip on his turn signal and check his blind spot before switching lanes.

It's like watching Daniel Craig scoop up cat litter, or Scarlett Johansson trim her fingernails.

And it's mesmerizing.

Realizing that I'm staring at Kai like a grade-A creeper, I tear my gaze away and watch the pickup truck in front of us like it's the most fascinating thing I've ever seen.

"So, Dr. North," Kai says finally. "He seemed very concerned about the state of your engine."

I can't tell if the innuendo is intentional, and I adjust the AC vent to blow in my direction lest I turn lobster red.

"Well, I struggle with adulting in a way that always drove him crazy," I explain. "You know, neglecting to get my oil changed or forgetting to rotate the mattress every three months. I was always just more focused on work, and he couldn't stand it."

"He sounds like a prick," Kai says plainly.

Huh. I think Kai's the only person in the world who's ever called him that. "Well, my grandmother loved Nick," I say. "And her best friend would have drop-kicked me if it meant getting a shot with him."

Nobody said it after the breakup, but I knew what Nona and Trudy and my co-workers thought: *Poor Lucy. If she can't make it work with sweet, agreeable Nick, who reminds her to pay her taxes and tolerates her work schedule, who can she?*

"Well, I vote prick," Kai says, and I wish I could record his statement with my phone and play it for Trudy the next time she pesters me about my ex. "Was he?"

"No," I say quickly. "Of course not."

Nick wasn't a prick. He spent his Saturday mornings performing free spays and neuters on the homeless animals at Columbus Humane, and he changed Trudy's flat tire, and he supported my decision to turn down work trips to the San Diego Zoo and a lemur rescue in Madagascar when I worried that Zuri's intestinal blockage would return once I left.

But then I remember the last three months of our relationship, when Nick side-eyed me whenever a Pampers commercial came on, like he was waiting for me to fall to my knees and announce that yes, finally, the crawling baby on the screen lit a fire in my cold, bitchy ovaries and convinced me to open my dusty womb to motherhood. I think of brunch at his parents', when his mother clutched her infant granddaughter to her chest and said, "I don't understand people who don't want children, they're just so *selfish*," her eyes darting toward me, and Nick didn't defend me or follow when I excused myself to go to the bathroom. I remember when we attended his college reunion and one of his buddies' wives asked if we had kids and Nick said *No, not yet, but maybe someday,* rubbing small circles on my back with his hand, even though I'd insisted earlier that morning that I wouldn't change my mind.

Nick wasn't a prick for dumping me, but maybe he was for trying to pressure me into accepting a life I didn't want. For assuming I would give in, and for acting like I was less of a woman when I didn't.

"Actually, yes," I tell Kai. "He kind of was."

I don't say what else I'm thinking: that I was kind of a prick to myself, too, for putting up with it.

"Nick wanted kids, but I didn't," I say, not sure why I'm sharing this. "Not that wanting kids makes someone a prick. It's just that he suddenly started dreaming about a wedding and toddlers and a 529 plan when all I wanted was a promotion. It's still all I want." I shrug. "Maybe that makes me selfish, but I'd rather be selfish without kids than selfish with them."

I don't tell him that I know what it's like to have a mom who puts you last, and that I'd never put myself in the position of doing that to a child.

"I don't think that makes you selfish," Kai says, and it's so unlike the petty insults we usually lob at each other that I'm surprised it isn't sarcasm. "Besides, no offense to your ex, but anyone who wears those shoes with tube socks should think twice about reproducing."

I laugh, and the knot of anxiety that formed in my stomach when I saw Nick and Margo loosens.

Kai glances sideways at me as he turns onto a main road. "It was cool of you to help me out back at the bar. I don't usually get tripped up over my words like that."

"Well, I get tripped up over my words all the time, so I recognize a fellow deer in headlights when I see one."

Kai smiles, but it doesn't reach his eyes. "The Taji stuff catches me off guard sometimes, even after all these years. People see me as the guy on TV who swims with eels and dives off rocks with sea lions, and they forget that I'm, you know . . ."

"A person?" I suggest when he trails off.

He nods. "Yeah. A person. They don't realize that bringing Taji up out of the blue is like walking up to a burn victim and saying, 'Hey, remember the day your house burned down? Give me all the details!' For them, it's just something that happened in a movie. But I was there when he died, you know? I was *there*. And it's crazy how casually people mention it. Like, one second I'm sitting at a bar eating spring rolls, and the next, someone's asking me about a massacre like we're chatting about the score of the Yankees game."

I can only imagine how that would feel. If a bartender came up to me and said, "Hey, remember when your mom abandoned you? That was just so *sad*, now sit still and smile while I ask you fifty questions about it," I'd fling my drink across the lounge and refuse to leave home again.

"Have you ever thought of just telling people no?" I ask. "Like if they bring up Taji, just refusing to engage?"

He shakes his head. "I've tried, but it doesn't go over well. When people see you on their TV screen every week, they start to think they know you. The real you. And when the real-life version doesn't measure up, well, next thing you know, there's a Page Six article about how Kai Bridges made a five-year-old cry by refusing to take a selfie.

"I took a selfie with the five-year-old," he explains when he sees my raised eyebrows. "What I would not do is autograph his mother's right butt cheek."

"Just the left one, then?" I say, and this time when Kai smiles, it's effervescent.

"I don't mean to sound like a spoiled rich kid," he says, turning where I direct him to. "I just wanted to say thanks for not hanging me out to dry. Even if you did drop a bomb on everybody with that scorpion horror story."

"No problem." I tap my temple with my index finger. "I've got more horrifying animal facts stored in here than I know what to do with."

Kai laughs. "I bet I've got you beat."

Recalling his accusation that I'm afraid of a challenge, I decide it's time to drop the gauntlet. "Okay, Mr. Big Shot, beat this: beavers produce anal liquids that get added to vanilla ice cream."

He rolls his shoulders back as if to say, *You're on.* "Some frogs make their homes out of elephant dung."

"Storks pee on themselves to stay cool."

"Horror frogs break their own bones to grow claws," Kai counters.

"Koalas have chlamydia."

"Honeybees boil hornets to death," he says.

"This is my stop," I say suddenly, realizing I've been so focused on shouting out disturbing animal facts that I almost let Kai pass Nona's house.

"Cows kill—" Kai starts to drop another fact, then pauses. "What?"

"—more humans than sharks do," I finish for him. "Yep, I know that one, too. And this is where I live. The house with the red tile roof."

He hits the brakes and puts the van in reverse, letting out a low whistle as he slows to a stop at Nona's curb.

"And you accused *me* of being in an international crime ring?" he asks.

I glance at Nona's Spanish Colonial, with its garden of lush roses blooming in the courtyard. "It's not mine. I just rent a room. My landlord's a cardiologist." I neglect to mention that my landlord is also my grandma, who still makes me crustless peanut butter and jelly sandwiches when I'm not feeling well.

Some things are better left unsaid.

I unbuckle my seat belt and slide out of the car. "Thanks for the ride."

"No problem," Kai says, giving me a salute. "See you around, Lucy."

I make a concerted effort not to trip over my own feet as I cross the yard, and I've almost made it to the front door when Kai, tires squealing as he circles out of the cul-de-sac, lowers his window.

"Hey, Lucy Rourke!" he calls, causing Joey Macoroy from next door and Mrs. Elgine two houses over to look up from their front porches. "Fruit fly swarms! They're just massive orgies! I win!"

Kai zooms off like a madman, leaving scandalized Mrs. Elgine's mouth shaped like a perfect O.

When I step inside the house, still laughing, I find Trudy and Nona playing a round of rummy in the sitting room.

"What happened to salsa?" I ask, dropping my purse.

"Canceled tonight," Nona explains. "Enrique broke his fibula. What was all the ruckus outside?"

"Oh, nothing. Just a friend dropping me off."

"It sounded like a man," Trudy says, peering at me over her cards. "Was it Nick? Are you two getting back together? I hope you've come to your senses about him, because he is *such* a nice young man."

It's a stark contrast to my conversation in the car with Kai, and annoyance prickles my skin. "It wasn't Nick, actually," I tell her. "And you know what? I don't want to hear about him anymore. If you think he's so great, *you* ask him out. It might just work, since you share the same taste in shoes."

And before her jaw even drops in response, I turn on my heel and stride toward my bedroom. I've got work to do.

Chapter Eighteen

After that, Kai and I aren't mortal enemies anymore. It's hard to view someone as a smarmy asshole when you've seen him drive a mid-range minivan, and even though he's still the jerk who stole my book, he's a jerk who knows a lot of freaky animal facts and may or may not have some lingering PTSD—two qualities I can relate to.

Plus, our little game of Who Knows More Deranged Facts About Animals? is kind of fun.

"Male koalas have two penises," I tell him when we pass each other in the Ape House hallway.

"A pig's orgasm lasts thirty minutes," he whispers as he helps me adjust my mic.

Maybe we're not friends, exactly, but I no longer wish him death by way of Rosha the tiger. One thing's for sure: I am *not* growing a crush on Kai Bridges. When I spend fifteen minutes crafting a "messy" bun and putting on mascara, it's not because I know I'll run into him. It's because I want to look nice for baby Keeva's arrival. And when I spend my bike ride to work thinking of more bizarre animal facts, it's not because I want to keep our game going. It's just a help-ful way to interrupt a stress response, like counting to ten.

Regardless, I don't have time to give in to Bad Lucy's desire to scroll through Kai's shirtless Instagram pics. Because the day after my car breaks down, four-month-old baby Keeva arrives at the zoo.

She's a nine-pound bundle of fluffy fur and gangly limbs, and as soon as Miami's Alexandra St. John carries her from a zoo transport van to the nursery, I know I've died and gone to heaven.

"Hi, Keeva," I say as the infant peeks out at me from where she's curled up in Alexandra's arms.

She opens her mouth and yawns, letting out an adorable squeak, and Lottie almost passes out from the cuteness. Between her wrin-kled face and the generous floof of black fur on top of her head, Keeva looks like a pint-sized mad scientist, and I fall instantly in love with her.

During her first few hours in the nursery, Keeva clings to Alex-andra, daring to approach me only when she realizes that yanking my bun is an incredibly fun game. By the end of my first shift, I've lost a good chunk of hair, but it's worth it when Keeva lets me feed her a bottle. She doesn't crawl into my lap like she does Alexan-dra's, but I don't blame her one bit: building a bond with a gorilla takes way longer than a day, and if I lost my whole family and got shuffled to two new homes within a month, I'd be reluctant around strangers, too.

By the end of Keeva's third day, though, she's comfortable enough with our keeper team that she doesn't scurry behind Alexandra's back when we enter the nursery, and she's found a best friend in a red rub-ber ball that she enjoys launching at Jack's head. I've gotten accus-tomed to wearing the heavy, hairlike vest that mimics the texture of a mother gorilla's fur and gives Keeva's agile fingers material to grab on to, and I'm decent enough at imitating soothing gorilla belch vocalizations that Keeva doesn't look at me like I'm speaking Mandarin at her.

When it's time for Alexandra to return to Miami, leaving her charge in my care, she clutches Keeva to her chest and makes soft grunt vocalizations, stroking the unruly fur on the infant's head.

"You're my brave girl, and you can do this," she whispers. "You can do anything." Then, wiping tears from where they've escaped her surgical mask, she passes Keeva to me.

When Keeva crawls off in pursuit of her ball, Alexandra takes her leave, but not before turning back to look at me.

"I've worked with my share of gorillas over the years," she says, "but never one I'm rooting for this much. Take care of her."

"I will," I promise, and I mean it with every fiber of my being. I know that Keeva is to Alexandra what Zuri is to me, and I'll do everything in my power to honor that bond.

And by everything, I mean everything. Day and night, I rotate through the nursery, trading off shifts with Jack and Lottie. I feed Keeva, burp her, change her diaper, and let her climb on me like I'm a jungle gym that feels no pain. I crawl around in the hay for hours, Keeva riding on my back like young gorillas ride on their mothers'. I sleep on a leaky air mattress that I park outside the nursery and subsist on microwaved lasagna, and even though I wake up every morning with a stiff neck and a craving for a homemade dinner, I'm having the time of my life.

Because while introducing a new gorilla into a troop, particularly a gorilla as vulnerable as a baby, is a risky, exhausting process, if Ozzie's troop accepts Keeva, it'll be a miracle—the story of an orphaned infant who survived a deadly infection and found a new, fulfilling family.

And I'll get to be a part of it.

. . .

Even though Keeva is cuter than all the world's puppies combined, life isn't all sunshine and roses. There's still the little matter of the cameras, and the only way I can cope is to ignore them completely. When Kai and his crew show up to shoot, I pretend that I'm wearing an invisibility cloak, and while it's probably not the most promising tactic to ensure good TV, I haven't yet fainted or embarrassed myself and everyone in my vicinity by rambling about bonobo sex habits.

Besides, Kai wasn't entirely wrong. I'm about as likely to get comfortable with the cameras as the kids from *It* are to get comfortable with Pennywise the dancing clown, but it *is* easier to be less cognizant of their presence when I'm focused on my work. When he says, "Camera two, ready!" and motions for Skippy to line up his shot, I still get a heart-pounding, fluttery-bones sensation that makes me dizzy. But if I look at Keeva and focus on the feel of her soft fur and the breathy snoring noises she makes when she sleeps, I can ward off a panic attack.

A week after Keeva's arrival, Phil gives me the okay to move the female gorillas from Ozzie's troop—Zuri, Tria, and Inkesha—into the "bedroom" next to Keeva's nursery. The mesh barrier separating the spaces will let the girls smell, see, and hear Keeva and even reach through it to touch her without getting close enough to cause injury.

Hopefully.

"Okay, ladies," I say, marching back and forth in front of Tria, Zuri, and Inkesha with a bucket of protein biscuits. "If we give you these treats, you have to promise that you'll be nice to Keeva. And I mean all of you."

I side-eye Inkesha, who's the orneriest of the bunch. "*Especially* you."

"Keeva is a tiny baby," Lottie explains as the gorillas stare at us blankly. "She needs your help. She needs a mommy."

Tria, ignoring her daughter Piper's attempts to grab a fistful of lettuce from her hand, grunts as if to say *I don't give a fuck who needs a mommy; I need those biscuits.* Inkesha crosses her arms over her chest and scratches her armpits. Zuri grabs a handful of hay and places it on top of her head like a sun hat.

"God help us," Lottie whispers.

Jack and Phil wait with Keeva in the nursery as Lottie and I prepare to open the gate to allow the girls into the bedroom. My heart pounds so loudly that I swear I can hear it over the sound of Keeva smacking her ball against Jack's head. What if none of the gorillas show interest in her? Worse, what if they feel threatened and try to reach through the mesh and rip her to shreds? What if I fail in my mission to usher her into the troop, and she moves from zoo to zoo forever, unloved and alone?

"It's go time," Phil says over the walkie-talkie system, and I push away my doubts and wait for Lottie's signal.

"And three, two, one, open!" she calls. Uttering a silent prayer to Jane Goodall, Charlotte Kimber, and the spirit of Ruth Bader Ginsburg, I lift a metal lever to open the gate. Lottie and I littered the area with the girls' favorite goodies—lettuce, watermelon, and enough popcorn to feed an entire movie theater—and they grunt with excitement as they scurry into their new space.

My pulse races as Keeva, first hearing and then seeing the commotion, lets out a cry of confusion and flings herself into Jack's arms. Tria scoops up an armful of lettuce and approaches the mesh but growls when she sees Keeva's tiny face peeking out at her. Zuri, startled by Tria's reaction, runs to the mesh and smacks it, hard, sending a terrified Keeva sprint-crawling to cower on the other side of the nursery.

"Yikes," Lottie says as Tria grabs a squirmy Piper by the ankle and rushes her away while Inkesha, disconcerted by the chaos and always happy to make trouble, runs bipedally along the mesh, letting out an aggressive hiccup bark. She dashes off after Tria and Piper while Zuri gathers up as much popcorn as she can carry and climbs to the highest platform in the bedroom, as far from Keeva as she can get.

"Be patient, guys," Phil instructs as Jack comforts a terrified Keeva and Lottie shoots me a look that says, *This is worse than the time Kyra the bonobo bit Scotty on the ear.*

I know Phil's right; just like you can't throw a random group of humans together and expect them to be besties, gorillas are no different. But I'd hoped for at least some positive interaction, and right now, the only connection that's forming is the one between Zuri and her mountain of popcorn.

By the end of the second day, when the girls still haven't shown more than a passing interest in the baby, I'm panicking. None of the tricks we've used, like stacking treat cups and peanut-butter-filled toys along the mesh, have enticed them to approach her. Even busting out their favorite enrichment items doesn't work. Zuri takes one look at the paint and butcher paper I assemble for her and makes a pig grunt sound before scampering off.

By the fourth night, when the girls are still staying as far from the mesh as possible, I can tell Phil's starting to worry, too. We can't force anyone to adopt Keeva as a surrogate, and putting her in the same quarters as a hesitant adult gorilla could have dangerous, if not deadly, consequences. So when Phil calls the senior keepers into a meeting and rumors swirl about the possibility of sending Keeva to the Pittsburgh Zoo, I offer to take an extra overnight shift. I need to think, and there's no better place to do it than sprawled out on some hay with a baby gorilla.

"See you in the morning, Lucy," Lottie says, yawning as she exits the nursery around midnight.

"See you." Keeva bounces on my right leg, hopping up and down on my knee while she clutches my hands.

"What are we gonna do with you, sweetheart?" I ask, my voice cracking with worry.

Keeva only grabs a handful of my hair and tugs, letting out an amused chuckle. She has no idea that I'm failing her, or that we're in a desperate race against time.

Chapter Nineteen

By three a.m., Keeva's fast asleep in my arms and I'm scribbling ideas in my logbook like a madwoman. What if we bake a humongous, gorilla-friendly cake and place it near the mesh as enticement for the females to get closer? Inkesha loves cake, and while there's a solid chance she'll fling frosting at Keeva instead of eat it, I'm willing to try anything. Heck, if I could bargain with the girls in English, I'd promise them each a pony if they'd just give her a chance.

As I jot down another desperate idea—*slather Keeva in peanut butter?*—I hear footsteps in the corridor, and I wonder if I'm finally cracking under the pressure and having auditory hallucinations. Jack, Lottie, and the summer interns left hours ago, and according to the last message Scotty sent over the walkie-talkie, he's in The Islands checking on the orangutans.

I grab my logbook, prepared to use it as a bludgeon. If someone broke into Ape House to steal this baby gorilla, I *will* fuck them up.

"Drop the weapon," a deep voice instructs, and I glance down the dim hallway to see Kai striding toward me, a duffel bag slung over his shoulder. "I come in peace." When he reaches the nursery, he gives me a once-over and grins. "Killer outfit, Lucy. Too bad you didn't run into your ex in that ensemble."

I glance down at my black faux-fur vest. I look like Big Bird if someone dipped him in mud, but I only roll my eyes. "You wish you could look this good."

Kai actually looks very good, a fact that Bad Lucy picks up on immediately. A day's worth of stubble covers his jaw, and his thick mane of hair is mussed like he just rolled out of bed. Maybe Lars forgot to restock his mousse.

"It's the middle of the night," I tell him. "Shouldn't you be resting in your luxury penthouse?"

"We're in the middle of Ohio. So if by luxury penthouse you mean my moderately appointed room at the Marriott, then no. I just wrapped up shooting Brutus the grizzly's emergency surgery. And before you freak out, yes, he's stable now. Besides," he adds, tugging at the draw-string of his hoodie, "I wanted to see you."

Bad Lucy, still running amok outside her cage, raises her middle fingers at me in a *Suck it!* gesture, and my breath catches in my throat. Kai wanted to see *me* at three o'clock in the morning? I guess our weird animal-fact-trading game got him all hot and bothered.

What a little freak, in the best sense of the word.

"You precious little munchkin, you," he continues in a singsong voice, and I realize he's talking to Keeva.

Of course he is. Of course Kai didn't come to Ape House after hours to see me in a vest that makes me look like I'm headed to a furry convention.

"Aw, don't be disappointed, Lucy-goosey," he teases as he pauses outside the nursery to slip on the Latex gloves, plastic booties, and surgical mask necessary to protect Keeva from germs. "I'm happy to see you, too."

"Call me Lucy-goosey again and see what happens," I threaten. "I promise you won't like it."

He smirks at me as he enters the nursery. "Or maybe I will."

I'm grateful for the dim nighttime lighting that hides the blush creeping over my cheeks, and I pretend I didn't hear him.

"Seriously, you can see Keeva anytime. Why so late?" I raise an eyebrow at him. "Is a SWAT team camped outside the Marriott? I knew I was onto something with the crime ring theory."

Kai settles into the hay across from Keeva and me. "May I?" he asks.

I nod and transfer the infant to his arms, careful not to jostle her awake. She's only nine pounds, but the long hours of carrying her have exhausted my biceps, and I'm grateful for a break.

"Hi, precious," Kai says, smiling as she nestles her head into his chest. "Hi, baby girl."

I don't lose my marbles over every cute thing I see like Elle and Lottie, but I have to admit that the sight of a handsome man cuddling a baby gorilla is almost more than I can handle. It's like Kai's shirtless Penny-the-puppy post on steroids, and before Bad Lucy gets up to no good, I scramble up from the hay to check on Keeva's formula supply.

"If you must know, the gravest crime I've ever committed was forgetting to return a *Scary Movie* DVD to Blockbuster. I know this disappoints you, but there's no SWAT team coming to whisk me away," Kai says. "I'm just not much of a sleeper. I'm lucky if I get five hours a night."

I have no idea how someone who barely sleeps manages to look that good, and I can only conclude that he sold his soul to the devil.

"That sucks," I say. "I'd be a total bitch if I slept that little."

He gives me a long look, as if to say, *In contrast to the total sweet-*

heart you are now? and shrugs. "I'm used to it, I guess. Been dealing with it my whole life."

"Seriously?" I ask, running a bottle under hot water. "Your whole life?"

Maybe that's why he acted like a jerk the first few times we met. Maybe Elle was right, and a combination of jet lag and decades of sleep deprivation caused his grouchiness.

"Well, since I was a kid," he says, cradling Keeva's head. "Since Taji, actually. And sometimes no sleep is better than the nightmares."

"I'm sorry. That must be awful."

He nods and clears his throat. "They've gotten better over time. Pretty embarrassing, really, that I'm a thirty-four-year-old man who still has bad dreams about something that happened when I was eight."

The thought of Kai, who wouldn't think twice about submerging himself in alligator-infested waters for a good shot, waking up from a nightmare in a cold sweat tugs at my heartstrings. Imagining him being frightened is like picturing Elle in a bout of road rage. It's almost impossible.

"That's not embarrassing," I assure him. "Plenty of adults have nightmares."

"See?" he says, grinning. "I knew I could tell my Lucy-goosey anything."

"I swear to Jane Goodall, I will feed you feetfirst to Roary the lion."

Before Kai can laugh at my threat, my phone, which I left sitting on my logbook in the hay, vibrates quietly.

"Lucy Rourke," he says, shaking his head. "Tsk, tsk, tsk. Booty call on a Wednesday?"

I roll my eyes. The last time I answered a booty call was in grad school, and it was from a dental student named Tad, who was decent in bed but insisted on flossing for twenty minutes before anything exciting happened. If I'm getting a text this late, it's either Phil checking up on Keeva or an Amber Alert.

"Oh, it's just an email," Kai says, glancing at my phone with no regard for boundaries. "Looks like somebody's having a birthday party."

"Huh?" I set the bottle down and scoop my phone up from the hay, giving Kai and his prying eyes a dirty look.

MIA'S TURNING 11! the email preview shows, and against my better judgment, I unlock my phone and open the message. It's an invitation from Karina to Mia's upcoming birthday party: Our Junior Scout is turning 11! Please join us August 11 for an afternoon campout to celebrate. Tents optional, s'mores mandatory.

I want to fling my phone across the nursery. How is it that I spent my eleventh birthday crying over my cake, hoping against hope that Karina would show up at Nona's, and Mia gets the camping-themed bash of her dreams? Worse, Karina hates camping, which makes the fact that she's not forcing Mia to host a Kardashian-themed party even more painful. She's putting aside her own preferences to make her daughter happy.

Because she loves her.

"Bad news?" Kai asks, studying my face.

I slide my phone into my pocket, trying to keep my expression neutral. "Nope, everything's fine."

"Sure it is. And I'm David Attenborough."

I return to the sink, determined to finish washing Keeva's bottles, but hot tears prick my eyes. It's not that I want Mia to spend her eleventh birthday like I did, crying so hard that she can barely inhale enough air to blow out her candles. I don't want her staring at the door, praying for Karina to walk through it, or for her to be too distraught to open the presents Nona wrapped.

But I don't want it for eleven-year-old me, either. And it's easier to forget how badly my mom's absence hurt when I'm not forced to look at a Paperless Post invitation to the exact opposite scenario. I would have chopped off my right pigtail to get Karina to visit on my birthday, let alone throw me a party with s'mores and hot dogs.

"Lucy," Kai says, and I've been so focused on holding back my tears that I didn't hear him join me at the sink. He cradles Keeva in one arm and places a hand on my back.

"Whoa," he says after a beat, his fingers caressing the vest. "I didn't expect you to be so hairy."

It's the dumbest joke I've ever heard, but in a moment when I'm fighting to keep my shit together, I'm grateful for it.

"Here," Kai says, passing a sleeping Keeva back to me. "The baby gorilla makes all the pain go away. Promise."

I wonder if that's why he came here tonight, because tending to Keeva helps push away the nightmares of Taji's horrific fate. But instead of asking, I let him place the infant in my arms. He's right; within seconds of hearing her soft snores, I'm a fraction calmer.

"So," Kai says when we settle along the mesh, sitting in the hay again. "Do you want to tell me why you look like you just got invited to Cruella de Vil's birthday party?"

I blink away any lingering tears, keeping my gaze on Keeva. "Not particularly."

He nudges my bootied foot with his. "C'mon. I know you think I'm a raging asshole, but I swear I'm a good listener."

I shake my head. I don't think he's a raging asshole, not after he saved me from the Nick-and-Margo carpool of hell. And especially not after he confessed to having nightmares about Taji.

"I don't think you're a raging asshole. I just think maybe, on occasion, you suffer from asshole tendencies. Besides, why do you care about my opinion? I could think you were the next Charles Manson and it wouldn't matter. You'd still have a three-year deal with Animal Planet and look like a Bridgerton brother."

He grins. "That's a compliment, right?"

"No, Kai. Charles Manson was a monster."

He rolls his eyes. "Come on. I told you about my nightmares. Do you, like, hate parties? Did you have a run-in with a clown when you were a child and now refuse to participate in anything birthday related?"

That does sound like something that might happen to me, but I shake my head. "No. The email was just an invitation to my half sister Mia's eleventh birthday. You know, your number one fan."

"I have an infinite number of number one fans," Kai teases. "But of course I remember Mia. She seems like a great kid."

"She is a great kid."

"Then why do you look like you're stepping on hot coals when you say that?" he asks.

I sigh. "Look, Mia's great. She really is. She's smart and curious, and she refuses to give up on learning the harmonica even though she sounds like a dying cat. It's our mother I don't get along with."

"Ah, yes," Kai says. "The great Kitty Conway."

"You mean Karina. And Kitty wasn't that great. She missed all the clues that Tommy Tomko was the Surfboard Strangler, even when they were glaringly obvious. Who has that many broken surfboards in his garage?"

"Hang on a second." Kai leans closer, and I do my best not to inhale his heady scent. "I thought you said you didn't watch *Guilty Pleasures*."

Busted, I watch the rise and fall of Keeva's chest to avoid his gaze. "Whatever. I still don't know who the Malibu Fish Hook Killer was."

"Dammit," Kai says. He crosses his arms over his chest and fixes me with a knowing smirk. "Well, well. Isn't Lucy-goosey just a little liar?"

"Maybe I lied, but you stole my book," I counter. "Stealing's a crime."

"I didn't steal. I only took it because you were looking at me like you were about to clobber me over the head with it."

He has a point, because I did consider clobbering him over the head with *Majesty on the Mountain*. "Well, I only lied about watching *Guilty Pleasures* because I didn't want you pestering me about it."

Kai brings a hand to his chest like I've wounded him. "Ouch, Lucy. How annoying do you think I am?" After I stare at him for a beat, he blanches. "Never mind. Point taken."

"When I was a kid," I continue, "watching the show was the only way I could see my mom." I have no idea why I'm admitting my crippling mommy issues to Kai, other than he's now the only person in the world who knows that I watched *Guilty Pleasures*. And even if I confessed that to him by accident, it felt good. Freeing. It's a lot easier to share personal things with someone once you've watched him drive a minivan.

"She dumped me at my grandmother's when I was ten," I tell him. "She told me she'd be back in a week to get me, but she never came. She changed her mind. She called Nona, my grandmother, and explained that it was too much for her to care for me and star in the show at the same time."

It's probably a mistake to reveal something so private, but after this summer, I'll never see Kai again—and if I can't pair Keeva with a surrogate mother and have to shuttle her off to the Pittsburgh Zoo soon, he won't have new material to shoot at Ape House anyway.

"That's awful," Kai says. "I'm sorry." His tone is earnest, stripped of its usual cockiness.

"Thanks. Anyway, I somehow convinced myself that she'd show up for my eleventh birthday. I mean, moms get busy, but they don't miss their kid's birthday, right? But she didn't come." I remember insisting to Nona that we make a carrot cake for my birthday because it was Karina's favorite. I didn't even like carrot cake; I still don't.

"So yeah, I'm jealous of Mia," I admit. "I'm jealous that she gets the party I dreamed of." I've never admitted my envy to anyone before, and the words sound petty and small coming out of my mouth. "It's pathetic, I know, to be jealous of a little girl."

"No, it isn't. It's not pathetic at all." Kai shifts his leg so that it's touching mine. "I mean, if my mum had another kid after me and did everything right with him, I'd be jealous, too."

I don't think Kai, whose mother made the ultimate sacrifice to protect him, can understand how I feel, but I appreciate his empathy.

"It's funny you say that," I tell him, "because when I was little, I was jealous of *you*. After Karina ditched me and my grandmother brought me to the zoo to meet Zuri, I pretty much became obsessed with all things gorilla. And you had everything I dreamed of." I remember my childhood fantasy of traipsing through the jungle with Dr. Kimber. "You had your very own mountain full of gorillas. And you had a mother who would do anything to take care of you."

The concern on Kai's face vanishes, and his jaw tenses. "You shouldn't have been."

"Huh?"

"You shouldn't have been jealous. Things weren't—" He pauses, his mouth puckering like it did when Mia and I saw him on the phone outside the nursery. He shakes his head and runs a hand through his hair. "I know I had major advantages because of who my mum is, but being Charlotte Kimber's kid wasn't all happy gorillas and movie premieres. I mean, I could live to be a hundred, and people will still see me as the stupid little boy who got Taji killed."

His admission catches me off guard, and I realize that Kai and I have more in common than I thought. I might be gunning for my dream job, but I still see myself as the hopeful little girl refusing to cut into her carrot cake. Kai might be the most charismatic wildlife explorer since Steve Irwin, but he still views himself as the sobbing eight-year-old stuck in a snare.

"What happened to Taji was not your fault," I say gently. "You tripped on a poacher's snare by accident, and your mom had no choice but to turn back for you. It's what anyone would have done."

When Kai inhales sharply and a faraway look comes over his eyes, I wonder if he's still here in the nursery with me—or if he's trapped in the thick leaves of the jungle, begging for his mother's help.

"Hey, I mean it," I say. He looks so forlorn that I automatically reach for his hand. "It wasn't your fault."

At first, his hand stays limp, and I think I might have overstepped. But then he curls his fingers around mine, and the pressure is firm and steady against my skin.

"The thing is, Lucy," he says, gripping my hand tighter, "gorillas are an endangered species. Humans are a dime a dozen. Maybe she made the wrong choice."

His face is wracked with guilt, and I wonder how much time Kai's spent on Mount Karisimbi since he was a child, how many times he's visited that lush green forest while he tries to fall asleep at night, remembering and imagining and blaming himself for something completely out of his control. Before I know what I'm doing, I tear my hand out of his grip and place it on his cheek, as if I can touch the guilt away.

"You are *not* a dime a dozen," I tell him. "You are anything but."

I didn't realize it at first, but he's not the arrogant jerkface I thought he was. He's a man who rescues puppies and snuggles baby capybaras and helped me keep my job, all while bearing the crushing weight of decades of self-blame. And right now, his eyes flickering with emotion, he's more vulnerable than I've ever seen him.

"Lucy," he says, his stubble rough against my hand, "what I said about you, that it doesn't matter what some keeper in Ohio thinks of me . . ." He traces a line over my thumb and covers my hand with his own. "I was an idiot. You're not just some keeper. You're anything but."

His admission lingers in the air between us, and I want to respond with one of my own—*I was an idiot, too; let's start over and give each other a second chance*—but just thinking it makes me feel exposed, naked, and I lose my nerve before I can get the words out.

"Slugs have four noses," I whisper, because I'm Lucy Rourke, and of course I do.

Kai laughs against my palm. "Some butterflies drink blood."

"Eagles can strike harder than rifle shots."

Kai reaches forward to cup my face with both hands, and his closeness causes my heart to pound so loud that I'll never be able to hear whatever animal fact he spouts off next.

"Hey, Lucy," he says. "Hold still, okay?"

He strokes my cheek with his thumb, and I fight off a shiver. The gentleness of the gesture feels more intimate than anything Nick and I did in the entire two years we dated, and I can't resist leaning into Kai's touch.

I should pull away, should remind myself that letting someone get close only leads to heartbreak, but I don't. Because when Kai's rough palm cups my face, the burdens I carry—my desperation to help Keeva, my jealousy over Mia's party, the sheer panic that overwhelms me when the cameras roll—suddenly don't feel so unbearably heavy. And even though I should grab my logbook and sprint to my office before I blur the lines between work and romance, between the Kai I met on day one and the Kai who's gazing at me now, his eyes ablaze with something between awe and desire, I won't. Because Kai Bridges, protector of pilot whales and my former enemy, is going to kiss me.

And I'm going to kiss him back.

"Okay," I whisper, breathless. Trembling, I close my eyes and wait for the welcome pressure of his lips on mine.

But it doesn't come. Instead, Kai's thumb brushes across my hairline, and he lets out a satisfied noise. "Ah. Got it."

Confused, I open my eyes to find him holding a piece of straw between his thumb and index finger.

"You had hay in your hair," he explains. "I didn't want it to fall into your eyes."

He might as well have dumped a bucket of ice water over my head, and the heavy yearning that overwhelmed me quickly morphs into sheer humiliation. I can't believe I misinterpreted his friendly gesture as a sexy overture; worse, I can't believe I welcomed it. I'm supposed to be saving Keeva, not entertaining imagined advances that were nothing of the sort.

"Thanks," I say quickly, brushing my cheek with my fingertips as if I can erase all evidence of Kai's touch.

"Of course. And thanks for listening to me complain about the nightmares. It's not something I share with many people."

I nod, thankful for the darkness hiding my blazing-hot cheeks. Why did I think the fact that he opened up about his trauma meant he wanted to jump my bones? How did I let his endless supply of weird animal facts and killer forearms knock me off my game? Dear God, did he see me close my eyes in anticipation as he leaned into me?

"You okay?" Kai asks, studying me with a look that the Lucy of forty seconds ago would have mistakenly regarded as amorous.

"Yep," I insist, reminding myself that he was only looking out for my corneas. Kai was never going to kiss me, and certainly not while I was wearing a vest made of hair. "Just hungry. Living off microwaved dinners is starting to catch up to me."

Kai blinks as if he doesn't quite believe me, and I force myself to stare at Keeva instead of into his searching gaze.

"Lucy," he says, "I—"

I cringe as I imagine what he's about to say—*Lucy, don't worry, women embarrass themselves like this around me all the time*—but his phone rings at full blast to interrupt him. The noise startles all three of us, and Keeva jolts awake in my lap and lets out a screech of terror, flinging herself against my chest.

"Dammit," Kai grumbles, rummaging through his duffel as I make soothing vocalizations to Keeva. His phone must be buried under a mountain of exclusive *Wild Side* baseball caps, because he still hasn't found it when it finally stops ringing. But after a beat of silence, the ringing starts again, and Keeva lets out another cry and punches my arm with a tiny fist.

"Um, I know this isn't helpful now," I say as Kai flings a hat, three pairs of socks, and a toiletry kit out of the duffel, digging around for the noisy culprit. "But have you heard of vibrate mode?"

He mutters under his breath but manages to find his phone just as the caller strikes for the third time. "Aha!" he cries, pulling it out of his bag.

He silences it, but not soon enough for poor, disoriented Keeva, who grabs my ponytail and yanks like her life depends on it. Tears spring to my eyes, and there's nothing I want more than to throw Kai's phone into the penny fountain outside Adventure Cove.

"Sorry," he mutters.

I motion for him to grab Keeva a bottle, but he ignores my request and points behind me. "Lucy," he whispers. "*Look.*"

"What?" I hiss, the nape of my neck aching from Keeva's tug. But when I turn around, I forget that she almost yanked my head off. Because there, sitting at the barrier between the nursery and the bedroom, is Zuri.

"Oh my God," I say, trying not to freak out. It's been days since any of the girls got half this close to Keeva, let alone came all the way up to the mesh, and hope blossoms in my chest.

"Your phone," I whisper to Kai. "Give me your phone."

"What?" he asks. "Why?"

"Zuri," I explain. "She loves phones. It must have been the ringing that enticed her to come over."

"And?" Kai prods.

"And if we let Keeva hold the phone, Zuri will want it. It might be enough to get her interested in Keeva."

"This is a brand-new iPhone," Kai says, crossing his arms over his chest. "I'm not giving it to a baby gorilla."

"Fine," I grumble. I wrestle my own from my pocket and set Keeva on the ground with my phone beside her. She might pick it up and fling it across the nursery like the little wrecking ball she is, but that's a small price to pay if it helps foster a connection.

183

I step away from the mesh, watching as Zuri glances at the phone with wide eyes. She reaches for it, pressing her fingers through the mesh, but it's just out of her grasp. She draws her hand back and then tries again, but this time little Keeva, her eyes wide and a piece of hay sticking out of her mouth, reaches out to brush Zuri's fingers with her own.

It's a cautious, hesitant gesture, but Zuri doesn't pull her hand away. She lets Keeva press her tiny fingers to her enormous ones, and when the infant lets out a hoot bark of excitement, Zuri makes a belch vocalization back to her. I hold my breath as Keeva crawls closer to the mesh, and Zuri tilts her head as if to say, *Who are you, little girl? And why are you wearing a diaper?*

"Oh my God," I cry, my heart nearly leaping out of my chest. "Oh my God, Kai, it's *working*!"

"It's working," he repeats, his mouth dropping open in awe as he watches the interaction.

Tears of relief and hope spring to my eyes, and I bounce up and down on my toes and grab a fistful of Kai's T-shirt in excitement. "We're doing it!" I cheer.

He nods and lets out a whoop of triumph, looping an arm around me and joining in on my impromptu victory dance. "Hell yeah. *You're* doing it."

Kai's face is so close to mine that his words are warm against my ear, and the realization snaps me back to my senses. I unclench my grip on his shirt and pull away, determined to keep my hands to myself.

"The camera," I say quickly, trying to cover up the awkward shift in mood. "This could be a major breakthrough."

Nodding, Kai grabs his camera and sets it up with smooth efficiency. I back out of the shot as the two gorillas continue to make vocalizations to each other, Keeva still clutching Zuri's index finger like it's my ponytail.

"This is amazing footage," Kai says as Keeva attempts to stuff Zuri's finger into her mouth. "Here. Come look."

He waves me toward him and moves aside to give me access to the camera. I peer into the lens, watching the baby gorilla marvel at her larger counterpart. We just might be witnessing the start of a powerful bond, and even though I'm still embarrassed about misreading Kai's intentions, I can't help but grin.

"You're right, it is. Might just win you that fourth Emmy."

Kai laughs, and despite my best efforts, the sound of it sends a spark of electricity through me.

"I should grab my logbook," I say, determined to fill my head with sober thoughts. "Phil will want good notes on this."

I move to hurry past Kai, but I'm flustered from my excitement over Zuri's progress and the heady scent of his aftershave, and my hip bumps the tripod.

"Dammit!" I cry, grabbing for the camera before it crash-lands in the hay. Kai reaches for it at the same time, and our hands meet as we scramble to keep it steady.

"Oops," I whisper. "Close one."

Kai breathes a sigh of relief and fixes me with a smirk. "What am I gonna do with you, Lucy Rourke?"

Well, you could have kissed me, the saucy, carefree version of me wants to tell him, and if I didn't know better, I'd think he was flirting. But I do know better now, and I tell myself that it's only walkie-talkie static, not sexual tension, that's causing the air to crackle.

"Logbook," I say, glancing around for my satchel and refusing to meet Kai's gaze. "Where's my logbook?" I will myself to peel my hands away from the camera, where Kai's fingers still brush against mine, but I'm frozen by lust and the alarming realization that I don't want to stop touching him. In fact, I want him to touch me *more*.

"Lucy," Kai says, the lines of his face softening as if he can read my thoughts.

I scramble to think of more animal facts or zoo gossip to prattle on about, anything that will snap me back into reality and knock me out of this trance.

"Seriously," I continue, forcing myself to look every which way but at Kai, searching the nursery for my notes. "Where the hell's my logbook?"

"*Lucy,*" he says, his tone so entreating, so wanting, that I abandon my search. "Can you forget about your damn logbook for a second?" Kai draws his hands away to run them through his hair, and the loss of his touch feels foreign. Wrong.

"I didn't mean to say *damn*," he says quickly. "I know your logbook is very important to you, and I would never disrespect that. I only meant . . ." He trails off, swallowing hard, and fidgets with the collar of his T-shirt. It's a far cry from the confident, unruffled guy he plays on TV, and if I didn't know better, I'd think he was nervous.

"That day I followed you inside after camera training," he says, stepping closer to me. "I said I only did that to get my mic back. I lied."

A shiver runs down my spine as he draws nearer, and the taut angle of his jawline makes me want to rip off my fur vest and propose a literal roll in the hay.

"I didn't give a damn about the mic," Kai says plainly, and even though I try to talk myself out of reading anything into his actions, his lingering gaze on my mouth makes it really freaking difficult.

"Um, okay." *Logbook-logbook-logbook*, I shout silently at myself, but my hormones pay my brain no attention.

Kai sighs as if I'm not understanding. "What I mean is, I followed you because I wanted to check on you. I'm always checking on you, Lucy."

The sincerity in his tone warms my blood, and I think of how he took my hand in the Huli Huli parking lot and helped me save face in front of Nick. I think of the private, assuring glances he sneaks my way when his crew films at Ape House, his subtle way of boosting my confidence and keeping me calm. I think of how he showed up here tonight, after hours of shooting and days of travel, to check on Keeva. To check on me.

"Why?" I ask, remembering the solid pressure of his hand on my cheek.

"Because I was completely wrong about you. You're anything but incompetent, and you're clearly not afraid of a challenge. You call me on my bullshit, which hardly anybody does anymore, and you went to bat for me with that bartender. Plus, you look at me like that."

"Like what?" I ask, brushing my hair out of my face.

"Like *that*," Kai says, his gaze meeting mine. He steps closer, mere inches from me now, and if he keeps talking in that full, throaty tone, I'm going to have a hell of a time keeping my wits about me.

"I'm confused," I admit, not sure what game he's playing. I won't make the same mistake twice, and I push away the possibility that I'm not alone in my desire. "Why didn't . . . ?" *Why didn't you kiss me?* I want to ask, but the words tangle in my throat. "I thought . . ." I tear my gaze away from Kai's, embarrassed, and glance at the spot where I thought he was making a move on me in the hay.

Kai follows my gaze with his own before looking back at me. "You thought I wanted to kiss you."

I could deny it, but I'm not a convincing liar, and besides, if we can be open with each other about his nightmares and my abandonment issues, maybe I can be open about this, too.

"Yes," I tell him, and it takes more courage for me to say that than to look into a thousand cameras. "I did."

"I wanted to." Kai's voice is quieter than usual, as if this takes courage for him, too. "But I wasn't sure if you did."

He tilts his head, studying me, and the shift in his posture is a question. An invitation.

"Did you want me to kiss you, Lucy?" he asks, his tone low. Guttural. "Do you want me to kiss you now?"

My fingers tremble, and I tuck them into my palms. If I say no, I'll be playing it safe and staying focused on the one thing that's supposed to matter to me: work. I'll be protecting myself from the risk of being vulnerable, of being hurt, of the messy ramifications that come from mixing business with pleasure.

But I'll also be denying what every cell in my body screams for.

"Yes," I say, choosing to dive headfirst into uncharted waters. "I do."

My heart thuds in my chest as Kai lowers his face toward mine, but he doesn't kiss me yet. Instead, he cups my face in his palms and caresses my cheek with his thumb. It's a lingering, delicious moment, and despite the warnings flashing in my head, I'm eager for what comes next.

So this time, I don't wait for him to make a move. I place a hand over his, savoring the feel of him, and lean forward to press my lips to his.

Because like I told him all those days ago, I'm not afraid of a challenge.

Chapter Twenty

I've made a huge mistake. I realize it as soon as I hear a loud clang from the hallway, and I pull away from Kai with a jolt.

"Scotty," I realize, wiping my mouth with the back of my hand. He must have finished checking on the orangutans and reentered Ape House.

"What's—" Kai starts, but I shush him and only speak again once I hear Scotty's footsteps leading toward the break room and away from the nursery.

"This was a bad idea," I say, scanning the hallway to check that it's empty. I let Bad Lucy get all kinds of ideas in her horny little head about Kai's biceps and triceps and delicious-smelling hair, and I succumbed to the dark side.

"We should not have done this," I tell him, panic rising in my chest. If Scotty had seen me kissing Kai, our romance would be the talk of the zoo tomorrow, and my name would be synonymous with hookup drama instead of professional expertise.

I got lucky, this time.

"I should go," I continue, smoothing the front of my ridiculous vest. "You should go. We should both definitely go."

Kai raises an eyebrow at me. "Well, I'm pretty sure one of us should stay and tend to the baby gorilla. And since you're the one who works here, it should probably be you."

"Right," I say, crossing my arms over my chest and trying to slow my pounding heart. "I stay. You go. Me: baby gorilla. You: anywhere else."

"Are you okay?" Kai asks, reaching out to touch my shoulder. "I'll admit, it's been a while and I'm a little out of practice, so if I, like, bit you or something, I'm really sorry."

My brain gets tripped up over the revelation that it's been a while since he kissed anyone, and before I can ask him what *a while* means—two weeks? four months?—I force myself to lock Bad Lucy up and throw away the key.

"No," I assure him. "It was nothing like that. I just absolutely, positively cannot kiss you again."

The kiss was good; it was too good, actually. Kai's lips were full and butter soft, and the way he stroked my cheek was a strong indication that he's very good with his fingers.

"Um, okay," he says, his brow furrowed in confusion. "But if I, like, scraped you with my teeth at all—"

"You didn't," I insist. "Your teeth were perfect. The kiss was perfect." It was the almost getting caught that ruined it and brought me back to reality.

Kai's characteristic smirk returns. "Perfect, huh?"

I roll my eyes, annoyed at myself for letting my budding crush get the best of me. I need to get our relationship back to safer ground, and I need to do it fast.

I grab my phone from the hay, and Zuri lets out an annoyed pant but doesn't leave her spot near the mesh.

"Look," I tell Kai, trying not to remember how good his hands felt on me. "I've done the whole workplace romance thing before, and it's a terrible idea. I mean, one second I was meeting the new vet at Ozzie's cataract surgery, and the next thing I know, he'd signed us both up for emails from Pottery Barn Kids. I won't let that happen again."

I think of what I learned the hard way from Nick: that commitment seems like an okay idea until it blows up in your face, leaving you with a stack of moving boxes and an extra fifteen pounds of post-breakup ice cream weight.

"Please don't compare me to Nicholas New Balance," Kai says. "It's downright offensive. I saw him at the manatee pool this morning wearing Croakies. *Croakies.*" His tone is light, joking, and frustration simmers in my stomach. Does he not realize how close we just came to disaster?

"I'm serious," I insist. "What if Scotty had walked in on us kissing? God forbid, what if *Phil* had? I'd be endless fodder for the zoo rumor mill. When Nick and I broke up, everyone from Norm the security guard to Elle's interns knew about it by the next morning. And we're nobodies! Can you imagine what would happen if people thought Lucy from Primates was fucking Kai Bridges?"

Kai flinches. "I never said anything about fucking."

I barrel on undeterred, even though I'm not sure which one of us I'm trying to convince. "I've spent my whole life dreaming of a chance like the one Phil's given me this summer. The senior keeper spot is finally within my reach, and I won't sacrifice my shot at it for—"

"For what?" Kai asks, his eyes blazing. "For an overhyped, over-paid, egotistical moron?"

The hurt in his voice slows my roll. "That's not what I meant."

"So what did you mean?" he asks, scooping up his duffel and

slinging it over his shoulder. "Because if you want to act like that kiss never happened, fine. I can handle that; no big deal."

The words sting even if I said them first, but Kai's not done.

"But if you really believe I'd ask you to sacrifice your shot at a promotion for me, then your opinion of me hasn't changed at all since we met. And if that's the case, we had no business kissing in the first place."

I shake my head, wishing I could get him to understand my position. "You don't get it," I tell him. "No matter what happens this summer, you'll still be Kai Bridges. You'll still have millions of fans and a passport full of stamps and people who scream 'Wowza!' at you everywhere you go. You won't have to worry about student loans or proving that your work actually means something. I have no such luxury."

I point to Keeva, who's trying to catch the stray bits of popcorn Zuri drops through the mesh. "They mean everything to me," I say. "This job, this zoo, these animals, they're my whole world. And if I screw that up, it's game over."

"Your whole word, huh?" Kai shakes his head. "I'm going to tell you a secret, Lucy. Your world is as big as you make it. One day you're going to wake up and realize that your life is only small because you made it that way."

His words hang heavily between us, and I take a step backward.

"I didn't mean that the way it sounded," he says, reaching for my hand.

I jerk away from him. "Yes, you did."

I was stupid to think, however briefly, that we had enough in common to understand each other. What could Kai Bridges, born with the world at his feet, know about making mine bigger? Absolutely nothing. I can't believe I told him about Karina and my eleventh birthday. I can't believe I told him what it was like to be abandoned. I thought that maybe, because of what he went through with Taji, he could understand.

I was wrong.

"You may think my life is small, but at least I earned it," I tell him. "Everything I have, I worked my butt off for. And if I had a mother who wrote a masterpiece like *Majesty on the Mountain*, you can bet I'd have read it."

"*Majest*— What are you talking about?" Kai asks.

I wish I could say I'm surprised that he doesn't get it. "That first day we met after the Critter Chat," I explain. "You said I was wrong about Dr. Kimber's nickname. I wasn't. So don't tell me how to make my world bigger when you can't even recognize that you got yours on a silver platter."

Kai holds his jaw taut, like a rubber band about to snap. "Is that what you want to hear? That you were right and I was wrong?"

I remember what he said when I overheard his phone call at Huli Huli: *I want things to be different.* Well, I want things to be different, too, and I won't let one misguided moment of false intimacy threaten my odds of making that happen.

"I want my book back," I tell him. "And I want to forget the kiss ever happened."

And for perhaps the first time since we met, Kai doesn't try to argue with me.

"Done and done, Lucy." He strides past me, his body a knot of muscle and tension, and when he leaves the nursery, he doesn't stop to look back.

Chapter Twenty-One

The next morning, after I run home for fresh underwear and to prove to Nona that I haven't fallen off the face of the earth, I return to Ape House to find my dog-eared copy of *Majesty on the Mountain* sitting on my desk. Kai left it tucked next to my Dr. Kimber bobblehead and my purple *Wild Side* hat, and I try to ignore the sinking feeling in my stomach when I slide the book into a drawer.

I know he didn't set out to insult me by calling my life small, but his words still held a painful kernel of truth. My life must seem downright claustrophobic from his perspective; forget going on the *Oprah* show, I can't keep it together long enough to shoot a ninety-second news clip about Poppet the lemur. And sure, I'd love to go to Rwanda and the Congo to see gorillas in the wild, but my place is here with Zuri. She helped repair my broken ten-year-old heart, and I can't just up and leave her.

The fact that Kai doesn't understand that confirms I was right: the kiss was a mistake, and we're better off acting like it never happened. Just because we're both passionate about gorillas and have childhood trauma doesn't mean we share a special connection. Hell, that description fits half the global population, and it's not enough to bridge the massive gulf between our lifestyles. Besides, even if the kiss was hotter than anything I've experienced before—even if the pressure of Kai's lips on mine made my skin tingle hours after they were gone—I have to focus on rearing Keeva, not waste time and energy on a pointless summer fling.

So when I reach the nursery and find Freya helping the crew set up instead of Kai, I tell myself that it's for the best.

"Lucy, can you believe it?" Lottie asks, tucking a clipboard under her arm. "Zuri hasn't left Keeva's side all morning."

Beaming, she points toward the mesh, where Zuri watches as Keeva flips herself upside down, grasping Phil's hands like they're gymnastics rings. "Phil says that if Zuri's still this interested in a day or two, we can try putting them together." She claps her hands and leans toward me, lowering her voice. "Also, Kai said he's going to see if he can get me a tiny hat and T-shirt for Ernest so I can do a *Wild Side*–themed photoshoot. Isn't he the best?"

I force myself to nod. I am absolutely not jealous that Kai's helping Lottie coordinate her pet hedgehog's wardrobe. Why wouldn't he help? After all, Ernest doesn't have a small life; he has twenty thousand Instagram followers.

I push away all thoughts of Kai as Keeva, abandoning her acrobatic routine, grabs her red ball and tries to pass it to Zuri through the mesh. But the ball is too big to fit through the gap, and she lets out a grunt of frustration and launches it at Phil. Zuri reaches past the barrier to stroke the top of Keeva's head.

My heart soars at the display of interest and affection, and I watch as Jack passes Zuri a biscuit and Keeva does her best to catch the crumbs.

"What do you think?" I ask Phil, grinning at the sight of my boss in the hairy vest. He looks like he's half-dressed to take his kids trick-or-treating.

"I think you're doing a great job, Lucy." He smiles back at me, and it's an even better reward than Nona's tiramisu. "And I think we might have found our surrogate mom."

His praise fills me with pride, and even the presence of the cameras can't dull the spark of joy that ricochets all the way from my toes to the top of my still-sore-from-Keeva's-pulling hair.

"Let's tentatively plan on putting Zuri and Keeva in the same space tomorrow if the rest of the day goes smoothly," he adds. "Does that sound good to you?"

I'm so surprised that Phil's asking for my opinion that I almost cough on my own saliva. "Sounds like a plan," I say, trying to muster up a senior-keeper level of confidence. "I'll make sure everything's set for their official introduction."

He gives me a thumbs-up as Keeva, a blur of black fur and gangly limbs who doesn't give a damn about introductions, flies at him with her ball in hand.

Unlike the first days of Keeva's arrival, when none of the girls showed interest in her besides a strong desire to scare her silly, the chances of successfully incorporating her into Ozzie's troop are finally looking up. Plus, I'm learning to coexist with the cameras, and my chances of getting the promotion are better than ever.

Everything I've ever wanted is within reach, and nothing else should matter.

So why do I wish Kai were here to witness it?

. . .

The next morning, I give Keeva her bottle through the mesh instead of holding her in my lap. If the process of letting her and Zuri in the same space goes smoothly, we'll need to start feeding her through a barrier, since keepers can't safely enter the quarters of an adult gorilla. Keeva seems to have no problem with the change, because she does her best to wrench the bottle out of my hands. After her meal, a weigh-in, and a temperature check, we're ready to roll.

Lottie transfers Zuri out of the bedroom, and Jack and I deposit fresh lettuce, browse, popcorn, and orange slices throughout the space. Then Phil carries Keeva to the bedroom and deposits her in the hay, giving her a pat on the head as she makes a beeline for the fruit. She's not a smooth walker yet, and when she waddles bipedally toward a chunk of orange, she falls sideways and lands on her butt with a clunk.

"Are we clear?" Lottie asks, checking to make sure the area is secure and human-free.

"Clear," I answer, butterflies swarming in my stomach.

"Camera one, ready," Freya calls, and Phil holds up a hand to signal to Lottie.

"Three, two, one, go!" he instructs, and Lottie lifts the lever granting Zuri access to the bedroom from her current quarters. A gate rises, and Zuri, spotting a breakfast buffet of her favorite foods, knuckle-walks through the open gate. Keeva sees the larger gorilla running toward her and lets out a high-pitched alarm call, scurrying toward the nursery as fast as her tiny limbs will let her.

At first, Zuri is more interested in stuffing popcorn in her mouth than tending to Keeva, and I wonder if we should have stocked up on snacks she likes just a little bit less. But after Zuri spends five minutes digging through the hay and swallowing orange slices, Keeva gets brave enough to wander away from the mesh. She approaches Zuri gingerly, closing the distance between them a few feet at a time. Finally, she plants herself two feet from Zuri and picks up a leaf, stuffing it halfway into her mouth.

I wait to see if Zuri gives any indication that she's frustrated or annoyed—a loud hoot, a thump of her hand against the ground—so that we can separate the pair at the first sign of aggression. But she only chews calmly, glancing at the baby as if to say, *Oh hi, it's you; you can sit near me, but don't get any ideas about my popcorn.*

Finally, Zuri abandons the popcorn and stretches her giant hand toward the baby. Keeva cowers as Zuri gives her a gentle poke, but then she sees an open invitation and wobble-walks to Zuri's side. They sit there, hips touching, as Zuri lifts handfuls of lettuce to her mouth and Keeva watches, mesmerized.

It's the first time she's been in direct contact with another gorilla since losing her troop, and the simple beauty of the moment causes my eyes to swell with tears. I blink them away, determined to maintain my professionalism. I can sob over the adorableness in my office later, with a Diet Coke and my Dr. Kimber bobblehead for company.

The most promising sign of a successful surrogate match will be if Zuri decides to hold Keeva, and sure enough, around six that evening, while my knees scream from being locked in a crouching position all day, Zuri grabs Keeva by one of her tiny arms and clutches her to her massive chest. Keeva grasps Zuri's fur with her little fingers—just like she did with my ponytail—and Zuri glances at me, Phil, Jack, and Lottie and carries Keeva to the far end of the bedroom.

I do my best not to anthropomorphize the animals in my care, but it's hard not to interpret Zuri's actions as a declaration: *This is my baby, and the rest of you can GTFO.*

"Hell yes!" Jack cheers, albeit at a low enough decibel not to startle the gorillas.

"It's a great start, Lucy," Phil says as I finish another page of notes in my logbook. "I just texted Alexandra, and we have a long way to go, but she's happy."

I nod. We do have a lot of work ahead of us; even if Keeva and Zuri take to each other, they'll need time to bond privately before we give more troop members access to Keeva. It'll be a staggered approach—we'll reintroduce the pair to females Tria and Inkesha first, along with little Piper, before including the rowdier youngsters Tomo and Risa and the teenage blackback Mac. The real test will be the final addition of Ozzie, whose ultimate acceptance or rejection of Keeva will determine her fate in the troop. In the gorilla world, the silverback's vote trumps everything, and I can only hope that our hard work pays off.

"It is a good start," I agree. "But we've still got our work cut out for us."

Phil nods. "I can see that you're working hard, but when was the last time you slept?"

Wow, I must really look like shit. I know several days of sleeping on a lumpy air mattress hasn't done wonders for my appearance, but I was starting to consider the bags under my eyes a badge of dedication.

"Um, a few hours this morning," I tell my boss. I fell asleep at my desk while typing up my observation notes, and I woke up with a stiff back and a protein bar wrapper stuck to my cheek.

"Rest is important, Lucy," he says, and I wonder if the wrapper might still be stuck in my hair. "You're not scheduled tonight, right? Go home. Sleep. Take a shower. I'll see you back here in the morning."

Take a shower? I give my armpits a subtle sniff. Damn, if I'm ripe enough that people can smell me over the pungent stench of gorilla, it's a wonder Lottie and Jack haven't staged an intervention.

"Yes, sir."

I *am* exhausted, but I don't want to take the night off. Because while it feels like I haven't seen my own bed and my good ol' Jack and Rose poster in ages, when I'm not working, I have time to think. And if my brain isn't laser focused on Keeva and Zuri, it might wander places it shouldn't—like the passenger seat of a minivan, or behind a potted plant at Huli Huli, or the nursery after hours, with a strong hand gripping the back of my head and a pair of lips mere inches from mine.

Because unlike what Kai said on his mysterious phone call, *I'm* not all about doing what I want and letting the chips fall where they may. The Lucy Rourke approach to life is planned, careful, scheduled. And now more than ever, I need work to keep me focused.

Chapter Twenty-Two

Luckily, I don't have to face an evening of sitting in my bedroom alone, watching a marathon of *My 600 lb. Life* and trying not to think about Kai. Because when I text Elle and Sam to let them know I'm off-duty tonight, Elle sends back a flurry of happy-face emojis. Perfect, come over! There's something I've been wanting to ask you guys. Nadeem will make a charcuterie board.

If I have to be apart from Zuri and Keeva, Nadeem's charcuterie board will at least make the separation easier. He's very into table-scapes and fancy appetizers, and our last get-together at Elle's featured a cranberry-rosemary cheese roll that was better than sex with Nick.

It was not better than the kiss with Kai, but I push that thought out of my mind as I head to Elle's. She and Nadeem live in a cozy Cape Cod in Grandview with a blue door and a bird bath in the front yard, and I take my work boots off before stepping inside. Elle will murder me if I track anything from Ape House onto her hard-wood floor. Actually, she'd probably say nothing and then attack the floor with a Swiffer later, but I don't want to lose my access to the cheese roll.

"We're in here!" Elle calls when she hears me enter, and I follow her voice through the kitchen and into the living room. It's a cooler-than-usual evening, and she's opened the windows to let in a gentle breeze. Hoping that will ward off some of my lingering gorilla odor, I plop down in a modular armchair across from the couch, where Elle and Sam are curled up with Trixie the Jack Russell mix.

"We were just saying that we're starting to forget what your face looks like," Sam says, handing me a can of strawberry-flavored Bubly. She studies me for a moment. "Just as pretty as I remember, but with some seriously alarming under-eye circles." She squints. "Can I ask out of nothing but pure love: what's going on with your hair?"

Blushing, I run a hand over my ponytail. I haven't washed my hair in a few days, and it got so oily this morning that I tried to use Jack's baby powder as dry shampoo despite Lottie's warnings.

"I substituted baby powder for dry shampoo. Big mistake," I admit. "Anyway, Elle, what do you want to ask us?"

I'm slightly terrified she's going to announce that she's planning a home birth and wants Sam and me to assist with it. I've attended my fair share of primate births, so I know things can get pretty gnarly, and while I'm happy to help Elle however I can, I'd much rather wait outside with flowers and a bottle of champagne.

"Later," Elle says. "Sam was just catching me up on things between her and Freya." She nudges Sam with her elbow, and Trixie lets out an exasperated sigh until Elle starts rubbing her ears again.

I'm shocked when Sam, who's given us play-by-plays of most of her sexual encounters, some so detailed that Elle just stared into space for a good ten minutes afterward, actually blushes. "Well, there's not much to tell. Freya's great. She's so smart—like, she's given me so many ideas for the blog—and she's funny as hell. Honestly, she got me to laugh at a dad joke the other day, and I once broke up with a guy for reading me the riddle on the end of a Popsicle stick."

"Oh my God," Elle says, clapping her hands. "You love her."

"Whoa. Slow down, Nora Roberts," Sam says. "It's only been a few weeks. But yeah, I like her a lot, and I can see things going in that direction."

I want to be happy for Sam, but doubt pops into my head instantly. What's going to happen at the end of the summer when Freya and Kai and the rest of the crew pack up their tripods and peace out? How can Sam maintain a relationship with someone who changes continents like Nona changes espadrilles? Oh my God, what if she falls so deeply in love that she quits her job and follows Freya around the globe, only coming home to visit once a year? I take a long sip of sparkling water and try not to hyperventilate. Things are changing too quickly around here; one minute the three of us are singing a terrible, off-key rendition of Lizzo's "Truth Hurts" at karaoke night, and the next Elle's popping out a baby and Sam's trading her corner-window office for a suitcase and a travel-sized bottle of moisturizer.

I understand that my friends and I want different things out of life, and sometimes that means we'll grow in different directions. But I remember the stinging message Kai delivered to me in the nursery: *Your life is only small because you made it that way.* I can't help thinking that my friends' lives are getting bigger and bigger, and I worry they'll get so big that they'll outgrow me.

But I don't want to rain on Sam's parade, so I clap my hands like Elle did. "That's so exciting."

Sam smiles. "Thanks. I was hoping you guys would join us for dinner sometime next week. Maybe Friday? You usually have Friday nights off, Luce, and I'd love for you both to get to know Freya. I'm thinking Café Istanbul. She loves Mediterranean food, and they have great sigara borek."

"Of course," Elle says, not missing a beat.

I have no idea what sigara borek is, but the excitement on Sam's face is undeniable, and I have no good reason to decline. Sure, I want to spend every waking moment working on the surrogacy project, but I owe it to Sam to be there for her.

"Sounds good," I tell her. "I'll make sure I'm free."

"Moving on," Sam says, tucking her legs underneath her. "A little bird told me that our very own Lucy Rourke left Huli Huli with none other than Kai Bridges. Do you have anything you'd like to share with the group, Lucy?"

Ugh, I should have known. The zoo really is a rumor mill on steroids, and anything that happens within five miles of its gates is bound to be witnessed by someone.

"Was it Akilah from Invertebrates?" I ask, scowling. I thought I saw her parking her SUV when I hopped into Kai's minivan.

"And Mary-Claire from Amphibians," Elle adds. "Who heard it from Charlie from Guest Relations, who I'm assuming heard it from Margo."

I shake my head. "Well, my car wouldn't start, and Kai saved me from having to carpool home with Nick. That's all."

I'm not ready to tell my friends about Kai's strange phone call and how I rescued him from Courtney the bartender with a disgusting fact about scorpions, and I'm definitely not about to tell them we kissed in the nursery. For one thing, I don't want to listen to a good-natured chorus of "we told you so's" about my initial contempt for him. And I certainly don't want to recount the argument Kai and I had afterward, where I freaked out over losing my focus and he implied that my life was pathetic. They'd either try to convince me that commitment isn't always so terrible, or they'd feed me chocolate and give each other knowing looks that say, *Oh, Lucy, our poor little work-obsessed friend, can't she ever just be normal?* And even if they somehow understood why I panicked after the kiss, I'm not ready to share that moment with them yet. Kai might think I'm a cowardly ding-dong in a furry vest, but the kiss, like my *Guilty Pleasures* confession, was just between the two of us. And I want to keep it that way, at least for now.

At least until I can get the memory of his breath against my skin out of my mind.

"He drives a minivan," I add, lest Elle and Sam sense that I'm holding something back. "Not a Lamborghini."

"Freya says Kai's very down to earth," Sam says, petting Trixie's head. "Apparently he donates the majority of his earnings to different wildlife foundations."

Elle sighs. "That's so sweet."

"Right?" Sam agrees. "Plus, Kai and Freya and a couple guys from Small Mammals are taking some animals to the Ronald McDonald House next weekend to cheer up the families."

I make a focused effort not to picture a Crocodile Dundee hat–wearing Kai bringing smiles to the faces of sad children, delighting them with tales of his jungle adventures while Poppet the lemur rests on his shoulder. My effort does not go well.

Dammit.

"Ladies," Nadeem greets us, strolling into the living room carrying a wooden tray. "I present to you: a summer charcuterie board. Today's edition includes smoked chorizo, bacon-onion jam, and pearl mozzarella marinated in herbs and spices." He sets the food on the coffee table, and Trixie sniffs the spread, getting dangerously close to swiping a cracker.

"Thank you, honey," Elle says, standing up to give him a peck on the cheek.

"Yes, thank you, honey," Sam echoes, her mouth already stuffed with chorizo. "We love you very much."

"We love you the most," I agree, going straight for the pearl mozzarella. It's been a while since I've eaten anything besides KIND bars or Pita Pockets, and it tastes like heaven. Besides, Nadeem's interruption probably stopped Sam from revealing some other devastatingly charming tidbit about Kai, like the fact that he's single-handedly developing a cure for cancer or funding a rescue farm for orphaned alpacas.

"So, Elle," I say, aiming for a swift change of subject, "what's the big question?"

"If you're proposing marriage, I'm in," Sam says. "I'll be a throuple with you and Nadeem if he promises to keep bringing me cheese."

"A quople," I correct her. "No, a quadrouple? Whatever it is, don't leave me out. This chorizo is incredible."

Sam narrows her eyes at me. "I thought you weren't into commitment."

I hold up a cracker. "I'll commit to this jam no problem."

Laughing, Elle reaches for a cracker as Nadeem, probably worried that we're going to force him to watch *The Bachelorette* with us, heads back to the kitchen.

"Okay, so, Nadeem and I were talking, and we think the baby needs godparents." She places a hand on her belly. "He's going to ask his brother to be godfather, and I wanted to know if you guys would be godmothers!"

"Godmothers?" I ask. "But I haven't been to church since Nona forced me to make my First Communion. And I got in trouble then for complaining that the bread was stale."

Elle laughs. "Yes, godmothers, but not in a religious sense. As you know, Nadeem's family is Hindu, and I'm Christian, but we don't want to push any particular religion on the baby. You'd be godmothers in the symbolic sense. Like, people he or she can talk to when Deem and I drive them crazy. Special aunts who spoil them with love and an extra helping of ice cream. Role models. I don't have sisters, but you guys are as good as."

"Oh my God, Elle," Sam says, almost choking on an olive. "Are you serious? I would love to! Aunt-Fairygodmother Sam is going to spoil the shit out of that kiddo. I'm talking ball pit, pony, that mini Mercedes G-Wagon Kim Kardashian's kids have. I can't wait."

"No ponies!" Nadeem calls from the kitchen. "They're against city ordinance!"

"Ordinance, schmordinance," Sam says, wrapping an arm around Elle. "Of course we'll be godmothers! Right, Luce?"

Panic floods me. Does being a godmother mean I'm next in line to raise the baby should the unthinkable happen to Elle and Nadeem? I picture myself squeezing a crib into my cramped office. I'd be like Katherine Heigl in that terrible movie where she and Josh Duhamel raise her late friend's baby, except I'd do a crappy job and there'd be no Josh Duhamel.

I am not cut out for legal guardianship.

"So," I say, "um." The cracker in my hand falls to the floor, and Trixie ditches the couch to rescue it. "That's, like, such an honor. To be asked to fulfill, you know, such an important role." I sip my Bubly, wishing it were spiked. "Thank you. But let's be real: that's more of a Sam job than a Lucy one, and we all know it."

"That's not true," Sam says.

Elle shakes her head. "You're both equally important to me, and to this baby. I wouldn't ask you if I didn't want you to accept."

I stuff another piece of cheese in my mouth to buy myself time. It's not that I'm not excited for Elle's baby; I am, even if I worry that once she becomes a mom, she won't have time for my bullshit anymore. I'm happy to be Auntie Lucy, who brings over toys and treats and babysits the nugget so Elle and Nadeem can have date night. But godmother—*role model*, as Elle said—is something more.

Elle's baby needs a role model like Sam, who can be professionally successful and manage a budding relationship at the same time. The baby doesn't need a role model who has to be told not to wear khaki to important events, or whose boss kindly but firmly implies that she reeks. It doesn't need a role model who can't remember to get her engine light checked.

And it definitely doesn't need a role model who refers to it as "it."

"I just don't think I'd be very good at it," I admit, hating the crestfallen look on Elle's face.

Karina taught me there's no commitment that can't be broken, and Nick showed me that making one only ends in misery. I don't want to let the baby down before they're even born by making promises I can't deliver.

"Can I think about it?" I ask, worried that if I outright reject the offer, Elle will burst into tears. The last thing I want to do is hurt her, and I need time to figure out how to decline in a way that won't break her heart.

"Of course," Elle says. "Take all the time you need."

Sam, already on track for Godmother of the Year, tosses out some theme ideas for a late-fall baby shower, and Elle compiles them into a list on her phone. Trixie, sniffing me intently, jumps up on my lap and starts licking up cracker crumbs. I try to join in on the shower ideas, but I know as much about baby showers as I do about carburetors, and after a few minutes, I'm just eating jam by the spoonful while my friends ooh and ahh over Pinterest suggestions.

But no matter how many olives and mozzarella pearls I swallow, I can't get rid of the gnawing feeling that Kai was right—that my friends' lives are expanding, evolving, while I'm staying exactly where I am. That my life, whether I want to admit it or not, is small.

Chapter Twenty-Three

I don't see Kai for an entire week. According to Lottie, he spends most of it camped out at The Wilds, the zoo's off-site safari park, where his crew shoots footage of the African painted dogs. He also goes to New York to make an appearance on the *Today* show, and Katie the summer intern plays the clip on repeat in the Ape House breakroom.

"Unf," she says as Kai, sporting his trusty safari hat, chats with Hoda Kotb about the future of critically endangered rhinos.

I don't care that Katie finds Kai attractive, nor do I want to assign her poop-scoop duty for watching the clip fourteen times in a row. Absolutely not. After all, he *is* attractive, and pretending he's not would be like denying that chocolate chip cookies are addictive. I don't have ownership rights to Kai or chocolate chip cookies, even if I do enjoy having them both in my mouth. So Katie can *unf* over Kai all she wants, because I have Keeva and Zuri to focus on.

But she is due for laundry duty.

I'm not sure if Kai's avoiding me or if his schedule has kept him out of Ape House by coincidence, but by Friday morning, I'm no longer peeking around corners before I enter a room or craning my neck toward Phil's office to check for Kai before I join my boss for a conference call. I can't hide from him forever, and I'm sure he doesn't care enough to hide from me.

Even so, when I stride into the breakroom to brew a much-needed cup of coffee, I almost drop my mug when I find Kai inside, leaning against the refrigerator in a way that should look ridiculous but somehow does not. My first instinct is to run away fast, and the fact that his gaze is glued to his phone gives me an opening. I scurry toward the door, and I'm halfway into the hallway when Kai calls after me.

"Lucy?"

Damn. Caught, I step back into the breakroom, letting the door swing shut behind me.

"Oh, hey, Kai," I say brightly, as if I'm not the most awkward person alive. "I didn't see you there."

He raises an eyebrow. "No? Then why'd you run out of here so quickly?"

"Well," I say, wishing I'd put on mascara this morning and then wishing I hadn't wished that, "I came to make coffee. But then I thought I forgot my mug. And then I realized I didn't. It's actually right here!" I hold up my mug as if that somehow proves my point, but then I remember it's one I borrowed from Lottie and reads, *I HEART MY ABYSSINIAN CAT* in glaring black letters. A picture of her grandmother's late feline, Prince von Meowington III—may he rest in eternal peace—stares out at Kai. I lower the mug, wondering if I can drink enough coffee to caffeinate myself to death.

"Right," Kai says, studying me for a long moment. He scratches his cheek, and I work hard to block out the memory of how good his stubble felt under my palm. "You know, Lucy, things don't have to be weird between us."

"Weird?" I ask. "Who's weird? Not me. Not you. We're not weird. We're cool. Too cool for school." I realize I'm making uninterrupted eye contact with Prince von Meowington, and I force myself to look away from the mug.

"Look, I'm sorry about the other night," he says. "I shouldn't have kissed you, and I shouldn't have said what I did afterward."

"I'm sorry, too," I say, my gaze darting toward the door to make sure no one's within earshot. "And for what it's worth, you didn't kiss me. I mean, you did, but I also kissed you. We kissed each other. It was, you know, a mutual kissing."

"Yep," Kai says, the hint of a smirk tugging at his mouth. "That is usually how kissing works."

I nod. "Right."

A beat of silence passes where I try not to think how strange it is that a week ago, I was telling Kai about my childhood and cupping his face in my hand, and now we're staring at each other across the room like a pair of awkward middle schoolers at the Winter Wonderland Dance.

"How's Keeva?" Kai asks at the same moment that I say, "How's Hoda?"

Neither of us answers, and half of me wants to fling my arms around him and say screw forgetting about the kiss. The other half—the sensible, pragmatic half that knows how to focus on her career and not accept a godmother role she doesn't deserve—wishes I could lock myself in the refrigerator until my frozen brain forgets that Kai ever existed.

"Hey, Kai," Katie the summer intern says, popping her head into the breakroom. "Freya's looking for you. She's heading to Asia Quest and wants to make sure you're good to stay here with the crew."

"Tell her sure thing," he says, flashing Katie his signature grin.

"Okay," Katie says, batting her eyelashes at him. "See you out there?"

He nods, and I roll my eyes as she flounces off toward the nursery. Of course she'll see him out there; they literally just discussed it.

"Everything okay over there?" Kai asks, smirking like he knows exactly what I'm thinking.

"Everything's peachy keen," I tell him, which is a phrase I have never before uttered in my life. "See you out there, Kai."

I'll brew my coffee later, when there's not a six-foot-two brick house blocking my path to the Keurig.

"Hey, Lucy," he says as I head for the hallway.

I turn around to face him, and I can't deny that part of me hopes he'll stride toward me like a bat out of hell and take my hands in his and say, *I'm sorry for saying you have a small life. You have a big, astronomical life, and you were right about everything except the fact that we should forget the kiss. Because I can't, not for a single second.*

But he only smiles at me, cocking his head to one side. "After male bees mate, their testicles explode."

It's not a grand romantic gesture. It's the extension of a peace treaty, a demonstration of his willingness to go back to Lucy and Kai 1.0, the versions of us who traded barbs and horrifying animal facts and didn't confess their darkest secrets or press their lips to each other's skin. He's waving a white flag, and it's up to me to accept it or not.

So I make the only choice I can.

"Ladybugs eat their own young," I say, forcing myself to return his smile with one of my own.

Kai nods, as if to say, *So we're in agreement, then, the kiss never happened*, and I nod back and stride out of the breakroom, clutching my mug so tightly that my fingers hurt.

Because if I'm getting everything I want—one step closer to the promotion and a return to normalcy with Kai—then why does it all feel so wrong?

Chapter Twenty-Four

By Thursday of the following week, Zuri and Keeva are inseparable. Keeva only accepts a bottle through the mesh if her new surrogate mother sits beside her, and when she gets a surge of energy and crawls off to explore her surroundings, Zuri keeps a close eye and grabs her by the ankle if she ventures too far away. Around midday, we restrict public access to the outdoor Gorilla Villa so that Zuri and Keeva can enjoy it in privacy, and my heart almost explodes out of my chest as I watch them nap together on a hammock in the sun.

"Atta girl, Zuri," I whisper, scribbling in my logbook as the older gorilla uses a stick to dig honey out of a manmade anthill. Everything she does—fashioning sticks into tools, gathering hay to assemble a night nest, foraging through the grass for leftover bits of food—is a tutorial in Gorilla 101, and Keeva's a fast learner. Even when Keeva disrupts Zuri's painting time by grabbing the brush and flinging it across the yard, sending blue paint flying, Zuri only grunts at her as if to say *tsk, tsk* before retrieving the brush and making sure to hold it high enough that the infant can't reach.

On Friday, Phil grants me permission to let Tria, her daughter Piper, and Inkesha into Gorilla Villa with the pair, reasoning that giving them access to twenty-six thousand feet of outdoor space might help prevent skirmishes. I'm not too worried about Tria, since I know she'll focus more on Piper than Keeva, but I hold my breath as Inkesha runs into the Villa and makes a beeline for the baby. It's unclear if she's just curious about Keeva or wants to drag her around by her ears, but she doesn't get more than six feet from the infant before Zuri, launching into mama-bear mode, lets out a warning growl and beats her chest with her fists. It's a powerful display of strength, and after she struts back and forth in front of Inkesha a few times, the other female shifts into a crouching position and contents herself with bending a slab of cardboard into various shapes. Zuri lets curious, wide-eyed little Piper sit about three feet from Keeva, but she positions herself between the infant and the toddler to ensure no funny business happens.

It's a hugely successful day, and even though Katie the summer intern breathes down Kai's neck for most of it, peppering him with questions about everything from his favorite *Wild Side* episode (He can't choose! He loves them all!) to his relationship status ("Well, Katie, the show is my one great love"), I don't pay them much attention. After all, Kai's business is his own, and if he wants to date someone who practically has the same name as him and was born so late that she's never seen an episode of *Boy Meets World*, that's his prerogative. I'm definitely not jealous, and it definitely doesn't take me an hour longer than usual to update my spreadsheets because I can't stop imagining them hiking the Matterhorn together, not a strand of hair out of place between them.

"Hey, Lucy," Lottie says, poking her head into my office as I map out a plan for next week, when we'll let the rest of the troop—minus silverback Ozzie—mingle with Zuri, Keeva, and the girls. "You have visitors."

I set my pencil down, confused. I don't get visitors at work. Jack's fiancé appears occasionally to drop off Starbucks for him and say hi to Ozzie, and Phil's kids pop in once a month or so to decorate his office with adorably messy paintings and macaroni art, but nobody stops by for me.

"Who is it?" I ask Lottie. But she's already gone, so I close my logbook with a sigh and make my way out of the office.

As soon as I round the corner toward the indoor gorilla exhibit, where Ozzie, Tomo, Risa, and Mac are taking their afternoon nap, I spot Mia waiting by the glass with three Pyrex containers in her arms.

"Lucy!" she says, hopping with excitement. She's sporting the hat Kai signed for her, and it bobs up and down on her head as she moves.

"Hey, Mia. What are you doing here?"

She grins. "Mom had the day off, so we decided to come to the zoo. And I brought you a surprise." She hoists the Pyrex into my arms, and I'm pretty sure they weigh more than Keeva. "It's fairy bread. A whole week's supply!"

"Oh. Wow," I say, my arms almost buckling under the weight. All those early-morning harmonica rehearsals must be giving my half sister some serious upper arm strength.

The hopeful optimism that crosses Mia's face as she waits for my reaction softens my heart, and I remind myself it's not her fault she gets a camping-themed birthday and I got a lifetime supply of crippling insecurity. "This is awesome," I say, trying on a smile so wide, it makes my cheeks hurt. "How'd you know I had a craving?"

"Mom!" Mia calls. "Mom, she loves it!"

I glance behind her to see Karina, dressed in a blue jersey wrap top and rouge trousers she probably got at Ann Taylor and carrying what I can only assume is a Tupperware container of more fairy bread. I suck in my breath, forcing myself to think of three horrific animal facts to stay calm. The zoo is my Karina-free zone, the one place in the world where I can go about my days without her asking me to meet for coffee or ice cream or a seaweed-wrap mani-pedi. Where there's not a walking, talking, Girl-Scout-vest-wearing reminder that she's perfectly capable of being a responsible mom; she just didn't care enough to be one for me.

"Luce, hi!" Karina says, waving, and I scramble for more facts before my brain launches into panic mode. *Female dragonflies fake their own deaths to ward off unwanted sexual advances. Nine-banded armadillos carry leprosy.* I'm tempted to make like a dragonfly and fake my own death as Karina catches up to Mia.

"I hope you don't mind us stopping by," my mother says, giving me a bashful smile. "We planned to leave your food with the security guard, but he let us in the back gate. We haven't seen you at Nona's in weeks, so we figured you must be incredibly busy."

"Super busy," I agree. I've also been taking special care to avoid them, but I keep that to myself.

"Mia thought you'd like some fairy bread, and I baked sugar cookies," Karina continues. "I know you always liked those."

When I lived with her in LA, when a guilty pleasure was just the occasional dessert we ate for dinner and not a primetime show, I thought my mother baked the tastiest sugar cookies in the world. She could never get the timing right, so we always ended up with black-bottomed cookies that tasted faintly of ash, but Karina only made them when she was in a good mood. She'd put on an Amy Grant CD and dance around the kitchen, and I'd crack the eggs and try not to spill flour everywhere. I still can't appreciate a sugar cookie unless it's burnt on the bottom.

"I left them in the oven a little too long," she says, scrunching her nose as she hands me the Tupperware.

"Oh. Um, thanks. Thank you." There's so much I want to say to her—*A batch of cookies doesn't make up for ditching me; I can't bring myself to attend Mia's birthday party; do you remember how we used to watch* Who Wants to Be a Millionaire? *and eat Pop-Tarts in our pajamas?*—but they're the mopey, self-pitying thoughts of my inner child, and I shove them back down where they belong.

"I better get back to work," I say. "Thanks for the fairy bread, Mia."

"Oh," Karina says. "Well, we were going to grab lunch at the Congo River food court, and we thought maybe—"

Jack's voice crackles over the walkie-talkie, asking someone to please bring a squeegee to the colobus monkey exhibit, stat. Even though it's a message meant for an intern, I tap my radio like I have to respond.

"Sorry, gotta take care of that. But thanks again."

I hurry back to my office, refusing to feel guilty about Mia and Karina's matching crestfallen looks. They clearly hoped this would turn into a special mother-daughter hangout, but I don't have time to skip off for a long lunch. And even if I did, I'd rather eat dirt. I drop the containers of food on my desk and head to check on Keeva and Zuri. But when I step into the hallway, Karina's voice floats toward me from around the corner.

". . . big fan of your work," she's saying, and I wonder if she and Mia ran into Ellie the Elephant, the zoo's ambassador mascot. I spent a summer during high school making minimum wage to wander around the zoo in the heavy fur suit, and I passed out twice during a particularly scorching week in July.

"That's so kind. Thank you," Kai says back to her, and my heart sinks all the way down to my toes.

Great. Now Kai and Karina can bond over their shared success and mutual respect for Diane Lane's glossy hair. Fire burns in my belly, and I wish Karina had never set foot in Ape House.

"I'm actually in the business, too," my mother continues, like she and Kai have anything in common. Like her soapy, melodramatic series ever had a shot in hell of winning a Peabody. Kai might drive me insane with his over-the-top on-screen energy and refusal to stop saying "Wowza!"—but at least *Wild Side* teaches people something about the world around them. "Or I was, anyway. I played Kitty Conway on *Guilty Pleasures.*"

Her tone is eager, almost desperate, like a high school QB who won't shut up about his championship passing stats thirty years after the fact, and despite my best efforts, I feel a pang of something like pity for her. But it evaporates when I realize what's coming next: Kai, seizing a once-in-a-lifetime opportunity, is going to feed right into her need for attention. He's going to score one for Aunt Susan by asking who the Malibu Fish Hook Killer was, and he's going to make Karina feel less like a washed-up star in the process. He won't mean to, but it'll feel like a betrayal anyway, and I turn on my heel to head back to my office.

Because I can't bear to listen.

But his answer stops me in my tracks.

"I'm sorry, I've never heard of that," Kai says, his tone full of confusion. Like he has no idea what the hell she's talking about. "*Guilty Pressures*, was it?"

I'm huddled just around the corner, so I can't see Karina's face, but I imagine a pink blush creeping over her cheeks. This never happens to her. As soon as she mentions her show, people's eyes light up like she was on *Seinfeld*.

"*Pleasures*," Karina says, her voice a tiny bit louder than necessary. "*Guilty Pleasures*."

"No, I'm sorry, I must have missed that one." Kai's voice floats around the corner. "Wait, was it the sitcom about the skinny mum who was always dieting and arguing with her bumbling husband? Did it have a canned laugh track?"

I cover my mouth to prevent a gasp from escaping. There's nothing Karina hates more than laugh tracks, except maybe varicose veins, and she'd probably rather be asked if *Guilty Pleasures* was a porno.

"No," she says, quieter this time. "It was a drama about PIs in Malibu. Maybe you're familiar with the theme song?" She hums a few bars, and Kai must shake his head, because she stops suddenly. "Well, maybe you've heard of the Malibu Fish Hook Killer? The show was canceled before we could reveal the murderer, but turns out—"

"No, I'm sorry," Kai says, cutting her off before she can reveal the answer to the question he's spent decades asking. "We didn't get cable on Mount Karisimbi, and to be honest, I was more into cartoons anyway."

"Right. Of course. Mia, time to go, sweetheart!" Karina calls, evidently embarrassed enough to haul her spinning-toned ass out of Ape House. "Great to meet you, Kai."

"And you as well, Katrina," his voice booms back to her. "I'll keep my eyes peeled for *Guilty Pressures* next time I'm browsing Netflix."

I hot trot it back to my office, my heart pounding. I'm so shocked by Kai's display of loyalty that my knees tremble, something that hasn't happened since he took my face in his hands and kissed me. He had no reason to pretend he wasn't a *Guilty Pleasures* fan, other than to deny Karina the satisfaction. He tanked his chances of ever solving the Malibu murders, and he did it for me, without even knowing I was there to witness it.

I just can't figure out why. He owes me nothing, especially after my blowup in the nursery. *You were wrong, you know,* he told me that first day after the Critter Chat, when he wore the hardened scowl of a man who just stepped on a Lego. I wasn't wrong about Dr. Kimber's nickname, but maybe I was for how harshly I judged Kai. For assuming he was just another condescending asshole. For thinking I could kiss him and somehow forget about it, or for deeming him incapable of having my back. Maybe I was wrong for wanting to act like the kiss never happened; not for wanting to put work above a hookup, but for denying the possibility that Kai was worth the risk.

Before I know it, I've polished off a half dozen of Karina's lightly burnt sugar cookies, but I'm still not satiated. Because as much as I want to deny it, a hunger gnaws at my core, and it's got nothing to do with baked goods and everything to do with the hazel eyes and rock-solid biceps of the one and only Kai Bridges.

Chapter Twenty-Five

I've made up my mind to tell Sam and Elle about Kai and me. Not that there *is* a Kai and me—my post-kiss freakout made certain of that—but if I don't share some of the confusion robbing me of my ability to focus exclusively on work, my head might pop off my body. So after work, I rush home to shower, blow-dry my hair, and change into something other than a furry vest and khakis. I settle on a mint button-front sundress that Nona bought for me at her favorite boutique in German Village. It's not as eye-catching as one of Elle's bold rompers or Sam's sleek jumpsuits, but it's better than my usual look, and it's cute enough that I won't stick out like a sore thumb from Freya and my friends.

Café Istanbul is only a few miles from Nona's, and as I cruise down Riverside Drive, I try to formulate a SparkNotes version of events to rattle off to my friends the instant Freya disappears to the bathroom. *I thought I hated Kai,* I'll say. *But then I saw him holding a baby gorilla, and how could I stop myself from smashing my face against his? Have you SEEN that man when he smiles? And have you seen that baby gorilla? No fair, right?*

As I enter the restaurant, an open, airy space decorated with thick Turkish rugs and a wrought iron chandelier, I get a text from Sam: Freya and I are running late. Bad accident on 270. Can whoever gets there first grab our table? Reservation's under my name.

"Hi, reservation's for Samira Rahimi," I tell the hostess. She marches me past rows of tables decorated with white cloths and single roses and leads me outside. The patio features granite tables guarded from the sun by red umbrellas, and lights strung overhead add a touch of charm.

"Here you are, ma'am," the hostess says as she guides me to a table overlooking the Scioto River.

But before I can thank her, the words get stuck in my throat. Because there's a *man* at my table. And that man is Kai Bridges.

"I'm sorry," I tell the ponytailed hostess, "but there must be some confusion. The table I'm looking for is reserved under Sam Rahimi."

"What a coincidence," Kai says, tapping his menu like it's a drum. "Because *this* table is reserved under Sam Rahimi."

"What are you doing at Sam's table?" I ask.

"I'm stealing it, Lucy," he says dryly. "What do you think I'm doing? I'm waiting for Freya and Sam, just like you."

"Oh," I say as the information registers with me. It makes sense that just like Sam wants Elle and me to get to know Freya, Freya wants Kai to get to know Sam. "Right."

The hostess deposits my menu on the table and shakes her head at me as she walks away, probably wondering how anyone could be dumb enough to look such a crazy-hot gift horse in his very chiseled face.

"You know," Kai says as I glance at the river and wonder if I can throw myself over the railing and swim home. "You have a lot of excellent qualities, but an ease with manners isn't one of them."

I try not to blush. I *do* have a lot of excellent qualities, including—or so I thought—the ability to keep my wits about me even though Kai looks like a tall glass of water in a seafoam green button-down that makes his eyes pop. He must notice my lingering gaze, because he smirks and rolls his sleeves up to his forearms before opening the top button to reveal a hint of chest hair.

"Sure is warm out," he says, his eyes on mine as he adjusts his collar. "Don't you think?"

"Um, yeah. Sure. Warm." I stare at the pink geraniums stuffed into a pot on the railing, scrambling to get my brain and my mouth on the same page long enough to say something else, even if it's as dumb as *It's not the heat, it's the humidity.*

"It's not the heat," I say finally, hating how flustered I sound. "It's the humidity."

Kai grins, and it's like looking at a glorious sunrise on the savanna. At least I assume it is, because I've never been anywhere close to the savanna. "So it is. Care to sit down?"

I realize I'm still standing beside the table like I'm waiting to take his order, and I slide into the chair across from him with such haste that my butt almost misses the cushion.

"Of course," I say as if it were my idea. "I love sitting down."

Kai browses the menu while I contemplate hiding in the bathroom to stop myself from saying anything else as asinine as *I love sitting down.* My phone vibrates with a text message from Elle: Nadeem and I are stuck in the same traffic. Must be a bad accident. Hope no one was injured:(

I also hope no one was injured, but not as fervently as I hope the traffic clears soon so I'm not forced to sit here alone with Kai. When the waiter comes to check on us, Kai orders an old-fashioned while I stick with water and Diet Coke. I want a glass of wine like nobody's business, but between Kai's bulging forearms and the knowing smirk that crosses his face whenever he catches my gaze drifting toward his collarbone, I need to keep a sober head. But as I peruse the menu, staring at the same appetizer list for three minutes because my brain has decided to stop working, I swear I notice him sneak a peek at the trace amount of cleavage I'm showing. I guess Nona was onto something when she bought this dress after all.

How far away are you? I text my friends. Can you abandon your cars and walk? I worry that the longer I'm forced to sit here and try not to stare at Kai's broad chest, the harder it will be to forget how his tongue felt in my mouth. Because there's not enough sigara borek on the planet to distract me from that.

"Traffic jam on the interstate," I tell Kai, waving my phone at him. "Everybody's running behind."

He nods but doesn't say anything, and I scour my brain for inane, G-rated discussion topics that will distract me from the forearm vein that pulses every time he moves his hand.

"So," I say, sipping my water. "Marionettes: yay or nay?"

Kai looks at me like one of my eyeballs fell out of its socket and landed on the table. Then he rests his elbows on the table in a way that Miss Manners would not approve of and leans toward me. "I met your mother today."

I'd much rather have a heated debate about the puppets—Kai could argue the pro position while I take the con and deliver an impassioned monologue about the terrifying glassiness of their eyes—than let the conversation shift toward anything personal. But I'm still taken aback by the way he coolly pretended like he'd never heard of Kitty Conway, and I can't help the confession that spills out of my mouth.

"I overheard you," I admit. "Accidentally."

Kai raises an eyebrow. "Aha. And did you just happen to be hiding behind a large potted plant again?"

"No," I say, blushing. "I was hiding in the hallway to avoid Karina." The waiter drops off an order of calamari, and I wait for him to leave before I ask the question that's plagued me all day. "Why did you pretend like you'd never heard of *Guilty Pleasures*? She would have told you who the Malibu Fish Hook Killer was. She was practically dying to."

He shrugs. "It didn't seem worth it. I'm still Team Lucy, you know. Even if the kiss that totally happened never happened." He raises his drink to his mouth while my lips tingle at the memory. "Besides, I'm convinced it was Detective Wiles. Any other answer would have left me disappointed."

I can't stop the little bubble of happiness that floats around in my stomach, and I steal a piece of his calamari without asking permission. "Well, I appreciate it."

Kai scoops half the calamari onto a side plate and slides it toward me. "I have a question for you, but you don't have to answer if you don't want to."

I freeze mid reach for the plate. Even though it goes against everything I've been telling myself for the past two weeks, part of me hopes his question has nothing to do with *Guilty Pleasures* or Keeva and Zuri. Part of me hopes he'll ask me to reconsider my stance on the whole kissing situation, and I'm not sure if I trust myself to decline.

Maybe I should fake appendicitis.

"Shoot," I say, grabbing a piece of calamari and chewing so quickly I barely taste it.

"I know this is a tough subject for you," Kai says, causing a wave of forbidden excitement to wash over me, "but I wanted to talk about the camera situation."

The wave crashes, and I wish I weren't so disappointed. "The camera situation?"

"I've been thinking about what you told me about Karina, and I've been wondering: Is the tension between you two the reason you hate being on camera? Like, because cameras were her thing, you have an automatic panic response when one's pointed at you?"

I'd rather lead a day camp class of unruly five-year-olds than discuss my phobia, but it's a safer conversation topic than anything kissing related, so I force myself to answer.

"I . . . it's more complicated than that."

Kai stays silent, waiting for me to say more, and he shakes his head when I don't. "Okay, that's a serious nonanswer."

I want to tell him to drop it, that talking about my stage fright is about as comfortable for me as talking about Taji's tragedy is for him. But I don't, because the way Kai's looking at me—like I really could ramble for twenty minutes about creepy puppets and he wouldn't judge me for it—makes me think it might be okay to be vulnerable. After all, he didn't judge me for admitting that I'm jealous of Mia, and besides, Kai's the reason I haven't passed out on camera since shooting started. He set aside time to help me practice and told Phil it was all my idea, so if anyone deserves an explanation, it's him.

"My stage fright started when I was little," I say. "My mom was young when she had me, with dreams of making it big, and she wasn't about to let a pregnancy and a deadbeat boyfriend get in the way. We moved to LA when I was three, and she had a whole plan for the two of us to eventually become a mother-daughter dream team, like Goldie Hawn and Kate Hudson."

Kai frowns. "That's a pretty big assignment for a toddler."

I nod and nudge a piece of calamari around my plate with a fork. "I think she expected me to be just like her. A mini-me. But I wasn't even close. She looked like a bigger-boobed Charlize Theron, and by the time I was seven, I looked like Helga Pataki from *Hey Arnold!* She wanted to win an Oscar and marry Richard Gere, and I wanted to live in a cabin and marry the brothers from *Zoboomafoo.* Karina just didn't know what to make of me. And even though I tried to be like her because I knew it would make her happy, I was hopeless."

I sip my water and try to stop the long-buried hurt from making my voice crack. "I bombed the singing lessons she signed me up for. And when she made me audition for a children's production of *Annie,* the only part I landed was Sandy's third understudy."

Kai does a double take. "Wasn't Sandy Annie's dog?"

"Yes," I say, cringing. "It was awful. *I* was awful. My mom just didn't get me, and as hard as I tried to learn baton and crimp my hair and follow in her footsteps, I couldn't do it. I failed miserably, and my anxiety about it got worse and worse. By second grade, I was so afraid of public speaking that I faked a stomachache to get out of show-and-tell. And in third grade, when I dropped out of a dance recital last-minute because I couldn't stop hyperventilating backstage, she pretty much gave up on me."

"What do you mean, gave up on you?" Kai asks. He reaches forward slightly, as if he's going to grab my hand, but stops and fidgets with his water glass instead.

I remember the look on Karina's face as I followed her to the car after the disastrous recital, her mouth a thin line as her eyes flashed with anger. *What a disappointment,* she said, gripping the steering wheel so tightly that her knuckles paled. And while she could have been talking about the botched performance, I knew she meant me.

That I, Lucy Rourke, with my frizzy hair and total lack of courage, made her ashamed to be my mom.

"I mean she quit dragging me to voice lessons and kids' acting classes. And when she started getting more work—a McDonald's commercial, a brief stint on *General Hospital*, and then *Guilty Pleasures*—she didn't have time for me anymore. The summer after *Guilty Pleasures* premiered, she flew me to Ohio to stay with Nona and said she'd be back for me in a week."

I glance out over the river, where a family of ducks waddles along the shore. "A week turned into two, and that became a month, and then she missed my birthday. After that, it was like she wasn't even my mom anymore."

I cough, trying to conceal the emotion in my voice. I shouldn't be spilling this to Kai, because sharing these broken pieces of my heart with him makes me want to share more than just my feelings. But maybe I've spent so much time hiding, whether behind potted palm trees or buried in my work at Ape House, that I've forgotten how to show anyone the real Lucy.

And maybe it's time to try.

"The reason I hate the cameras so much is that I'm afraid," I continue, forcing the words out. "I'm afraid that my mom was right to call me a disappointment. I'm afraid Nick was right when he said there was something fundamentally wrong with me for refusing to compromise on kids. I'm terrified the camera will capture the truth and broadcast it for the whole world to see: That I'm not good enough. That I never will be."

The threat of tears stings my eyes, and as I blink them back, Kai sets down his glass and reaches across the table to wrap my hand in his.

"You are enough, Lucy. You're a force of nature. *That's* what the world will see—a passionate, brilliant zookeeper who's changing the world one baby gorilla at a time." He squeezes my hand, and his touch is so comforting that I can't help but squeeze back.

"I believe that with every fiber of my being," Kai promises. "But you need to believe it, too."

Nodding, I dab my eyes with my napkin. Kai's delivery is so impassioned, so unquestioning, that it soothes the ache that took root in my chest the instant he mentioned the cameras. "I'll keep working on it."

"I think you're brave," he says. "And for what it's worth, Helga Pataki is an icon."

I can't help but laugh, and suddenly the weight that's crushed me all these years—the weight of letting Karina down and comparing myself to others, then coming up short—feels a little bit lighter. I can't remember the last time someone called me brave, if ever, and hearing those words from Kai helps me see myself in a new light.

"Maybe that's why I love reality TV so much," I say. "Because it's ridiculous and sometimes trashy, but the people on those shows don't let cameras stop them from doing anything. In a way, they're fearless."

Kai grins. "I've seen a few episodes of *Teen Mom 2*. I'm not sure being fearless is always a good thing."

I smile back at him, but the mention of fearlessness makes me think of the phone call I overheard at the tiki bar. *I don't want to do it anymore*, Kai said. *So we let the chips fall where they may . . . I want things to be different.* I know my struggle with self-worth holds me back from feeling comfortable on camera, but what's holding Kai back from not doing whatever the "it" he doesn't want to do anymore is? What's stopping the man in front of me—the guy who camped in the Arctic and got breathtakingly close to a green anaconda in the Amazon—from doing whatever the hell he pleases?

"My turn to ask a question?" I say. Kai's hand is still wrapped around mine, and I know the responsible thing to do would be to pull away, but I can't bring myself to do it. "That day at Huli Huli, when I heard you on the phone. What was that about?"

Kai blanches, and I worry I've gone too far. Maybe admitting my insecurities doesn't entitle me to his private information. But he sips his drink and nods.

"I was on the phone with my mother," he says. "In September, NBC is airing a special to raise money for the Charlotte Kimber Research Center. It's the twentieth anniversary of *Majesty on the Mountain*. Diane Lane's going to be there, and my mum, of course, and everyone expects me to make an appearance, too."

I imagine what it must be like to have Dr. Charlotte Kimber's number in your phone. For me, it's the equivalent of having the ghost of Ruth Bader Ginsburg on speed dial.

"And you don't want to?" I ask.

Kai shakes his head. "It's not that I don't care about supporting the research center. I do. It's that the instant that damn movie came out, my name became synonymous with Taji's death. It still is, but I've worked hard to build an identity outside of my past. But the second I sit down with my mother and Lester Holt or whoever wants an interview, I'll be right back in that position again."

"Can't you just say no?" I wonder.

He shakes his head, and a rueful smile crosses his face. "You'd think so, but Charlotte Kimber is a difficult person to say no to. Plus, I feel like I owe it to Taji, you know? Like if I don't do it, I'm dishonoring his memory. And I don't think I could live with that."

He blinks, and his shoulders sag in a way that reminds me of the fleeting moment of exhaustion I thought I witnessed at Picnic for Paws, just as the cover band singer called Kai to the stage. I try to imagine how much energy it must take, how much sheer force of will, to strut around in a safari hat like his life is easy breezy lemon squeezy. Like he's not shouldering years' worth of guilt that weighs roughly as much as a silverback gorilla.

"Hi," a forty-something mustached guy says, startling me when he pops up beside our table. "I'm sorry to bother you, but you're Kai Bridges, right? From *On the Wild Side*? My wife and daughter are huge fans, and I was hoping we could trouble you for a picture."

Quick as lightning, the weariness on Kai's face disappears, replaced by an effortless smile. "Of course," he says. "I'd be happy to."

The man waves his family over, and his raven-haired wife and daughter cluster around Kai like they can't believe their good fortune as I snap a picture.

"Thank you so much," the mom says, shaking Kai's hand for the fifth time as the little girl prattles on about Penny the puppy.

My phone buzzes with a text from Sam: Traffic's not moving. I don't think we're going to make it to dinner. I'm so sorry, Lucy! Twenty seconds later, Elle echoes her sentiments.

"So," Kai says, glancing at his menu once the family returns to their table. "What sounds good to you?"

From the corner of my eye, I spot an older couple across the patio glancing toward Kai and whispering to each other, and I know it's only a matter of time until a line snakes around the table to meet him like he's a mall Santa the day after Thanksgiving. And even though I know it's a bad idea, that I'm going against everything I told Kai in the nursery and letting Bad Lucy out to play again, I want to get out of here. I want to be somewhere with Kai where I don't have to share him, where he can let himself look as exhausted as he feels without putting on a happy smile for his admirers.

Someplace where Kai can just be Kai, and I can just be Lucy, and the cameras and his Taji guilt and my insecurities don't exist, at least for a while.

"Actually," I say, knowing I might regret this later, "I have an idea."

Chapter Twenty-Six

Kai is right: his room at the Marriott is no penthouse. But it does have a balcony that overlooks the Scioto River, and after we open Styrofoam containers of the five dishes we ordered to go from Café Istanbul, it smells of sizzled meat and feta cheese.

"This was a great idea," Kai says, his knee touching mine as we sit cross-legged on his king bed, our food spread out in front of us. "You're a genius. A *brave* genius."

His repeated use of the compliment thrills me, and I don't move my leg away. I know that parking my butt on Kai's bed is like playing with fire, but I tell myself that it's only because there's no place else to sit where we can both see the TV.

"Okay, so," I say, pointing Kai's Fire TV Stick remote at the screen, "prepare to be addicted. We'll start with season three so you can meet Mark and Nikki."

I scoop up a forkful of moussaka as the *90 Day Fiancé* opening credits roll, and Kai bumps me with his elbow and rolls his eyes.

"Why don't we just watch paint dry, or something else equally stimulating?" he asks. "It's been ten seconds, and I can feel my brain rotting."

"Hush." I grab a grape leaf and nod toward the screen. "Just wait."

Sure enough, by the time he's eaten his way through two steak kebabs, Kai's mesmerized. "But she's nineteen," he marvels, reaching for a bite of spinach pide. "And he's *fifty-eight*."

"I know. You can't look away. Just wait until she rearranges his bookshelf and he acts like she set the house on fire."

We eat in companionable silence, munching on kebabs and french fries as Mark tries to make his twenty-year-old daughter give poor Nikki her old hand-me-downs. By the third episode, Kai deposits the empty containers on a desk near the window and bumps my leg with his as he returns to the bed. It's after nine, so the waning sunlight streaming through the window gives the room a twilight glow, and even though I should gather my purse and leave, I don't.

Because I don't want to.

"Thank you, Lucy," Kai says, running a hand through his hair. "I needed this."

"Obviously—*90 Day Fiancé* is an essential part of the reality TV canon. And just wait for Chantel and Pedro in season four."

He laughs. "No, I mean, I can see why you're into the show, but thank you for just hanging out with me. It's not very often that I get to switch off my 'Wowza!' mode and relax."

"What do you mean?"

He sighs. "When I first got the idea for a wildlife show, I didn't even want to be on camera. I wanted to stay behind the scenes, like David Attenborough. But I was good on camera, you know? And the more over-the-top I went, the more times per episode I shouted 'Wowza!' like a goofball, the more people liked it. And before you know it, I had a whole crew relying on me for their incomes, and a catchphrase that people love shouting at me at airports."

"I'll admit, it does roll nicely off the tongue."

"Sometimes I wish I could make something less flashy, you know? Like a nice, quiet documentary about the gorillas of Rwanda where I don't appear on-screen or scream at anybody to stay wild. Something a bit more serious. Less schtick-y. Something a little more me."

I remember his words on the phone: *I want things to be different*. I guess no one's immune to feeling like their life is small, not even Kai.

"So why don't you?" I ask.

He shakes his head. "Trust me, I'd love to pass the reins to Freya for a season while I go shoot in the jungle. But I have to think about our sponsors and what Animal Planet wants. I have to think about what makes money."

I nudge his foot with mine. "Well, what about what you want?"

He smirks, but there's no malice in it, only wistfulness. "I let go of what I wanted a long time ago."

Despite my best intentions, I can't stop my hand from wandering across the bed to touch his. "Well, maybe it's time to get it back."

He leans toward me, the wistful look on his face shifting to something more like longing. "What if there's something else I want? Something I'm not supposed to. Something I shouldn't." His tone is husky, gruff, and whatever hope I had of triumphing over Bad Lucy disappears when he lets go of my hand and snakes his behind my head, caressing my ear with his thumb. "What should I do then?"

A wave of desire crashes over me, and I reach up to place my hand over his. My heart pounds, the rhythm wild and frantic, and I grab his other hand and place it against my chest so he can feel it. "That depends. What is it that you want?"

"You, Lucy," he whispers. "I want you."

I know that if I respond the way I want to, there will be no going back. There will be no returning to Lucy and Kai 1.0, no unrolling the die I've cast. But I don't care. Because he knows me, at least as well as I've let anyone know me, and I want to know him, too. And because I've got plenty of nerve after all.

"I want you, too," I say, and when he lifts his hand from my chest and runs it along my cheek, sliding his fingers all the way down to the ends of my hair, the part of me that ever thought he was an asshole melts into nothingness.

"I've never seen your hair down before," he says, twirling a lock between his fingers like it's pure gold. "It's beautiful. So soft."

I edge closer to him on the bed and do what I've been wanting to since I sat next to him in Phil's office. I rake a hand through his hair, and he leans forward to press his lips to my collarbone. We sit like that for a moment, his hair thick between my fingers and his breath hot against my neck. When he rights himself, his hair mussed from my touch, there's a question in his glinting hazel eyes.

"Lucy," he says. "I thought we were going to pretend the kiss didn't happen."

I arch my body toward his, every inch of my skin aching for his touch. "I tried," I whisper, nuzzling my face into his neck. "But I can't."

It's the final bit of encouragement he needs, and he groans and gently grips my hair, tilting my head back to press his lips to mine. His kiss is a slow burn at first, his tongue patient and yielding, until I let out a soft moan and lean forward to wrap my arms around his neck. Then his patience disappears, and the feel of his mouth against mine is needy, wanting. Aching. We stay like that for a few minutes, his hands strong on my back as our mouths meet, part, and meet again, until the work of staying upright is too much and Kai shifts me onto my back, his broad chest looming over me as I wrap a leg around his waist.

As his mouth finds his way back to mine, my insistent fingers wrestle with his shirt, and Kai laughs at the disgruntled noise I make when the buttons don't yield to me immediately.

"Let me help," he whispers against my neck, and he pushes himself off the bed and smiles, almost bashful, as he works one button at a time. When he finally takes the shirt off and drops it to the floor, he leans over me, his strong arms boxing me in, and the sight of his flexed biceps and broad chest and easy smile above me is the hottest thing I've ever witnessed. It's better than Aragorn flinging open the doors in slow motion after the Battle of Helm's Deep in *The Two Towers*. It's sexier than a locked-up Leonardo DiCaprio doing shirtless triceps dips in *The Departed*. It's more erotic than Darcy's infamous hand flex after his fingers grazed Elizabeth's in the 2005 version of *Pride & Prejudice*.

It's incredible.

"No fair," I say, placing my hand on Kai's chest. "Are you sure you're human?"

He rocks his hips against me, as if to demonstrate how very human he is, and I shut the hell up and go back to kissing him with everything I have. He reaches one hand under my skirt and caresses my thigh while the other cups my breast, and there's nothing I want more than to rip off my dress.

"Wait," I say suddenly, scooting out from under him.

Kai retracts his hand from my skirt immediately, and his forehead wrinkles in concern. "Too fast? We can slow down, Lucy, or stop altogether."

I look at him like he suggested we rob a bank naked. "Are you crazy? I don't want to stop. I just want to close the curtains." The sun has set, but I want to ensure our privacy, and I cross the room in a few quick strides and tug the curtains closed. Before I can even turn away from the window, Kai's arms snake around my waist, and I laugh as he moves my hair aside to kiss the back of my neck. "You weren't supposed to follow me over here."

His words are warm against my ear. "I'm not supposed to do a lot of things."

When I turn around, reaching for Kai in the darkness, he wraps his arms around my hips and scoops me off the ground, and I close my legs around his waist as he carries me toward the bed, his forehead pressed to mine the whole time. He sets me down to stand at the foot of the bed and sits before me. I run my hands through his hair as he kisses the hollow between my breasts and gives my ass a gentle squeeze. I reach for the bottom of my dress, but he gets there first, and he stands as he tugs it over my head and tosses it aside. Then he picks me up again, this time lowering me onto the bed so slowly that it feels like it's happening in slow motion.

When Kai settles over me, I buck my hips against him, and he lets out a soft moan but gently pushes me back down to the bed, bending forward to leave a trail of kisses from my mouth to my clavicle. When he goes lower, kissing the exposed skin at the top of my breasts, I try to wiggle out of my bra, but he reaches behind me and does the work for me. I smile when it takes him three attempts to unhook it, but once it's gone, he cups a breast in one hand and lowers his mouth to the other, kissing and licking the nipple as I writhe my hips against him. Kai keeps one hand on my chest as his mouth works its way past my belly button and down to the band of my underwear. He kisses the lowest part of my stomach and then lifts his mouth to mine again, and his hand abandons my breast as he uses it to cup the space between my legs. I let out a soft groan and grind against his hand, and he massages my clit through my underwear as his tongue curls around my own.

"Lucy," he whispers, tearing his mouth away from mine, "tell me what you like. Tell me what feels good."

I'm usually shy about stating my preferences, at least at first, but something about the way Kai says it—like we're a team in this, like making each other feel good is the only thing in the world that matters—puts me at ease.

"Touch me," I whisper against his cheek, and he tugs my underwear low enough that I can kick it off. Then, his mouth enveloping mine in a kiss that's the opposite of a slow burn—it's urgent, desperate, like he could never get enough—he reaches between my legs, exploring the now-uncovered territory. It's delicious, the feel of his body against mine as he rubs my clit, and it's not long before I can sense my orgasm on the horizon. But as if he can sense it, too, Kai stops and scoots me lower down the bed until my legs hang over the end of it before gently guiding my knees apart. I let out a frustrated moan at the sight of him standing between my legs, and I reach up to grab for his belt buckle.

"Do you have a condom?" I ask, breathless.

He smiles. "Yes, but I don't think it's time for that yet. Do you?" Not giving me time to answer, he bends down to the ground and slides a finger inside me as he kisses the inside of my thighs.

"Lucy," he says, "let me taste how sweet you are. Please."

I want to laugh at how positively polite he is when requesting to do something that's anything but, but I only let out an enthusiastic moan.

Kai kneels on the carpet before the bed, gripping the backs of my thighs. When he lowers his head to the ache between my legs, everything ceases to exist except the flick of his tongue against me.

He takes his time, increasing the pressure and speed of his movements and then slowing them down, as if he's savoring every single second of my pleasure.

"Kai," I say after a few minutes, almost breathless. "I'm close."

Like a man on a mission, he slides a finger into me and licks my clit with even more vigor, and it's only a matter of seconds until the pressure swells and climbs until it combusts, and an explosion of heat and satisfaction have me crying out in pleasure.

"Hey," Kai says when I've finished, crawling back onto the bed to kneel over me. "Come here." He lifts my chin toward his and kisses me again, and I reach forward blindly to unbuckle his belt.

"Are you sure?" he asks as I fumble with the buckle and finally manage to open it.

I raise an eyebrow at him and run a hand over the bulge in his pants, and he lets out a little moan as it grows harder. "I'm sure," I whisper, cupping his cock through the denim. He stands up to kick them off, revealing a snug pair of gray boxers underneath, and he pads across the room to fish something out of his wallet.

When he returns to the bedside, he goes to open the condom, but I crawl to the end of the bed and snatch it away, depositing it next to me. "I don't think it's time for that yet," I say with a grin, reaching out to stroke him through his boxers. "Do you?"

I tug his boxers down until his cock is unsheathed, and as Kai stands naked before me, I take a second to marvel at how beautiful he is—the broadness of his chest, the sculpted-but-not-to-the-point-of-being-intimidating abdomen, the smooth cock that begs for my touch. When I lower myself toward him and take him in my mouth, he grunts in response and reaches out to run his hands through my hair. He moans before I've even started to move, and when I slide my curled fist and my mouth up and down his cock in unison, Kai lets out a guttural noise that tells me it won't take long for him to finish this way.

Maybe he wasn't lying in the nursery; maybe it *has* been a while. Before long, he gently pulls himself out.

"Lucy," he whispers. "That was so good, that was . . ."

I kiss him before he can say anything else, because I want him inside me, and I want him inside me *now*. Sensing my urgency, Kai reaches to unwrap the condom and slide it over his cock, and then he lowers himself onto his elbows over me.

"Lucy, are you—"

"I'm sure," I tell him, grazing his chest with my fingers. "I want you."

He leans forward to kiss me, and I open my legs to give him unhindered access. Kai reaches down to guide his cock inside me with a groan of pleasure, and he keeps himself there for a moment, just kissing me and tracing my breast with his fingers, and then he starts to move. Somehow it's an even more delicious feeling than the pressure of his fingers and mouth against my clit, because it's him, it's *Kai*, and he's *inside* me, and we're moving together, taking each other to a place we've never been before.

Kai slows his pace, trying not to get ahead of himself, but I buck against him to encourage him to go at whatever pace he wants.

"Lucy," he says as a moan escapes my lips. "*Lucy.*"

I know he's checking to see if I want him to hold back, to last longer, but all I want is to earn his release. To feel what it's like for Kai to lose all control, when the swagger and smugness and ridiculously well-fitted jeans are stripped away and all that's left is him. The real him.

"Come," I tell him, reveling in the fire in his gaze as we lock eyes.

"Lucy," he says again, and I keep one arm wrapped around his neck and use the other to squeeze his ass as he rides me, thrusting faster and faster until he lets out an earth-shattering, guttural cry and presses his tongue into my mouth, getting as much of his body inside mine as he can.

We stay like that for a long moment, his forehead resting against mine, and after he eases off me and gets up to dispose of the condom, he crawls onto the bed and takes me into his arms, planting kisses on my jawline.

"Well, I was right about one thing," he says when he's caught his breath, stroking my hair with his hand. "You are a goddamn force of nature."

Chapter Twenty-Seven

I stay the night. I didn't plan on it, but when Kai asks me to, I agree, and we stay up until four in the morning watching ill-conceived relationships crash and burn on *90 Day Fiancé* and trading random life stories. I tell Kai about my first kiss—I was thirteen, and it was during a game of Seven Minutes in Heaven at summer camp with Timmy Falcone, who smelled like pencil eraser and refused to wear anything besides a Cleveland Browns jersey. He tells me the real reason he broke up with his last girlfriend, a human-rights lawyer named Antonia: not because of her inability to pronounce *wolf*, but because he suspected she was dating him only to meet Amal Clooney.

"I've never even met *George* Clooney," he says, scratching his chin. "The closest I've come is watching *One Fine Day* a bunch of times with my aunt Susan."

He tells me about Susan, too; how his mother's sister, with whom he spent all those summers in Montana, gave him the closest thing to a slice of "normal" childhood he ever experienced. How he rotated time between Mount Karisimbi with his mom and London, New York, and Sydney with his dad and felt like he belonged everywhere and nowhere all at once. I tell him how guilty I feel sometimes about keeping Mia at arm's length, and how badly I wish I could forget the hurt Karina caused me. We talk and laugh and trade more depraved animal facts, and the next thing I know, it's Saturday at noon and I'm waking up to the sight of Kai doing push-ups on the hotel room floor.

"Hey," he says when he sees that I'm awake. He's wearing a T-shirt and khakis, and his hair's still wet from a shower. "Sorry, douchey habit, I know."

I don't care about the push-ups, but I do care that it's noon and I haven't even glanced at my phone yet. What if Phil's tried to call me with news about Keeva and Zuri?

"Can you hand me my phone, please?" I ask.

It's the first morning since my breakup with Nick that I haven't sat outside the gorilla quarters with my sketchbook, and when Kai hands me my phone, I unlock it quickly. Thankfully, there aren't any missed calls or texts from work, and I breathe a sigh of relief.

"So I was thinking," Kai says, with none of the morning-after awkwardness I expect, "what sounds good for breakfast? I know it's noon, but I was thinking I could run out and grab something from the bakery down the street."

I'd planned on rushing home to change before heading to the zoo, but the happy smile on Kai's face—and the memory of how exceptional he was last night—gives me pause. My one-night vacation from the rigors of being Lucy Rourke was the most fun I've had in a while, and who says I can't make it last for part of today, too? After all, I'm not scheduled for today, and we won't move any more members from Ozzie's troop in with Keeva and Zuri until Monday. I can't remember the last time I actually ate breakfast, let alone breakfast in bed, and Kai's offer sounds tempting.

"You don't have to shoot today?" I ask, suddenly conscious of the fact that I'm naked under the covers.

He shakes his head. "I'm free for a couple hours, and then I need to head to the Ronald McDonald House at three."

"You know, you already got into my pants," I tell him. "You don't need to woo me with pastries and charitable deeds. But if you're offering, I wouldn't say no to a cinnamon roll."

Kai nods approvingly. "That's my girl," he says, grabbing his wallet from the bedside table. "Be right back."

When the door closes behind him with a thud, I realize my heart's pounding. *That's my girl?* Does he think we're, like, a thing now? I loved everything we did last night, including our conversations, but I'm not anyone's girl but my own. I told Kai that work was my focus, and I meant it. One blissful night rolling around in bed together can't change that. I won't let it.

By the time he returns with two cups of coffee and a to-go container of cinnamon rolls and fruit, I'm circling panic territory.

"Thanks," I say, accepting the coffee Kai passes me. "But before we eat, maybe we should talk."

He smiles and adjusts his watch as he sits at the edge of the bed. "Are you spiraling, Lucy? Because you don't need to spiral."

"I am *not* spiraling." I take a sip of my coffee as if that proves how calm and stable I am. "I just think we need to reflect on last night's . . . activities."

"Last night's activities?" he asks, raising an eyebrow at me. "You mean when we made each other come and spent all night talking afterward?"

"Um, yes." I take another sip of coffee even though it's so hot, it makes my eyes water. "Those activities. While they were fun—very,

very, *very* fun, I just want to remind you that my work is my priority. I'm not looking for anything else."

"How many *very*s was that again?" Kai asks, smirking. He dodges the napkin I toss at him. "And yes, I understand and respect your priorities. As I tried to tell you that night in the nursery, I would never ask you to sacrifice career advancement for me. Nor would I jeopardize your professional reputation by sharing our private business with anyone. I don't kiss and tell."

I nod and trace the lid of my cup with my fingers. "Okay."

"That being said," he continues, "I had a very, very, very, *very* fun time last night, and I don't just mean the banging. I mean all of it."

"Oh my God," I say, lifting the cinnamon roll to cover my face. "Don't say *banging*!"

"And I like you, Lucy. I know I'm only here for the summer, and you're busy saving a baby gorilla, but I'd like to keep hanging out. Whether or not we keep"—he pauses, as if trying to come up with a substitute word for *banging*—"making love."

"That's so much worse," I groan. "Do not say *making love*."

"Well, whatever you want to call it, I'd like to keep doing it. And I'd like to keep talking to you about everything from Zuri to reality television. But it's entirely up to you."

I take a bite of gooey cinnamon roll to give myself time to think. I refuse to compromise my career ambitions for any kind of commitment—I learned that the hard way with Nick, after he, too, claimed to admire my work ethic only to later declare it selfish—but as long as Kai understands, what's wrong with a casual summer fling? After all, it felt good to take a break from stressing about Phil and Zuri and Keeva, and the orgasm Kai gave me felt even better.

"So you're on board with no commitment, no strings attached, and no one at the zoo finding out about this?" I ask, licking stray icing off my finger. "And you agree that at the end of the summer, we'll go our separate ways with no drama?"

Kai nods. "I'll go off to make an appearance on the NBC special, and you'll march into your new job as senior keeper. And no one will be the wiser."

The icing sticks to my hands, and I lick another glob of it off my wrist. "Okay then."

"Lucy, if you keep licking things like that, you're gonna make it very difficult for me to make it to my three o'clock appointment."

I mutter in protest as Kai takes the cinnamon roll from my hand and places it back in its plastic container. But when he joins me under the covers, pressing his warm body against mine, I stop complaining.

Chapter Twenty-Eight

By Monday afternoon, every member of Ozzie's troop except the silverback himself has been introduced to Keeva—all under Zuri's watchful eye. Youngsters Tomo and Risa make a game out of trying to dart past the older gorilla to drag Keeva around by the ankle, but it's typical play behavior, and Zuri tolerates it until Keeva lets out an alarmed cry. Then she snatches the baby back and clutches her to her chest, grunting to reprimand the troublemakers. Blackback Mac stares at the infant for several minutes before returning to his enrichment puzzle, and even Inkesha, bored of trying to harass Keeva, mostly leaves her alone.

But when Phil calls me into his office on Tuesday for an unexpected meeting, I'm paranoid that he somehow found out about Kai and me. Did someone spot me leaving the Marriott on Saturday and put two-and-two together? Did Akilah from Invertebrates see Kai and me walking the Olentangy Trail together on Sunday, when Nadeem flew out of town for work and Elle, still fighting morning sickness into her second trimester, asked me to take Trixie for a walk? I know nobody cares *that* much about my sex life, but I want to make sure

Phil sees me as a dedicated, competent professional, and romantic drama spilling into the workplace won't help my case.

"You've been doing a terrific job with Keeva, Lucy," Phil says, adjusting a framed drawing that sits next to his computer. One of his daughters made it for him, and it's supposed to be a sketch of her holding hands with Mickey Mouse, but she made Mickey's fingernails so long that he looks like Freddy Krueger.

"Thank you, sir. It's been a great team effort."

"A team effort, yes, but one led by you. You've risen to the challenge this summer. That's why I want you to go to San Diego at the end of the month."

"San Diego?" I ask. If I'm doing well, why is Phil sending me *away* from the zoo?

Phil nods. "The American Zoological Association Conference is being held there this year, and I'd like you to attend and do a poster presentation on Keeva's progress."

"Me? Don't Todd and Daiyu usually go to the AZA stuff?" Todd and Daiyu, two of the senior keepers, travel to conferences and symposiums all over the world on behalf of our zoo.

"Yep, and they still are. They'll be meeting with reps from the Species Survival Program to discuss the chimpanzee conservation project."

"So it'll be me . . . and some senior keepers," I say, feeling like a Minor League Baseball player getting called up to the World Series. "Look, Phil, I'm honored, but are you sure you don't need me here? Keeva's progressing really quickly, and there's so much work to do."

I don't mention that, as a serious helicopter mom, I worry that something will happen to our animals while I'm gone. I know they're in excellent hands even when I'm not around, but the one time Nick convinced me to take a weekend off and visit the Michigan dunes with him, Zuri suffered an intestinal blockage that resulted in emergency surgery. It wasn't my fault, sure, but I'll never forget the sickening fear that took root in my heart as I sped the whole way home, desperate to get back to her. She made a full recovery, but I never would have forgiven myself if the unthinkable happened while I was out frolicking on the beach.

"I know it's outside your comfort zone," Phil says. "And that's part of why I want you to go. If you want to be a senior keeper, you need to demonstrate that your passion extends to all primates, not just the ones here in Columbus. Traveling to conferences and stepping outside our zoo bubble is crucial to staying on top of your game."

He's telling me to suck it up and put on my big-girl pants, and I tell myself that it's only a weekend conference. Zuri and Keeva can survive without me for two days.

"Besides, Dr. Kimber will be there to receive a lifetime achievement award," Phil adds. "This might be your chance to finally meet your idol."

"Seriously?" I ask, my jaw dropping.

"Seriously," Phil says, grinning. "Maybe she'll even sign your bobblehead."

The next day, Phil gives us the green light to let four-hundred-pound Ozzie into Gorilla Villa with the rest of his troop, plus Keeva. I'm so nervous that I can't even eat the cinnamon roll that mysteriously appears on my desk that morning, and even bright-eyed, bushy-tailed Lottie looks like she might be sick. Ozzie is a gentle giant, but silverbacks don't take kindly to strangers encroaching on their territory, and there have been documented cases of infanticide in the wild when two troops merge. On the off chance that the situation spirals out of control, we have a veterinary team on standby with a tranquilizer, but I pray we don't have to use it.

Tensions run high among the staff, and even Skippy seems jumpy as he sets his camera up outdoors. My heart pounds as I let Ozzie into the overhead chute that grants him access to Gorilla Villa, and when I step outside, Kai catches my gaze and gives me a brief nod. *You're fine*, he's saying. *You've got this, Lucy.* But I don't; not really. I can try to make the environment as calm as possible for Ozzie, but there's no guarantee that when he finds a strange baby in the middle of his yard, he won't fling her across the grass—or worse.

"Stations, everyone!" Phil calls, directing keepers with buckets of treats to disperse outside the perimeter. Hopefully, if a scuffle breaks out, the presence of treats might be enough to calm the troop down.

"Here he comes," I say into the walkie-talkie as Ozzie clambers through the metal chute and emerges in the exhibit. "Hang tight, everyone."

I hold my breath as he knuckle-walks into the grassy yard, his massive arms wide as pillars. The other troop members, noticing his presence, seem to gravitate toward Keeva instinctively. Even Inkesha drops her handful of lettuce and scurries closer to the baby, as if responding to a biological drive to protect the young. Ozzie pauses to examine a pile of hay and scoops it up, carrying it under one arm as he maneuvers toward the surrogate mom and baby. As he approaches the pair, Zuri lets out a warning growl, and the majestic silverback stops in his tracks. He's only ten feet or so from Keeva, and the baby crawls behind her surrogate mother, who juts her chest out toward Ozzie in a defensive posture.

"I can't watch," Lottie whispers, pulling her polo up to cover her eyes.

"You go, mama bear," I whisper as Zuri pulls the infant closer.

But Lottie's panic turns out to be unfounded, as Ozzie drops his pile of hay and plops down on top of it. Within seconds, the demeanor of the whole troop relaxes. Inkesha resumes eating her lettuce, Tria stops clutching Piper's ankle and lets her clamber toward Keeva, and youngsters Tomo and Risa return to their feisty wrestling match. When Zuri calms down enough to let the baby slide off her back, I'm so relieved that tears spring to my eyes. The transition isn't done yet—it'll probably be weeks before Phil deems it safe to leave the troop together overnight—but success, and Keeva's chances of living a healthy, fulfilling life with other gorillas, are on the rise.

"Great work, Lucy," Kai says as he passes me on his way into Ape House. He glances around to check for witnesses before nudging my shoulder with his. "That deserves a much better reward than cinnamon rolls."

And later that night, when I leave the zoo and drive straight to his hotel, he proves it.

Chapter Twenty-Nine

The next week passes in a blur. Every day, the expanded troop spends a little more time together in Gorilla Villa, and by the end of the week, we leave them together for a twelve-hour stretch. Zuri continues to be an excellent surrogate mother, devoting her time and energy to her growing charge, and Ozzie seems perplexed the first time Keeva waddles toward him but tolerates her antics, even when she flings her red ball at his head like he's Jack or Phil.

When I'm not monitoring the troop, I'm logging notes at my computer or working on the poster Phil wants me to present in San Diego, and I'm totally swamped. So when Jack and Lottie offer to stay after hours with me a couple evenings and help me practice the presentation, I'm more than grateful. And when Kai continues to surprise me by leaving random treats on my desk—a bag of Swedish Fish one day, a twelve-pack of Diet Coke the next—I'm grateful for that, too.

I'm even more grateful for the time we spend together in his hotel room a couple times a week, when I need a break from tracking Keeva's weight gain and staring at poster fonts. Sometimes our clothes don't stay on for longer than it takes Kai to carry me from the door to the bed, and sometimes we just eat takeout and watch *90 Day Fiancé* while we trade stories about our day. Sam reschedules the dinner with Freya, and when Elle, Nadeem, Kai, and I meet up with the new couple at Tucci's, no one notices when he caresses my thigh under the table. Or at least I *think* no one notices, but the look Elle gives me when I meet her in the waiting room of her OB's office gives me pause.

Nadeem, trying to finish all his work travel before the baby comes, had to fly to Dallas last-minute, so when Elle asks Sam and me to accompany her to a routine ultrasound, I can't say no. I'm already letting her down by waffling on the whole godmother thing, and if I have time to let Kai go down on me for twenty minutes in his ridiculous minivan, I can make time for my friend's significant life milestone.

"You look different," Elle says as I slide into an uncomfortable plastic chair next to her and Sam. "Why do you look different?"

"Well, I spent two hours shoveling the bonobo exhibit yesterday and forgot to wear sunscreen," I tell her. "Also, I washed my hair recently."

She shakes her head at me. "That's not it."

"I agree," Sam says, peering at me over a brochure titled *My Health, My Life* that has a colorful illustration of a daisy next to a giant speculum. "Something's changed."

I squirm as if my friends can count on my face the orgasms Kai's given me. But before I can make up an excuse for whatever strange aura I'm exuding, a nurse calls Elle's name, and we follow her down a hallway and into an ultrasound suite.

"We don't want to know the sex of the baby," Sam tells the tech, as if Elle's offspring belongs to all of us and we're just a very modern family. When the tech nods and goes off to grab a fresh bottle of ultrasound gel, Elle squeezes my hand.

"I'm nervous," she says, clutching my fingers so hard, she reminds me of Keeva. "What if something's wrong? What if—"

"We have no reason to think anything is wrong," Sam assures her.

"Still, I'm freaking out." Elle tilts her head toward the ceiling as if she's trying not to cry. "Someone distract me with something. Anything."

"Um, did you know this clinic offers vaginal rejuvenation surgery?" Sam asks, dangling a brochure in front of Elle's face. When Elle only starts to inhale rapidly like she's in labor, Sam bites her lip. "Right, sorry. Not helpful."

"I'm sleeping with Kai Bridges," I blurt out as Elle's respirations approach panic-attack levels.

She calms down immediately, turning to stare at me with wide eyes. "What?"

"What?" Sam asks, dropping the pamphlet.

"What?" Nadeem asks, and I roll my eyes when I realize Elle's FaceTimed him into the appointment.

"You could have told me Nadeem was listening in," I grumble.

"I didn't know you were about to confess to sleeping with *Kai Bridges!*" Elle whispers, as if her husband didn't already overhear. "Besides, don't worry about him. He's just one of the girls anyway."

"Um, excuse me," Nadeem says, clearing his throat. "I am not."

"You little hussy," Sam says, giving me a mischievous smile. "I *knew* there was something up with you two. I saw the way your hands touched over the breadbasket at Tucci's. No wonder you look different. You're getting laid!"

I blush as Elle claps her hands like a little kid on Christmas morning. "See? We told you he wasn't terrible!"

"Yeah, well, don't get too excited," I tell her, shaking the fingers she practically squeezed to death. "It's casual. No strings attached. You guys know I don't do commitment, and Kai and I agreed that once shooting finishes at the end of the summer, we'll part ways and go on with our very separate lives."

"Famous last words," Nadeem says, and I lift Elle's phone to stick out my tongue at him.

But before anyone can ask for the dirty details, the ultrasound tech returns, and we fall silent. And a minute later, when she squirts some gel onto Elle's belly and places the probe on it, we're staring at the black-and-white image of the cutest little baby that ever existed.

"There's the heartbeat," the tech says, pointing to the flicker on the left side of the screen. "Nice and strong."

Elle squeezes my hand again, and when I see the joy radiating from her face, I squeeze back. Because I may not want children of my own, but I can't deny the magic of this moment. I can't deny Elle's happiness or the goose bumps that appear on my arms, and even though I'm dying to check my phone in case I miss a message from Phil or the team, I'm grateful to be right where I am.

But the magic of the ultrasound doesn't stop my friends from peppering me with questions as soon as we leave the office.

"Is Kai good in bed?" Sam asks. "Does he yell 'Wowza!' when he climaxes?"

"Are you sure you're not falling for him?" Elle asks. "Are you *sure* commitment is such a bad idea?"

"Yes, no, yes, and yes," I answer, hightailing it toward my Chevy before Sam can ask for a play-by-play of our sexual encounters. "I'm *this* close to getting promoted, and Kai's just a fun distraction from all the stress." There's a tiny voice in my head that whispers otherwise, but I silently tell it to shut the eff up.

"If you say so," Elle says with a shrug. "But will you promise me one thing?"

"No, I do not promise to catch the baby when it exits your vagina," I tell her.

She smiles as she reaches her car. "Can you promise me that if you start having doubts about your whole casual, no-strings-attached policy, you'll at least consider listening to them? Because you deserve a promotion, Luce, but you also deserve joy. And happiness and success are not the same thing."

I love Elle, and I know she means well, but she sounds like one of the inspirational quote calendars with a page you tear off every day. Maybe all the pregnancy hormones are making her even more sentimental than usual. I don't want to make her cry, so I nod as she climbs into her SUV.

"I promise," I tell her.

And I mean it. But I know it won't come to that. Because I will be happy and fulfilled once I get the promotion. Maybe happiness and success aren't the same for most people, but I'm not most people. I'm Lucy Rourke, future senior keeper. And they're the same for me.

Chapter Thirty

The week before the San Diego conference—the one Kai's also attending to promote *On the Wild Side*—I'm doing afternoon rounds on the colobus monkeys and Ozzie's troop when I notice Zuri's acting differently. And not in a Lucy-acting-differently-because-she's-getting-railed-by-the-world's-favorite-wildlife-host kind of different. Bad different. Worryingly different.

My first clue something's up is that when I round the corner to the indoor exhibit with a trayful of individualized protein drinks, Zuri doesn't scamper toward me like usual. Instead, Inkesha and Tria beat her to the mesh, and I glance around to find Zuri curled up in some hay while Keeva sits on her arm, tossing lettuce into the air. It's not a major red flag, because gorillas get belly aches just like humans, but it's enough to give me pause. And five minutes later, when I watch her facial muscles strain like she's in pain while she tries to do her business, I whip out my walkie-talkie and page the veterinary team.

"What's wrong?" Kai asks when he returns from a lunch break, seeing the panic on my face, but I can't stop to talk. I yell for Jack and Lottie, and they help separate the rest of the troop from Zuri and Keeva by luring them into the neighboring exhibit with the protein drinks. If what's causing Zuri to grimace in pain and lose her appetite is what I think it is—an intestinal blockage, just like the one she had two years ago—we're running on borrowed time. Blockages can result in bowel tearing, infection, and even death, and just like in humans, some are medical emergencies. Of course, she could also just be constipated, but this is Zuri we're talking about, and I'm not taking any chances.

Within minutes, Nick, a second vet, and a couple of techs arrive on the scene, and my pulse races as I explain Zuri's strange behavior. I call her to the mesh so Nick can listen to her heart and lungs with a stethoscope while a tech wheels in an ultrasound machine, and little Keeva lets out a frightened cry.

"Zuri, touch," I say, pressing my fist to the mesh. "Stomach, touch."

She knows what I'm asking thanks to her daily training, and she leans her abdomen into the mesh.

"Good girl," I tell her, forcing myself not to cry. "That's my smart girl."

Nick bites his lip as he presses the probe to her stomach, and I offer a silent prayer that we don't find anything—that she's just constipated, and I'm paranoid for no reason. But as Nick lowers the probe, I see it at the same time he does: a fuzzy gray bull's-eye-like cluster of matter where it shouldn't be.

"What is it?" I ask, trying to stay calm.

He moves the probe even lower, his eyes darting across the screen. "It's her bowel. One section of her intestine is sliding into another. Intussusception."

My heart drops into my stomach, and I want to panic, but there's no time for that. There's only time for action.

"She needs surgery," Nick announces. "Now. Let's go, guys. Get her out."

His fellow vet approaches the mesh, holding a syringe full of anesthetic that will knock Zuri unconscious, and my voice cracks as I instruct her to lift her arm toward the mesh.

"Zuri, arm," I tell her, swallowing down my tears, and like the amazing gorilla she is, she presses her arm to the mesh so the vet can inject the anesthetic.

It only takes her a few minutes to grow drowsy and pass out into the hay, and a terrified Keeva lets out an alarmed cry and smacks her surrogate mother's leg.

"You go with Zuri," Jack says, scrambling to open the gate so we can load her onto a stretcher and into the van that will transport her to the Animal Health Center. "Lottie and I will stay with Keeva."

I nod at him, grateful, and then step back as Phil, Kai, and a couple of guys from the vet team work to load Zuri onto a gurney. Norm backs the van right up to the Ape House entrance, and within two minutes, Zuri, Phil, the two vets, and I, plus Kai with his camera, scramble into the back. Putting a gorilla under anesthesia—and keeping her there—is no small task, and Nick monitors her vitals during the five-minute ride to the health center on the far side of the zoo.

"Heart rate's climbing," he warns. "We need to move fast."

The last thing anyone wants is a pained, pissed-off Zuri waking up in the back of a cargo van, and Norm steps on the gas. By the time we reach the health center, a team waits outside to usher Zuri to the surgical suite, and I hop out of the van and reach out to touch her arm as the medical staff rushes toward her.

"I love you," I whisper, willing her to make it. "You're my strong, smart girl, and I love you."

"Lucy," Kai calls after me as I turn to follow my favorite gorilla into surgery. He reaches for my hand, but I pull away before anyone sees. "Are you okay?"

I shake my head. "I'll be okay once Zuri is."

And then I jog after the gurney, my heart pounding out of my chest.

Two hours later, I emerge from the OR with trembling hands. Usually only Phil and the senior keepers attend surgeries, especially emergency ones, but perhaps knowing the depth of my dedication to Zuri, my boss let me stay. Kai, who stood at the edge of the room with Skippy and their cameras, spent the whole procedure glancing between me and the hands of the surgeon working diligently to fix the obstruction in the gorilla's abdomen. Dr. Trotter was able to repair the obstruction before it perforated, but as she explains to Phil and me in a debriefing afterward, it's no guarantee that we'll have the same luck next time.

"Just like some people are prone to seizures or cardiac incidents, some are prone to these kinds of blockages," she tells me, looping a stethoscope around her neck. "Same goes for gorillas. And sometimes it's caused by a tumor or a polyp that we can remove, but that's not the case for Zuri."

"So it's basically just bad luck?" I ask. "Is there anything we can do to prevent it?"

The gray-haired surgeon shakes her head. "I'd recommend regular abdominal scans to check for any developing masses, but just like in humans, we're not always sure why intussusception happens. Your best bet is to keep a close eye on her moving forward and hope it was just a fluke."

I roll my eyes when the vet walks away. I appreciate her life-saving surgery skills, but *hope* is not the foolproof solution I want.

"I'll look in the international database to find other zoos who've dealt with recurrent intussusception in their gorillas," Phil says, rubbing his eyes. "Maybe they know more than we do. And when you go to San Diego, talk to other primate keepers. They're a wealth of information."

My jaw drops. "You still want me to go to the conference? But it's six days away, and I can't leave Zuri." I motion toward the surgical suite, where Zuri will receive fluids and monitoring overnight before Dr. Trotter clears her to return to the troop.

"She'll be in good hands," Phil assures me. "I know it's hard to concentrate on anything else when one of our animals is sick, but it's essential to the job. You can do it, Lucy. I know you can."

He pulls out his walkie-talkie radio to update the team at Ape House, and I manage to keep the WTF off my face until I've rounded the corner to an empty hallway of the health center. I know Phil's trying to shape me into the best keeper I can be, but Zuri's not just *one of our animals*. She's the reason I started smiling again all those years ago. She's the reason I fell in love with gorillas and dedicated my life to working with them. She's *Zuri*, my smart, strong girl, and she could have died.

She could have *died*.

Before I know it, the tears fall fast and furious, and I'm grateful that no one's here to see me fall apart. But within seconds, footsteps round the corner, and I glance up from where I'm wiping away snot with my shirt sleeve to see Kai striding toward me, his brow furrowed in concern.

"Luce," he says, crossing the distance between us, but I shake my head as he approaches.

"I can't deal with the cameras right now," I tell him, my voice choked. "I just can't." During Zuri's ordeal, I'd forgotten about the cameras for the first time all summer, but I can't fathom the thought of staring into one right now.

"No cameras," Kai promises, wrapping his arms around me. "Just me, okay? Just me."

He rubs my back and strokes my hair, pulling my face into his chest, and suddenly I'm glad I'm not alone anymore. I'm glad he's here with me.

Even though when he lowers his face to press his lips against my forehead, it feels anything but casual.

Chapter Thirty-One

I don't leave Zuri's side for three days. After two nights in the health center, she returns to her troop, and Keeva snuggles against her chest like no time has passed at all. Zuri's eating and drinking normally, which points toward a full recovery, but I still sleep on my air mattress outside the gorilla quarters just in case. On my third night sleeping in Ape House, Kai whips out his own sleeping mat and sets it a safe distance from my air mattress.

"What?" he asks as I eye him suspiciously. "If anyone sees me here, they'll just assume I'm getting footage. Which I am." He points to the camera beside him. "I'm definitely not here to keep you company."

I can't help but smile. "I have company," I say, nodding toward the troop.

"Let me clarify: human company. I don't need you going full Jane Goodall and moving in with the gorillas."

I laugh. "They're better company than most people."

"I don't disagree."

Zuri makes little grunting noises in her sleep, and I watch as she shifts her weight from one side of her night nest to the other.

"I still wonder if I should tell Phil I can't go to San Diego," I tell Kai. "It doesn't feel right to leave her while she's recovering."

"I know it's hard, but just think how close you are to that promotion," he says. "Plus, you'll get to hang out with me. And in case you've forgotten, I'm really good with my hands. And my mouth. And my—"

"Stop," I insist. Three days of not leaving the zoo means three days of not visiting Kai in his hotel, and I don't need any reminders of what I'm missing. My body knows it all too well.

He smirks. "Fine. But don't forget, if you come to San Diego, you'll get to meet the one and only Dr. Kimber. And I'm pretty sure that's on the Lucy Rourke bucket list, right under running Ape House and marrying the brothers from *Zoboomafoo*."

"I'd settle for one brother," I joke, causing Kai to scrunch his nose in mock annoyance. "But yes, I can't believe I'll actually get to meet your mom." I remember all the times I read her book and watched *Majesty on the Mountain* as a kid, wishing I could have a mother as great as her. "Is she as marvelous in person as she seems?"

For a split second, Kai's jaw tenses, and I wonder if I've said something wrong. God, does he think I'm sleeping with him just to get to Dr. Kimber? Does he think I'm like Antonia, only with worse fashion sense? But then he flashes his characteristic stay-wild grin, and the moment passes before I'm sure it happened at all.

"She's one in a million," Kai promises, and I make a mental note to pack my bobblehead. He pulls out his laptop and a set of AirPods and passes one of the earbuds to me. "Wanna watch our show? I want to see if Melanie and Devar actually get married."

For a second, I think "our show" refers to *Wild Side*, but I quickly realize he's talking about *90 Day Fiancé*. The realization that Kai and I have a show sends a jolt of electricity through me. Isn't "our show" a couple-y thing to have? Do friends with benefits sleep on uncomfortable-looking pads that sit three inches off the cement floor to keep each other company? And do they share AirPods and Snickers bars and kiss their friend's forehead while she sobs against their chest?

"We can watch *Tiny House Nation* if you're burned out on bad relationships," Kai offers, still holding the earbud toward me.

"*90 Day Fiancé* is perfect," I say, accepting the earbud. I slide it into my ear as Kai slides one into his, and he sets his laptop on the floor between us so we can watch Kyle and Noon's Buddhist temple wedding.

I don't know if I'm doing this whole no-strings thing correctly. If I don't want a commitment, then why do I want to curl up next to Kai on his pathetic sleeping pad and snuggle into the nook between his neck and shoulder? If this is only a fling, why does the thought of him packing up at the end of the summer, leaving me to watch crappy reality TV all by myself, sound so unbearable? And why can't I get Elle's warning—*happiness and success are not the same*—out of my head, even if I know she's wrong?

"Hey, Lucy," Kai whispers, shifting his weight onto his elbow and turning sideways to face me. "Owls don't have eyeballs."

I don't know the answers to my own questions. But I do know that when Kai holds his hand out toward me, bridging the gap between his mat and mine, I want to reach out and grasp it.

And so I do.

Chapter Thirty-Two

By Friday morning, when I'm scheduled to leave for the conference, Zuri's almost back to her old self. It's clear that her incision is causing some discomfort—she doesn't let Keeva rest on the lower half of her abdomen, and she moves more gingerly than normal—but all things considered, she's in good shape, and I pass her a biscuit through the mesh as I bid her farewell.

"I'll be back on Monday," I promise. "Don't get into any trouble while I'm gone, okay?"

She makes a belch vocalization as if to say, *I make no promises*, and when I tap my fist to the mesh, she places her giant hand against it.

"I love you," I tell her. "Take care of Keeva."

Zuri spots Jack passing out handfuls of pumpkin on the far side of the exhibit, and I'm not offended when she trots off to join the excitement. Pumpkin is more enticing than a protein biscuit, and it warms my heart to see her passion for food returning.

"Lucy, you ready?" senior keeper Todd calls from down the corridor. "We're leaving in five."

"Ready!" I answer, surprised that Todd's speaking to me. I regard the senior keepers the same way young soccer players look up to Alex Morgan, and the fact that I'm traveling to San Diego with Todd and Daiyu feels like a trip to the big leagues.

I grab my suitcase from my office, making sure my Dr. Kimber bobblehead is tucked inside my carry-on in case my checked luggage gets lost.

"Hey, Lucy," Lottie says as I wheel my suitcase toward the exit. "Here, I got you this for the flight." She fishes a packet of Orbit gum out of her pocket and hands it to me. "In case your ears pop. Mine always do."

"Wow," I say, genuinely touched. "Thank you, Lottie. That's so nice."

She nods, pleased by my happiness in a way that reminds me of Mia. "Also, this might be a big ask, but if you happen to see any small souvenirs while you're in San Diego, like a tiny T-shirt or a little hat that you think might fit Ernest, could you grab it for me? I'm working on an Ernest Goes on a Road Trip post, and I don't have anything for the West Coast."

"I'll keep my eyes peeled," I promise, and when Lottie reaches forward to wrap me in a hug, I freeze for only a second before returning the affection.

Kai's on the same flight, but he sits near the front of the plane with Freya while Todd, Daiyu, and I are toward the back. He winks at me when I shuffle past with my carry-on, giving me a look that says, *I'm going to make you come later*, and when Daiyu asks if I'm okay, I tell her I'm only sweating because flying makes me nervous. During a layover at Dallas Fort Worth, Kai makes small talk with keeper contingents from Reptiles and Aquatics, but when I pop into a Hudson News to buy a bag of trail mix, he follows me in under the pretense of buying a magazine.

"I can't wait to be inside you," he whispers as he passes me, giving me goose bumps as I try to select an overpriced bag of carbohydrates. I grab a pouch of sweet-and-salty mix and nudge him as he flips through the latest edition of *Ladies' Home Journal*.

"Your room or mine?" I ask, and a thrill runs through me as his gaze meets mine over an article about easy ways to polish your summer wardrobe.

"Mine," he answers, and it's a good one, because I'm pretty sure I'm assigned to bunk with Daiyu.

By the time we land in San Diego and Uber to the Gaslamp Quarter Hilton, less than a mile from the convention center, I'm hornier than a bonobo, and before I can give Daiyu an excuse as to why I'm disappearing to the fifth floor, she announces that she's going to visit a cousin and leaves me alone in our two-queen room. I change out of my leggings and button-down and into a sleeveless shift dress that Sam insisted I borrow after I refused to pack a tube top. Kai's texted me his room number—he, being a guest of honor at the convention, does not have to share a room—and I've barely knocked once on his door when he flings it open and grabs my hand to pull me inside.

"That was the longest flight of all time," he murmurs, spreading his arms on either side of me as I lean against the door.

"Haven't you flown to, like, Singapore?" I ask, confused, but I understand when he presses his lips to the ticklish spot behind my right ear. "Oh. Never mind."

It's been a week since Zuri got sick and since I last visited him at the Marriott, so we're both eager to make up for lost time. It's only a matter of minutes until Kai's clothes, along with the not-long-for-this-world shift dress, end up in a pile on the floor, and he gets me off with his mouth so intensely that I swear to God I see stars. And when he buries his face in my shoulder as he inserts himself inside me, I get a warm, heavy feeling in my bones, and it's the sensation of being exactly where I'm supposed to be. As if Kai entering me, his cock filling up the place between my legs, is a destiny. A providence. A coming home.

"Lucy," he says, his thrusts getting faster and deeper, and I don't close my eyes as he gazes down at me. "Lucy, sweetheart," he moans, his hazel eyes ablaze, and the look that he gives me as he finishes—wanting, adoring, *knowing*—is enough to break my heart and put it back together again.

The conference doesn't start until tomorrow, so after we reacquaint ourselves one more time, Kai suggests we grab dinner, and we wander a few blocks from the hotel until we find a Mexican place decorated with colorful flags and simple furnishings. We each get an order of carne asada tacos and split a bucket of lobster tails, and even though I check my phone every five minutes in case Phil or Lottie tries to reach me, I'm having the time of my life. While I'm nervous to be away from the zoo and anxious to get my poster presentation over with, it feels good to know I don't have to worry about cameras for the next three days. And it feels even better to be with Kai, whose easy laugh and willingness to let me eat the last lobster tail make me feel like I can do anything.

When we get back to the hotel and curl up on Kai's bed, we watch *Bridesmaids* on HBO while I teach him how to play Egyptian Ratscrew.

"It's a card game, so contain yourself," I say when he raises his eyebrows at the game's title, and by the time the movie ends, he's as good at it as I am.

"Are you just, like, naturally skilled at everything?" I ask, rolling my eyes when he beats me again.

He smiles. "I'm only naturally skilled at spending time with you." It should sound like a stupid pickup line, but it doesn't, and I don't even cringe when he doubles the cheesiness factor by pecking me on the lips.

"Lucy," he says before I can turn the kiss into more R-rated fun. "I'm going to present my mother with her lifetime achievement award tomorrow. Will you join me backstage beforehand?"

"Will I join you and *Dr. Charlotte Kimber* backstage at the convention center?" I ask, dropping my eight of spades. "Um, yes. Of course I will."

"You sure?" His tone is hesitant, as if by agreeing to join him with my idol backstage, *I'm* the one doing *him* a favor.

"Of course." I'd consider walking on hot coals if Kai asked me to, even though that's the opposite of no strings attached, and the realization that his happiness matters to me doesn't fill me with the frantic anxiety it once would have.

"You want to play another hand of Egyptian Ratscrew?" he asks, nuzzling against my cheek.

"Nope," I say, shoving the cards aside and rolling over to straddle him.

Afterward, when we're naked under the sheets and his hands stroke my butt with comfortable familiarity, Kai props himself up on his elbow and looks at me intently.

"I know I shouldn't say this," he tells me, tracing a line down my arm with his index finger, "but this feels . . ."

He leaves the sentence unfinished, but I know what he means: *This feels right. This feels real. This feels very, very, very unlike a summer fling.*

"I know," I tell him, because I do.

I just don't know what to do about it.

Chapter Thirty-Three

For a woman who threw up six times from nervousness on the way to her seventh-grade science fair, my presentation on Keeva's surrogacy goes remarkably well. It helps that it takes place in a conference room the size of a football field where hundreds of other people hang out awkwardly in front of their own posters, so there are never too many pairs of eyes on me at once. It also helps that every time I start to stumble over my words or sweat off my mascara, Kai walks by and says, "Wowza, great poster!" in the thickest accent he can muster.

I fought tooth and nail over trying not to appear on camera this summer, and even though I'll probably never be able to deliver more than a few lines into the lens without running a cold sweat, I can't help but think that spending so much time outside my comfort zone has helped me expand it by a mile. Daiyu snaps a picture of me alongside my poster and I send it to Sam, who uploads it to the zoo's Facebook page with a caption that reads, Primate keeper Lucy spreading knowledge and making waves in San Diego!, and although looking at pictures of myself usually makes me cringe, I like this one. I look happy, even confident, in my slate gray power suit, like a woman who'd never ramble about hyena pseudopenises or pass out during a Critter Chat.

I look like I know what I'm doing.

I don't see Kai for most of the day, because he's busy doing interviews and promoting *Wild Side* with Freya, but I mingle with representatives from other zoos and attend two lectures, one on advancements in gorilla cardiac health and another on the effects of anti-inflammatory drugs on the gut flora of colobus monkeys. I mention to other keepers that I'm looking to gather more research on the prevention of intussusception, and I even meet a keeper team from St. Louis that inquires about visiting Columbus to learn more about our surrogacy program. We trade numbers and business cards, and the fact that I'm doing what Phil hoped I would—talking to other keepers, seizing an opportunity—fills me with pride.

The conference's keynote speaker, Priya Kumar-Tyler, founder of the Global League for the Prevention of Wildlife Trafficking, is scheduled to give her lecture at eight, and the awards and honors presentations will occur just beforehand. At seven thirty, I meet Kai in the lobby outside the amphitheater, and he looks like an absolute snack in a navy blue suit that fits him like a glove.

"Sexy can I," I mutter. "Want to run back to the hotel for a quickie?"

I expect him to jokingly suggest we find an empty closet instead, but he only flashes me a tight smile. "Ready?"

"Ready," I say, patting my purse. "Bobblehead locked and loaded."

"Great." He nods, and there's something in his expression I haven't seen before: a tension coiled around the tight lines of his mouth and a hard glint in his eyes.

Is he regretting his decision to invite me backstage? Does he find my Dr. Kimber bobblehead embarrassing?

"I don't have to bring the bobblehead," I tell him. "I can get my book signed instead."

"The bobblehead is fine, Lucy." Kai's tone is stiff, almost sharp, and I'm not sure anyone's ever uttered the word *bobblehead* so tensely.

"Hey, you okay?" I ask, reaching out to touch his hand. "If this is about last night, about what you started to say about this thing between us feeling, you know . . ." *Real*, I want to say. *Meaningful*. But Kai cuts me off before I can finish the sentence he left open-ended last night.

"It's not." He runs a hand through his hair and shakes his head, sighing. "I'm sorry. I know I'm tense, but it doesn't have anything to do with you. I'm glad you're here." He squeezes my hand, and the brief smile he gives me tells me his words are genuine. "I'm just nervous."

He might as well have announced that he transforms into Bigfoot at every full moon. "Nervous? You?"

How does a man who went cage diving with great white sharks in season four of *Wild Side* get nervous about presenting his mom with an award?

"You know the saying, 'Never meet your heroes'?" Kai asks, fiddling with the top button of his shirt. "Well, my mum is . . . she can be . . . difficult. Mercurial. And she's not my biggest fan."

He tilts his head from side to side, rolling out his neck, and the anxiety emanating off him is palpable.

"I don't understand. Why isn't she?" Based on my experience, moms love Kai more than scented candles and uninterrupted baths. Wouldn't Dr. Kimber, who dedicated her life to protecting gorillas, be ecstatic that her son dedicated his to sharing that love for wildlife with the world?

Kai glances at his smartwatch. "We better head backstage." He slips a laminated pass out of his pocket and pins it to my jacket, and I can't resist the opportunity to place my hand against his cheek.

"You sure you're okay?" I ask, trying to solve the mystery in his eyes.

He nods and presses his forehead to mine for the briefest of moments. "I'm okay. Just ready to get this over with." Then he smooths his jacket and nods toward the amphitheater. "Let's go."

I want to ask more questions and give him the same steady assurance he tried to give me that first day with the cameras outside the bonobo exhibit but he's striding toward the amphitheater with a confidence that betrays none of the agitation I saw on his face. I hurry after him, wondering why the silly figurine tucked safely in my purse suddenly feels like it's made of brick.

Chapter Thirty-Four

The first thing I notice about Dr. Kimber is how petite she is. Perhaps because of the outsized influence she had on my childhood, I expect her to be roughly the height of an Amazon warrior from the Gal Gadot *Wonder Woman* movie. But she's at least seven inches shorter than me, and I feel like I'm standing next to a gorilla-saving Polly Pocket.

"Hello, I'm Charlotte," she says, extending a hand toward me. The raven braid she wore on the cover of *Majesty on the Mountain* has been cut into a slick-straight bob, and wispy bangs end at a pair of hazel eyes identical to Kai's. Strands of gray weave through her hair, and she wears a black jumpsuit that Sam would thoroughly approve of. This is the woman whose book changed my life, who marched into the jungle with a travel guide and a tent and decided to change the course of history. This is the woman whose decades of work ensured the survival of mountain gorillas, at least for now.

And she's talking to *me*.

When I'm too awestruck to speak, Charlotte raises an eyebrow in a way that reminds me of her son.

"This is Lucy Rourke," Kai says, swooping in to help. "She's a soon-to-be senior keeper at the Columbus Zoo and Aquarium, where she's heading up a gorilla surrogacy project."

"Nice to meet you, Lucy," Charlotte says, her hand still outstretched toward me.

Suddenly coming to my senses, I reach for her hand. "I'm, your, well, biggest. Fan," I tell her, barely able to get the words out.

Dr. Kimber, still shaking my hand despite the fact that I sound like I'm having a stroke, smiles. "That's very sweet."

"*Majesty on the Mountain* changed, um, my life," I continue. "I used to trek around the woods behind my grandmother's house and, um, pretend I was tracking gorillas with you. In Rwanda. I wanted to be just like you."

"It's always delightful to hear that I had an effect on a young person's life," she says, tucking a strand of hair behind her ear to reveal a smooth pearl earring.

Before I can grab my bobblehead from my purse and ask her to sign it, she turns her attention toward Kai. "I thought we agreed you'd wear a black suit. Did I misunderstand?"

I glance sideways at Kai, whose jaw tenses imperceptibly. Why does Dr. Kimber, who I imagined only worried about big stuff like saving endangered species, care about something as inconsequential as a suit color?

"The black suit had a tear," Kai says quietly. "I didn't realize it until this morning and didn't have time to replace it."

Dr. Kimber smiles at him, but it's not the warm, patient smile she gave me. It's polite, almost cold, like how Karina probably smiled at Kai when he asked if *Guilty Pleasures* was a sitcom. "I suppose I should be grateful that you're here at all. I know how busy you are with your little program."

I imagine my eyes popping out of my skull with surprise like a cartoon character's. Did she seriously just call *Wild Side* a "little program"? Besides being cruel, it's also factually inaccurate; Kai's show has strong ratings and performs even better on streaming platforms, and more important, there are families across the world who wouldn't know the difference between a gorilla and a chimpanzee if it weren't for his docuseries.

I wait for Kai to correct her, or at least say something to defend himself, but he only looks at her with the sloping shoulders of someone who's heard this a thousand times before.

"Actually, Dr. Kimber," I say, suddenly finding my voice, "with all due respect, *On the Wild Side* is not a little program. It's huge. Kai's won three Emmys, and I've seen how hard he and his crew work. It's really impressive."

"Of course, Lucy," she says with a nod. "I didn't mean to imply that the show isn't successful. I'm only saying that some of us, like you and I, do the grunt work of being in the field and getting our hands dirty. And others jet around in first class and parade around on camera like a dancing monkey. Not that there's anything wrong with being an entertainer."

Her tone is calm, collected, without a trace of malice or spite, and that's almost as unnerving as her words.

"Kai's more than just an entertainer, though," I tell her. "He's an educator."

I think of Kai taking time out of his nonstop schedule to help coach me for the camera, and helping to load Zuri onto the stretcher, and staying at the zoo all hours of the day and night to capture Keeva's arrival and Brutus the grizzly's surgery and the birth of Phoebe the Asian elephant's new calf. I think of him autographing a hat for Mia and beaming for the camera even when he doesn't want to, even when he's so sick of saying "Wowza!" that he wants to scream. Because he knows there are a lot of people—and animals—counting on him.

Dr. Kimber smiles. "I think this one likes you, Kai," she says, reaching out to flick a speck of imaginary dust off his shoulder. He flinches but doesn't respond, only setting his jaw in a tight line.

Confusion and annoyance prick my skin. I'm not defending Kai because I like him, even though I do—I'm defending him because it's the truth, and because it's unbearable to watch Dr. Kimber treat her son with the same dismissive coldness my mother showed me. I didn't deserve it when I was ten, and he doesn't deserve it now.

I give Kai my best what-the-hell-is-going-on-here look, but he only shakes his head and gives my hand a brief squeeze.

"So, Lucy," Dr. Kimber says, studying me like she didn't just insult her own flesh and blood so cruelly, "tell me about your surrogacy project."

Before I can fashion a response, however, a frazzled-looking woman with an earpiece and a clipboard marches toward us. "Mr. Bridges, you're on in five minutes," she says. "We'll play a short video about Dr. Kimber's work, you'll say a few words, and then you'll present her with the award. Any questions?"

"No questions, thank you," Kai says.

"I'm beyond honored," Dr. Kimber says with a smile.

The woman almost drops her clipboard. "I can assure you, Dr. Kimber, the honor is mine," she says before glancing my way. "Want to follow me to your seat?"

I don't want to leave Kai, but he only nods when I look at him with a question in my eyes. "Go ahead," he says. "Enjoy the presentation, and I'll see you after."

"Are you sure?" I whisper as Dr. Kimber watches placidly.

He nods and brushes a lock of hair away from my face. "Positive."

I'm not convinced, but I can't very well hold up the evening, so I don't press further. "Okay then. Break a leg."

"Hey, Luce," he calls after me as I follow the clipboard-bearing woman past a tableful of finger foods.

When I turn back, Kai's grinning at me, but it's a few watts short of its usual voltage. "In grassy areas, there are fifty thousand spiders per acre."

I want nothing more than to wrap my arms around him and convince him we should blow this Popsicle stand, but I only smile back. "For every human on earth, there are one million ants."

Then I follow the attendant to my seat, wondering how my beloved childhood idol turned out to be so rude and condescending toward her own son. I guess Kai was right, that you should never meet your heroes, because once this presentation is over, I plan to march straight down to the beach and fling my cherished copy of *Majesty on the Mountain* and my bobblehead into the Pacific.

Chapter Thirty-Five

I'm seated in the front row like I'm a VIP, and I settle in as music swells from the amphitheater speakers and images of Dr. Kimber's storied life grace the giant screen in front of me. There are entertaining clips of her as a thirty-something adventurer, rolling around in the grass with a baby mountain gorilla as the baby's troop looks on. There's a snippet of her 2001 testimony to Congress, where she advocated for increased spending on conservation, followed by a minute-long reel of a braided Diane Lane sobbing in the immediate aftermath of Taji's death. Pictures of Dr. Kimber with President Obama, Greta Thunberg, and Betty White grace the screen, and the applause of the audience turns deafening when the music fades and Kai, looking dapper as hell in his navy suit, strides onto the stage and approaches the microphone.

"Hi, I'm Kai Bridges, host of *On the Wild Side*," he greets the audience, looking every bit the confident, unflappable expert he is on-screen. "And today, I have the privilege of presenting my hero with the American Zoological Association's lifetime achievement award for her work protecting mountain gorillas and many species of animal all over the world. I'm talking, of course, about my mother, the one and only Dr. Charlotte Kimber."

The audience cheers, because the thousands of keepers and veterinarians and journalists sitting behind me have no idea what I witnessed backstage. And Kai gives no indication that his relationship with his mother is less than ideal; he rhapsodizes about her dedication to gorillas and the joys—and occasional heartbreak—of spending a chunk of his childhood on Mount Karisimbi. And when Dr. Kimber joins him onstage, she wraps him in a hug so warm and maternal that I half wonder if I didn't imagine the events that unfolded minutes earlier.

"Thank you, Kai," she says, beaming as he steps away from the microphone and she looks out over her adoring fans. "To be chosen for an award like the one I'm receiving tonight is such a special honor. But it's made even more special by the fact that my son, a trailblazer in his own right, is here to share the moment with me."

I shift so suddenly in my seat that my purse almost slides off my lap. Ten minutes ago she accused him of parading around like a dancing monkey, and now he's a trailblazer?

"And while I'm so proud to receive the AZA's lifetime achievement award, no prize could ever rival the honor of being Kai's mother. So thank you, Kai, for being here with me tonight, and for the hard work you do to bring the magic of wildlife to so many people."

The audience cheers again, and Kai flashes a wide smile and gives a little bow before descending from the stage.

"Um, not to be rude," I whisper as he slides into the seat next to mine, "but what the hell's going on?"

He brushes my hand with his but doesn't respond, and we both sit back and watch as Dr. Kimber gives a speech about the majesty of mountain gorillas, the significance of family, and the importance of standing up for what you believe in—even if you must take on a corrupt government and rogue poachers to do it. Her message earns a standing ovation, and while I'm interested in what Priya Kumar-Tyler has to say about preventing wildlife trafficking, all I want is to get Kai someplace private so he can explain what's going on.

But after her presentation, there's a reception with fizzy drinks and cake, and Kai, Dr. Kimber, and Priya Kumar-Tyler smile for what seems like an endless round of pictures. Finally, after Kai and his mother make the rounds and sign more than a few autographs, the crowd starts to thin.

"Hey," Kai says, appearing beside me as I scarf down another crab cake before the catering staff clears what's left of the hors d'oeuvres. "You ready to get out of here?"

I've been ready to get out of here since Dr. Kimber referenced his "little program," and I swallow the rest of the crab cake and nod. "Abso-freaking-lutely."

But before we make it out of the conference room, Dr. Kimber weaves a path toward us.

"What a pleasure it was to meet you, Lucy," she says, her voice smooth as silk. "Will you be joining Kai and me for breakfast tomorrow?"

I glance at Kai skeptically. He's already subjected himself to a dose of her mistreatment backstage, and now he's signing up for breakfast, too?

"We're making plans for an NBC special in September," Dr. Kimber adds, noticing my confusion. "It's the twentieth anniversary of the release of *Majesty on the Mountain*. It's a big deal for our family."

I remember the rueful smile Kai wore at Café Istanbul when he told me about the special and admitted that he wanted no part in it.

"Oh," I say, caught off guard. "I wasn't aware Kai had agreed to appear in that just yet."

Dr. Kimber's eyes flash in a way that suggests maybe it hasn't been such a pleasure to meet me after all, but then it passes, replaced by an imperturbable smile.

"Of course he'll appear," she says, fingering her pearl earring. "After all, he owes it to Taji. And he knows that. Right, Kai?"

Kai doesn't answer. Instead, he looks straight ahead, wearing the same sunken, defeated look he wore when Courtney the bartender peppered him with questions about Taji and Oprah Winfrey.

"I'll see you two tomorrow," Dr. Kimber says, nodding at us. "Breakfast Republic at ten. Don't be late."

And then, with the quiet, graceful motions of one used to hiking through every manner of terrain, she's gone.

"Okay," I say once Kai and I reach his room, where I kick off my heels and wiggle out of my jacket. "What the fuck was that?"

Kai loosens his collar. "As I told you, my mother isn't my biggest fan."

"No, *my* mother isn't my biggest fan. Yours does a killer impression of Mother Gothel from *Tangled*."

"I've never seen *Tangled*."

"Well, she's a charismatic villain who gaslights Rapunzel in a sweet tone of voice."

Kai raises an eyebrow. "I wouldn't refer to my mother's tone as particularly sweet."

"Well, what's her deal? The way she insulted you and your show—"

"Is a lot like the way you insulted me at Picnic for Paws, right?"

he asks, removing his cufflinks. "So maybe she's actually onto some-thing."

I freeze. "I didn't know you when I insulted you at Picnic for Paws. You know that. And you know I changed my mind about you completely. So that's not fair."

He nods and sits on the edge of the bed, then takes my hand and tugs me down gently to sit beside him.

"You're right," Kai says. "It wasn't fair, and I'm sorry. It's just that being around my mum brings up a lot of insecurities."

When he wraps an arm around my waist, I don't pull away. "Well, I can see why. She's a real peach. I mean, the way she just assumed you'd do the anniversary special, and how she tried to use Taji to guilt you into doing it—that's beyond the pale, Kai. You see that, right?"

He shrugs. "I guess I'm used to it. I mean, she has a point."

"But she doesn't," I insist. "Taji's death was not your fault. She's the one who brought an eight-year-old child into dangerous terrain. She's the one who put you in harm's way. And it was her choice to turn back and help you when you got caught in the snare all those years ago. Are you supposed to spend the rest of your life fighting for her approval just because she made the same choice every mother would?"

"But she didn't, Lucy," Kai says, standing up from the bed so abruptly that I almost fall sideways when his weight disappears. "She didn't, okay? So please stop trying to give advice on a situation you know nothing about."

I watch, taken aback, as he strides toward the window, his ex-pression a storm of hurt and anger.

"What are you talking about?"

"She didn't turn back," Kai says, his voice breaking. "When I got caught in the snare, she didn't turn back. She saw that I was trapped, and she heard me screaming for her, but she kept going. Because she wanted to protect Taji. Because he mattered to her more than I did."

I stare at him, incredulous. "What? But in her book, she wrote how she had to choose between helping you and helping Taji, and she—"

"The book is a lie, Lucy," Kai says, his tone flat. "She never turned back for me. She tried to stop the poachers from getting to Taji. She couldn't, but she chose him. And the locals never called her *Nyiramacibiri*. The locals hated her because they used the land for hunting and farming, and she wanted to cut off their access to protect the gorillas. That's why I said you were wrong at the Critter Chat. Because you were, even if you had no way of knowing."

The news hits me like a hammer to the chest. "Why would she lie?"

"Because nobody roots for a woman who deserts her own kid," Kai explains, his eyes shining wet. "Telling the world she sacrificed her chance to save Taji for me made her a hero. Donations started pouring in like crazy, and Hollywood came knocking, and next thing I knew, Diane Lane was winning an Oscar for her moving portrayal of my mum."

I shake my head. "So why keep the secret all these years? Why not tell the truth? It's not fair that anyone ever blamed you for Taji's death, but it's especially unfair when you know what really happened."

"His death is still my fault, Lucy," Kai says, wiping his eyes with his sleeve. "I did slow her down. I was only eight, and I was small, and she had to worry about me, too, in addition to Taji's troop. She didn't even want me there on the mountain, but I begged. Because I wanted to spend time with her, because she was my mum."

I know the feeling so intimately that my heart twists, and I reach forward to grab Kai's hand. "None of that is your fault."

"If I hadn't been at camp," he says, running a hand through his hair, "she would have left earlier that morning to go tracking. She would have moved through the brush faster. She might have gotten to the troop soon enough to ward off the poachers, and Taji might have lived."

His tone is empty, hollow, like he's reciting something he's been told a thousand times since childhood. Probably because he is.

"Hey," I say, standing up and taking Kai's face in my hands. "Just because that's what she told you doesn't make it true."

He's weeping openly, tears streaming down his face, and I can't stop myself from pressing a kiss to his moist cheek. "You aren't responsible for what happened to Taji," I tell him, my voice getting choked up, too. I remember the strain in Kai's voice during his phone call at Huli Huli and the sour look that crossed his face every time his phone rang. I can only imagine the cruel words Dr. Kimber used to manipulate him into playing along with her ruse. "You don't owe anyone an NBC special, and you don't owe it to your mom to keep perpetuating her lies."

He shakes his head. "It's not that simple."

I lower my hands to Kai's chest and press my lips to his briefly. "I heard you tell her that you want things to be different. And they can be. You don't have to do the special. And if you want to take a season off *Wild Side* and let Freya handle things while you work on your dream documentary, you can do it. Hell, if I can coexist with a camera all summer and not lose my mind entirely, you can do anything you want." I wipe a tear from his cheek and smile at him. "I believe in you, and I'll stand by you."

The anguish on his face evaporates, replaced by something like wonder. "But aren't we— I mean, I thought you only wanted . . . I thought you wanted things between us to stay casual."

I had, and I had meant it with every fiber of my being. But somewhere along the line, maybe when Kai spent the night with me by Zuri's side or wrapped his arms around me in the health center or trusted me with the backbreaking secret he's kept all these years, that changed. Somewhere along the line I realized that having Kai by my side didn't distract me from my job; it made me better at it.

"If I'm being honest," I say, wrapping my arms around his neck, "nothing's ever been casual between us. Not since the first time we met. I just didn't want to admit it."

He peers at me like he can't quite believe what he's hearing. "So you're saying you want . . . more? Commitment?"

"I'm saying I want you. And I'm going to keep wanting you past the end of the summer. And I'm going to want you whether you're shouting 'Wowza!' in your Dundee hat or watching Danielle and Mohamed make terrible life decisions on *90 Day Fiancé*."

Kai laughs, and it's the best thing I've heard all day. "Danielle and Mohamed are a train wreck."

I smile at him. "They sure are."

He lowers his mouth to mine, and his kiss is soft, tender, like our lips are meeting for the very first time.

"Hey, Lucy," he says, touching his forehead to mine.

I can't help but roll my eyes. "I know, I know. It's weird animal fact time. Scientists have done brain surgery on cockroaches."

He laughs again and leans back to meet my gaze. "I was going to say that I'm falling in love with you."

"Seriously?" I ask, my heart thudding. "You say that right after I drop a line about cockroaches?"

"Seemed like the perfect moment," he says with a shrug, laughing as I swat him on the arm.

"I'm falling in love with you, too," I tell him, marveling at the words as I say them aloud. Elle's going to lose her mind.

He kisses me again, and soon our clothes, like the secrets we kept to ourselves for so long, are stripped off and discarded.

Chapter Thirty-Six

The next morning, I wake up to find Kai sipping coffee in bed, one hand resting on my back.

"How are you always up first?" I ask, blinking against the sunlight streaming through the window. "And please say you got me coffee, too."

"I told you, I don't sleep." Kai kisses my bare shoulder before reaching toward the bedside table to grab a second cup. "And of course I did."

"Thanks," I mumble, sitting up and taking the steaming cup. "So, what's on the agenda for today?"

He smiles. "You mean, do I still plan on meeting my occasionally kind, sometimes vicious, always narcissistic mother for breakfast? Why yes, I do. I'm going to enjoy a delicious frittata and tell her I've decided not to participate in the anniversary special."

I raise an eyebrow at him. "Cool. She might poison your food, though, so maybe you should get the frittata to go."

"Ah, but I'm bringing you with me, so you can keep an eye out for misdeeds," Kai says, leaving a trail of kisses down my arm. "If you're comfortable joining, of course."

I'm not entirely comfortable, but then again, I've spent all summer doing something that makes me uncomfortable, so I think I can handle a short breakfast. "Wouldn't miss it."

After a shared shower that leads to other, less-squeaky-clean shared activities, we dress and take an Uber to the restaurant, a bright, open space with a chrome exterior and a slanted cedar awning. We're ten minutes early, but Dr. Kimber is already seated at a table on the patio, wearing a royal blue wrap and white slacks. She's nothing like the braided, smiling woman I remember from the cover of her book, and I feel a pang of nostalgia for simpler times when I thought she was a real-life superwoman. And maybe she is when it comes to saving gorillas, but she's no hero when it comes to being Kai's mother.

And for some reason, that's what matters more to me.

"Sit," Dr. Kimber says, smiling as we reach her table. "Welcome. You're both looking well."

I want to say something cutting, like, *Looks can be deceiving, can't they?* but old habits die hard, and for a split second, I forget she's no longer my idol.

"I love your wrap," I tell her, and then I immediately want to kick myself.

She smiles. "I ordered you grapefruit juice, Kai. I didn't know what you'd like, Lucy, so I just guessed a mimosa."

I love mimosas, but I'm determined to stay loyal to Kai, so I keep my enthusiasm to a minimum. "Thank you."

"Now," Dr. Kimber says, stirring a mug of coffee, "I know it's uncouth to get down to business before you've even looked at the menu, but we have a lot to cover." She turns her attention to Kai, who crosses his arms over his chest in a way that works very well for his biceps.

"I had a conference call with the network producer yesterday afternoon," she continues, "and it looks like most of the *Majesty on the Mountain* cast will appear on the special. And after the taping, they want you and me to do a quick segment on *Jimmy Fallon*, which I know you'll enjoy. You've always liked him, right?"

"Jimmy Fallon's great," Kai says. "But here's the thing, Mum." He pauses, a bit of the color draining from his cheeks, and I put my hand on his thigh under the table to remind him that it's okay.

"I've decided not to do the special," he says.

There's a long pause where no one speaks, and I wonder if I should track down a waiter and order that frittata stat.

"Of course you're going to do it," Dr. Kimber finally says with a forced laugh. "I need you there. We're a team."

What she probably means is that Kai's popularity benefits her, too, and that she needs him to sit in a leather chair across from Lester Holt and cry about poor Taji's murder so the money keeps rolling in.

"Actually, I don't think we've been a team for a very long time," Kai says, running a hand through his hair. "Since I was about eight years old, I'd say. Don't you think?"

Dr. Kimber's mouth puckers, and her gaze darts toward me for the briefest of moments. Then she takes a sip of coffee and shakes her head. "I know things haven't always been easy for you. And some of that is my fault. But we have responsibilities. *You* have responsibilities."

"And sometimes people fail at their responsibilities," he says, my hand still perched on his thigh. "If you know what I mean."

He's thrown down the gauntlet, and his mother smiles tightly at Kai like he's an annoying child who needs a good timeout. "I'm happy to discuss that with you another time," she says, raising her mug to her lips. "But make no mistake: you're participating in the special."

"I said no, and that's final." Kai reaches under the table to wrap his hand around mine. "I'm not a scared little boy anymore, Mum. Besides, I thought you didn't like dancing monkeys."

Dr. Kimber drops her mug, spilling coffee on the table, and she scrambles to set it upright. "Kai," she says plaintively, "you can't just—"

"I can do whatever I want, actually," he says, standing up from the table. "This has been a fun reunion, Mum, but I'm gonna see about a frittata to go. Come on, Lucy."

Kai strides toward the dining room, and I get up to follow, but Dr. Kimber reaches out to grasp my arm.

"Lucy, wait," she says. "Please, just wait a moment."

I don't want to spend a second more of my time with her, but Kai's already inside the restaurant, and his mother, who I spent decades idolizing, blinks at me like she might be on the verge of tears. I sit down hesitantly, hoping Kai hurries back.

"You seem like a nice girl," Dr. Kimber says, her tone congenial. "You and Kai seem to care about each other. And if you care about him, I'm sure you don't want him making any irrational decisions."

I narrow my eyes at her. She might be a real-life Mother Gothel, but I'm no Rapunzel. "I want Kai to make whatever decisions he thinks are right for him."

Dr. Kimber nods as if we're in agreement. "Of course. I just mean, you seem to have a certain amount of influence over him. I'm sure you wouldn't want to steer him wrong."

"He's perfectly capable of steering himself," I say, angered by her insinuation and the fact that I don't have a mimosa to toss at her.

"I understand. But look, Lucy, I have influence, too. Kai says you want to be a senior keeper, right? I'm friendly with Shira Woodrow, and I'd be happy to make a call on your behalf. Women like you and me are achievers. We rise to the top, and I can help you get there."

At the start of the summer, if someone had told me that Dr.

Charlotte Kimber would offer to call the zoo's CEO and help me get my dream promotion, I would have thought they were crazy—and I might have jumped up and down for joy. But the fact that she'd stoop so low as to bribe me into manipulating her own son makes me nauseous.

"We're nothing like each other," I tell her, sitting ramrod straight in my chair. "And I know the truth about what happened the day Taji died. Kai told me. So please, don't try to give me any lessons about rising to the top."

She doesn't flinch at my admission. "Kai's a storyteller. It's what he does. He's entitled to his version of the story, but I wouldn't go around spreading rumors if I were you."

"I believe Kai," I tell her, my voice so loud that other diners glance over. "And by his version of the story, I think you mean the truth."

Charlotte gives a tepid smile. "I can see that you mean well, Lucy, but don't be foolish. Get Kai to do the special, and I'll make the call to Shira. It's a win-win for both of us."

It might be a win-win for us, but it wouldn't be a win for Kai, and even though I started the summer hating his guts, we've come so far together. Too far to accept a promotion through her influence when I can get it with hard work.

"You know, Dr. Kimber," I say, "you used to be my hero. I worshiped you. And I admire everything you've done for gorilla conservation, but that's not enough to stop me from telling you that you seriously, seriously suck."

I get up from my chair, sliding my purse over my shoulder. "A friend of mine told me that success and happiness aren't the same. It took me a long time to realize she was right. And one day, I hope you realize it, too, while you still have a chance to make things right with Kai."

I strut away from the table with the confidence of a peacock, but I can't resist turning back to deliver one final blow. "And not that it matters, but he looked fine as hell in the blue suit."

Then, leaving my longtime idol speechless, I march off to join Kai.

Taking our frittatas to go, we venture to La Jolla Cove beach and eat breakfast with sand squished between our toes. The tranquil sounds of the ocean waves crashing are the perfect soundtrack to our meal, and afterward, we walk along the shoreline and look for seashells.

"I feel so at peace," Kai says, looping an arm around my waist and holding up a dome-shaped shell for me to admire. "With my decision. And with you. Thank you, Lucy."

"The ocean sure doesn't hurt, either," I say, venturing out to dip my toe in the water.

"I know how you feel about cameras, but what do you say to a selfie?" Kai asks, fishing his phone out of his pocket.

I narrow my eyes at him. "Do I have to say 'Stay wild'?"

He laughs. "No. You can say whatever you like."

"Okay then."

Kai stands beside me with our backs to the ocean, and he holds his phone out as we both give our cheesiest grins.

"Say 'Wowza!'" I say, leaning into Kai.

"Say 'hotel sex,'" he says, laughing as I elbow him in the ribs.

He snaps the shot and sends it to me, and it's a good one. My hair's blowing in the breeze, blocking part of Kai's face, but his smile is undeniable, and we look happy. Carefree. So I forward the picture to Elle and Sam, along with a one-word caption: Joy.

. . .

It's a storybook kind of day, and I feel like I'm living in a rom-com movie montage. We spend hours holding hands as we walk along the beach, stopping for ice cream cones and lemonades and eating dinner at a tiny seafood restaurant as the sun sets over the ocean. When we return to the hotel, we shower off the sand and roll around under the covers, christening this new stage of our relationship with every inch of our bodies.

It's well past midnight when I realize I never heard back from my friends, which is odd—I fully expected Elle to send me an all-caps text with at least ten exclamation points and fourteen emojis. But when I reach for my phone to make sure the text went through successfully, I realize I must have accidentally switched the setting to Do Not Disturb. I have fifteen missed calls and twice as many texts, a bunch of them from Phil and Lottie. My fingers trembling, I tap my most recent voice mail message and lift the phone to my ear.

"Lucy," Lottie says, her voice shaky and breathless. "Are you getting my messages? Call me back as soon as you can. It's Zuri. She's sick, Lucy. And it's not looking good."

Chapter Thirty-Seven

"I need to get to the airport," I tell Kai, scrambling out of bed and pulling on my sand-wrinkled sundress. "Now."

He rolls over, a sleepy, dazed look in his eyes. "Huh?"

"I need to fly home right now. Zuri's sick." I'm already crying so hard that I can barely see well enough to find my flip-flops.

Kai's out of bed in an instant, crossing the room to hug me. "Okay. I'll call Freya and we'll book the first flight out. It's gonna be okay."

"You don't know that." My voice is choked, panicked, with a flinty edge. I'm sick of people offering empty words of consolation that they have no way or intention of seeing through. *I'll be back in a week*, Karina told me. *I don't want kids, either*, Nick promised me early on in our relationship. *You're enough for me*. It was bullshit, all of it, and even though Kai's doing his best to calm me down, there's no guarantee that everything will turn out okay. There's no guarantee they'll turn out anywhere close.

"I should never have come here," I tell him, grabbing my purse off the floor. "I shouldn't have left Zuri. And I shouldn't have spent the whole day frolicking on the beach like an idiot instead of checking on her."

"Lucy, come on," Kai says, hurriedly putting on a pair of jeans. "Zuri was doing well when we left. You had no way of knowing that wouldn't last."

Oh, but I did. "Of course I did," I insist, hot tears stinging my eyes. "Good things never last. It's the way of the world, in case you haven't noticed. And maybe I would have known if I'd been at the top of my game. Maybe she had symptoms or signs that she wasn't healing completely, and I didn't notice because I was too busy watching *90 Day Fiancé* and playing house with you."

Kai sucks in his breath. "I know you're upset, but let's not lash out at each other. Let's stay calm and get to the airport."

But I'm not really lashing out at him. I'm lashing out at myself, for doing the one thing I promised myself I wouldn't: losing my bull's-eye focus on work for something as fickle and fleeting as a summertime hookup. I think of Zuri, the gorilla who changed my life all those years ago, sick and suffering and probably scared out of her mind more than two thousand miles away. I should be there with her. I should have never left.

And I have no one but myself to blame.

We manage to get a six thirty a.m. flight, but I still have to spend five agonizing hours waiting for the plane to take off. I pace around the San Diego International Airport, my phone pressed to my ear as I get updates from Phil and Lottie and even Nick. They don't know exactly what's going on with Zuri; Jack first noticed her pressing a fist to her chest yesterday afternoon, as if she was in pain, and a stat call to the veterinary team determined her heartbeat was irregular. They suspected a pulmonary embolism, a rare postsurgical complication. Imaging showed a small clot, but when they administered blood thinners to dissolve it, her heart rate didn't stabilize.

Kai tries to hold my hand as we wait to board, but I can't stand to be touched. All I want is to get home to Zuri, for her to be okay, and to never leave her again. It's late afternoon eastern time when we land in Columbus, and Freya stays behind to grab our checked luggage while Kai and I sprint to passenger pickup, where Sam waits with a box of Kleenex and a lead foot. She breaks a dozen road safety laws as we rush to the Animal Health Center, and I try to open the car door before she even switches the gear into park.

I sprint inside the health center with Kai behind me, and when I round the corner to the surgical suite, I find Phil, Lottie, Jack, Scotty the intern, and Dr. Trotter clustered around an anesthetized Zuri. Everyone's eyes are red, and Lottie gasps when she sees me.

"Lucy," she says, grabbing my hand and guiding me toward Zuri's side. "You got here just in time."

Just in time for what? In time for Dr. Trotter to do chest compressions? In time to help administer another round of anticoagulant drugs?

"It's time for her to go, Lucy," Phil says, placing a hand on my shoulder.

No. It can't be. Three days ago she was scurrying across the exhibit to grab a chunk of pumpkin. Three days ago she was clutching her new surrogate baby to her chest. Three days ago I was telling her I loved her, that I'd be right back.

"But she was fine," I say, barely able to get the words out. "She was fine, and we just need to—"

Dr. Trotter shakes her head, and even though I want to rip off her stethoscope and fling it across the room, I know what she's thinking: fine three days ago doesn't matter. And she's right. Animals, just like people, can be fine one minute and dead the next, and sometimes all the medical interventions and life-saving techniques and love in the world aren't enough to stop it.

"Her blood pressure won't stabilize," the vet explains, her eyes wet. "She's clotting and bleeding and clotting and bleeding, and her body's just given up the fight. She's held on as long as possible, and we've done all we can."

I stare at her in disbelief before turning my attention to Zuri. Her chest rises and falls, but slowly, and when I reach out to touch her massive hand with my smaller one, she doesn't react.

"She's not in any pain," Dr. Trotter assures me.

It's only a small relief, because the pain ripping through me is a knife that shreds my insides, down to my very heart, and all that's left of me is sorrow and despair.

"Zuri," I whisper, lowering my face to her ear. "I love you. I love you so, so much, and you're my smart, strong girl. Always have been, always will be." I can hardly breathe because of the sobs wracking my body, but the vet and my colleagues back away slightly, and the message is clear: they've said their good-byes, and now it's my turn.

I press my hand to the beautiful blaze of copper fur that crosses Zuri's forehead and nuzzle my face against her chest. I think of all the days we've spent together, all the times she's listened to me pour my heart out to her in exchange for popcorn and protein biscuits. I think of how many children have visited the zoo to marvel at her and left with the same love for gorillas that she sparked in me when I was young. I think of how she saved Keeva from a lifetime of living without a troop, and how much better so many lives have been because of her existence.

I think that this is the last time I'll ever see her.

"I love you," I tell her again, my tears wetting her thick fur. "You saved my life and gave it purpose. I will make sure you are never forgotten."

The heart rate monitor beeps, followed by a long warning buzz, and I keep my face tucked into Zuri's chest as Dr. Trotter announces the time of death. I stay like that for a long time, sobbing and telling my favorite gorilla how sorry I am as Jack and Lottie and Scotty the intern try their best to comfort me. Finally, when it's time to transport Zuri's body for a necropsy, I lift my head up. Despite my desperate claims that I never should have let myself get distracted by Kai, I need him right now. I need him to wrap his arms around me and tell me it's going to be okay, even if I can't believe him. Even if I still have to wake up tomorrow, and every day after that, and live without the gorilla who changed my life.

But when I turn away from Zuri, expecting to find Kai waiting with open arms, what I see knocks the air out of my lungs. Because his arms aren't open at all. They're holding up the camera he's got hoisted over his shoulder, the one he's pointing straight at me.

Chapter Thirty-Eight

"Luce," Kai says, lowering the camera when he sees the stricken look on my face. "It's not, I wasn't—"

If my heart wasn't just ripped out of my body, I might laugh, because it's the most clichéd excuse of all time: *This isn't what it looks like.* But it's exactly what it looks like; Kai knows I hate the cameras, and he still decided to record the single most devastating moment of my life. He decided to exploit my pain. So much for love, or even like, and for standing by each other.

"I think it's exactly what it looks like," I tell him in a shaky voice, not caring that Jack and Lottie and Phil are within earshot. "I think you recorded me saying good-bye to my most beloved friend so you could use it to pump up your ratings. Everybody likes a tearjerker, right?"

"No," he says, setting the camera aside and reaching for my hand, but I yank it away from him. "No. It's not like that."

I do laugh this time, and it's a dry, devastated sound that sends Kai reaching for me again. "You're a storyteller," I say, shrugging off his attempt to touch me. "And what am I but a good story, right?"

"Lucy," Kai says, his tone pleading. "Let me explain."

"You don't need to. You were never the moron, Kai. It was me, all along, for letting you in. For believing that you cared about me, about something more than your little program."

He takes a step back like I've slapped him, but he doesn't storm out. Instead, he raises his hands in apology. "I do care about you. I care about you more than anything. I'll delete the footage if that's what you need. What can I do, Lucy? Just tell me what you want and I'll do it."

I want a time machine so that I can stay in Columbus instead of going to San Diego. I want to take all the hours I wasted with Kai and spend them with Zuri instead. But I can't, and the crushing heartbreak almost brings me to my knees.

So Kai can't give me what I want, but maybe he can give me the next best thing.

"I want you to stay away from me," I tell him, the words choked with tears. "And I never want to see you again."

Unable to bear another second inside the health center, I stride away from the surgical suite and out of the building to find that Sam, wonderful, loyal Sam, is still parked outside.

"Oh, Luce," she whispers when she sees my tear-streaked face. "I am so, so sorry."

She wraps her arms around me as I climb into the passenger seat, pulling me close. It's exactly the comfort I needed from Kai, and I cry harder as I lean into her touch.

"What can I do?" she asks, her voice breaking. "How can I help?"

I pull away from her to press a tissue to my face. "Can you just take me home?"

The next day, I do something I've never done in my entire career: I call out from work.

"Take all the time you need," Phil says when he answers my phone call. He assures me that Keeva, still housed with Ozzie's troop, is doing okay—she keeps peering through the mesh, as if waiting for Zuri to return, but she shared a night nest with Tria and little Piper, and none of the troop members are causing her trouble. And whatever my boss thought of the harsh words I exchanged with Kai, he doesn't even broach the subject.

I spend an entire day holed up in my bedroom, crying beneath an enamored-looking Jack and Rose. Nona brings in trays of tiramisu and red velvet cake, but I only get through half a slice before I think of a lifetime without Zuri and collapse into sobs. Elle and Sam come over in the evening and sit silently on either side of me while I wipe my tears and watch an episode of *The Little Couple*, and even Trudy slips a sympathy card under my bedroom door. It has a basketful of basset hound puppies on the front, and the inside reads, "I'm paws-itively sorry for your loss," and it's the nicest thing she's ever done for me.

But nothing makes the pain better. Nothing can fill the hole in my heart that belongs to Zuri. And no amount of baked goods can make me forget the raw sting of betrayal I felt when I found Kai pointing his camera at me like I was a particularly interesting insect instead of the woman he proclaimed to be falling in love with. His first instinct wasn't concern for me but an impulse to document my devastation for viewers across the world to watch while they eat dinner or fold laundry. And even though I wish it didn't hurt, even though I wish I'd never let myself get close enough to him to care, I can't ignore that it wounds me worse than any snare ever could.

On my third day off work, when I've entered the smelling-like-old-socks-but-not-caring part of the grieving process, Nona knocks on my bedroom door.

"Luce?" she asks, peeking inside my room. "I know you said no more baked goods, but your sister came to see you. She brought fairy bread, and she really wants to help cheer you up."

"Half sister," I correct my grandmother, too depressed to bite my tongue. "And tell her I said thank you, but I don't want to see anyone."

But before Nona can respond, Dynamite lumbers into my bedroom and Mia trots in after him, a Tupperware container in one arm and a backpack in the other.

"Now's not a good time, Mia," I say, trying to keep my voice gentle, but it's hard, because I have a throbbing headache from crying for three days straight. "I don't want company, okay?"

She doesn't hear me, because Dynamite, spotting an untouched slice of cake on a plate next to me, lets out an enthusiastic bark and lunges onto the bed, his hundred-and-seventy-pound bulk landing on my chest and knocking the air from my lungs.

"Get out!" I yell, coughing as Dynamite nudges the plate with his nose and swallows the cake in one quick bite. "Please just get out!"

"What's going on?" Karina asks, appearing in the doorway beside Nona. She glances from me to Dynamite to Mia, who stares openmouthed at me like I swore at her.

"I'm sorry," Mia says, dropping the Tupperware on my bed. "Mom said you were sad about Zuri, and I wanted to bring you your favorite food." She smooths the front of her Girl Scout vest and bites her lip. "I was really sad when my dog Pinecone died last year, so I know how you feel. But Mom read me a poem about the Rainbow Bridge that animals cross when they die, and it made me feel better. Do you want me to read it to you?"

Karina reaches out to smooth Mia's hair, and it's such a loving, easy gesture that it makes me want to scream. Because my heart is broken, and my temple's throbbing, and where was she to smooth my hair and read me poems when I was Mia's age? None of this—Zuri's death, Kai's betrayal, Karina's abandonment—is Mia's fault, but I want her gone anyway.

"Pinecone was a dog, Mia," I say, surprised by the venom in my tone. "I'm sorry he died, but Zuri was a gorilla. A critically endangered gorilla. She was much more than just a pet, so you have no idea how I feel. And I hate to break it to you, but there's no Rainbow Bridge, and your mom doesn't know jack shit about anything. She's a liar who doesn't keep her promises, and it's only a matter of time until she ditches you like she ditched me."

Mia's eyes fill with tears, and I instantly wish I could take my cruel words back. But I can't, and she drops her backpack and flies out of my bedroom, a barking Dynamite hurrying after her. Nona goes after the pair, calling for Mia, but Karina stays put, standing in the doorway of my bedroom with one hand on the knob.

"I'm sorry, Lucy," she says, her voice cracking on my name. "I'm so, so sorry."

Then she leaves, closing the door behind her, and I'm regretful and I'm furious, but at least I'm alone.

Chapter Thirty-Nine

That afternoon, I force myself to take a shower and then pad into the kitchen for a glass of water. Nona and Trudy sit at the table, slicing cucumbers and tomatoes and dumping them into a plastic bowl.

"Before you say anything, I know I was terrible to Mia," I tell Nona. "And I'll apologize to her tomorrow."

Nona sighs and gets up from the table, opening the refrigerator to pull out a sandwich. "Turkey, your favorite. And I'm glad you're going to apologize to Mia, but I owe you an apology, too." She tugs at the cashmere scarf looped around her neck and gives me a sad smile. "Ever since Karina and Mia moved here last year, I kept hoping you would bond with Mia. But I think I wanted everyone to get along so badly that I never gave your feelings the consideration they deserved. Karina's my daughter, and I'm glad she's on a good path now. But that doesn't change how much she let you down, and I know that better than anyone."

She places a hand on my arm and squeezes, and I'm surprised by the tears that spring to my eyes. "Mia wasn't the right target, but you had every reason to say what you said. I'm sorry for trying to push a relationship with her and your mother on you. I'm going to try to respect your boundaries moving forward."

My grandmother takes me into her arms, and I breathe in the familiar scent of Chanel No. 5.

"What did you say to Mia?" Trudy asks, always one for gossip.

Nona and I both roll our eyes at her, but before I can reply with a witty retort, the doorbell rings.

"I'll get it," Nona says, patting my arm. "You eat your sandwich."

She waltzes off to answer the door, and I pour myself a glass of water and watch as Trudy, wearing a collared vest with a polyester kitten on it, resumes slicing vegetables.

"Um, Lucy?" Nona calls after a moment. "It's for you."

It's probably Karina and Mia again, and I'm grateful for a chance to apologize to Mia. I carry my sandwich down the hallway and into the foyer, but I almost drop it when I see who's waiting for me.

It's Kai.

"Hi," he says, running a hand through his hair as Nona stares at him as if Harrison Ford just appeared in our home.

"Who is it?" Trudy calls, barreling after me down the hallway in her cat vest. She freezes when she sees Kai. "Holy fuckballs!"

"We'll leave you two alone," Nona says, giving me a sly wink as she grabs a protesting Trudy by the elbow and leads her back toward the kitchen.

Once they're gone, I cross my arms over my chest and wish I weren't holding a half-eaten turkey sandwich. With pale circles under his eyes and a wrinkled T-shirt, Kai looks like he hasn't slept much in days, and the part of me that was falling in love with him wants to take him into my arms. But the sting of betrayal I feel when I look at him stops me.

"I know you said you didn't want to see me, but I had to come by and tell you how sorry I am," Kai says, his hazel eyes meeting mine. "And to bring you this." He reaches into his pocket and pulls out a flash drive, holding it out toward me. "It's the footage of you and Zuri."

I shake my head in disgust. "That's the last thing I'd ever want to see. I lived through that pain once. I don't need to watch it again."

"You don't have to watch if you don't want to," Kai says. "But if you do, I don't think pain is the only thing you'll see."

When I don't reach out to accept the drive, he sets it on Nona's oak entry cabinet, along with a paper bag.

"I brought you Diet Coke and a cinnamon roll, too," he says, nodding toward the bag. "That sounds pretty stupid now that I say it out loud." He thrusts his hands into his pockets and studies me. "I'm so sorry that I hurt you, Lucy. And I miss you. And I really, really hope we can work things out."

Then, without another word, he leaves.

I leave the flash drive but take the cinnamon roll and the Diet Coke, because it's not their fault my life's in shambles. Around eight thirty, I'm back in my bed, watching my fifth episode of *Breaking Amish*, when Nona knocks on my door again.

"Lucy?" she asks, entering without waiting for an answer. "Has Mia called you?"

I shake my head. She's never called me; I've never given her my number. "Why?"

Nona sighs. "She told Karina she was going to watch Netflix in her room around five, and Karina just went to check on her, but she's not there. She's not anywhere at home, and she's not here, and Karina's freaking out."

"Mia's missing?" I push my covers off. "Where would she have gone?"

"Karina's not sure. She called all of Mia's friends' parents, but she's not at any of their houses, and Alfie's driving around looking for her now."

Guilt fills my belly. If Mia got so upset by my outburst that she ran off, she could be in danger. And it's all my fault.

"I'm gonna drive to Handel's and see if Mia got it into her head to take herself out for ice cream," Nona says. "I'll call you if I hear anything."

I nod, stunned, but she's already gone. Mia is *missing*? I roll out of bed and grab a pair of shorts to slide over my underwear, and when I slip them on, I notice Mia's backpack on the floor. Not sure what I'm looking for, I grab it and riffle through its contents. There's a phone charger and a pair of headphones, a sheet of cupcake stickers, and a half-eaten bag of Cheez-Its. I also find her JoJo Siwa notebook, and I open the first page to see that she's scribbled MIA'S NOTEBOOK. STAY OUT!!! in threatening red pencil.

Now doubly guilty for invading her privacy on top of yelling at her, I flip past drawings of Dynamite until I find a page simply marked LUCY. I feel like the worst human on earth when I see that Mia's doodled pictures of the two of us, with matching smiles and unruly hair, doing things we've never done together: Strolling around the zoo. Visiting Cinderella's Castle at Disney World. Riding what I think are supposed to be horses but look more like gigantic chunky hamsters.

Lucy's Likes, she's written on one page, followed by a list: Gorillas. Kai Bridges' mom. Strawberry chunk ice cream. Research. Fairy bread. Khaki. Dynamite (sometimes). On the next page, titled Dislikes, she's written: Girl Scouts. Voice lessons. Kai Bridges. Licorice. Hats. Dynamite (sometimes). It's a preteen's field guide to Lucy Rourke, and the realization that Mia's paid such close attention to me, even when I dismissed her attempts to hang out or develop any kind of sisterly bond, breaks my heart. I certainly didn't deserve how Karina treated me all those years ago, but maybe I don't deserve Mia, either.

I continue flipping through the pages, finding a chunk titled Mia's Nature Adventures. She's drawn a sketch of the weeping willow tree that separates Nona's backyard from the stretch of forest behind it, and suddenly I have an idea. If Mia's as much like me as I think she is—and our equally untamed hair, soft bellies, and weird childhood notebooks indicate that she is—then I might know where to find her.

I traipse past the willow tree, careful to avoid a mound of poison ivy. I haven't explored the woods behind Nona's since I was a teenager, but except for new overgrowth and a stash of dirty cigarette butts under a maple tree, it's the same as I remember. I stroll along for a quarter mile, passing a babbling brook and a fallen tree sprouting mushrooms, and sure enough, when I reach the small clearing where I did my most successful "gorilla tracking" as a kid, I spot Mia sitting on a log, a Nintendo Switch resting on her lap. Dynamite lies beside her, eating a chunk of grass.

"Mia!" I call.

Her brow furrows in confusion when she sees me, as if she has no idea how I found her secret hiding place. As if it's not a four-minute walk from our grandmother's house.

"Hey," I say, stopping beside her. "Mind if I join you on your log?"

She shrugs, and I plop down next to her.

"How'd you find me?" she asks, like I tracked her across the Atlantic Ocean.

"Well, this used to be one of my favorite hangout spots when I was your age. I haven't been in a while, but it's held up pretty well."

We're quiet for a minute, listening to the hum of cicadas and the singing of birds and Dynamite's deafening panting.

"I'm sorry for what I said earlier," I tell her. "I was upset, and I took it out on you. I shouldn't have."

She pushes a curl out of her eyes. "Is it true there's no Rainbow Bridge?"

"Honestly? I have no idea. There might be. I don't know any more than you do."

"But you're all grown up," Mia says.

I can't help but smile. "A lot of the time, grown-ups don't actually know more than kids. In fact, a lot of the time we know less."

She nods, as if this is just confirmation of what she already suspected. "Do you think I'll see Pinecone again?"

I reach out to pet Dynamite, who's making a valiant attempt to eat my shoelaces. "I don't know. I hope so. And I hope to see Zuri again one day, but I'd be lying if I said I knew for sure."

She nudges Dynamite away from my shoe. "Is it true what you said about Mom? That she's a liar?"

I take a deep breath. "It's true that when I was your age, Karina—Mom—made a lot of mistakes. But people can change, I guess, and it seems like she has. She loves you a whole lot, Mia. And she's not going to ditch you."

I have no guarantee of that, but as I say the words aloud, I realize I really do believe them. It's part of why I've been so jealous of Mia all this time.

"She loves you, too, you know," Mia says, turning to face me. "She tells me all the time."

"She does?" I ask, surprised by the ball of emotion that swells in my throat.

Mia nods. "Did you think she didn't? Is that why you don't like us?"

It's a sincere, simple question, and I try to give her the same kind of answer. "I felt very hurt for a very long time, but that has nothing to do with you. I like you just fine, Mia, and I'm sorry I haven't let myself love you the way you deserve. But I'd like to work on that, if you'll let me."

"Really?" she asks, her face lighting up like I announced that I'm joining her Junior Girl Scout troop.

"Really. After all, you're the only sister I've got."

She pokes a stick with her foot. "Do you think you'll work on loving Mom, too?"

I give her my honest answer. "I don't know. Maybe one day we'll get there. But in the meantime, I'd really like to stop by one of your Girl Scout meetings and talk about gorillas. If you want me to."

"Seriously?" Mia asks, her voice rising several decibels. "Um, yes! That would be so cool. None of the other girls' siblings have cool jobs. Olivia's sister is a boring old Target cashier."

Olivia's sister is probably also sixteen, but I don't point that out. "Nona and Mom are worried about you. What do you think about heading home?"

She shrugs. "I just wanted some time alone, but it is getting dark. Plus, my Switch battery is about to die."

As if that settles it, she clambers up from the log and grabs Dynamite's leash. I follow them past the mushroom-ridden tree and the weeping willow and through Nona's backyard, and I take my little sister home.

Chapter Forty

When I get back to Nona's, she and Trudy decide to relieve the stress of the past hour by sipping wine on the patio. They invite me to join, but I grab my laptop and carry it into the living room, where I post up on the couch with Doritos and a determination to catch up on my work emails. Returning to an Ape House without Zuri in it might be the hardest thing I'll ever have to do, and my stomach drops at the thought, but I can't grieve at home forever. Keeva still needs me, and besides, it might help me to be around Jack and Lottie and other people who loved Zuri.

I'm skimming through a summary of the orangutans' biannual dental exam when I'm interrupted.

"Luce?"

I glance up from my laptop to see Karina entering the living room. She glances at the two bags of Doritos, one on either side of me, but if she has thoughts about them, she keeps them to herself. "Hi. Do you . . . do you mind if I sit with you for a moment?"

My immediate inclination is to say no, but I pause before I can reject her with a polite excuse. If I can learn to be in the same room as my mother without feeling uncomfortable, it'll make my life at Nona's easier. And it might add some joy to Mia's, which makes me think it could be worth a shot.

For Mia, then, I shove one of the Doritos bags aside. "Okay."

Karina settles next to me onto the couch and crosses one leg over the other. She has the stiff, nervous posture of someone who's about to get a root canal, and I realize she's as uncomfortable as I am.

"What are you working on?" she asks.

"Oh. Work stuff."

She nods, and I wait for her to make an innocuous comment about the weather.

Instead, she takes a deep breath and rests her hands in her lap. "Thank you for finding Mia today. It meant so much to her, and to Alfie and me, that you went looking for her. She told me what you two talked about."

I nod. "It's a conversation that was a long time in the making."

"When she came home, she had some hard questions for me. About the kind of mother I was to you—am to you—versus the kind of mother I am to her."

The thought of Mia holding Karina's feet to the fire fills me with satisfaction, because Mia's not one to let anybody off the hook, but it also fills me with a new brand of sadness. It sucks for Mia to learn that the mom who she thinks hung the moon is actually a flawed, complicated person, and I wish it was a lesson she didn't have to learn.

"I'm sure she wasn't easy on you," I say, recalling the time Mia interrogated Trudy for an hour over her failure to properly recycle a soda can.

"Mia's not easy on anybody who wrongs someone she loves. And she loves you more than you know."

I think of her doodles of imaginary sisterly activities. "I think I'm starting to understand."

"She asked me what happened when you were her age," Karina continues, her voice raw with emotion. "Why I left you with Nona. How I could stand to leave you. Why I never told her, and if I'd do the same to her."

I picture my indignant sister in her Girl Scout vest yelling questions at Karina, and the thought of her standing up for me almost brings me to tears. "What did you tell her?"

Karina looks up from her hands to study me, her blue eyes glistening. "I told her the truth: that I had a lot of problems when you were little. I was so young, and I thought my career was the most important thing in the world. I didn't know how to be a mom, and I didn't care to learn. I was selfish and immature, and the only thing I cared about was making sure that people knew my name. And in doing that, I ruined my relationship with the one person who should have mattered."

She's full-on crying now, but she doesn't stop to wipe her tears. "I told her that I won't do the same to her, not because my love for her is different, but because I'm different. I've learned and changed, but that does nothing to repair the damage I've done, and I will forever regret the awful choices I made."

She's only been sitting next to me for a minute, but this is already the longest, most intense conversation we've had since I was a kid, and a ball of emotion swells in my throat. The woman pouring her heart out next to me isn't the mom who glared at me on the way home from my botched recital, or the Karina who tiptoes around me when she sees me at Nona's, like she's scared I might lunge at her if she says the wrong thing. She's earnest, open, a woman I've never been able to let myself know.

Karina tucks a strand of hair behind her ear, her hand shaking. "I know you don't want anything to do with me, Lucy. And I don't blame you. But I want you to know that I'm deeply, deeply sorry for how I treated you when you were younger, and in all the years since. I've been a terrible mother to you, and I tried to do the opposite for Mia, but I can see how that might have hurt you even more."

I listen, not saying anything, and my hands are shaking, too. Because I know she's decades too late to fix the damage she caused, but maybe hearing her acknowledge that damage in the first place is a start. I wonder what Kai would give to hear Dr. Kimber admit her wrongs and apologize for them, and I realize that at least in this small way—and granted, the bar is incredibly low—Karina has a big head start on her.

"Anyway," she continues, clearing her throat and sniffling. "I know I've asked you to coffee and brunch and dinner a thousand times since we moved here, and I understand that you don't want to spend time with me. And I don't blame you one bit. But I want you to know that you are twice the woman I could ever hope to be. You are. And I know you're too old to need a mom, but if you ever want a friend, or even an acquaintance, or somebody to scream at when you're mad or sad or heartbroken, I'd like to try to be there for you. When you're ready, if that time ever comes."

Karina runs a hand across her cheek, smearing a trail of ruined mascara. Despite my distrust of her, I find myself believing that the emotion on her face and in her wavering voice is genuine. She might have been a well-known actress, but she wasn't a particularly talented one, and she looks a lot like Mia when she cries. She probably looks a lot like me, too, even if I can't quite see it.

"Anyway," she says. "I just wanted you to know that."

I'm silent as I look at Karina, with her perfect bob and gleaming white teeth and enough baggage to fill a flight from Columbus to San Diego. Nona's been more of a mother to me than she ever has, and I've got the two best friends I could ask for in Elle and Sam. I don't need another, but I suppose I could use a break from the decades of resentment I've carried. I suppose I could give things the chance to be different.

"I like pastries," I say finally. "Cinnamon rolls. Maybe one weekend you and I can go get some together. With Mia."

Karina sniffles again. "I would love that. I like cinnamon rolls, too."

I nod back at her, and we just sit quietly next to each other for a moment. The silence is peaceful but awkward, and that's okay. After all, Rome wasn't built in a day.

"Mind if I just chill here for a bit?" Karina asks. "Mia asked for space and that I respect her boundaries, which means she doesn't want me home for at least half an hour."

I can't help but laugh at Mia's forthrightness. "Sure, I guess, if you don't mind being bored to tears watching me read emails. Feel free to turn on the TV if you want."

Karina nods and switches on the TV, sorting through streaming options until she settles on *Married at First Sight*. I'm not sure if she actually enjoys the show or just knows I do, but she gives me a small smile as she wipes her eyes again.

I don't reach over to pat her hand or wrap an arm around her, because we're not there yet. We might never be, and that's okay. But I do pass her a bag of Doritos, and she reaches in and pulls out a handful, crunching loudly through her tears.

A few hours after Karina goes home to make peace with Mia, my laptop blinks a low battery warning. When I grab the charger, I notice

Kai's flash drive resting where he left it on the entry cabinet, and I can't stop myself from picking it up. Watching it means subjecting myself to total emotional devastation, but I miss Zuri so desperately that I'll do anything to see her face again. She was always my comfort when I was feeling down, and after the emotional roller coaster of my fight with Kai and conversations with Mia and Karina, I need her more than ever.

I take my computer to my bedroom, where I can sob in private. Tears well in my eyes before I even insert the flash drive, and my mouth goes dry as I click on the file that pops up. I expect a tragic clip of Zuri's final moments to play immediately, but it doesn't. The first thing I see is a reel of me hanging out with Zuri while she paints, laughing as she drops her brush on the paper and accidentally splashes me with paint. Next is footage of me conducting one of her daily wellness checks, pressing my fist against the mesh as she meets it with her enormous hand. Kai didn't give me some devastating gorilla snuff video; it's a twenty-minute montage of the moments I shared with her, big and small: Zuri grunting with excitement as I carry a bucket of watermelon toward her; me cheering like a crazy person as she slides Keeva onto her back; Lottie, Jack, and me laughing as Zuri fashions a piece of cardboard into a very stylish hat.

My tears fall fast and furious as I reminisce on each special memory, but I find myself laughing, too, at the more comedic scenes. It feels good to laugh, even if it's against a backdrop of heartache, and I wish the reel could go on forever.

But then Kai's video moves on to the clip I dread: footage of me bent over Zuri in the health center, whispering to her about how much I love her and that she will always be my smart, strong girl. It's devastating and beautiful all at once, and I don't even bother to wipe my tears as I sob into my hoodie. I watch my on-screen self say good-bye to the best gorilla of all time, and it takes ten minutes of counting to ten over and over until I feel like I can breathe again. But when I can, I feel for the first time since Zuri's passing that, somehow, I'm going to be okay.

Because everything I've been through this summer—navigating life with the cameras, falling in love with Kai, learning the truth about Dr. Kimber, losing Zuri—has cracked my heart open and transformed it. I'm a new Lucy, and as I watch myself touch the streak of copper fur on Zuri's head, I realize Kai was right.

Because when I look at that video, at that woman and the beloved gorilla, I don't see only pain. I see something brighter, something deeper, something that will last until the end of time and long after that.

I see love.

Chapter Forty-One

The day I return to work, it's pouring rain. Thunder sounds overhead as I step inside Ape House, shaking water droplets from my hair. I usually hate getting caught in the rain, but Zuri always loved stomping in puddles after a storm, and my eyes well up as I remember how much joy she got from splashing around like a preschooler.

"Lucy!" Lottie says when I find her carrying a bucket of lettuce in the hallway. "You're back!" She sets the bucket down to hug me, and when she releases me from her embrace, she smiles like I've been gone for months instead of four days. "We really missed you."

"We seriously did," Jack says, echoing her sentiments as he rounds the corner to join us, a mop in one hand and a towel in the other. "You're the only one Scotty listens to. I caught him watching *BoJack Horseman* when he was supposed to be doing rounds, and when I threatened to tell Phil, he looked at me and said, 'I'm not scared of you. You're not Lucy.'" Jack rolls his eyes and pretends to smack an invisible figure with the mop.

"Are you doing okay?" Lottie asks. "We've been worried."

A month ago, I would have shrugged and assured my coworkers

that I was fine, reluctant to show them any vulnerability. Today, I take a breath before giving an honest answer.

"I'm not great," I say. "But I'll be okay eventually. I think it's just going to take some time."

Lottie and Jack both nod, and then Lottie takes my hand and leads me toward the indoor gorilla exhibit. "I want to show you something."

When we reach the exhibit, we find silverback Ozzie snoozing on his back while Tomo and Risa engage in a wrestling match next to him. Inkesha plays with her feet while Mac the blackback tries to poke her with a stick.

"Look," Jack says, pointing toward a hammock strung between two artificial trees.

Tria lies sideways on the hammock as little Piper sits beside her, clutching a red ball in her hands.

"Piper's playing with a ball," I observe. "Cool, I guess?"

Lottie grins. "Just wait for it."

I have no clue what I'm waiting for, but ten seconds later, the answer reveals itself when baby Keeva pops up from behind Tria. She climbs over the adult gorilla, who doesn't seem bothered in the slightest, and tries to grab the ball from Piper's hands. The two youngsters battle for the toy until Tria, awoken from slumber by their commotion, grabs Keeva and places her on her chest.

My breath catches in my throat. "Tria's . . . Tria's taking care of Keeva?"

"Tria's taking care of Keeva," Lottie says with a smile. "I know that Tria's not Zuri, and no one can ever replace her, but this means Keeva can stay in the troop. She can stay here in Columbus with her new family."

Tears spring to my eyes again as I watch Keeva cuddle against

Tria's chest. Seeing her like that makes Zuri's death even more real, but it also means that the love and affection Zuri showed the infant— the willingness to open her heart to her—were not in vain. And neither was all our hard work.

"I know it's going to be really difficult for a while," Lottie says, brushing her bangs out of her face. "I know how much you loved Zuri. But we're here for you, Jack and me. And we'll be here for you every step of the way."

I grab Lottie's hand and squeeze it. I'm lucky to have colleagues who care as much about me as they do our gorillas, and I'm ashamed it's taken me so long to realize it.

"Thank you, guys. That means so much to me."

Jack nods. "We can't bring Zuri back, but we can make sure that we keep you busy and distracted. So you're coming to karaoke night with us this weekend, and we won't take no for an answer."

I bite my lip. "Are you sure you want me crashing the party? I might cry."

Lottie laughs. "Just wait until Jack and Patrick do their rendition of 'Wannabe.' You won't be the only one in tears."

"I do a killer Sporty Spice," Jack says.

"Kill people's ears, you mean," Lottie counters.

Their banter lasts a few minutes, and just as Jack challenges Lottie and me to a Spice Girls sing-off, Lottie raises her eyebrows at him and gives him a knowing look.

"Jack, I think I just heard Phil calling for us," she tells him. "Let's go."

"Oh yeah," Jack says, grabbing his mop. "He definitely called for us. Coming, Phil!" he yells over his shoulder, even though I haven't heard or seen Phil at all. They hurry off toward the offices, and I'm trying to figure out what the heck's going on when a deep voice behind me explains their sudden departure.

"Hi."

I turn around to find Kai standing behind me, his hands in his pockets.

"Oh," I say, watching as a swinging door closes behind my fellow keepers. "Now I get it."

Kai nods. "They're very smooth."

"Something like that."

We stare at each other for a minute, and as I scramble for an animal fact to break the tension, Kai takes a step toward me.

"I am so sorry," he says, regret written all over his face. "I never meant to hurt you when I filmed you and Zuri in the health center. I thought if I captured your last moments together, it would give you something to remember her by and help you see yourself the way other people see you. The way *I* see you. I thought I was gathering evidence that you filled her life with peace and love, right to the very end. I thought it might bring you comfort. But I promise you, Lucy, that footage will never see the light of day. You're what matters to me, not ratings."

His voice is raw, raspy, and I don't retreat when he takes another step closer.

"I know," I tell him. "At least, I know now. As soon as I watched the footage, I understood. You're right; it did bring me comfort. And I'm grateful. I'm grateful for the time I had with her, and to you for memorializing some of it. And I want you to use the footage."

Kai does a double take. "Are you sure?"

I nod. The old Lucy would have demanded that he burn the flash drive. After all, it's way more comfortable to fall back on old tendencies than to put myself out there. It's the same reason I assumed the worst about Kai in the surgical suite. It's the reason I couldn't accept Elle's offer to be godmother to her baby, and why I lashed out at Mia instead of giving her the chance to console me. Because it's easy to keep things the way they are, to deal with the pain you know instead of opening yourself up to something new—even if that something could rock your world.

But now I want things to be different.

"You were right," I tell him. "What I saw in the footage wasn't only pain. It was love and friendship and beauty, too, and if people don't get a chance to see that, they'll never know who Zuri was or what she meant. What she'll always mean. I want you to share it with the world so that she's never forgotten."

Kai nods. "I can do that." He takes another step closer to me so that he's only an arm's length away. "And I owe you a thank-you. For believing in me, and for helping me stand up to my mother. I'm not ready to share the truth about Taji with the world yet, but I am ready to start making changes. I'm going to Rwanda to work on my mountain gorilla documentary."

He grins, and it might be the happiest I've ever seen him. "I'm finally going to tell the story I want to tell."

"That's amazing, Kai. When?" My heart sinks at the prospect of his departure, but the grin on his face eases my sadness.

"December. I'm only going for a month to start, because I have contractual obligations with the show. But I'm more excited about this than I've been about anything in a long, long time." Joy flickers in his eyes. "Except for you."

"You're going to make an incredible documentary," I tell him, and I mean it.

He crosses his arms over his chest. "I'm gonna try. But it would certainly help if I had a gorilla expert to join me on my adventure. What do you think?"

My heart skips a beat. "Are you asking me to leave my job and travel to Mount Karisimbi with you?"

He reaches out to brush a lock of hair behind my ear. "I'm asking you if you'd like to take a monthlong sabbatical to go see gorillas in the wild. Something tells me you've got a few years' worth of vacation days saved up."

I loop my arms around his neck. "Are you asking me to be your wingman, Kai Bridges?"

He laughs, and the sound of it dulls a little of the ache in my chest. "No, Lucy-goosey. I'm asking if I can be yours." He reaches to boop my nose but draws his finger back when he sees the glare on my face.

"Don't even think about it," I warn him. "My promise to feed you to the polar bears still stands."

He sighs but shrugs. "Fair enough. What if I kiss you instead?"

In answer, I lean forward to press my lips to his, and the sensation of our bodies coming together melts away some of the anguish in my chest.

"Hey, Lucy," Kai mumbles into my hair. "A shrimp's heart is located in its head."

"Hey, Kai," I whisper back, cupping his cheek in my hand. "Koalas have two vaginas."

He laughs, and when my lips meet his again, I don't even care that we're kissing in the middle of Ape House, in full view of Ozzie and his troop. Because we might be animal-fact-spouting weirdos, but we're weirdos who were made for each other.

Always have been, always will be.

Chapter Forty-Two

December

"Did you remember to pack dental floss?" Elle asks as she follows me through the sliding-glass doors of John Glenn Columbus International Airport.

"Did you remember to pack lingerie?" Sam asks, maneuvering one of my suitcases past a yellow caution cone.

Elle shoots her a look. "She's gonna be traipsing through forests and mountains. I hardly think lingerie's a priority."

"She's gonna be traipsing through forests and mountains *with Kai*," Sam corrects her. "And it's not like a chemise takes up a lot of room."

"I packed all the necessities," I assure my friends. "Although 'necessity' is relative."

Sam shrugs. "Well, when I go visit Freya next week, you better believe I'm taking at least five different teddies."

I don't point out that she and Freya are staying at the Four Seasons in Maui, and Kai and I will be sleeping in a tent. Instead, I deposit my luggage at the Delta kiosk and make my way toward security, where an entire contingent awaits my send-off.

"You've got enough fairy bread for the flight, right?" Mia asks, adjusting her pigtailed buns.

Over the past four months, much about my relationship with Mia has changed, but her obsession with wearing her Girl Scout vest has not.

I smile at her. "I think eight sandwiches is plenty."

She grins and wraps me in a tight hug. "I'm gonna miss you, Lucy."

I'm pretty sure my sister's squeezing the air out of my lungs, but I hug her back anyway. "I'll miss you, too. But I'll only be gone a month."

"And then we can have Sister Saturdays again?"

I nod. "Yep. It's already on my calendar."

Every other Saturday, I make it a point to spend time with Mia. Sometimes we see a movie or go to Handel's to stuff ourselves with strawberry-cheesecake-chunk ice cream. Sometimes we walk Dynamite in the woods behind Nona's house, jotting notes in our logbooks about the rabbits and deer and wild mountain gorillas that cross our path. Occasionally Nona and Karina join us, but most of the time, it's just Mia and me. And believe it or not, we're becoming rather good friends.

"You've got your cookies, too?" Karina asks once Mia releases me from her iron grip.

I pat my carry-on and nod. "Sugar cookies locked and loaded and ready to be eaten as soon as the seat belt sign goes off."

Karina and I aren't good friends yet—I'm not sure that's something I'll ever be ready for—but we've met up for coffee a few times since the summer, and although our conversations still contain a lot of awkward silences, at least there are conversations to speak of. And that's something I couldn't have imagined happening just a few short months ago.

"Sorry it took us so long to get inside," Nadeem says, power walking to join our group near security. "Parking lot was busy, and this one had a blowout." He hoists up the drowsy newborn in his arms, and I reach for my goddaughter and take her into my arms.

"Hi, Elsie," I whisper, straightening the daisy headband that's half the size of her body. "Auntie Lucy will miss you so much, but I'll bring you back an awesome souvenir."

She opens one eye to peer at me, as if to ask, *What kind of souvenir can you buy in the jungle?* and she's so cute, I can hardly stand it. Becoming a godmother was one promotion I wasn't sure I wanted, but now that Elsie's here, I can hardly remember life without her.

"Tell Mommy not to cry," I whisper to the baby as I pass her to Elle. "Tell her Auntie Lucy will be back in thirty-one days."

"You better call us whenever you have service," Elle says, sniffling. "And don't you dare get malaria or dengue fever or Lyme disease."

"But do get laid a ton," Sam says, lowering her voice so Mia doesn't overhear.

I laugh and wrap them both in a group hug, giving Elle time to shed a few tears before I wave to Nadeem and Karina and make my way toward Nona.

She smooths my hair and smiles at me. "I'm so proud of you, Lucy. Who knew that the surly ten-year-old I dragged to the zoo would turn out to be a wonderful big sister, a world traveler, *and* a senior keeper?"

I grin. "To be fair, I'm still pretty surly. And this is my first trip out of the country, so 'world traveler' is a bit of a stretch. Plus, I'm not officially a senior keeper until January."

When Phil called me into his office and offered me the promotion in early September, just after filming ended, it was a dream come true. But I accepted it on two conditions: that I could take

December off to study mountain gorillas, and that he'd let me start a fundraiser to raise money for the Zuri Award, a scholarship for local high school students who demonstrate a passion for wildlife conservation.

"January, Schmanuary," Nadeem says. "It's time to order new business cards."

I laugh and hug Nona, and then I make my way through the maze of barriers toward security, blowing kisses at my friends and family and trying not to laugh as Sam bites into one of Karina's lightly burnt sugar cookies and spits it right back out.

"Love you guys!" I call, waving like a madwoman as I pass my ID and boarding pass to the TSA agent.

I glance back one more time as I head toward the metal detectors, smiling as Mia leans against Karina and Nona, and Nadeem coos at Elsie and Sam links an arm through Elle's.

And then I take a deep breath and head off toward adventure.

"We're almost there," our guide Keza says, climbing over a fallen log and waiting for Kai and me to catch up.

We've been trekking through steep, sometimes muddy terrain for six hours straight, and my quads are screaming for a break, but I press on. Because the prize that awaits us at the top of the mountain will be better than any promotion.

Kai, who's carrying a pack full of supplies, plus his camera, grimaces, but he maneuvers over the log and extends a hand toward me to help me climb over it.

"Almost," Keza repeats, and I will my calves and glutes and tolerance for mosquitoes not to give up as I scramble after her.

"Here," she says after we hike for another ten minutes, my boots covered in leaves and mud. "Here they are: the most striking animals in all the world."

Keza points to the lush valley below us, and my heart races as I rush to catch up with her. When I reach her, I place my hands on my knees and gasp for air, but the sight in front of me takes my remaining breath away. Because there, only two hundred yards beneath us, is a troop of wild mountain gorillas resting in the afternoon sun. I watch, speechless, as a young gorilla steals a handful of browse from its mother and scampers off to enjoy it in peace. The pair reminds me of Zuri and Keeva, and my eyes fill with tears—both for the beauty in front of me and in memory of the gorilla who changed my life forever.

"What do you think?" Keza asks, grinning as Kai and I watch the troop in open-mouthed disbelief.

But I can't speak, and Kai only reaches for my hand and squeezes it.

"Shouldn't you get your camera out?" I ask him.

He shakes his head. "Not now. Now I just want to be here with you."

I nod and squeeze his hand back, and when I glance out over the valley at the majesty below me, there's only one word that sums it up.

Wowza.

Acknowledgments

The Columbus Zoo and Aquarium is one of my favorite places in the world, and I am grateful to the many people who work so hard to make it special. On countless visits, I've encountered keepers and docents whose commitment to animal care and educational outreach is unparalleled. While Lucy, her colleagues, and the animals in their care are entirely fictional, the passion she has for her work mirrors the very real dedication of CZA staff and volunteers. I encourage you to visit the zoo if possible. Information about the gorilla surrogacy program and the zoo's extensive conservation efforts, as well as the sustainable palm oil shopping guide Lucy mentions in Chapter One, can be found at: https://columbuszoo.org.

My research resources included the Gorilla Species Survival Plan, *Voices from the Ape House* by Beth Armstrong, *Woman in the Mists* by Farley Mowat, *Gorillas in Our Midst* by Jeff Lyttle, and *Gorillas in the Mist* by Dian Fossey. I am grateful for these illuminating works and for the ongoing projects of experts dedicated to the conservation of gorillas in the wild.

I'm thankful for the team that brought this book to life: agent extraordinaire Jessica Watterson, my powerhouse editor Angela Kim, Hello Marine, and the entire Berkley team, including Daché Rogers, Jessica Plummer, and the production and art departments.

ACKNOWLEDGMENTS

Many thanks to the Pitch Wars community, especially the class of 2017, and Susan Bishop Crispell, Melissa West, Kerry Winfrey, Kelly Siskind, kc dyer, Sarah Smith, and Laura Heffernan.

Thank you to the readers who sent me lovely messages about *The Wedding Ringer*. I cherish them.

To my husband, Chris Rea: We've endured so much together, and you're the best teammate anyone could ask for. Thank you for making me laugh every single day and for loving me so deeply. You're an amazing husband and dad, and spending life with you is an absolute joy. I love you. Reas never give up.

To Finn: Thank you for bringing back the light. Thank you for showing Daddy and me how much joy is possible. I love you, I love you, I love you.

To Ciaran: Daddy and I miss you so much, but we know you're still with us. Thank you for sending your baby brother. Thank you for showing us that love is brave and infinite. There's never a moment when I'm not thinking of you, my wild, beautiful boy.

Kelly: I don't have to say because you already know. I love you. Thank you.

Mom and Dad: Thank you for making me a reader. I love you. Mom, thank you for watching Finn so I could get some work done!

Special thanks to the best godmother on the planet, Audrey Roncevich, and to Brittany Angarola, as well as the many friends whose support and companionship have made my days brighter. I am also grateful for my extended family, including the Reardons, Reas, McVeys, and Corletzis.

And finally, thank you to all the beloved animals who've run along ahead of us, especially Riley.